No Surrender!
A Tale Of The Rising In La Vendee

by
G. A. Henty

No Surrender!
A Tale Of The Rising In La Vendee
by G. A. Henty

Copyright © 2024

All Rights reserved.

No part of this publication may be reproduced, stored in a retrieval system, or transmitted in any form or by any means, electronic, mechanical, photocopying or Otherwise, without the written permission of the publisher.
The author/editor asserts the moral right to be identified as the author/editor of this work.

ISBN: 978-93-64285-33-9

Published by

DOUBLE 9 BOOKS
2/13-B, Ansari Road
Daryaganj, New Delhi – 110002
info@double9books.com
www.double9books.com
Tel. 011-40042856

This book is under public domain

ABOUT THE AUTHOR

English author and war correspondent George Alfred Henty lived from 8 December 1832 to 16 November 1902. He is most well-known for his historical fiction and adventure books, including The Dragon & The Raven (1886), For The Temple (1888), Under Drake's Flag (1883), and in Freedom's Cause (1883). (1885). He was a British journalist who served as G. A. Henty's war correspondent. He was raised in Cambridge and finished his education there at Gonville and Caius College. He continued to cover important wars that followed, such as the Italian and Austro-Italian Wars. He wrote 122 books, most of which were geared toward young readers. He also wrote non-fiction, adult fiction, and short tales. In Henty's stories, the main character is a boy or young man who is going through a challenging situation. His characters are consistently low-key, astute, courageous, truthful, and resourceful with a lot of "pluck." The date was put at the bottom of the title page of each of Henty's 122 historical fiction works in their first printings.

CONTENTS

Preface 7

Chapter 1
  A French Lugger 8

Chapter 2
  The Beginning Of Troubles 20

Chapter 3
  The First Successes 35

Chapter 4
  Cathelineau's Scouts 49

Chapter 5
  Checking The Enemy 63

Chapter 6
  The Assault Of Chemille 79

Chapter 7
  A Short Rest 92

Chapter 8
  The Capture Of Saumur 105

Chapter 9
  Bad News 119

Chapter 10
  Preparations For A Rescue 134

Chapter 11
  The Attack On Nantes 149

Chapter 12
　A Series Of Victories 162

Chapter 13
　Across The Loire 175

Chapter 14
　Le Mans 187

Chapter 15
　In Disguise 201

Chapter 16
　A Friend At Last: 215

Chapter 17
　A Grave Risk 228

Chapter 18
　Home 242

Preface

In the world's history, there is no more striking example of heroic bravery and firmness than that afforded by the people of the province of Poitou, and more especially of that portion of it known as La Vendee, in the defence of their religion and their rights as free men. At the commencement of the struggle they were almost unarmed, and the subsequent battles were fought by the aid of muskets and cannon wrested from the enemy. With the exception of its forests, La Vendee offered no natural advantages for defence. It had no mountains, such as those which enabled the Swiss to maintain their independence; no rivers which would bar the advance of an enemy; and although the woods and thickets of the Bocage, as it was called, favoured the action of the irregular troops, these do not seem to have been utilized as they might have been, the principal engagements of the war being fought on open ground. For eighteen months the peasants of La Vendee, in spite of the fact that they had no idea of submitting either to drill or discipline, repulsed the efforts of forces commanded by the best generals France could furnish; and which grew, after every defeat, until at length armies numbering, in all, over two hundred thousand men were collected to crush La Vendee.

The losses on both sides were enormous. La Vendee was almost depopulated; and the Republicans paid dearly, indeed, for their triumph, no fewer than one hundred thousand men having fallen, on their side. La Vendee was crushed, but never surrendered. Had the British government been properly informed, by its agents, of the desperate nature of the struggle that was going on; they might, by throwing twenty thousand troops, with supplies of stores and money into La Vendee, have changed the whole course of events; have crushed the Republic, given France a monarch, and thus spared Europe over twenty years of devastating warfare, the expenditure of enormous sums of money, and the loss of millions of lives.

G. A. Henty

Chapter 1
A French Lugger

Some half a mile back from the sea, near the point where the low line of sandy hill is broken by the entrance into Poole Harbour, stood, in 1791, Netherstock; which, with a small estate around, was the property of Squire Stansfield. The view was an extensive one, when the weather was clear. Away to the left lay the pine forests of Bournemouth and Christ Church and, still farther seaward, the cliffs of the Isle of Wight, from Totland Bay as far as Saint Catherine Point. Close at hand to the south was Studland Bay, bounded by Handfast Point. Looking towards the right was a great sheet of shallow water, for the most part dry at low tide, known as Poole and Wareham Harbours, with its numerous creeks and bays.

Netherstock was an old house, with many nooks and corners. The squire was a justice of the peace but, unless there was some special business on, he seldom took his place on the bench. He was a jovial man, who took life easily. He was popular among his neighbours, especially among the poorer classes; for whom he had always a pleasant word, as he rode along; and who, in case of illness, knew that they could always be sure of a supply of soup, or a gill of brandy at Netherstock.

Among those of his own class it was often a matter of wonder how James Stansfield made both ends meet. The family had, for two or three generations, been of a similar temperament to that of the present holder; men who spent their money freely, and were sure to be present whenever there was a horse race, or a main of cocks to be fought, or a prizefight to come off, within a day's ride of Netherstock. Gradually, farm after farm had been parted with; and the estate now was smaller, by half, than it had been at the beginning of the century.

James Stansfield had, however, done nothing further to diminish it. He had a large family, but they could hardly be said to be an expensive one, seeing that little was spent upon the fashion of their clothes; and beyond the fact that the curate in charge of the little church in the village of Netherstock came over, every morning for two or three hours, to give the boys and girls the elements of education, they went very much their own way. Mrs.

Stansfield had died, five years before this. Polly, the eldest girl, aged twenty, acted as mistress of the house. Next to her, at intervals of little more than a year, came Ralph and John; two strongly built young fellows, both fearless riders and good at all rustic games. What supervision the farm work got was given by them.

Patsey, the second girl, was generally admitted to be the flower of the Stansfields. She was bright, pretty, and good tempered. She was in charge of the dairy, and the Netherstock butter was famous through the country round, and always fetched top prices at the market. The youngest of the family was Leigh, who was now fourteen. He was less heavily built than his brothers, but their tutor declared that he was the quickest and most intelligent of his pupils; and that, if he had but a chance, he would turn out a fine young fellow.

The boys were all fond of boating and sailing, which was natural enough, as the sea washed two sides of the estate. They had two boats. One of these lay hauled up on the sands, a mile to the east of the entrance to the harbour. She was a good sea boat and, when work was slack about the place, which indeed was the normal state of things, they would often sail to Weymouth to the west, or eastward to Yarmouth or Lymington, sometimes even to Portsmouth. The other boat, which was also large, but of very shallow draught of water, lay inside the entrance to the harbour; and in her they could go either north or south of Brownsea Island, and shoot or fish in the many inlets and bays. There were few who knew every foot of the great sheet of water as they did, and they could tell the precise time of the tide at which the channels were deep enough for boats drawing from two to three feet of water.

The most frequent visitor to Netherstock was Lieutenant, or, as he was called in courtesy, Captain Whittier, the officer in command of the coast guard station between Poole and Christ Church; his principal station being opposite Brownsea Island, the narrowest point of the entrance to the harbour. He was a somewhat fussy little officer, with a great idea of the importance of his duties, mingled with a regret that these duties did not afford him full scope for proving his ability.

"Smuggling has almost ceased to exist, along here," he would say. "I do not say that, across the harbour, something that way may not still be done; for the facilities there are very much greater than they are on this side. Still, my colleague there can have but little trouble; for I keep a sharp lookout that no boat enters by the passage south of the island without being searched. Of course, one hears all sorts of absurd reports about cargoes being run; but we know better, and I believe they are only set on foot to put our officers from

Swanage Westward, and beyond Christ Church down to Hurst Castle, off their guard."

"No doubt, captain; no doubt," James Stansfield would agree. "Still, I fancy that, although times are not what they were, it is still possible to buy a keg of brandy, occasionally, or a few yards of silk or lace, that have never paid duty."

"Yes, no doubt occasionally some small craft manages to run a few kegs or bales; and unfortunately the gentry, instead of aiding his majesty's representatives, keep the thing alive by purchasing spirits, and so on, from those who have been concerned in their landing."

"Well, you know, Captain Whittier, human nature is pretty strong. If a pedlar comes along here with ribbons and fal-lals, and offers them to the girls at half the price at which they could buy them down at Poole, you can hardly expect them to take lofty ground, and charge the man with having smuggled them."

"I do not think the young ladies are offenders that way," the officer said, "for I have never yet seen them in foreign gear of any sort. I should, if you will allow me to say so, be more inclined, were you not a justice of the peace, to suspect you of having dealings with these men; for your brandy is generally of the best."

"I don't set up to be better than my neighbours, captain," the squire said, with a laugh; "and if the chance comes my way, I will not say that I should refuse to buy a good article, at the price I should pay for a bad one in the town."

"Your tobacco is good, too, squire."

"Yes, I am particular about my tobacco, and I must say that I think government lays too high a duty on it. If I had the making of the laws, I would put a high duty on bad tobacco, and a low duty on a good article; that would encourage the importation of good wholesome stuff.

"I suppose you have heard no rumours of any suspicious looking craft being heard of, off the coast?"

"No, I think that they carry on their business a good deal farther to the west now. My post is becoming quite a sinecure. The Henriette came into Poole this morning, but we never trouble about her. She is a fair trader, and is well known at every port between Portsmouth and Plymouth as such. She always comes in at daylight, and lays her foresail aback till we board her, and send a couple of men with her into Poole or Wareham. Her cargo is always consigned to well-known merchants, at all the ports she enters; and consists of wines, for the most part, though she does occasionally bring in brandy.

"He is a fine young fellow, the skipper, Jean Martin. I believe his father is a large wine merchant, at Nantes. I suppose you know him, squire?"

"Yes, I have met him several times down in the town, and indeed have bought many a barrel of wine of him. He has been up here more than once, for I have told him, whenever he has anything particularly good either in wine or spirits, to let me know. He talks a little English, and my girls like to have a chat with him, about what is going on on his side of the water. He offered, the other day, to give Leigh a trip across to Nantes, if I was willing.

"Things seem to be going on very badly in Paris, by what he says; but he does not anticipate any troubles in the west of France, where there seems to be none of that ill feeling, between the different classes, that there is in other parts."

The departure of Captain Whittier was always followed by a broad smile on the faces of the elder boys, breaking occasionally into a hearty laugh, in which the squire joined.

"I call him an insufferable ass," Ralph said, on this particular evening. "It would be difficult, as father says, to find an officer who is, as far as we are concerned, so admirably suited for his position."

"That is so, Ralph. There is scarcely a man, woman, or child in this part of Dorsetshire who does not know that there are more goods run, on that piece of water over there, than on the whole south coast of England. I sincerely trust that nothing will ever bring about his recall. Personally, I would pay two or three hundred a year, out of my own pocket, rather than lose him. There is no such place anywhere for the work; why, there are some fourteen or fifteen inlets where goods can be landed at high water and, once past the island, I don't care how sharp the revenue men may be, the betting is fifty to one against their being at the right spot at the right time.

"If the passage between our point and the island were but a bit wider, it would be perfect; but unfortunately it is so narrow that it is only on the very darkest night one can hope to get through, unnoticed. However, we can do very well with the southern channel and, after all, it is safer. We can get any number of boats, and the Henriette has only to anchor half a mile outside the entrance. We know when she is coming, and have but to show a light, directly she makes her signal, and the boats will put out from Radhorn passage and Hamworth; while messengers start for Bushaw, and Scopland, and Creach, and a dozen farmhouses, and the carts are sure to be at the spot where they had been warned to assemble, by the time the boats come along with the kegs; and everything is miles away, in hiding, before morning.

"If it is a dark night the Henriette makes off again, and comes boldly in the next afternoon. If one of the revenue boats, either from here or Studland, happens to come across her before she gets up anchor, there she is--the crew are all asleep, with the exception of a man on watch; she is simply waiting to come in, when there is light enough to enable her to make her way up the passage."

James Stansfield was, in fact, the organizer of the smuggling business carried on at Poole, and the adjacent harbours. There was not a farmhouse, among the hills to the south of the great sheet of water, with which he was not in communication. Winter was the season at which the trade was most busy, for the short summer nights were altogether unsuited for the work; and when the cold weather drove the wildfowl in for shelter, there was splendid shooting, and Ralph and John were able to combine amusement with business, and to keep the larder well stocked.

The night signals were made from a cleft in the sand hills, half a mile from the house; the light being so arranged that it could not be seen from Brownsea Island, though visible to those on the south side, from Studland right away over the hills to Corfe Castle, even to Wareham. It was shown but for half a minute, just as the bells of Poole Church struck nine. At that hour, when the lugger was expected, there was a lookout at the door of every farmhouse and, the moment the light was seen, preparations were made for the landing at the spot of which notice had been given, by one or other of the boys, on the previous day. Then, from quiet little inlets, the boats would put off noiselessly, directly there was water to float them; for it was only at high tides that the shallows were covered. They would gather in the channel south of Brownsea, where the boys and often their father would be in their boats in readiness, until a momentary glimmer of a light, so placed on board the lugger that it could only be seen from the spot where they were awaiting it, showed the position of the craft and their readiness to discharge cargo.

It was exciting work, and profitable; and so well was it managed that, although it had been carried on for some years, no suspicion had ever entered the minds of any of the revenue officers. Sometimes many weeks would elapse between the visits of the lugger, for she was obliged to make her appearance frequently at other ports, to maintain her character as a trader; and was, as such, well known all along the coast.

It was only a year since the Henriette had taken the place of another lugger, that had previously carried on the work, but had been wrecked on the French coast. She had been the property of the same owner, or rather of the same firm; for Jean Martin, who had been first mate on board the other craft, had invested some of his own money in the Henriette, and assumed the command. It was noticed, at Poole, that the Henriette used that port more frequently than her predecessor had done; and indeed, she not infrequently came in, in the daytime, with her hold as full as when she had left Nantes.

It was on one of these occasions that Jean Martin, on coming up to Netherstock, had a long talk with the squire.

"So you want my daughter Patsey?" the latter said, when his visitor had told his story. "Well, it has certainly never entered my mind that any of my girls should marry a Frenchman. I don't say that I have not heard my boys making a sly joke, more than once, when the Henriette was seen coming in, and I have seen the colour flying up into the girl's face; but I only looked at it as boys' nonsense. Still, I don't say that I am averse to your suit. We may be said to be partners, in this trade of yours, and we both owe each other a good deal. During the last eight years you must have run something like forty cargoes, and never lost a keg or a bale; and I doubt if as much could be said for any other craft in the trade.

"Still, one can't calculate on always being lucky. I don't think anyone would turn traitor, when the whole countryside is interested in the matter; and I wouldn't give much for the life of anyone who whispered as much as a word to the revenue people. Still, accidents will take place sometimes. Your father must have done well with the trade, and so have I.

"At any rate, I will leave it in Patsey's hands. I have enough of them, and to spare. And of course, you will be able to bring her over, sometimes, to pay us a visit here.

"I think, too, that your offer of taking Leigh over with you helps to decide me in your favour. They are all growing up and, if anything were to put a stop to our business, this place would not keep them all; and it would be a great thing, for Patsey, to have her brother as a companion when you are away. The boy would learn French, and in your father's business would get such a knowledge of the trade with Nantes as should serve him in good stead. At any rate, he will learn things that are a good deal more useful to him than those he gets from the curate.

"Well, you know you will find her in the dairy, as usual. You had better go and see what she says to it."

It is probable that Jean Martin had already a shrewd idea of what Patsey's answer would be, and he presently returned to her father, radiant. Patsey, indeed, had given her heart to the cheery young sailor; and although it seemed to her a terrible thing, that she should go to settle in France, she had the less objection to it, inasmuch as the fear that the smuggling would be sooner or later discovered, and that ruin might fall upon Netherstock, was ever present in her mind, and in that of her elder sister.

To her brothers, engaged in the perilous business, it was regarded as a pleasant excitement, without which their lives would be intolerably dull. It was not that she or they regarded the matter in the light of a crime, for almost everyone on that part of the coast looked upon smuggling as a game, in which the wits of those concerned in it were pitted against those of the revenue men. It brought profit to all concerned, and although many of the gentry found it convenient to express indignation, at the damage done to the king's revenue by smuggling; there were none of them who thought it necessary to mention, to the coast guard, when by some accident a keg of brandy, or a parcel with a few pounds of prime tobacco, was found in one of the outhouses.

Patsey had suffered more than her sister, being of a more lively imagination, and being filled with alarm and anxiety whenever she knew that her father and the boys were away at night. Then, too, she was very fond of Leigh, and had built many castles in the air as to his future; and the thought that, not only would he be with her, but would be in the way of making his road to fortune, was very pleasant to her. She knew that if he remained at Netherstock he would grow up like his brothers. His father might, from time to time, talk of putting him into some business; but she understood his ways, and was certain that nothing would come of it.

Martin had, before, expressed to her his doubt as to whether her father would consent to her going away with him; but she had no fear on the subject. In his quiet, easygoing way he was fond of his children; and would scarcely put himself out to oppose, vehemently, anything on which they had set their hearts. He had, too, more than once said that he wished some of them could be settled elsewhere; for a time of trouble might come, and it would be well to have other homes, where some of them could be received.

"Patsey has consented," Jean Martin said, joyously, as he rejoined the squire.

"Well, that is all right. I think, myself, that it is for the best. Of course, it must be understood that, in the matter of religion, she is not to be forced or urged in any sort of way; but is to be allowed to follow the religion in which she has been brought up."

"I would in no way press her, sir. We have Protestants in France, just as there are Catholics here; though I must admit that there are not many of them in La Vendee. Still, the days when people quarrelled about religion are long since past; and certainly at Nantes there is a Protestant congregation, though away in the country they would be difficult to find. However, I promise you, solemnly, that I will in no way try to influence her mind, nor that of the boy. He will still, of course, look upon England as his home, and I should even oppose any attempt being made to induce him to join our church. You have plenty of Frenchmen in this country, and no question as to their religion arises. It will be just the same, with us."

Six weeks later, the Henriette returned. In her came Monsieur Martin, whose presence as a witness of the ceremony was considered advisable, if not absolutely necessary. He had, too, various documents to sign in presence of the French consul, at Southampton, giving his formal consent. The marriage was solemnized there at a small Catholic chapel, and it was repeated at the parish church at Poole, and the next day the party sailed for Nantes.

It was two months before the lugger again came in to Poole. When it returned, it took with it the squire and Polly, to whom Monsieur Martin had given a warm invitation to come over to see Patsey, in her new home.

They found her well and happy. Monsieur Martin's house was in the suburbs of Nantes. It had a large garden, at the end of which, facing another street, stood a pretty little house that had been generally used, either as the abode of aged mothers or unmarried sisters of the family, or for an eldest son to take his wife to; but which had now been handed over to Jean and his wife. This was very pleasant for Patsey, as it united the privacy of a separate abode with the cheerfulness of the family home. She had her own servant, whose excellent cooking and, above all, whose scrupulous cleanliness and tidiness, astonished her after the rough meals and haphazard arrangements at Netherstock.

Whenever she felt dull during Jean's absences, she could run across the garden for a talk with his mother and sister; at meals and in the evening she had Leigh, who spent most of his time at the cellars or in the counting house of Monsieur Martin; learning for the first time habits of business, and applying himself eagerly to acquiring the language.

The squire was put up at Monsieur Martin's, and Polly slept in the one spare room at her sister's, all the party from the pavilion going over to the house, to the midday meal and supper. The squire and Polly were much pleased with their visit. It was evident that Patsey had become a prime favourite with her husband's family. Jean's sister Louise was assiduous in teaching her French, and she had already begun to make some progress. Louise and her mother were constantly running across to the little pavilion, on some errand or other; and Patsey spent as much of her time with them as she did in her own house.

Jean's absences seldom exceeded ten days, and he generally spent a week at home before sailing again. He had driven her over to stay, for three or four days, at a small estate of his own, some forty miles to the southeast of Nantes, in the heart of what was called the Bocage--a wild country, with thick woods, narrow lanes, high hedges, and scattered villages and farms, much more English in appearance than the country round Nantes. The estate had come to him from an aunt. Everything here was very interesting to Patsey; the costumes of the women and children, the instruments of husbandry, the air of freedom and independence of the people, and the absence of all ceremony, interested and pleased her. She did not understand a single word of the patois spoken to her by the peasants, and which even Jean had some difficulty in following, although he had spent a good deal of his time at the little chateau during the lifetime of his aunt.

"Should you like to live here, when not at sea, Jean?" asked Patsey.

"Yes, I would rather live here than at Nantes. Next to a life at sea, I should like one quite in the country. There is plenty to do here. There is the work on the place to look after, there is shooting, there is visiting, and visiting here means something hearty, and not like the formal work in the town. Here no one troubles his head over politics. They may quarrel as they like, in Paris, but it does not concern La Vendee.

"Here the peasants love their masters, and the masters do all in their power for the comfort and happiness of the peasants. It is not as in many other parts of France, where the peasants hate the nobles, and the nobles regard the peasants as dirt under their feet. Here it is more like what I believe it was in England, when you had your troubles, and the tenants followed their lords to battle. At any rate, life here would be very preferable to being in business with my father, in Nantes. I should never have settled down to that; and as my elder brother seems specially made for that sort of life, fortunately I was able to go my own way, to take to the sea in the lugger, and become the carrier of the firm, while taking my share in the general profits."

"How is it that your brother does not live at home? It would seem natural that he should have had the pavilion, when he married."

"He likes going his own way," Jean said shortly. "As far as business matters go, he and my father are as one; but in other matters they differ widely. Jacques is always talking of reforms and changes, while my father is quite content with things as they are. Jacques has his own circle of friends, and would like to go to Paris as a deputy, and to mix himself up in affairs.

"Though none of us cared for the lady that he chose as his wife, she had money, and there was nothing to say against her, personally. None of us ever took to her, and there was a general feeling of relief when it was known that Jacques had taken a house in the business quarter.

"He looks after the carrying business. Of course, my lugger does but a very small proportion of it. We send up large quantities of brandy to Tours, Orleans, and other towns on the Loire; and have dealings with Brittany and Normandy, by sea, and with the Gironde. He looks after that part of the business. My father does the buying and directs the counting house. Though my art is a very inferior one, I have no reason to complain of my share of the profits."

The first eighteen months of Patsey's married life passed quietly and happily. She could now speak French fluently and, having made several stays at the country chateau, could make herself understood in the patois. Leigh spoke French as well as English. Fortunately he had picked up a little before leaving home, partly from his tutor, partly from endeavouring to talk with French fishermen and sailors who came into Poole. He frequently made trips in the Henriette, sometimes to Havre and Rouen, at others to Bordeaux. He had grown much, and was now a very strong, active lad. He got on very well with Monsieur Martin; but kept as much apart as he could from his eldest son, for whom he felt a deep personal dislike, and who had always disapproved of Jean's marriage to an Englishwoman.

Jacques Martin was the strongest contrast to his brother. He was methodical and sententious, expressed his opinion on all subjects with the air of a man whose judgment was infallible, and was an ardent disciple of Voltaire and Rousseau. It was very seldom that he entered his father's house, where his opinions on religious subjects shocked and horrified his mother and sister. He lived with an entirely different set, and spent most of his time at the clubs which, in imitation of those of Paris, had sprung up all over the country.

"What is all the excitement about, Jean?" Leigh asked his brother-in-law, one evening. "There are always fellows standing on casks or bales of timber along the wharf, shouting and waving their arms about and, sometimes, reading letters or printed papers; and then those who listen to them shout and throw up their caps, and get into a tremendous state of excitement."

"They are telling the others what is being done at the Assembly."

"And what are they doing there, Jean?"

"They are turning things upside down."

"And is that good?"

"Well, there is no doubt that things are not as well managed as they might be, and that there is a great deal of distress and misery. In some parts of France the taxation has been very heavy, and the extravagance of the court has excited an immense deal of anger. It is not the fault of the present king, who is a quiet fellow, and does not care for show or pageants; but it is rather the fault of the kings who preceded him, especially of Louis the Fourteenth--who was a great monarch, no doubt, but a very expensive one to his subjects, and whose wars cost an enormous sum.

"You see it is not, in France, as it is with you. The nobles here have great power. Their tenants and serfs--for they are still nothing but serfs--are at the mercy of their lords, who may flog them and throw them into prison, almost at their pleasure; and will grind the last sou out of them, that they may cut a good figure at court.

"In this part of France things are more as they are in England. The nobles and seigneurs are like your country gentlemen. They live in their chateaux, they mix with their people and take an interest in them, they go to their fetes, and the ladies visit the sick, and in all respects they live as do your country squires; paying a visit for a few weeks each year to Paris, and spending the rest of their time on their estates. But it is not from the country that the members of the Assembly who are the most urgent for reforms and violent in their speech come, but from the towns. There were two writers, Voltaire and Rousseau, who have done enormous mischief. Both of them perceived that the state of things was wrong; but they went to extremes, made fun of the church, and attacked institutions of all sorts. Their writings are read by everyone, and have shaken people's faith in God, and in all things as they are.

"I do not say that much improvement could not be made, but it will never be made by sudden and great changes, nor by men such as those who are gradually gaining the upper hand in the Assembly. The people ought to have a much stronger voice than they have in their own taxation. They see that, in England, the ministers and parliament manage everything; and that the king--although his influence goes for a good deal, and he can change his ministers as often as he likes--must yet bow to the voice of parliament. I think that that is reasonable; but when it comes to a parliament composed largely of mere agitators and spouters, I, for my part, would rather be ruled by a king."

"But what is it that these people want, Jean?"

"I do not think they know in the least, themselves, beyond the fact that they want all the power; that they want to destroy the nobility, overthrow the church, and lay hands on the property of all who are more wealthy than themselves. Naturally the lowest classes of the towns, who are altogether ignorant, believe that by supporting these men, and by pulling down all above them, it would no longer be necessary to work. They want to divide the estates of the nobles, take a share of the wealth of the traders, and of the better class of all sorts; in fact they would turn everything topsy-turvy, render the poor all powerful, and tread all that is good and noble under their feet. The consequence is that the king is virtually a prisoner in the hands of the mob of Paris, the nobles and better classes are leaving the country, thousands of these have already been massacred, and no one can say how matters will end.

"Here in Nantes there is, as you see, a feeling of excitement and unrest; and though as yet there has been no violence, no one could venture to predict what may take place, if the moderate men in the Assembly are outvoted by the extremists, and all power falls into the hands of the latter. But I still hope that common sense will prevail, in the long run. I regard the present as a temporary madness, and trust that France will come to her senses, and that we shall have the satisfaction of seeing the scoundrels, who are now the leaders of the mob of Paris, receive the punishment they deserve.

"However, as far as we are concerned I have no uneasiness for, if troubles break out at Nantes, we can retire to my chateau, in the thickest and most wooded part of La Vendee, where there is no fear that the peasants will ever rise against their masters."

Chapter 2
The Beginning Of Troubles

"Things are getting more and more serious, Patsey," said Jean one evening. "I don't know what will come of it. The excitement is spreading here, and there can be no doubt that there will be very serious troubles, ere long. The greater portion of the people here are with the Assembly, and approve of all these decrees against the priests, and the persecution of the better classes. You know what has taken place in Paris, and I fear that it will be repeated here.

"We are split up. My father, dear good man, thinks that he has only to attend to his business, and to express no opinion whatever about public affairs, and that the storm will pass quietly over his head. My brother has thrown himself heart and soul--that is to say, as far as he has a heart to throw--into what he calls the cause of the people; and which I consider to be the cause of revolution, of confiscation, of irreligion, and abomination generally.

"I am told that my name has freely been mentioned, in his club, as that of a dangerous man, with opinions contrary to the public good. I hear, too, that that brother of mine was there, at the time; and that he got up and said that in a case like this his voice must be silent, that true patriots place their country before all things; and then affected to speak mildly in my favour, but at the same time doing me as much harm as he could. I believe the fellow is capable of denouncing his own father.

"From the Bocage I hear that the whole country is in confusion. The people, of course, side with their priests. The nobles and land owners are naturally royalists, and are furious that the king should be held in what is practically subjection; by men of low degree, and who, although they may have some virtuous men among them, have also sanguinary scoundrels who gradually gain in power, and will soon be supreme.

"They, however, can do nothing at present. The peasants know nothing about the king, to them he is a mere name; but this persecution of their priests angers them greatly; and if, as is said, orders have been given to raise an army, and to drag men away from their homes whether they like to go or not, you may be sure that, ere long, there will be trouble there.

"Now you see, dear, I am a sort of double character. At sea I am Captain Jean Martin, a peaceful trader with, as you know, but little regard for the revenue laws of your country. On the other hand, in La Vendee I am Monsieur Jean Martin, a landed proprietor, and on friendly terms with all the nobles and gentry in my neighbourhood. It is evident that I cannot continue to play this double part. Already great numbers of arrests have been made here, and the prisons are half full. I hear that a commissioner from the Assembly is expected here shortly, to try these suspects, as they are called; and from what we know already, we may be sure that there will be little mercy shown.

"They are almost all people of substance; and the people, as they call themselves, are on principle opposed to men of substance. Now, if I remain here, I have no doubt that I shall be denounced in a very short time; and to be denounced is to be thrown into prison, and to be thrown into prison is equivalent to being murdered. I have no doubt, Patsey, that you would share my fate. The fact that you are an Englishwoman was among the accusations brought against me, in the club; and although, so far as I can see, the majority of these scoundrels have no religion whatever, they venture to make it a matter of complaint that you are a Protestant.

"I have seen this coming on for some time, and must now make my choice; either I must take you and the child over to England, and leave you there with your father until these troubles are over, while I must myself go down and look after my tenantry, and bear my share in whatever comes; or you must go down there with me."

"Certainly I will go down with you, Jean. It is your home, and whatever dangers may come I will share them with you. It would be agony to be in England, and to know nothing of what is passing here, and what danger might be threatening you. We took each other for better or worse, Jean, and the greater danger you may be in, the more it will be my duty to be by your side.

"I should be very happy down at the chateau. More happy than I have been here with you, for some time past; for one cannot but be very anxious, when one sees one's friends thrown into prison, and knows that you are opposed to all these things, and that it may be your turn next. Nothing would persuade me to leave you."

"Very well, wife, so be it. I am sure that there, at least, we shall be safe. It is only in the towns that these rascals are dangerous, and in a country like ours there is little fear that the knaves will venture to interfere, when they see that they are stirring up a nest of hornets. They have plenty of work to satisfy even their taste for confiscation and murder, in the large towns. There is an army gathering, on the frontier, and they will have their hands full, ere long.

"And now, about Leigh. My brother has always shown a dislike for him and, as it is certain that he cannot remain here, he must either return to England or go with us."

"I am sure that he would choose to go with us, Jean. You say yourself that he talks French like a native now, and although he has often told me that he would never settle in France--for naturally he is as horrified as I am with the doings in Paris, and the other great towns--still I am sure that he would choose to remain with us, now. You see, he is strong and active, and has made so many trips with you, that he is almost a sailor. He is within a few months of sixteen, and of late he has several times said to me that he would like to go some long voyages, and have some adventures, before settling down in business, in England, as an agent of your house."

"I should like to have him with us," Jean said heartily. "In the first place, he is a lad after my own heart, full of life and go, and already strong enough to take his own part; in the next place, although I hope for the best, a man can never say exactly what will take place. I may be away at times, and should be glad to know that you had a protector; and if he is willing to go, I shall be more than willing to have him.

"Then, too, it would be useful to have someone whom one could trust to carry messages. My idea is that I shall not leave the lugger here for, if I am denounced, it would certainly be seized. Pierre Lefaux, my mate, is a shrewd as well as a faithful fellow. I shall appoint him captain. I shall tell him to leave here, at once, and employ the lugger in coasting voyages; making Bordeaux his headquarters, and taking what freights he can get between that town and Rochelle, Brest, or other ports on this coast. So long as he does not return here, he might even take wines across to England, or brandy from Charente. He knows his business well and, as long as we are at peace with England, trade will still go on.

"The best thing would be for him to be at Bordeaux once every fortnight, or three weeks, so that we shall know where to find him. I have a great friend at Bordeaux, and shall get him to have the lugger registered in his name, and give him a receipt for her purchase money; so that in case the people here learn that she is trading at Bordeaux, he will be able to prove that she is his own property. Then, if the very worst should come, which I cannot bring myself to believe, there will be a means of escape for us all to England.

"She will be sailing there in two or three days. I have fifty thousand francs lying in my father's hands. I shall send that over by Lefaux, and instruct him to ask your father to go with him to the bank, at Poole, and pay the money in to my account. Then, if we should have to leave France, we shall have that to fall back upon, and the lugger. I should, of course, transfer her to the English flag, and have no doubt that we should be able to get on very fairly. So you see, I am preparing for all contingencies, Patsey."

"It seems very dreadful that the country should be in such a state, Jean."

"It is dreadful, and I am afraid that things have by no means got to the worst, yet.

"Ah, here comes Leigh! After supper I shall go in and have a talk with my father. I have very little hope of having much success with him; but at least, when he sees the steps that I am taking, it cannot but make him think seriously of his own position, and that of my mother and sisters."

Leigh was delighted when he heard Jean's proposal. His own position had been unpleasant, of late. He had long since ceased to go to Jacques Martin, for the dislike between them was mutual and, do what he would, he failed to give satisfaction. And of late, even in Monsieur Martin's cellars and storehouses, he had met with a good deal of unpleasantness; and would have met with more, had it not been that he had, on one occasion, knocked down one of the chief clerks, who had sworn at him for some trifling act of carelessness. As the clerk knew that the merchant would have been very angry at the insult he had offered to Leigh, he had not ventured to make a complaint; but in many ways he had been able to cause numberless petty annoyances. Many of the others were inclined to follow his lead, and would have done so more openly, were it not that they held in respect Leigh's strength, and readiness in the science they called le boxe.

The talk that there might be troubles in La Vendee heightened his satisfaction at leaving Nantes, and going down to stay in the country. The thought of a life spent at Poole, or Weymouth, as a wine merchant and agent of the house of Martin had, for some time past, been unpleasant to him. The feeling of general unrest that prevailed in France had communicated itself to him, and he thought possibly that something might occur which would change the current of his life, and lead to one more suited to his natural activity and energy.

"You had better pack up quietly, tomorrow," Jean said to his wife, after his return from his father's. "If there were any suspicion that I was thinking of going away, it might bring matters to a head. I will get the lugger's boat down to the wharf, and four sailors shall come up here and take the boxes down, in one of the hand carts, with a tarpaulin thrown over them. I will arrange for a cart and a carriage to be waiting for us, on the other side of the river.

"There is no moving my father. He cannot persuade himself that a man who takes no part in politics, and goes about his business quietly, can be in any danger. He has, however, at my mother's entreaty, agreed for the present to cease buying; and to diminish his stock as far as possible, and send the money, as fast as he realizes it, across to England. He says, too, that he will, if things get worse, send her and my sister to England. I promised him that your father would find them a house, and see that they were settled comfortably there, for a time. He would not believe that Jacques could have been at the club when I was denounced, without defending me; for although himself greatly opposed to the doings in Paris, and annoyed at the line Jacques has taken up, he thought that there was at least this advantage in it--that in case of troubles coming here, he would have sufficient influence to prevent our being in any way molested. However, there can be no question that I have, to some extent, alarmed him; and he agreed not only to draw, tomorrow, my fifty thousand francs from his caisse, but to send over with it a hundred thousand francs of his own. Fortunately he can do this without Jacques knowing anything about it, for although Jacques and I have both a share in the business, he has always kept the management of the money matters in his own hands.

"So that is settled, as far as it can be settled. Fortunately the club does not meet this evening, so there is no fear of a demand being made, by it, for my arrest tomorrow. I have a friend who belongs to it--not, I think, because he at all agrees with its views; but because, like many others, he deems it prudent to appear to do so. It was from him that I heard what had passed there, and he promised to give me warning of anything that might be said, or done, against me. I shall go down to the lugger early, and remain on board all day, seeing to the stowage of the cargo we are taking on board, so that no suspicion can arise that I am thinking of leaving for the country."

The next evening the party started by unfrequented streets for the quay, the nurse carrying the child, now three months old. The boxes had gone half an hour before. It was nearly ten o'clock, and the quays were deserted. Monsieur Martin had himself gone down, in the afternoon, with the money to the lugger, and handed it over to Jean, and had a long talk with him and Pierre Lefaux, to whom Jean had also intrusted letters from himself and Patsey, to the squire.

As soon as the party had taken their seats in the boat, it was rowed two miles up the river, to a point where there was a ferry across to a road, leading into the heart of La Vendee. Here a light waggon and a carriage were waiting. The luggage was transferred to the former and, after a hearty farewell to Pierre Lefaux, who had himself come in charge of the boat, they started on their journey; and arrived at the chateau at nine o'clock in the morning, to the surprise of the man and woman in charge of it.

"Here we are safe," Jean said, as they alighted from the carriage. "It would take nothing short of an army to fight its way through these woods and lanes and, if the Assembly try to interfere with us, they will find it a much easier thing to pull down the throne of France, than to subdue La Vendee."

The news that the master had come down, and that he was going for a time to live among them, spread rapidly; and in the course of the day some fifteen of the tenants came in to pay their respects, few of them arriving without some little offering in the way of game, poultry, butter, or other produce.

"Our larder is full enough for us to stand a siege," Patsey said, laughing, "and I know that we have a good stock of wine in the cellar, Jean."

"Yes, and of cider, too. When the tenants are in any difficulty about paying their rents, I am always willing to take it out in wine or cider; for my father deals in both, and therefore it is as good as money. But I have not sent any to Nantes for the past two or three years and, as you say, the cellars are as full as they can hold.

"Tomorrow, Leigh, we will ride over and call upon some of our neighbours to hear the last news, for the Bocage is as far away from Nantes as if it were on the other side of France, and we hear only vague rumours of what is going on here."

The ride was a delightful one to Leigh. He had only once visited the chateau before, and then only for a day or two. The wild country, with its deep lanes, its thick high hedges, its woods and copses, was all new to him; for the country round his English home was, for the most part, bare and open. Some of the peasants carried guns over their shoulders, and looked as if accustomed to use them.

"Very few of them possess guns," Jean Martin remarked, "and that they should carry them shows how disturbed a state of mind all these people are in. They know that their priests may be arrested and carried off, at any moment; and no doubt the report that an order has been issued to raise thirty thousand men throughout France, and that every town and village has to furnish its quota, has stirred them up even more effectually. I don't suppose that many of them think that the authorities will really try to drag men off, against their will; but the possibility is quite enough to inflame their minds."

At the very first house they visited they received, from the owner, ample confirmation of Jean's views.

"There have been continual fracases between the peasants and the military," he said, "over the attempts of the latter to arrest the priests. They can scarcely be called fights, for it has not come to that; but as soon as the peasants hear that the gendarmes are coming, they send the priest into the wood, and gather in such force that the gendarmes are glad enough to ride away, unharmed. Of course, until we see that the peasants are really in earnest, and intend to fight to the last, it would be madness for any of us to take any part in the matter; for we should be risking not only life but the fortunes of our families, and maybe their lives, too. You must remember, moreover, that already a great number of the landed proprietors have either been murdered or imprisoned in Paris, or are fugitives beyond the frontier."

"If the peasants would fight," Jean Martin said, "it might not be a bad thing that there are so few whom they could regard as their natural leaders. If there are only a few leaders they may act together harmoniously, or each operate in his own district; but with a number of men of the same rank, or nearly of the same rank, each would have his own ideas as to what should be done, and there would be jealousy and discord."

"That is true," the other replied. "Of course, if this were an open country it would be necessary, to give us a chance of success, that some sort of discipline should be established; and none could persuade the peasants to submit to discipline, except their own lords. But in a country like this, discipline is of comparatively little importance; and it is well that it is so, for though I believe that the peasants would fight to the death, rather than submit to be dragged away by force from their homes, they will never keep together for any time."

"I am afraid that that will be the case. We must hope that it will not come to fighting but, if it does, it will take a large force to conquer La Vendee."

"What has brought you down here, Monsieur Martin?"

"It was not safe for me to stay longer in Nantes. If I think a thing I say it, and as I don't think well of what is being done in Paris, I have not been in the habit of saying flattering things about the men there. In fact I have been denounced and, as there is still room for a few more in the prisons, I should have had a cell placed at my disposal, if I had remained there many more hours; so I thought that I should be safer, down here, till there was some change in the state of affairs."

"And you brought madame down with you?"

"Assuredly. I had only the choice open to me of sending her across to England, and of making my home there, or of coming here. If there had been no prospect of trouble here, I might have joined the army of our countrymen who are in exile; but as, from all I heard, La Vendee was ready to take up arms, I determined to come here; partly because, had I left the country, my estates here would have been confiscated; partly because I should like to strike a blow, myself, at these tyrants of Paris, who seem bent on destroying the whole of the aristocracy of France, of wiping out the middle classes, and dividing the land and all else among the scum of the towns."

Three or four months passed quietly. There were occasional skirmishes between the peasants, and parties of troops in search of priests who refused to obey the orders of the Assembly. At Nantes, the work of carrying out mock trials, and executing those of the better classes who had been swept into the prisons, went on steadily. From time to time a message came to Jean, from his father, saying that he had carried out his determination to lessen his stocks, and that he had sent considerable sums of money across the Channel. So far he had not been molested, but he saw that the public madness was increasing, and the passion for blood ever growing.

Then came the news of the execution of the king, which sent a thrill of horror through the loyal province. Shortly afterwards it was known that the decree for the raising of men was to be enforced; and that commissioners had already arrived at Saumur with a considerable force, that would be employed, if necessary; but that the process of drawing the names of those who were to go was to be carried out by the local authorities, assisted by the national guards of the towns.

During the winter things had gone on quietly, at the chateau. There had been but little visiting, for the terrible events passing in Paris, and in all the large towns, and the uncertainty about the future, had cast so deep a gloom over the country that none thought of pleasure, or even of cheerful intercourse with their neighbours. Many of the gentry, too, had given up all hope; and had made their way down to the coast, and succeeded in obtaining a passage in smuggling craft, or even in fishing boats, to England.

Jean Martin and Leigh had spent much of their time in shooting. Game was abundant and, as so many of the chateaux were shut up, they had a wide range of country open to them for sport. Once or twice they succeeded in bringing home a wild boar. Wolves had multiplied in the forests for, during the last three years, the regular hunts in which all the gentry took part had been abandoned, and the animals had grown fearless.

One day, soon after the news of the king's death had been received, Jean, who had ridden over to Saumur on business, brought back the news that war had been declared with England.

"It would have made a good deal of difference to me," he said, "if I had still been on board the lugger; for of course there would be an end to all legitimate trade. However, no doubt I should have managed to run a cargo, sometimes; for they will want brandy and tobacco all the more, when regular trade is at an end; and prices, you may be sure, will go up. I have no doubt, too, that there will be a brisk business in carrying emigrants over. Still, of course the danger would be very much greater. Hitherto we have only had the revenue cutters and the coast guards to be afraid of, now every vessel of war would be an enemy."

As during their expeditions they were generally accompanied by half a dozen peasants, who acted as beaters, Leigh had come to understand the patois, and to some extent to speak it; and he often paid visits to the houses of the principal tenants of the estate, who not only welcomed him as the brother of their mistress, but soon came to like him for himself, and were amused by his high spirits, his readiness to be pleased with everything, and his talk to them of the little known country across the water.

It was evident, from the manner in which the drawing for the conscription was spoken of, that it would not be carried out without a strong resistance. Sunday, the tenth of March, had been fixed for the drawing and, as the day approached, the peasants became more and more determined that they would not permit themselves to be dragged away from their homes.

Three days before, a party of the tenants, together with some from adjoining estates, had come up to the chateau. Jean Martin at once came out to them.

"We have come, monsieur, to ask if you will lead us. We are determined that we will not be carried off like sheep."

"There you are right," Jean said; "but although I shall be ready to do my share of fighting, I do not wish to be a leader. In the first place, there are many gentlemen of far larger possessions and of higher rank than myself, who would naturally be your leaders. There is the Marquis de Lescure at Clisson, and with him are several other noble gentlemen, among them Henri de la Rochejaquelein--he is a cavalry officer. His family have emigrated, but he has remained here on his estates. Then, too, you have many other military officers who have served. There is Monsieur de Bonchamp, Monsieur d'Elbee, and Monsieur Dommaigne, all of whom have served in the army. If the insurrection becomes general, I shall head my own tenants, and join the force under some chosen commander; but I shall not appear as a leader. Not only am I altogether ignorant of military affairs but, were it known in Nantes that I was prominent in the rising, they would undoubtedly avenge themselves upon my relations there."

It was known that artillery and gendarmes had been gathered in all the towns of La Vendee. Two days before that appointed for the drawing, Jean said to Leigh:

"I shall ride tomorrow to the castle of Clisson. I know Monsieur de Lescure. He has wide influence, and is known to be a devoted royalist, and to have several royalist refugees now at his house. I shall be able to learn, from him, whether his intention is to take part in the insurrection. It is a long ride, and I shall not return until tomorrow.

"If you like, you can ride north to Saint Florent. If there should be any tumult, I charge you not to take any part in it. You had better leave your horse at some cabaret on this side of the town, and go in on foot. It is possible that there will be no trouble there, for they are sure to have made preparations against it; and it is more likely that there will be disturbances at smaller places. Still, it will be interesting to mark the attitude of the peasants.

"You see, if there is to be a war, it is their war. The gentlemen here would have fought for the king, had there been a shadow of a prospect of success, and had he given the smallest encouragement to his friends to rally to his support. They might even have fought against the disturbance of the clergy. But they would have had no followers. The peasants cared but little for the king and, though they did care enough for the priests to aid them to escape, they did not care enough to give battle for them. They are now going to fight for their own cause, and for their own liberty. They have to show us that they are in earnest about it, before we join them. If they are in earnest, we ought to be successful. We ought to be able to put a hundred thousand men in arms and, in such a country as this, we should be able to defy any force that the Convention can send against us; and to maintain the right of La Vendee to hold itself aloof from the doings of the rest of France.

"But, as I said, until we know that they are really in earnest, we cannot afford to throw in our lot with them; so if you go to Saint Florent, keep well away from the point where the drawing is to take place. Watch affairs from a distance. I have little doubt that those who go will go with the determination of defending themselves, but whether they will do so will depend upon whether there is one among them energetic enough to take the lead. That is always the difficulty in such matters. If there is a fight we must, as I say, simply watch it. It is, at present, no affair of ours. If it begins, we shall all have our work before us, plenty of it, and plenty of danger and excitement, but for the present we have to act as spectators."

It was a ride of fifteen miles to Saint Florent and, although Leigh had twice during the winter ridden there with Jean, he had some difficulty in finding his way through the winding roads and numerous lanes along which he had to pass. During the early part of the ride he met with but few people on the way. The church bells were ringing, as usual, and there was nothing to show that any trouble was impending; but when he arrived within two or three miles of the town, he overtook little groups of peasants walking in that direction. Some of them, he saw, carried pitchforks. The rest had stout cudgels.

Saint Florent stood on the Loire and, in an open space in the centre of the town, the authorities were gathered. Behind them was a force of gendarmes, and in the middle of their line stood a cannon.

Leigh had, as Jean had told him, left his horse outside the town; and now took up his place, with a number of townspeople, on one side of the square. As the peasants arrived, they clustered together at the end of the street, waiting for the hour to strike at which the drawing was to begin. A few minutes before the clock struck, some of the gendarmes left the group in the centre of the square, and advanced to the peasants. They were headed by an officer who, as he came up, exclaimed:

"What do you mean by coming here with pitchforks? Lay them down, at once!"

There was a low murmur among the peasants.

"Follow me!" he said to his men and, walking up to one of the men carrying a pitchfork, he said:

"I arrest you, in the name of the Republic."

In an instant a young man standing next to the one he had seized sprang forward, and struck the officer to the ground with his cudgel.

"Follow me!" he shouted. "Make for the gun!"

With a cheer the peasants rushed forward, overthrowing the gendarmes as they went. The municipal authorities, after hesitating for a moment, took to their heels in the most undignified manner. The gun had not been loaded. The gendarmes round it, seeing that they were greatly outnumbered, followed their example; and the peasants, with exultant shouts, seized the cannon and then, scattering, chased the gendarmes out of the town.

Never was a more speedy and bloodless victory. Headed by their leader, whose name was Rene Foret, the peasants went to the municipality, broke open the doors, took possession of the arms stored there, collected all the papers they could find, and made a great bonfire with them in the centre of the square. Then without harming anyone, or doing the slightest mischief, they left the town and scattered to their homes in the Bocage.

Leigh waited until all was over, returned to the cabaret where he had left his horse, and rode on. Passing through the little town of Pin a powerful-looking man, some thirty-five years old, with a quiet manner, broad forehead, and intelligent face, stepped up to him.

"Pardon, monsieur," he said; "but you have come from Saint Florent?"

"Yes," he replied.

"Has aught happened there?"

"Yes, the peasants attacked the gendarmes, who fled, leaving their cannon behind them. The peasants took what arms there were in the municipality, and made a bonfire of the papers. They then, without doing any damage, dispersed to their homes."

"They have done well," the man said. "They have made a beginning. My name, monsieur, is Cathelineau; my business, so far, has been that of a hawker. I am well known in this part of the country. Maybe, sir, you will hear my name again, for henceforth I am an insurgent. We have borne this tyranny of the butchers in Paris too long, and the time has come when we must either free ourselves of it, or die. You belong to another class, but methinks that when you see that we are in earnest, you will join."

"I doubt not that we shall," Leigh said. "I am but a lad yet; but I hope that, when the time comes, I shall do my part."

The man lifted his hat and moved off, and Leigh rode forward again. He was struck with the earnest manner of the man. He had spoken calmly and without excitement, expressed himself well, and had the air of a man who, having determined upon a thing, would carry it through.

"I expect I shall hear of him again," he said to himself. "A man like that, travelling round the country, no doubt has a deal of influence. He is just the sort of man the peasants would follow; indeed, as it seems to me, that anyone might follow."

It was late in the afternoon when he arrived home, and told his sister what he had witnessed.

"I am not surprised, Leigh," she said. "If I were a man I would take up arms, too. There must be an end to what is going on. Thousands have been murdered in Paris, men and women; and at least as many more in the other great towns. If this goes on, not only the nobles and gentry, but the middle class of France will all disappear; and these bloodstained monsters will, I suppose, set to to kill each other. I feel half French now, Leigh, and it is almost too awful to think of.

"It seems to me that the only hope is that the peasants, not only of the Bocage, but of all Poitou, Anjou, and Brittany, may rise, be joined by those of other parts, and march upon the towns; destroy them altogether, and kill all who have been concerned in these doings."

"That would be pretty sweeping, Patsey," Leigh laughed. "But you know I hate them as much as you do and, though I don't feel a bit French, I would certainly do all that I could against them, just as one would kill wild beasts who go about tearing people to pieces. It is no odds to me whether the men, women, and children they kill are French, or English. One wants to put a stop to their killing."

"I wish, now, that I had not brought you out with me, Leigh."

"In the first place, Patsey, I deny altogether that you did bring me out--Jean brought me out; and in the next place, I don't see why you should be sorry. I would not miss all this excitement, for anything. Besides, I have learned to talk French well, and something of the business of a wine merchant. I can't be taken in by having common spirit, a year or two old, passed off on me as the finest from Charente; or a common claret for a choice brand. All that is useful, even if I do not become a wine merchant. At any rate, it is more useful than stopping at Netherstock, where I should have learned nothing except a little more Latin and Greek."

"Yes, but you may be killed, Leigh."

"Well, I suppose if I had stayed at home, and got a commission in the army or a midshipman's berth in the navy, I might have been killed and, if I had my choice, I would much rather be killed in fighting against people who murder women and children, who have committed no crime whatever, than in fighting soldiers or sailors of another nation, who may be just as honest fellows as we are."

"I cannot argue with you, Leigh; but if anything happens to you I shall blame myself, all my life."

"That would be foolish," Leigh said. "It is funny what foolish ideas women have. You could not have foreseen what was coming, when you came over here; and you thought that it would be a good thing for me to accompany you, for a time. You did what you thought was best, and which I think was best. Well, if it doesn't turn out just what we expected, you cannot blame yourself for that. Why, if you were to ask me to come for a walk, and a tree fell on me as we were going along and killed me, you would hardly blame yourself because you asked me to come; and this is just the same.

"At any rate, if I do get killed, which I don't mean to be if I can help it, there is no one else who will take it very much to heart, except yourself. There are plenty of them at home and, now that I have been away nearly two years, they must almost have forgotten my existence."

"I consider you a very foolish boy," Patsey said, gravely. "You talk a great deal too much nonsense."

"Very well, Patsey; abuse is not argument, and almost every word that you have said applies equally well to your folly, in leaving a comfortable home in a quiet country to come to such a dangerous place as this.

"Now, I hope that supper is ready, for I am as hungry as a hunter."

Chapter 3
The First Successes

The next morning, at twelve o'clock, Jean Martin reached home.

"The war has begun," he said, as he leaped from his horse. "Henri de la Rochejaquelein has accepted the leadership of the peasants, at Clisson. Lescure would have joined also, but Henri pointed out to him that it would be better not to compromise his family, until it was certain that the insurrection would become general. The young count was starting, just as I got to the chateau. He is a splendid young fellow, full of enthusiasm, and burning to avenge the misfortunes that have fallen upon his family. A peasant had arrived the evening before, with a message from his aunt, who lives farther to the south. He brought news that the chevalier de Charette--formerly a lieutenant in the navy and a strong Royalist, who had escaped the massacres at Paris, and was living quietly on his estate near Machecoul--had been asked several times, by the peasants in his neighbourhood, to take the command, and had accepted it; and that the rising was so formidable, there, that it was certain the authorities in that part of Poitou would not succeed in enforcing the conscription.

"I have told Lescure that I shall be prepared to join, as soon as there is a general movement here; but that I should attach myself to whoever took the direction of affairs in this part, for that in the first place I knew nothing of war, and in the second place I have resided here so small a portion of my time that I am scarcely known, save to my own tenants.

"After our meal, we will ride round and see how they are off for arms and powder. That is our great weakness. I am afraid, taking the whole country round, that not one man in twenty possesses a gun."

This indeed was found to be the case, as far as those on the estate were concerned. The men themselves, however, seemed to think little of this.

"We will take them from the Blues," several of them said confidently. "It does not matter a bit. They will only have time to fire one volley, in these lanes of ours, and then we shall be among them; and a pike or pitchfork are just as good, at close quarters, as a bayonet."

That the whole country was astir was evident, from the fact that the sound of the church bells rose from the woods, in all directions. All work was suspended, and the peasants flocked into the little villages to hear the news that was brought in, from several directions.

Cathelineau had, in the course of the night, gathered a party of twenty-seven men who, at daybreak, had started out from Pin, setting the church bells ringing in the villages through which they passed; until a hundred men, armed for the most part with pitchforks and stakes, had gathered round him. Then he boldly attacked the chateau of Tallais, garrisoned by a hundred and fifty soldiers, having with them a cannon. This was fired, but the shot passed over the peasants' heads, and with a shout they dashed forward, and the soldiers of the republic threw away their arms and fled. Thus Cathelineau's followers became possessed of firearms, some horses and, to their great delight, a cannon.

Their leader did not waste a moment, but marched at once against Chemille, his force increasing at every moment, as the men flocked in from the villages. There were, at Chemille, two hundred soldiers with three guns; but some of the fugitives from Tallais had already arrived there, bringing news of the desperate fury with which the peasants had attacked them and, at the sight of the throng approaching, with their captured cannon, the garrison lost heart altogether and bolted, leaving their three cannon, their ammunition, and the greater portion of their muskets behind them.

The news spread with incredible rapidity. From each village they passed through, boys were despatched as messengers, and their tidings were taken on by fresh relays. By the afternoon all the country, for thirty miles round, knew that Cathelineau had captured Tallais and Chemille, and was in possession of a quantity of arms, and four cannon.

From Saint Florent came the news that, early in the morning, a party of Republican soldiers had endeavoured to arrest Foret, who led the rising on the previous day; but that he had obtained word of their approach and, setting the church bells ringing, had collected a force and had beaten back those who came in search of him.

Close by, a detachment of National Guards from Chollett had visited the chateau of Maulevrier. The proprietor was absent, but they carried off twelve cannon, which had been kept as family relics. The gamekeeper, Nicholas Stofflet, who was in charge of the estate, had served sixteen years in the army. He was a man of great strength, courage, and sagacity and, furious at the theft of his master's cannon, had gathered the peasantry round, and was already at the head of two hundred men.

"Things go on apace, Patsey," Jean Martin said, as they sat by the fire that evening. "We only know what is happening within some twenty or thirty miles of us, but if the spirit shown here exists throughout Poitou and Anjou, there can be no doubt that, in a very short time, the insurrection will be general. This Cathelineau, by their description, must be a man of no ordinary ability; and he has lost no time in showing his energy. For myself, I care not in the least what is the rank of my leader. Here in La Vendee there is no broad line between the seigneurs, the tenants, and the peasantry; at all rustic fetes they mix on equal terms. The seigneurs set the example, by dancing with the peasant girls; and their wives and daughters do not disdain to do the same with tenants, or peasantry. They attend the marriages, and all holiday festivities, are foremost in giving aid, and in showing kindness in cases of distress or illness; and I feel sure that, if they found in a man like Cathelineau a genius for command, they would follow him as readily as one of their own rank."

On the fourteenth the news came that the bands of Stofflet and Foret had, with others, joined that of Cathelineau. Jean Martin hesitated no longer.

"The war has fairly begun," he said. "I shall be off tomorrow morning. If Cathelineau is defeated, we shall have the Republicans devastating the whole country, and massacring women and children; as they did, last August, after a rising for the protection of the priests. Therefore I shall be fighting, now, in defence of our lives and home, wife."

"I would not keep you at home, Jean. I think it is the duty of every man to join in the defence against these wretches. I know that no mercy will be shown by them, if they conquer us. But you will not take Leigh with you, surely?"

Leigh uttered an exclamation.

"Leigh must choose for himself," Jean said quietly. "He is not French, and would have no concern in the matter, beyond that of humanity, were it not that you are here; but at present our home is his. Your life and his, also, are involved, if we are beaten. He is young to fight, but there will doubtless be many others no older, and probably much less strong than he is. Moreover, if I should be killed, it is he who must bear you the news, and must arrange with you your plans, and act as your protector.

"I do not say that I should advise your leaving the chateau directly, but if the Republicans come this way, it will be no place for you; and I should say that it would be vastly better that you should, at once, endeavour to cross to England. There are five thousand francs in gold in my bureau, which are worth three or four times their value in assignats; and should, if you can gain the coast, be amply sufficient to procure a passage for you to England.

"Do not weep, dear. It is necessary to leave you, on an undertaking of this kind, prepared for whatever may happen. At present the risk is very small. As we have heard, the fury of the peasants has struck such consternation into the National Guards, and newly-raised soldiers, that they will not await their onslaught; and it will not be until the Convention becomes aware of the really serious nature of the storm they have raised, that there will be any hard fighting. Still, even in a petty skirmish men fall; and it is right that, before I go, we should arrange as to what course you had best pursue, in case of my death.

"From the first, when we came here we did so with our eyes open. If we had merely sought safety, we should have gone to England. We came here partly because it is my home, and therefore my proper place; and partly because, in case La Vendee rose against these executioners of Paris, every man of honour and loyalty should aid in the good cause."

"I know, Jean, and I would not keep you back."

"The struggle has begun and, if the Republicans conquer La Vendee, we know how awful will be the persecutions, what thousands of victims will be slaughtered. Our only hope is in victory and, at any rate, those who die on the battlefield will be happy, in comparison with those who fall into the hands of the Blues."

"You wish to go, Leigh?"

"Certainly I do," the lad said. "I think that everyone strong enough to carry arms, in La Vendee, ought to join and do his best. I can shoot better than most of the peasantry, not one in twenty of whom has ever had a gun in his hands; and I am sure that I am as strong as most of them. Besides, if I had been at home I should, now the war has begun, have tried to get a commission and to fight the French--I mean the people who govern France at present--and in fighting them, here, I am only doing what thousands of Englishmen will be doing elsewhere."

"Very well, Leigh, then you shall go with Jean. I shall certainly be glad to know you are together, so that if one is wounded or ill, the other can look after him and bring him here. I shall do the best I can, while you are away."

"I think that we shall soon be back again, and that we shall be constantly seeing you," Jean said. "You may be sure that the peasants will not keep the field. They will gather and fight and, win or lose, they will then scatter to their homes again, until the church bells call them out to repel a fresh attack of the enemy. That is our real weakness. There will never be any discipline, never any common aim.

"If all the peasants in the west would join in a great effort, and march on Paris, I believe that the peasantry of the departments through which they pass would join us. It would only be the National Guards of the towns, and the new levies, that we should have to meet; and I believe that we might take Paris, crush the scum of the faubourgs, and hang every member of the Convention. But they will never do it. It will be a war of defence, only; and a war so carried out must, in the long run, be an unsuccessful one.

"However, the result will be that we shall never be very far away from home, and shall often return for a few days. You must always keep a change of clothes, and your trinkets and so on, packed up; so that at an hour's notice you and Marthe can start with the child, either on receiving a note from me telling you where to join us, or if you get news that a force from Nantes is marching rapidly in this direction. Two horses will always remain in the stables, in readiness to put into the light cart. Henri will be your driver. Francois you must send off to find us, and tell us the road that you have taken. However, of course we shall make all these arrangements later on, when affairs become more serious. I don't think there is any chance, whatever, of the enemy making their way into the country for weeks, perhaps for months, to come."

The next morning, Jean Martin and Leigh started early. Each carried a rifle slung behind him, a brace of pistols in his holsters, and a sword in his belt. Patsey had recovered from her depression of the previous evening, and her natural good spirits enabled her to maintain a cheerful face at parting; especially as her husband's assurances, that there would be no serious fighting for some time, had somewhat calmed her fears for their safety.

"The horses are useful to us, for carrying us about, Leigh," Jean Martin said, as they rode along; "but unless there are enough mounted men to act as cavalry, we shall have to do any fighting that has to be done on foot. The peasants would not follow a mounted officer as they would one who placed himself in front of them, and fought as they fought.

"I hope that, later on, we may manage to get them to adopt some sort of discipline; but I have great doubts about it. The peasantry of La Vendee are an independent race. They are respectful to their seigneurs, and are always ready to listen to their advice; but it is respect, and not obedience. I fancy, from what I have read of your Scottish Highlanders, that the feeling here closely resembles that among the clans. They regard their seigneurs as their natural heads, and would probably die for them in the field; but in other matters each goes his own way, and the chiefs know better than to strain their power beyond a certain point.

"As you see, they have already their own leaders--Stofflet the gamekeeper, Foret the woodcutter, and Cathelineau, a small peddling wool merchant. Doubtless many men of rank and family will join them, and will naturally, from their superior knowledge, take their place as officers; but I doubt whether they will displace the men who have, from the beginning, taken the matter in hand. I am glad that it should be so. The peasants understand men of their own class, and will, I believe, follow them better than they would men above them in rank. They will, at least, have no suspicion of them; and the strength of the insurrection lies in the fact that it is a peasant rising, and not an insurrection stirred up by men of family."

At ten o'clock they arrived at Cathelineau's camp. Just as they reached the spot, they encountered Monsieur Sapinaud de la Verrie. He was riding at the head of about a hundred peasants, all of whom were armed with muskets. They had, early that morning, attacked the little town of Herbiers. It was defended by two companies of soldiers, with four or five cannon; and the Republicans of the town had ranged themselves with the Blues. Nevertheless the peasants, led by their commander and his nephew, had fearlessly attacked them and, with a loss of only two or three wounded, defeated the enemy and captured the place, obtaining a sufficient supply of muskets to arm themselves.

As Jean Martin was known to Monsieur Sapinaud, they saluted each other cordially.

"So you are coming willingly, Monsieur Martin. There you have the advantage of me, for these good fellows made me and my nephew come with them, as their leaders, and would take no refusal. However, they but drew us into the matter a few days earlier than we had intended; for we had already made up our minds to join the movement."

"I come willingly enough, Monsieur Sapinaud. If I had remained in Nantes, I should have been guillotined by this time; and I made up my mind when I left there that I would, on the first opportunity, do a little fighting before I was put an end to.

"This is my brother-in-law. He has been out here now nearly two years, and has seen enough of the doings of the murderers at Nantes to hate them as much as I do."

The streets of the little village, which Cathelineau had made his headquarters, were thronged with men. Through these the four mounted gentlemen made their way slowly until, when they came to the church, they saw three men standing apart from the others.

"That is Cathelineau, the one standing in the middle," Leigh said.

"We have come to place ourselves under your orders," Monsieur Sapinaud said, as they rode up to him; and he named himself and his companions.

"I am glad indeed to see you, sirs," Cathelineau said. "You are the first gentlemen who have joined us here; though I hear that, farther south, some have already declared themselves. We want you badly.

"One of you I have seen already," and he smiled at Leigh. "I told you that you would hear of me, young sir; and you see I have kept my word.

"These with me are Stofflet who, as you may have heard, recaptured the cannon the Blues took at Clisson; and Foret, who had the honour of striking the first blow, at Saint Florent."

"Your names are all widely known in this part," Monsieur Sapinaud said, courteously. "Well, sirs, we have come to fight under your orders. I have brought a hundred men with me, and we have already done something on our own account; for we last night captured Herbiers, which was defended by two companies, with four cannon. We have gained a sufficient number of muskets to arm all our party."

"If I do not offer to give up the leadership to you, Monsieur de la Verrie," Cathelineau said gravely, "it is from no desire on my part to be a commander; but I am widely known to the peasantry of many parishes round Pin and, perhaps because I understand them better than most, they have confidence in me; and would, I think, follow me rather than a gentleman like yourself, of whom they know but little."

"They are quite right," Monsieur Sapinaud said. "The peasantry commenced this war. It is right that they should choose their own leaders. You and your two companions have already their confidence, and it is far better that you should be their leaders. I believe all other gentlemen who join you will be as ready as we are to follow you, and I am sure that the only rivalry will be as to who shall most bravely expose himself, when he faces the enemy."

"I thank you, sir," Cathelineau said. "I believe earnestly that, in many respects, it is best that the peasants should have their own leaders. We can associate ourselves with their feelings, better than the gentry could do. We shall have more patience with their failings.

"You would want to make an army of them. We know that this cannot be done. They will fight and die as bravely as men could do, but I know that they will never submit to discipline. After a battle, they will want to hurry off to their homes. They will obey the order to fight, but that is the only order one can rely upon their obeying.

"We are on the point of starting for Chollet. It is a town where the people are devoted to the cause of the Convention. At the last drawing for the militia they killed, without any pretext, a number of young men who had come, unarmed, into the town. Many inhabitants of adjoining parishes have been seized and thrown in prison, charged only with being hostile to the Convention, and expressing horror at the murder of the king.

"The capture will produce an impression throughout the country. They have three or four hundred dragoons there, and yesterday, we hear, they called in the National Guard from the villages round, though scarce believing that we should venture to attack them. Your reinforcement of a hundred men, all armed with muskets, will be a very welcome one; for they will hardly suspect that many of us have firearms. However we had, before your arrival, three hundred who have so armed themselves, through captures at Saint Florent and Chemille."

He now ordered the bell to be rung and, as soon as its notes pealed out, started; followed at once by the crowd in the village, without any sort of order or regularity. Jean and Leigh continued to ride with Monsieur de la Verrie and his nephew.

After some hours' marching, at two o'clock in the afternoon they approached Chollet. On the way they received considerable reinforcements, from the villages they passed through. As soon as they approached the town they saw the dragoons pouring out, followed by three or four hundred National Guards.

The Vendeans now fell into some sort of order. A short council of war was held. It was arranged that Monsieur de la Verrie with his hundred musketeers, and Foret with as many more, should advance against the dragoons; while Cathelineau and Stofflet, with a hundred musketeers and the main body of peasants with their pitchforks, should attack the National Guards.

The dragoons had expected that the mere sight of them would be sufficient to send the peasants flying, and they were amazed that they should continue to advance. As soon as they were within easy range, the peasants opened fire. At the first volley the colonel of the dragoons and many of his men fell. Reloading, the peasants advanced at a run, poured in a volley at close quarters; and then, with loud cheers, charged the dragoons.

These, being but newly raised troops, were seized with a panic, turned, and galloped off at full speed. Astounded at the defeat of the cavalry, in whom they had confidently trusted, the National Guard at once lost heart and as, with loud shouts, Cathelineau with his peasants flung themselves upon them, they, too, broke, and fled in all directions.

The peasants pursued them for a league, and then returned, exultant, to Chollet. Here the leading revolutionists were thrown in prison but, with the exception of the National Guards who attempted resistance after reaching the town, no lives were taken. A large quantity of arms, money, and ammunition fell into the hands of the victors.

Scarcely had the peasants gathered in Chollet, than the news arrived that the National Guard of Saumur were marching against them; and Cathelineau requested Monsieur de la Verrie and Foret, with their following, to go out to meet them. They marched away at once, and met the enemy at Vihiers.

Unprepared for an attack, the National Guard at once broke and fled, throwing away their arms and abandoning their cannon. Among these was one taken from the Chateau de Richelieu. It had been given by Louis the Thirteenth to the cardinal. On the engraving, with which it was nearly covered, the peasants thought that they could make out an image of the Virgin, and so called it by her name. With these trophies the party returned to Chollet.

The next day being Saturday the little army dispersed, the peasants making their way to their homes, in order to spend Easter there; while Cathelineau, with only a small body, remained at Chollet. From here messengers were sent to Messieurs Bonchamp, d'Elbee, and Dommaigne-- all officers who had served in the army, but had retired when the revolution broke out. Cathelineau offered to share the command with them, and entreated them to give their military knowledge and experience to the cause.

All assented. Thus the force had the advantage, from this time forward, of being commanded by men who knew the business of war.

Leigh had started for home as soon as the National Guards of Saumur were defeated; Jean Martin, at Cathelineau's request, remaining with him in order to join some other gentlemen, who had that day arrived, in calling upon the three officers, and inviting them to join Cathelineau in the command.

Leigh's sister ran out, as he rode up to the house. The news of the capture of Chollet, almost without loss, had already spread and, although surprised, she felt no alarm at seeing Leigh alone.

"I hear that you have taken Chollet, and defeated the dragoons and National Guards."

"Yes; and this morning we put to flight the guards of Saumur, without the loss of a single man. I don't know what it may come to, presently; but just now it can hardly be called fighting. The sight of peasants rushing on seems to strike these heroes with a panic, at once; and they are off helter skelter, throwing away their guns and ammunition."

"Have you come home only to tell me the news, Leigh?"

"I have come home because, at present, our army has evaporated into thin air. Tomorrow being Easter Sunday, the peasants have all scattered to their homes; so that it was of no use my staying at Chollet. Cathelineau is there, and the other leaders; among them Monsieur de la Verrie, a nephew of his, Jean, and several other gentlemen, who have just arrived there. They are going as a sort of deputation, tomorrow, to Bonchamp, d'Elbee, and another officer whose name I forget, to ask them to join Cathelineau in the command. I think that he will still remain as leader, and that they will act as his councillors, and in command of columns."

"Then your impression of this man is confirmed?"

"More than confirmed. Jean said, this morning, that he was a born leader of men. While all round him there is excitement and confusion, he is as calm and serene as if he were alone. He is evidently a man who has read a good deal, and thought a good deal; and I can quite understand the influence he has gained over the peasantry in his neighbourhood, and that it has long been their custom to refer all disputes to him.

"Stofflet is a different sort of man. He is tall and powerful in frame, stern and almost morose in manner. He has been sixteen years a soldier; and was, I hear, distinguished for his bravery."

"And Foret?"

"He is an active young woodman, evidently a determined fellow and, as he was the first to lead the peasants against the Blues, he is sure to have a following. They are three very different characters, but all of them well fitted to act as peasant leaders."

"And will Jean be a leader?"

"Not a leader, Patsey; that is to say, certainly not a general. He does not want it, himself. But he will no doubt lead the peasants on the estate, and perhaps those in the neighbourhood. You know that he would not have the church bell rung, when he started, because he did not wish the tenants to join until he had seen the result of the first fight; but when he comes home he will summon those who like to go with him."

"Yes, I have had to explain that, over and over again. Yesterday and today almost all the men have been up here, to ask why Jean did not take them. I told them that that was one reason; and another was that, had they started on foot when you did, they would not have arrived in time to take part in the fight at Chollet."

The conversation, begun as Leigh dismounted, had been continued in the house, the groom having taken the horse round to the stable.

"So the peasants fought well, Leigh?"

"They would have fought well, if the Blues had given them a chance; but these would not stop till they came up to them. If they had done so, I am convinced that the peasants would have beaten them. There was no mistaking the way they rushed forward and, upon my word, I am not surprised that the enemy gave way; although well armed, and not far inferior in numbers, they would have had no chance with them."

"And did you rush forward, Leigh?"

"We were with the party that attacked the cavalry. Jean and I fired our rifles twice, and after that we only saw the backs of the cavalry. If they had been well-drilled troops they ought to have scattered us like sheep; for everything must have gone down before them, had they charged. There was no sort of order among us. The men were not formed into companies. There was no attempt to direct them. Each simply joined the leader he fancied and, when the word was given, charged forward at the top of his speed. It is all very well against the National Guards, and these young troops; but as Jean said, it would be a different affair, altogether, if we were to meet trained soldiers.

"But the peasants seem to be quick, and I expect they will adopt tactics better suited to the country, when they come to fighting in these lanes and woods. You see, so far a very small proportion have been armed with guns, and their only chance was to rush at once to close quarters; but we have captured so many muskets, at Chollet and Vihiers, that in future a considerable proportion of the peasants will have guns and, when they once learn to use the hedges, they will be just as good as trained troops."

"Then I suppose Jean is more hopeful about the future than he was?"

"I don't say that, Patsey. He thinks that we shall make a hard fight of it, but that the end must depend upon whether the people in Paris, rather than keep fifty thousand men engaged in a desperate conflict, here, when they are badly wanted on the frontier, decide to suspend the conscription in La Vendee, and to leave us to ourselves. There can be no doubt that that would be their best plan. But as they care nothing for human life, even if it cost them a hundred thousand men to crush us; they are likely to raise any number of troops, and send them against us, rather than allow their authority to be set at defiance.

"Do you know, Patsey, when I used to read about Guy Fawkes wanting to blow up the Houses of Parliament, I thought that he must be a villain, indeed, to try to destroy so many lives; but I have changed my opinion now for, if I had a chance, I would certainly blow up the place where the Convention meets, and destroy every soul within its walls; including the spectators, who fill the galleries and howl for blood."

"Well you see, Leigh, as Guy Fawkes and the other conspirators failed in their attempt, I am afraid there is very small chance of your being able to carry out the plan more successfully."

"I am afraid there is not," Leigh said regretfully. "I should never be able to dig a way into the vaults, and certainly I should not be able to get enough powder to blow a big building up, if I could. No; I was only saying that, if Guy Fawkes hated the Parliament as much as I hate the Convention, there is some excuse to be made for him.

"Now, Patsey, I am as hungry as a hunter."

"I have a good supper ready for you," she said. "I thought it was quite possible that you and Jean would both come home, this evening; for I felt sure that most of the peasants would be coming back, if possible, for Easter Sunday; and I had no doubt that, if you did come, you would both be hungry."

"Have you any news from other districts?" he asked, after he had finished his supper.

"There is a report that Captain Charette has gathered nearly twenty thousand peasants, in lower Poitou; and that he has already gained a success over the Blues. There are reports, too, of risings in Brittany."

"There is no doubt that things are going on well, at present, Patsey. You see, we are fighting on our own ground, and fifty thousand men can be called to arms in the course of a few hours, by the ringing of the church bells. We have no baggage, no waggons, no train of provisions; we are ready to fight at once.

"On the other hand, the Blues have been taken completely by surprise. They have no large force nearer than the frontier, or at any rate nearer than Paris; and it will be weeks before they can gather an army such as even they must see will be required for the conquest of La Vendee. Up to that time it can be only a war of skirmishes, unless our leaders can persuade the peasants to march against Paris; and that, I fear, they will never be able to do.

"When the enemy are really ready, the fighting will be desperate. 'Tis true that the Vendeans have a good cause--they fight for their religion and their freedom, while the enemy will fight only because they are ordered to do so. There is another thing--every victory we win will give us more arms, ammunition, and cannon; while a defeat will mean simply that the peasants will scatter to their homes, and be ready to answer the next call for their services. On the other hand, if the Blues are defeated they will lose so heavily, both in arms and stores; and will suffer such loss of life, from their ignorance of our roads and lanes, that it will be a long time before they will again be able to advance against us."

The next morning, after the service at the church was over, the peasants came down in numbers to the chateau, to hear from Leigh a full account of the fighting at Chollet and Vihiers, a report of the latter event having arrived that morning. There were exclamations of lively pleasure at the recital, mingled with regret that they had not borne their share in the fighting.

"You will have plenty of opportunities," Leigh said. "Monsieur Martin has told me that, when he next leaves home, all who are willing to do so can go with him. But it may be some little time before anything of importance takes place; and as, at present, what fighting there is is a considerable distance away, he thinks it best that you should reserve yourselves for some great occasion; unless, indeed, the Blues endeavour to penetrate the Bocage, when, I have no doubt, you will know how to deal with them, when they are entangled in your lanes and woods."

"We will go, every man of us!" one of the peasants shouted, and the cry was re-echoed, with enthusiasm, by the whole of the men.

It was nearly an hour before Leigh and his sister were able to withdraw from the crowd, and make their way homeward.

"It is difficult to believe that men so ready and eager to fight can be beaten," she said. "Did you notice, too, that their wives all looked on approvingly? I believe that, even if any of the men wished to stay away, they would be hounded to the front by the women. I think that, with them, it would be regarded as a war for their religion; while with the men it is the conscription that has chiefly driven them to take up arms."

Chapter 4
Cathelineau's Scouts

For some days nothing happened. The insurrection spread like wildfire, in Poitou and Anjou; and everywhere the peasants were successful, the authorities, soldiers, and gendarmes for the most part flying without waiting for an attack.

The news that all La Vendee was in insurrection astonished and infuriated the Convention, which at once took steps to suppress it. On the second of April a military commission was appointed, with power to execute all peasants taken with arms in their hands, and all who should be denounced as suspicious persons. General Berruyer was sent down to take the command. The large army that had been raised, principally from the mob of Paris for the defence of that city, marched down; and Berruyer, at the head of this force, entered the Bocage on the tenth of April.

The time had passed quietly at the chateau. The peasants had dispersed at once and, except that the principal leaders and a small body of men remained together, watching the course of events, all was as quiet as if profound peace reigned.

Jean Martin had returned home. Two days after arriving, he had called all the tenants on the estate together, and had endeavoured to rouse them to the necessity of acquiring a certain amount of discipline. He had brought with him a waggon load of muskets and ammunition, which had been discovered at Chollet after the main bulk of the peasants had departed; and Cathelineau had allowed him to carry them off, in order that the peasantry in the neighbourhood of the chateau should be provided with a proportion of guns, when the day of action arrived. The peasants gladly received the firearms, but could not be persuaded to endeavour to fight in any sort of order.

"They did not do it at Chollet, or elsewhere," they exclaimed, "and yet they beat the Blues easily. What good did discipline do to the enemy? None. Why, then, should we bother ourselves about it? When the enemy comes, we will rush upon them when they are tangled in our thickets."

Leigh was somewhat more successful. The fact that he had fought at Chollet, and was their seigneur's brother-in-law, had established a position for him in the eyes of peasants of his own age; and as he went from house to house, talking with them, he succeeded in getting some twenty boys to agree to follow him. He had been nominated an officer by the three generals, who had picked out, without reference to rank or age, those who they thought would, either from position, energy, or determination, fill the posts well. Thus one company was commanded by a noble, the next by a peasant; and each would, on the day of battle, fight equally well.

Leigh's arguments were such as were suited to the lads he addressed.

"You see, if you go with the bands of men, you will be lost in the crowd. The men will rush forward in front, you will all be in the rear. You want to serve your country. Well, you can serve it much better by watching the movements of the enemy, and carrying word of it to the commander. Then, sometimes, we can have a little enterprise of our own--cut off a post of the enemy, or manage to decoy them into lanes where we know their guns will stick fast.

"It is not size and strength that are most necessary in war; but quickness, alertness, and watchfulness. You know that, already, the leaders have found that nothing can persuade the men to keep guard, or to carry out outpost duty. If we do this, even if we do nothing else, we shall be serving the cause much better than if we were to join in a general rush upon the enemy."

"But we shall have no muskets with us," one of the boys objected.

"Nor would you want them. You would have to move about quickly, and guns would be terribly inconvenient, if you had to push your way through a hedge or a close thicket. And besides, if you had guns they would not be of much use to you, for none of you are accustomed to their use, and it needs a great deal of training to learn to shoot straight.

"I am quite sure that if I were to march with twenty of you to Cathelineau's headquarters, and were to say to him, 'We have come here, sir, to act as scouts for you, to bring you in news of the movements of the enemy, and to do anything in our power to prevent you from being surprised,' he would be more pleased than if I had brought him a hundred men armed with muskets."

When twenty had expressed their willingness to go, Leigh asked Jean, who had warmly entered into the plan, to speak to the fathers of the lads and get them to consent to their going with him. He accordingly called them together for that purpose.

"But do you mean that they will be away altogether, master?"

"Yes, while this goes on."

"But we shall lose their labour in the fields?"

"There will not be much labour in the fields, till this is over; and by having scouts watching the enemy you will get early news of their coming, and have time to drive off your beasts before they arrive."

"But how will they live?"

"When they are in this neighbourhood, one or two can come back and fetch bread. If they are too far off for that, my brother will buy bread for them. In cases where they cannot well be spared, I will remit a portion of your dues, as long as they are away; but this will not be for long, for I can see that, ere many weeks are past, the Blues will be swarming round in such numbers that there will be little time for work on your land, and you will all have to make great sacrifices.

"You must remember that the less there is in your barns, the more difficult it will be for an enemy to invade you; for if they can find nothing here, they will have to bring everything with them, and every waggon will add to their difficulties. My brother tells me that one of the things he means to do is to break up the roads, when he finds out by which line the Blues are advancing; and for that purpose I shall serve out, from my store, either a pick or an axe to each of the band."

At last all difficulties were got over, and twenty lads were enrolled. Another three weeks passed. The peasants of Poitou and Anjou thought but little of the storm that was gathering round them.

General Berruyer had arrived from Paris, with his army. A portion of the army from Brest moved down to Nantes; and were in concert, with the army of La Rochelle, to sweep that part of La Vendee bordering on the coast. General Canclaus was at Nantes, with two thousand troops. General Dayat was sent to Niort, with six thousand men; and was to defend the line between Sables and Saint Gilles. Bressuire was occupied by General Quetineau, with three thousand men. Leigonyer, with from four to five thousand men, occupied Vihiers; while Saint Lambert was held by Ladouce, with two thousand five hundred. The right bank of the Loire, between Nantes and Angers, was held by fifteen hundred men of the National Guard.

Thus that part of upper Poitou where the rising had been most successful was surrounded by a cordon of troops; which the Convention hoped, and believed, would easily stamp out the insurrection, and take a terrible vengeance for what had passed.

When the storm would burst, none knew; but Jean one day said to Leigh that it was certain that it must come soon; and that, if he was still resolved to carry out his plan, it was time that he set out.

"I am quite ready to carry out my plans, Jean, as you know; but dangers seem to threaten from so many quarters that I don't like going away from home. While my company are scattered near Chollet, for instance, the Blues may be burning down your chateau."

"I don't think there is much danger of that, Leigh. It is quite certain that, as soon as these divisions begin to move, they will have their hands full. We may hope that in some cases they will be defeated. In others they may drive off the peasants, and march to the town that they intend to occupy, but they will only hold the ground they stand upon. They will not be able to send out detached parties to attack chateaux or destroy villages.

"For the present, I have no fear whatever of their coming here. We are well away from any of the roads that they are likely to march by. I don't say that any of the roads are good, but they will assuredly keep on the principal lines, and not venture to entangle themselves in our country lanes. There are no villages of any size within miles of us, and this is one of the most thickly wooded parts of the Bocage--which, as you know, means the thicket--therefore I shall, when the time comes, leave your sister without uneasiness. We may be quite sure that if, contrary to my anticipation, any column should try to make its way through this neighbourhood, it would be hotly opposed, and she will have ample time to take to the woods, where she and the child will find shelter in any of the foresters' cottages.

"She is going to have peasant dresses made for her and Marthe. She will of course drive, as we intended; and the two men will take the horse and vehicle to some place in the woods, at a considerable distance from here, and keep it there until we join her and carry out our original plan of making for the coast. Directly you are gone, I shall make it my business to find out the most out of the way spot among the woods; and ride over and make an arrangement, with some woodman with a wife and family living there, to receive her, if necessary; and I will let you know the spot fixed on, and give you directions how to find it."

In order to add to Leigh's influence and authority, Martin persuaded the village cure--who was a man of much intelligence, and perceived that real good might be done by this party of lads--to have a farewell service in the church. Accordingly, on the morning on which they were to start, all attended the church, which was filled by their friends; and here he addressed the boys, telling them that the service in which they were about to engage was one that would be of great importance to their country, and that it would demand all their energy and strength. He then asked them to take an oath to carry out all orders they might receive from their leader, the seigneur's brother; who would himself share in their work, and the many hardships they might have to undergo.

"Here," he said, "is a gentleman who is by birth a foreigner, but who has come to love the land that his sister adopted as her own; and to hate its enemies--these godless murderers of women and children, these executioners of their king, these enemies of the church--so much that he is ready to leave his home, and all his comforts, and to risk his life in its cause. Remember that you have voluntarily joined him, and accepted him as your leader. The work once begun, there must be no drawing back. There is not a man in La Vendee who is not prepared to give his life, if need be, to the cause; and you, in your way, can do as much or more."

He then administered an oath to each lad and, as had been arranged, Leigh also took an oath to care for them in every respect, and to share their risks and dangers. Then the cure pronounced his blessing upon them, and the service ended.

Very greatly impressed with what had taken place, the little band marched out from the church, surrounded by their friends. Jean Martin then presented hatchets or light picks to each, and a waist belt in which the tools should be carried. As a rule, the peasants carried leathern belts over the shoulders, in which a sword, hatchet, or other weapon was slung; but Jean thought the waist belt would be much more convenient for getting rapidly through hedges or thickets, and it had also the advantage that a long knife, constituting in itself a formidable weapon, could also be carried in it.

Patsey presented them each with a hat, of which a supply had been obtained from Saint Florent. These were of the kind ordinarily worn by the peasants, in shape like the modern broad-brimmed wide-awake, but made of much stiffer material. She had bought these to give a certain uniformity to the band, of whom some already wore hats of this kind, others long knitted stocking caps, while others again were bare headed.

She added a piece of green ribbon round each hat. Leigh objected to this, on the ground that they might sometimes have to enter towns, and that any badge of this sort would be speedily noticed; but as she said, they would only have to take them off, when engaged in such service.

A quarter of an hour after leaving the church they marched away, amid the acclamations of their friends; each boy feeling a sensation of pride in the work that he had undertaken, and in the ceremony of which he had been the centre.

"Now, lads," Leigh said, as soon as they were fairly away from the village, "instead of walking along as a loose body, you had better form four abreast, and endeavour to keep step. It is no more difficult to walk that way than in a clump; and indeed, by keeping step it makes the walking easy, and it has the advantage that you can act much more quickly. If we heard an enemy approaching, and I gave the order, 'Ten go to the right and ten go to the left!' you would not know which were to go.

"Now each four of you will form a section, and the order into which you fall now, you will always observe. Then if I say, 'First two sections to the right, the other three sections to the left!' every one of you knows what to do, instead of having to wait until I mention all your names.

"This is nearly all the drill you will have to learn. You can choose your places now, but afterwards you will have to keep to them, so those of you who are brothers and special friends will, naturally, fall in next to each other."

In a minute or two the arrangements were made, and the party proceeded four abreast, with Leigh marching at their head. For the first hour or so, he had some difficulty in getting them to keep step; but they presently fell into it, time being kept by breaking into one of the canticles of the church.

After a long day's march, they arrived at the village which Cathelineau now occupied as his headquarters; as it had been necessary, in view of the threatening circle of the various columns of the enemy, to remove the headquarters from Chollet to a central point, from which he could advance, at once, against whichever of these columns might first move forward into the heart of the country. The lads all straightened themselves up as they marched through the streets, the unwonted spectacle of twenty peasant lads, marching in order, exciting considerable surprise. Cathelineau was standing at the door of the house he occupied, conversing with Messieurs Bonchamp and d'Elbee.

"Ah, Monsieur Stansfield," he said, "is it you?" as Leigh halted his party, and raised his hat. "You are the most military-looking party I have yet seen. They are young, but none the worse for that."

"There is nothing military about them, except that they march four abreast," he said, with a smile, "but for the work we have come to do, drill will not be necessary. I have raised this band on Jean Martin's estate, sir, and with your permission I propose to call them 'Cathelineau's scouts.' It seemed, to my brother and myself, that you sorely need scouts to inform you of the movements of the enemy, the roads by which they are approaching, their force and order. I have therefore raised this little body of lads of my own age. They will remain with me permanently, as long as the occasion needs. They will go on any special mission with which you may charge them; and will, at other times, watch all the roads by which an enemy would be likely to advance."

"If they will do that, Monsieur Stansfield, they will be valuable, indeed; that is just what I cannot get the peasants to do. When it comes to fighting, they will obey orders; but at all other times they regard themselves as their own masters, and neither entreaties nor the offer of pay suffices to persuade them to undertake such work as you are proposing to carry out. Consequently, it is only by chance that we obtain any news of the enemy's movements. I wish we had fifty such parties."

"They would be valuable, indeed," Monsieur d'Elbee said. "The obstinacy of the peasantry is maddening.

"How do you propose to feed your men?"

"When we are within reach of their homes, two will go back to fetch bread for the whole; when we are too far away, I shall buy it in one of the villages."

"When you are within reach of my headquarters, wherever that may be, you have only to send in; and they shall have the loaves served out to them, the same as the band who remain here. We are not short of money, thanks to the captures we have made.

"I see that none of your band have firearms."

"No, sir. Jean Martin would have let me have some of the muskets he brought from here, but it seemed to me that they would be an encumbrance. We may have to trust to our swiftness of foot to escape and, at any rate, we shall want to carry messages to you as quickly as possible. The weight of a gun and ammunition would make a good deal of difference; and would, moreover, be in our way in getting through the woods and hedges."

"But for all that, you ought to have some defence," Cathelineau said; "and if you came upon a patrol of cavalry, though only three or four in number, you would be in a bad case with only those knives to defend yourselves.

"Do you know whether there are any pistols in the storehouse, Monsieur Bonchamp?"

"Yes, there are some that were picked up from the cavalrymen we killed. They have not been given out yet."

"Then I think we had better serve out a pistol, with a score of cartridges, to each of these lads.

"If you let them fire three or four rounds at the trunk of a tree, or some mark of that sort, Monsieur Stansfield, they will get to know something about the use of the weapons."

"Thank you, sir. That would be excellent, and would certainly enable us to face a small party of the enemy, if we happen to encounter them."

"Please form the boys up two deep," Cathelineau said. "I will say a word or two to them."

The manoeuvre was not executed in military style, but the boys were presently arranged in order.

"I congratulate you, lads," Cathelineau went on, "in having devoted yourselves to your country, and that in a direction that will be most useful. I trust that you will strictly obey the orders of your commander; and will remember that you will be of far more use, in carrying them out, than in merely helping to swell the number in a pitched battle. I have every confidence in Monsieur Stansfield. He has set a noble example to the youths of this country, in thus undertaking arduous and fatiguing work, which is not without its dangers.

"I was glad to see that you marched in here, in order. I hope that you will go a little further, and learn to form line quickly, and to gather at his call. These things may seem to you to make very little difference, but in fact will make a great deal. You saw that you were at least a couple of minutes forming in line just now. Supposing the enemy's cavalry had been charging down upon you, that two minutes lost would have made all the difference between your receiving them in order, or being in helpless confusion when they came up.

"I have no doubt that one of my generals here has, among his followers, someone who served in the army, and who will teach you within the course of an hour, if you pay attention to his instructions, how to form into line, and back again into fours."

"I will give them an hour myself," Monsieur Bonchamp said. "I have nothing particular to do, and should be glad to instruct young fellows who are so willing, and well disposed.

"Are you too tired to drill now? You have had a long march."

A general negative was the reply.

"Well, then, march to the open space, just outside the town, and we will begin at once."

Feeling very proud of the honour of being drilled by a general, the boys fell into their formation, and followed Monsieur Bonchamp and Leigh. They were at a loss, at first, to comprehend the instructions given them; but by the end of an hour, they had fairly mastered the very simple movement.

"That will do," Monsieur Bonchamp said. "Of course you are not perfect, yet; but with a quarter of an hour's drill by your commander, every day, at the end of a week you will be able to do it quickly and neatly; and you will certainly find it a great advantage, if you come upon the enemy."

A large empty room was allotted to them and, as they sat down on the floor and munched the bread that they had brought with them, they felt quite enthusiastic over their work. It was a high honour, indeed, to have been praised by Monsieur Cathelineau, and been taught by one of his generals. They even felt the advantage that the drill had given them, contrasting the quickness with which they had finally formed into line, with their trouble in arranging themselves before Monsieur Cathelineau. The fact, too, that they were next morning to be furnished with pistols was a great gratification to them and, over and over again, they said to each other:

"What will the people at home say, when they hear that Monsieur Cathelineau has praised us, that Monsieur Bonchamp himself has drilled us, and that we are to be provided with pistols?"

In the morning, the pistols and ammunition were served out. Leigh had, during the previous evening, seen Cathelineau and asked for orders.

"I cannot say exactly the line the Blues are likely to take. I should say that you had better make Chemille your headquarters. Berruyer, who is their new commander, has arrived at Saint Lambert. There is a strong force at Thouars, being a portion of the army from Saint Lambert. The enemy are also in force at Vihiers, and at Parthenay.

"It is from the forces at Thouars and Vihiers that danger is most likely to come. Doubtless other columns will come from the north, but we shall hear of their having crossed the Loire in time to oppose them; and with so small a band as yours, you will be amply employed in watching Thouars. There are many roads, all more or less bad, by which they may march; as soon as you ascertain that they are moving, and by which route, you will send a messenger to me.

"Any others of your band that you may have with you, send off to all the villages round. Give them warning, set the bells ringing, promise that aid will soon arrive, and urge them to harass the enemy, to fell trees across the road, and to impede their advance in every possible way.

"I will give you half a dozen papers, for the use of yourself and your messengers, saying that you are acting under my orders, and are charged with raising the country, directly the enemy advance. But above all, it is important that I should get the earliest possible information as to the route by which they are moving; as it will take us thirty-six hours before we can gather in anything like our full strength.

"It will be useful that you should spread false news as to our whereabouts. Your boys can say, in one village, that we are marching towards Tours; in another, that we are massed in the neighbourhood of Saint Florent; in a third that they hear that the order is, that all able-bodied men are to go west to oppose the force coming from Nantes, which has already taken Clisson, and carried Monsieur de Lescure and his family, prisoners, to Bressuire."

"We shall have to tell the villagers, sir, that we wish this news to be given to the Blues, if they should come there or, if questioned, they would tell them something else. I am sure that even the women would suffer themselves to be killed, rather than give any news that they thought would be useful to the enemy."

"You are right. Yes, you must tell them that this is what we want the Blues to believe, and that it is my wish that these are the answers to be given to any of them who may enter the village."

"The only thing, sir, is that they may find the villages empty, as they come along. The women and children will, no doubt, take to the woods. The men will, perhaps, offer some resistance; but when they find how strong the Blues are, will probably hurry to join you."

"There will probably be a few old people remaining in each village. However, we must trust much to chance. The great thing is for you to let me know, as soon as their main body is in motion. Whichever way they come, we must meet and attack them. It is in the woods and lanes that we must defend ourselves."

"I will endeavour to carry out your orders, sir; and shall start tomorrow morning, as soon as we get our pistols."

As soon as the little band was well away from the town, the pistols were loaded; and each of the lads, in turn, fired three shots at the trunk of a tree, at a distance of ten yards, under Leigh's directions. The shooting was quite as good as he had expected, and the boys themselves were well satisfied.

Then, the pistols being reloaded and placed in their belts, they resumed their march. They halted at a tiny hamlet, consisting of half a dozen houses, four miles from Thouars. The inhabitants were greatly surprised at their appearance, and an old man, who was the head of the little community, came out and asked Leigh who they were.

"We are Cathelineau's scouts," he replied. "We have orders to watch the movements of the enemy. We wish to be of no trouble. If there is an empty shed, we should be glad of it; still more so if there is a truss or two of straw."

"These you can have," the old man said. "If Cathelineau's orders had been that we were to turn out of our houses for you, we should have done so, willingly."

"A shed will do excellently for us. We shall be here but little. Half our number will always be away. If you can supply us with bread, I will pay you for it. If you cannot do so, I shall have to send two of my party away, every day, to fetch bread from Cathelineau's camp."

"I will see what can be done. It will not be for long?"

"No, it may possibly be only two or three days, and it may be a week."

"Then I think that we can manage. If we have not flour enough here to spare, I can take my horse and fetch half a sackful from some other village."

"Thank you very much. However, I think that we shall only occasionally want bread; for I shall be sending messengers, every day, to Monsieur Cathelineau, and these can always bring bread back with them."

The old man led them to a building which had served as a stable, but which was then untenanted.

"I will get some straw taken in presently, lads.

"As for you, sir, I shall be glad if you will be my guest."

"I thank you," Leigh said, "but I prefer to be with my followers. They come by my persuasion, and I wish to share their lot, in all things; besides, my being with them will keep up their spirits."

There was half an hour's drill, and then Leigh led the party to the shed, to which four or five bundles of straw had, by this time, been brought.

"Now," he said, "before we do anything else, we must choose two sub-officers. At times we may divide into two parties, and therefore it is necessary that one should be responsible, to me, for what is done in my absence.

"I will leave it to you to choose them. Remember it is not size and strength that are of most importance, it is quickness and intelligence. You know your comrades better than I do, and I shall be quite content to abide by your choice. I will go outside for a quarter of an hour, while you talk it over. I don't want to influence you, at all."

In ten minutes, two of the lads came out.

"We have chosen Andre Favras and Pierre Landrin."

"I think that you have done very wisely," Leigh said. "Those are the two whom I, myself, should have selected."

He had, indeed, noticed them as the two most intelligent of the party. They had been his first recruits, and it was in no small degree owing to their influence that the others had joined him. He returned to the shed.

"I approve of your choice, lads," he said. "No doubt Andre and Pierre will make very good sub-officers. When I am not present, you must obey their orders as readily as you do mine; and I shall be able to trust them to carry out my directions, implicitly.

"Now you will divide in two parties: the first two sections, and two of the third section will form one party, and will be under Andre's command, when acting in two parties; the other two of the third section, and the fourth and fifth, will form the second division, under Pierre. You will take it in turns to be on duty. We shall not need to watch by night, for there is no chance of the enemy venturing to enter our lanes, and thickets, after dark. The party not out on scouting duty will remain here, and will furnish messengers to carry news to Cathelineau, to fetch bread, or to perform other duties."

The next morning Leigh set out with the whole band, except two. He had gathered, from the people of the village, the position of the various roads and lanes by which troops, going westward from Thouars, would be likely to travel. When within two miles of the town, he placed two boys on each of these roads. They were not to show themselves, but were to lie behind the hedges and, if they saw any body of troops coming along, were at once to bring news to him, his own point being on the principal road.

Andre and Pierre were to leave their arms and belts behind them, to make a long detour, and to enter the town from the other side. They were to saunter about the place, listen to what was being said, and gather as much news as possible. Each was provided with two francs and, if questioned, they were to say that they had come in, from some village near, to buy an axe.

"I should have gone in myself, Andre; but although I can get on fairly enough in your patois, I cannot speak it well enough to pass as a native. However, you are not likely to be questioned. In a town crowded with troops, two lads can move about without attracting the smallest attention from the military. It would be only the civilian authorities that you would have to fear; but these will be so much occupied, in attending to the wants of the soldiers, that they will not have any time on their hands for asking questions.

"Be sure, before you enter the town, that you find out the name of some village, three or four miles on the other side; so as to have an answer ready, if you are asked where you come from.

"It is probable that you will find troops quartered in all the villages beyond the town, which could hardly accommodate so large a number as are there. Remember, you must try to look absolutely unconcerned as you go through them, and as you walk about the streets of the town. The great object is to find out how many men there are in and around Thouars, whether they are looking for more troops to join them from Saumur, and when they are expecting to move forward."

As soon as they had left he repeated, to the six lads who remained with him, the orders that he had given to those posted on the other roads.

"You are to remain in hiding," he said, "whatever the force may be. It is likely enough that patrols of four or five men may come along, to see that the roads are clear, and that there are no signs of any bodies being gathered to oppose their advance. It is quite true that we might shoot down and overpower any such patrols, but we must not attempt to do so. If one of them escaped, he would carry the news to Thouars that the roads were beset. This would put them on their guard--doubtless they imagine that, with such a force as they have gathered, they will march through La Vendee without opposition--and they would adopt such precautions at to render it far more difficult, than it otherwise would be, to check their advance when it begins in earnest. We are here only to watch. We shall have opportunities for fighting, later on.

"This is a good spot for watching, for we have a thick wood behind us; and plenty of undergrowth along its edge, by the road, where we can hide so closely that there will not be the slightest chance of our being discovered, if we do but keep absolutely quiet."

Three or four times during the day, indeed, cavalry parties passed along the road. They did not appear to have any fear of an attack, but laughed and jested at the work they had come to do, scoffed at the idea of the peasants venturing to oppose such forces as had gathered against them, and discussed the chances of booty. One party, of four men and an old sergeant, pulled up and dismounted, close to the spot where the lads where hidden.

"It is all very well, comrades," their leader said, "but for my part, I would rather be on the frontier fighting the Austrians. That is work for soldiers. Here we are to fight Frenchmen, like ourselves; poor chaps who have done no harm, except that they stick to their clergy, and object to be dragged away from their homes. I am no politician, and I don't care a snap for the doings of the Assembly in Paris--I am a soldier, and have learned to obey orders, whatever they are--but I don't like this job we have in hand; which, mind you, is bound to be a good deal harder than most of you expect. It is true that they say there are twenty thousand troops round the province--but what sort of troops? There are not five thousand soldiers among them. The others are either National Guards, or newly-raised levies, or those blackguards from the slums of Paris. Of the National Guards I should say half would desert, if they only had the chance, and the new levies can't be counted on."

Chapter 5
Checking The Enemy

"You see," Leigh said, when the patrol had ridden on, "the real soldiers do not like the work they are called upon to do, and they have no belief in the National Guards, or in the new levies. It will make all the difference, in their own fighting, when they know that they cannot rely upon some of the troops working with them. I have no doubt that what they say of the National Guards is true. They have had to come out because they are summoned, but they can have no interest in the war against us and, doubtless, many of them hate the government in Paris just as much as we do, and would give a great deal to be back again with their homes and families. It is just as hard for them to be obliged to fight us, as it is for us to be obliged to fight them."

It was late in the afternoon before Andre and Pierre returned. By the time they did so, the various cavalry patrols had all gone back to Thouars. From time to time, boys had come in from the other roads. One or two patrols, only, had gone out by each of the lanes on which they were posted. It was evident that the main road was considered of the most importance, and it was probable that the greater portion of the enemy's force would move by it.

"Well, what is your news?" Leigh asked, as his two lieutenants came down from the wood behind. "I hope all has gone well with you."

"Yes, captain," Andre replied; "we have had no difficulty. The troops in the villages on the other side of the town did not even glance at us, as we went through; supposing, no doubt, that we belonged to the place. Thouars was crowded with soldiers, and we heard that two thousand more are to arrive from Saumur, this evening. We heard one of the officers say that orders were expected for a forward movement, tomorrow; and that all the other columns were to move at the same time, and three of them were to meet at Chemille."

"That is enough for the present, Andre. You have both done very well, to pick up so much news as that. We will be off, at once."

Messengers were at once sent off, to order in the other parties and, as soon as these joined, they returned to the village, where they passed the night. On arriving there, Leigh wrote a report of the news that he had gathered; and sent off one of the band, who had remained all day in the village, to Cathelineau, and the other to Monsieur d'Elbee at Chollet.

The next day's watch passed like the first. Two or three officers, however, trotted along the main road with a squadron of cavalry, and rode to within a few miles of Chemille, and then returned to Thouars.

The next morning Leigh and his band were out before daybreak and, making their way to within a short distance of Thouars, heard drums beating and trumpets sounding. There was no doubt that the force there was getting into motion. The band at once dispersed, carrying the news not only to every village along the road, warning the women and children to take to the woods, and the men to prepare for the passage of the enemy, but to all the villages within two or three miles of the road, ordering the church bells to be sounded to call the peasants to arms; while two lads started to carry the news to Cathelineau and d'Elbee. When once the bells of the churches near the road were set ringing, they were speedily echoed by those of the villages beyond; until the entire district knew that the enemy were advancing.

On the way from Chemille, Leigh had kept a sharp lookout for points where an enemy might be checked; and had fixed upon one, about halfway between the two towns. A stream some four feet in depth passed under a bridge, where the road dipped into a hollow; beyond this the ground rose steeply, and was covered with a thick wood, of very considerable extent. As soon as he reached this point, he set his band to work to destroy the bridge. As groups of peasants came flocking along, and saw what was intended, they at once joined in the work.

As soon at it was done, Leigh led them to the spot where the forest began, some thirty yards up the hill, and set them to fell trees. This was work to which all were accustomed and, as many of them carried axes, the trees nearest to the road were felled to fall across it; while on each side facing the stream, they were cut so as to fall down the slope, and so form an abattis.

Before the work was finished, to a distance of two or three hundred yards on each side of the road, several hundred peasants had come up. Of these, about a third were armed with muskets. Seeing the advantage of the position; and that, in case it was forced, the forest offered them a means of retreat, all prepared for a desperate resistance. The men with firearms were placed in the front rank. Those with pitchforks, and other rural weapons, were to keep at work till the last moment, cutting underwood, and filling the interstices between the boughs of the fallen trees, so as to make it extremely difficult to force. They were ordered to withdraw, when the fight began, to a distance of two or three hundred yards; and then to lie down, in any inequalities of the ground, so as to be safe from cannon shot Only when the defenders of the abattis were forced back, were they to prepare to charge.

A young fellow with a cow horn took his place by Leigh's side. When he blew his horn, the front rank were to run back, and the reserve to come forward to meet them; and then they were to rush down again upon their assailants who had passed the abattis, and to hurl them into the stream.

The peasants all recognized the advantages of these arrangements. Those who had come first had found Leigh in command and, by the readiness with which he was obeyed by his own followers, saw at once that he was in authority. As others came up, he showed them Cathelineau's circular. These recognized its order, and informed the later arrivals that the young officer, who was giving orders, was specially empowered by Cathelineau to take command; and Leigh was as promptly obeyed as if he had been their favourite leader, himself. They saw, too, that he knew exactly what he wanted done, and gave every order with firmness and decision; and their confidence in him became profound.

It was three hours after he arrived at the river when a party of horse came down the opposite slope. Leigh had ordered that not a shot was to be fired, until he gave the signal. He waited until the enemy came to the severed bridge, when they halted suddenly; and as they did so he gave the word and, from the long line of greenery, fifty muskets flashed out. More than half the troop of horse fell; and the rest, turning tail, galloped up the hill again, while a shout of derision rose from the peasants.

Half an hour passed, then the head of the column was seen descending the road. It opened out as it came, forming into a thick line of skirmishers, some two hundred yards wide. Moving along, Leigh spread the musketeers to a similar length of front. At first, the enemy were half hidden by the wood at the other side of the slope; but as they issued from this, some twenty yards from the stream, a scattered fire broke out from the defenders.

The Blues replied with a general discharge at their invisible foes, but these were crouching behind the stumps or trunks of the felled trees, and the fire was ineffectual. Leigh's own band were lying in a little hollow, twenty yards behind the abattis; their pistols would have been useless, until the enemy won their way up to the trees, and until then they were to remain as a first reserve.

Exposed as they were to the steady fire of the peasants, the assailants suffered heavily and, at the edge of the stream, paused irresolutely. It was some fifteen yards wide, but they were ignorant of the depth, and hesitated to enter it; urged, however, by the shouts of their officers, who set the example by at once entering the stream, and by seeing that the water did not rise above their shoulders, the men followed. But as they gained the opposite bank, they fell fast. At so short a distance, every shot of the peasants told; and it was some time before a sufficient number had crossed to make an assault against the wall of foliage in their front.

Fresh troops were constantly arriving from behind and, encouraged by this, they at last rushed forward. As they did so, Leigh called up his own band; and these, crawling forward through the tangle as far as they could, opened fire on the enemy, as they strove to push their way through the obstacle.

For a quarter of an hour the fight went on. Then the assailants, having with great loss succeeded in passing over or pulling aside the brushwood, began to pour through. The moment they did so, Leigh's horn sounded; and at once the defenders rushed up the hill, pursued by the Blues, with exulting shouts. But few shots were fired, for the assailants had emptied their muskets before striving to pass through the obstacle.

Leigh and his men had run but a hundred yards into the wood when they met the main body of the peasants, rushing down at full speed. Turning at once, his party joined them, and fell upon the advancing enemy. Taken wholly by surprise, when they believed that victory was won, the two or three hundred men who had passed the abattis were swept before the crowd of peasants like chaff. The latter, pressing close upon their heels, followed them through the gaps that had been made.

The panic of the fugitives spread at once to those who had crossed the river, and were clustered round the openings, jostling in their eagerness to get through and join, as they believed, in the slaughter of those who had caused them such heavy loss; and all fled together. The peasants were at their heels, making deadly use of their pitchforks, axes, and knives, and drove the survivors headlong into the river. The horn again sounded and, in accordance with the strict orders that they had received, they ran back again to their shelter; a few dropping from the scattered fire that the troops on the other side of the stream opened against them, as soon as the fugitives had cleared away from their front.

Scarcely had the peasants gained the shelter when six pieces of cannon, that had been placed on the opposite slope while the fight was going on, opened against them.

Leigh at once ordered the main body back to their former position, scattering his hundred men with guns along the whole line of abattis, whence they again opened fire on the troops on the opposite side of the river. These replied with volleys of musketry; but the defenders, stationed as they were five or six yards apart, and sheltering behind the trees, suffered but little either from the artillery or musketry fire; while men dropped fast in the ranks of the Blues.

The cannon were principally directed against the trees blocking the road. Gradually these were torn to pieces and, after an hour's firing, were so far destroyed that a passage through them was comparatively easy. Then the enemy again began to cross the stream.

As soon as they commenced to do so, Leigh called up the men with muskets from each flank, and sent word to the main body to descend the hill again, as the cannonade would cease as soon as the attack began. Three times the assault was made and repulsed, the peasants fighting with a fury that the Blues, already disheartened with their heavy losses, could not withstand. As they fell back for the third time, Leigh thought that enough had been done, and ordered the peasants at once to make through the woods, and to proceed by-lanes and byways to join Cathelineau; who, he doubted not, would by this time have gathered a considerable force at Chemille.

By the time that the Blues were ready to advance again, this time in overwhelming force, the peasants were well away. The wounded, as fast as they fell, had been carried off to distant villages; and when the enemy advanced they found, to their surprise, that their foes had disappeared, and that only some thirty dead bodies remained on the scene of battle.

Their own loss had exceeded three hundred, a large proportion of whom were regular soldiers; and the National Guards, and the new levies, were profoundly depressed at the result of the action.

"If," they said to themselves, "what must have been but a comparatively small number of peasants have caused this loss, what will it be when we meet Cathelineau's main body?"

There was no thought of pursuit. A regiment was thrown out in skirmishing order, and advanced through the wood, the rest following in column along the road. General Berruyer had joined General Menou the evening before, with the force from Saumur and, as they moved forward, the two generals rode together.

"This is a much more serious business than I had expected," Berruyer said. "I certainly imagined that, with such forces as we have gathered round La Vendee, the campaign would be little more than a military promenade.

I see, however, that I was entirely mistaken. These men have, today, shown themselves capable of taking advantage of the wild character of their country; and as to their courage, there can be no question, whatever. If this is a fair sample of the resistance that we have to expect, throughout the whole country, we shall need at least fifty thousand men to subdue them."

"Fully that," Menou said, shortly. "There is no doubt that we blame the National Guards, who were so easily routed by the peasants on the tenth of March, more severely than they deserve. I rode forward to encourage the men, at their last attack. I never saw soldiers fight with such fury as did these peasants. They threw themselves on the troops like tigers, in many cases wresting their arms from them and braining them with their own muskets. Even our best soldiers seemed cowed, by the fierceness with which they were attacked; and as for the men of the new levies, they were worse than useless, and their efforts to force their way to the rear blocked the way of the reinforcements; who were trying, though I must own not very vigorously, to get to the front.

"The peasants were well led, too, and acting on an excellent plan of defence. They must have been sheltered altogether from our fire, for among the dead I did not see one who had been killed by a cannonball. The country must possess hundreds of points, equally well adapted for defence; and if these are as well and obstinately held as this has been, it will take even more than fifty thousand men to suppress the insurrection."

"The Convention is going to work the wrong way," Berruyer said. "The commissioners have orders to hang every peasant found in arms, and every suspect; that is to say, virtually every one in La Vendee. It would have been infinitely better for them to have issued a general amnesty; to acknowledge that they themselves have made a mistake; that the cures of Poitou and Brittany should be excepted from the general law, and allowed to continue their work in their respective parishes without interruption; and that for a year, at least, this part of France should be exempt from conscription. Why, if this campaign goes on, a far larger force will be employed here than the number of troops which the district was called upon to contribute, to say nothing of the enormous expense and loss of men.

"It is a hideous business altogether, to my mind. I would give all I possess to be recalled, and sent to fight on the frontier."

Two hours after the fight, Leigh with his band, of whom none had been killed, although several had received wounds more or less serious, arrived at Chemille. They had been preceded by many of the peasants, who had already carried the news of the fight, and that the column from Thouars had been delayed for three hours, and had suffered very heavy losses.

"It was all owing, Monsieur Cathelineau," the head of one of the peasant bands said, "to the officer you sent to command us. He was splendid. It was to him that everything was due. He was cutting down the bridge when we came up, and it was by his orders that we felled the trees, and blocked the road, and made a sort of hedge that took them so long to get through. We should have been greatly damaged by the fire of their guns and muskets; but he kept us all lying down, out of reach, till we were wanted, while the men with the guns defended the line of fallen trees. When we were wanted, he called us up by blowing a cow horn, and then we drove the Blues back into the stream, and returned to our shelter until we were wanted again.

"We did not lose more than thirty men, altogether; while more than ten times that number of the Blues have fallen. We thought at first that you had chosen rather a strange leader for us; but as always you were right, for if you had been there, yourself, things could not have gone better."

"But I sent no one as your commander," Cathelineau said in surprise.

"He had a paper that he read out, saying that he was acting on your orders. As I cannot read, I cannot say that it was written down as he read it; but if you did not send him, God must have done so."

"It is strange, Bonchamp," Cathelineau said to that officer, "for I certainly did not send anyone. I never thought of defending the passage of that stream. However, whoever it is who has commanded has done us great service, for that three hours which have been gained will make all the difference. They cannot arrive, now, until after dark, and will not attack before morning; and by that time, our force will have doubled."

"Here comes our officer, monsieur!" the peasant exclaimed; as Leigh, with his party, came down the street, loudly cheered by the peasants who had fought under him.

"Why, it is Jean Martin's young brother-in-law!" Monsieur Bonchamp exclaimed and, raising his voice, he called to Jean, who was talking to a group of other officers near.

Jean ran up.

"Monsieur Martin, it is your young Englishman who has held Berruyer in check, for three hours; see how the peasants are cheering him!"

Cathelineau advanced to meet Leigh, who halted his band and saluted the general. The latter stepped forward, and returned the salute by lifting his hat.

"Monsieur Stansfield," he said, "I salute you, as the saviour of our position here. Had Berruyer arrived this afternoon, we must have retired;

for we are not yet in sufficient force to withstand his attack. Tomorrow we shall, I hope, be strong enough to beat him. I have been wondering who this officer could be who, with but three or four hundred men, held the principal force of our foes, led by their commander-in-chief, in check for three hours; and, as I hear, killed three hundred of his best troops, with a loss of but thirty of ours. I ought to have thought of you, when they said that you read them an order, saying that you were acting in my name."

"It was great presumption on my part, general," Leigh said, "and I know that I had no right to use it for such a purpose; but I felt how important it was that you should have time to prepare for defence, and I thought it my duty, as there was no one else to take the matter in hand, to do so myself."

"You have done magnificently, sir, and the thanks of all La Vendee are due to you.

"I see that several of your lads are wounded," for five of them wore bandages, and a sixth was carried on a rough litter, by four of his companions. "Lads," he said, "I salute you. You have done well, indeed, and there is not a boy of your age in La Vendee but will envy you, when he hears how you, under your brave young commander, have today played the chief part in checking the advance of an army of five thousand men. I shall publish an order, today, saying that my scouts have rendered an inestimable service to their country."

"Well, Leigh," Jean Martin said, after the little band had fallen out, and one of the surgeons had taken charge of the wounded, "you have indeed distinguished yourself. I certainly did not think, when I persuaded your sister to let you go, that you were going to match yourself against the French general, and to command a force which should inflict a heavy check upon him. Cathelineau has asked me to bring you round to his quarters, presently, so that you can give him the full details of the affair; saying that a plan that had succeeded so well might be tried again, with equal effect. I cannot stay with you now, for I am going, with Bonchamp, to see to the work of loopholing and fortifying the church."

"I am going to look after my boys, Jean. They have had nothing to eat this morning, except a mouthful or two of bread each, and they have been up since two hours before daylight. Do you feel sure that the Blues will not attack tonight?"

"Yes, I think so. After the lesson you have given Berruyer of the fighting qualities of the peasants, it is pretty certain that he will not venture to attack us after a hard day's march, and a fight that must have sorely discouraged his men."

That evening, news came in from several quarters. Leigonyer had marched from Vihiers by three roads, directing his course towards Coron. Two of the columns had been attacked by the peasants and, being largely composed of new levies, had at once lost heart and retreated; the central column, in which were the regular troops, being obliged in consequence also to fall back. Another column had crossed the Loire and taken Saint Florent, without any very heavy fighting; and Quetineau had advanced from Bressuire to Aubiers, without meeting with resistance.

The news was, on the whole, satisfactory. It had been feared that the force at Vihiers would march north, and join that of Berruyer; and that they would make a joint attack upon the town. The disaster that had befallen them rendered this no longer possible. There was disappointment that Saint Florent had been recaptured, but none that Quetineau had advanced without opposition to Aubiers; for the whole of the peasantry from that locality were with Cathelineau.

In point of fact, Berruyer had not ordered the force at Vihiers to march to join him. On the contrary, he had intended, after capturing Chemille, which he expected to do without serious trouble, to march south and effect a junction with Leigonyer at Coron. He halted four miles from Chemille, harangued the new levies, reproaching those who had shown cowardice during the day's fighting, and exhorting them to behave with courage on the following day. No inconsiderable portion of them belonged to the force that had marched down from Paris, and these heroes of the slums, who had been foremost in the massacres in the prisons, and in their demand for the blood of all hostile to them, behaved throughout with abject cowardice, whenever they met a foe with arms in their hands.

After having had an interview with Cathelineau, and relating to him full particulars of the fight, Leigh, having nothing to do, strolled about the town. Presently he came upon a group of three or four peasants, who had been drinking more than was good for them. One of them, whose bearing and appearance showed that he had served in the army, was talking noisily to the others.

"You will see that I, Jacques Bruno, artilleryman, will be a great man yet," he said. "I shall soon be rich. I have had enough poverty since I left the army, but I shall have plenty of gold yet. You will see what you will see."

"How can you be rich?" one of the others said, with an air of drunken wisdom. "You are lazy, Jacques Bruno. We all know you. You are too fond of the wine cup It is seldom that you do a day's work."

"Never mind how I shall get rich. I tell you that it will be so, and the word of Jacques Bruno is not to be doubted;" and he turned away, saying, "I shall go for a few hours' sleep, now, to be in readiness for tomorrow."

"Who is that man?" Leigh asked sharply, going up to the others.

The scarf that he wore showed him to be an officer, and the peasants removed their hats.

"It is Jacques Bruno, monsieur. He is in charge of our guns. He is an old artilleryman. Cathelineau has appointed him to the post, as it needs an artilleryman to load and point the guns."

Leigh moved away. This fellow was half drunk, but not too drunk to know what he was saying. What did he mean by declaring that he would soon be rich? The peasants had said that he was lazy, and fond of the wine cup He could hardly be likely to acquire wealth by honest labour.

Perhaps he might be intending an act of treachery. Putting aside other considerations, he, as an old soldier, would scarcely care to mow down his former comrades, and his sympathies must be rather with the army than with the peasants. He had no personal interest in this revolt against conscription, nor was it likely that the cause of the cures concerned him greatly. He might, however, meditate some act of treachery, by which he would benefit his former comrades and gain a rich reward.

At any rate, it would be worth while watching. He returned to the room where his band were quartered.

"Andre," he said, "I want you and two others to keep watch with me until midnight, then Pierre and two of his party will relieve you. At that hour you will send one of your party, to guide Pierre to the place where I shall be. You will bring your pistols and knives with you, and if I come down and tell you to move forward, you will do so as noiselessly as possible."

"Shall we come at once, captain?" Andre asked.

"No, you had better lie down, with the two who are to come with you, and sleep till nine o'clock. I will come at that hour. We will say one o'clock instead of twelve for the watch to be changed; that will make a more even division for the night."

Going out again, Leigh inquired where the cannon had been placed. They were on an eminence outside the town, and commanded the road by which Berruyer's column would advance. Strolling up there, he saw Bruno lying asleep between two of the guns, of which there were five.

"It seems all right," he said to himself, "and as he cannot walk off with them, I don't see what his plan can be--that is, if he has a plan. However, there is no harm in keeping watch. The guns are against the skyline and, lying down fifty yards away, we shall be able to see if he does anything with them. Of course he might spike them, but I don't suppose that he would risk that, for the spikes might be noticed the first thing in the morning. I don't think that it would do for him to try that. It seemed a stupid thing even to doubt him but, half drunk as he was, he certainly was in earnest in what he said, and does believe that he is going to be a rich man; and I don't see how that can possibly come about, except by some act of treachery. At any rate, we will keep an eye upon the fellow tonight, and if we are not posted in any particular spot tomorrow, I will be up here with my band when the firing begins, and keep my eye on him."

He spent three or four hours with Jean Martin, and then went back to his quarters. Andre and two of the lads were in readiness. They moved out quietly, for the street was thick with sleeping peasants. There were no sentries to be seen.

"If the enemy did but know," he muttered to himself, "they might take the place without firing a shot."

Presently, however, he came upon an officer.

"Where are you going?" he asked sharply.

"I am Leigh Stansfield, and am going, with three of my party, to keep watch near the guns."

"That is good," the officer said. "I am on duty here, and Jean Martin has just ridden out. He is going a couple of miles along the road, and will give the alarm if he hears any movement of the enemy. When he gets within half a mile he is to fire off his pistols, and I shall have time to get the men up, long before their infantry can arrive. We have tried, in vain, to get some of the peasants to do outpost duty. They all say that they will be ready to fight, when the enemy comes; but they want a good sleep first, and even Cathelineau could not move them. It is heartbreaking to have to do with such men."

"I do not think that it is laziness. It is that they have a fixed objection to doing what they consider any kind of soldier work. Their idea of war is to wait till the enemy comes, and then to make a rush upon them; and when they have done that, they think their duty is ended. Some day, when the Blues have a sharp commander, and have gained a little discipline, we shall suffer some terrible disaster from the obstinacy of the peasantry."

With a word of adieu Leigh turned off the road, and made his way halfway up the eminence. Here the guns could be plainly made out. Leaving Andre and his two followers, he went quietly up the slope, to assure himself that the artilleryman was still there. Had he missed him, he was determined to go at once to Cathelineau, and state his suspicions, and his belief that Bruno had gone off to inform Berruyer that, if he advanced, he would find the place wholly unguarded, and would have it at his mercy. He found, however, that the artilleryman was still asleep, and returned to Andre.

"Now," he said, "there is no occasion for us all to watch. I, with one of the others, will keep a lookout for the next two hours and, at the end of that time, will rouse you and the others."

Leigh's watch had passed off quietly. There was no movement among the guns and, from the position in which Bruno was lying, his figure would have been seen at once, had he risen to his feet.

"If the man up there stands up, you are to awaken me at once, Andre," he said.

Overcome by the excitement and the heat of the day, Leigh dropped off to sleep almost immediately. An hour later, he was roused by being shaken by Andre.

"The man has got up, sir."

The artilleryman, after stretching himself two or three times, took up something from the ground beside him, and then went some distance down the side of the hill, but still in sight of the watchers.

"He has got something on his shoulder, sir. I think it is a shovel, and he has either a cloak or a sack on his arm."

"He is evidently up to something," Leigh replied, "but what it can be, I cannot imagine."

Presently the man stopped, and began to work.

"He is digging," Andre said, in surprise.

"It looks like it certainly, but what he can be digging for I have no idea."

Presently the man was seen to raise a heavy weight on to his shoulders.

"It was a sack he had with him," Andre said, "and he has filled it with earth and stones."

Leigh did not reply. The mystery seemed to thicken, and he was unable to form any supposition, whatever, that would account for the man's proceedings. The latter carried his burden up to the cannon, then he laid it down, and took up some long tool and thrust it into the mouth of one of the cannon.

A light suddenly burst upon Leigh.

"The scoundrel is going to draw the charges," he said, "and fill up the cannon with the earth that he has brought up."

Andre would have leapt to his feet, as he uttered an exclamation of rage.

"Keep quiet!" Leigh said, authoritatively. "We have no evidence against him, yet. We must watch him a bit longer, before we interrupt him."

After two or three movements, the man was seen to draw something from the gun. This he laid on the ground, and then inserted the tool again.

"That is the powder," Leigh whispered, as something else was withdrawn from the gun; "there, you see, he is taking handfuls of earth from the sack, and shoving it into the mouth."

This was continued for some time, and then a rammer was inserted, and pushed home several times. Then he moved to the next cannon.

"Now follow very quietly, Andre. Busy as he is, we may get quite close up to him, before he notices us. Mind, you are not to use your knife. We can master him easily enough, and must then take him down to Cathelineau, for his fate to be decided on."

Noiselessly they crept up the hill. When within five or six paces of the gun at which Bruno was at work, Leigh gave the word and, leaping up, they threw themselves on the traitor; who was taken so completely by surprise that they were able to throw him, at once, to the ground. Snatching up a rope that had been used for drawing the guns, Leigh bound his arms securely to his side; and then, putting a pistol to his head, ordered him to rise to his feet.

"Shoot me, if you like,"' the man growled. "I will not move."

"I will not shoot you," Leigh replied. "You must be tried and condemned.

"Now, Andre, we must carry him."

The four boys had no difficulty in carrying the man down. As they passed the officer on sentry, he said:

"Whom have you there, Monsieur Stansfield?"

"It is Bruno, the artilleryman. We have caught him drawing the charges from the guns, and filling them with earth. We must take him to the general."

"The villain!" the officer exclaimed. "Who would have thought of a Vendean turning traitor?"

Cathelineau was still up, talking with some of his officers as to the preparations for the battle. There was no sentry at his door. Leigh entered and, tapping at the door of the room in which he saw a light, went in. Cathelineau looked up in surprise, as the door opened.

"I thought you were asleep hours ago, monsieur," he said.

"It is well that I have not been, sir."

And he related the conversation that he had overheard, and his own suspicions that the man Bruno meditated treachery; the steps they had taken to watch him, and the discovery they had made. Exclamations of indignation and fury broke from the officers.

"Gentlemen," Cathelineau said, "we will at once proceed to try this traitor. He shall be judged by men of his own class.

"Monsieur Pourcet, do you go out and awaken the first twelve peasants you come to."

In a minute or two the officer returned with the peasants, who looked surprised at having been thus roused from their sleep.

"My friends, do you take your places along that side of the room. You are a jury, and are to decide upon the guilt or innocence of a man who is accused of being a traitor."

The word roused them at once, and all repeated indignantly the word "traitor!"

"Monsieur Stansfield," he said to Leigh, "will you order your men to bring in the prisoner?"

The man was brought in and placed at the head of the table, opposite to Cathelineau.

"Now, Monsieur Stansfield, will you tell the jury the story that you have just told me?"

Leigh repeated his tale, interrupted occasionally by exclamations of fury from the peasants. Andre and the other lads stepped forward, one after the other, and confirmed Leigh's statement.

"Before you return a verdict, my friends," Cathelineau said quietly, "it is but right that we should go up to the battery, and examine the cannon ourselves; not, of course, that we doubt the statement of Monsieur Stansfield and the other witnesses, but because it is well that each of you should be able to see for himself, and report to others that you have been eyewitnesses of the traitor's plot."

Accordingly the whole party ascended to the battery. There lay the spade and the sack of earth. The tool with which the work had been done was still in the mouth of the second cannon and, on pulling it out, the powder cartridge came with it. Then Leigh led them to the next gun, and a man who had a bayonet thrust it in, and soon brought some earth and stones to the mouth of the gun.

"We have now had the evidence of Monsieur Stansfield, and those with him, tested by ourselves examining the guns. What do you say, my friends--has this man been proved a traitor, or not?"

"He has!" the peasants exclaimed, in chorus.

"And what is your sentence?"

"Death!" was the unanimous reply.

"I approve of that sentence. March him down to the side of the river, and shoot him."

Three minutes later, four musket shots rang out.

"Thus die all traitors!" Cathelineau said.

Bruno, however, was the sole Vendean who, during the course of the war, turned traitor to his comrades and his country.

Chapter 6
The Assault Of Chemille

Few words were spoken, as the group of officers returned to the town. When they reached Cathelineau's quarters Leigh would have gone on, but the general said, "Come in, if you please, Monsieur Stansfield," and he followed the party in.

"This has been a trial, gentlemen, a heavy trial," the general said. "When I entered upon this work, I knew that that there were many things that I should have to endure. I knew the trouble of forming soldiers from men who, like ours, prize their freedom and independence above all other things; that we might have to suffer defeat; that we must meet with hardships, and probably death; and that, in the long run, all our efforts might be futile.

"But I had not reckoned on having to deal with treachery. I had never dreamed that one of my first acts would have been to try and to sentence a Vendean to death, for an act of the grossest treachery. However, let us put that aside; it was, perhaps, in the nature of things. In every community there must be a few scoundrels and, if this turns out to be a solitary instance, we may congratulate ourselves, especially as we have escaped without injury.

"That we have done so, gentlemen, is due solely to Monsieur Stansfield; who thus twice, in the course of a single day, has performed an inestimable service to the cause. There are few indeed who, on hearing the braggadocio of a drunken man, would have given the matter a moment's thought; still less have undertaken a night of watchfulness, after a day of the heaviest work, merely to test the truth of a slightly-founded suspicion that might have occurred to them. It is not too much to say that, had not this act of treachery been discovered, our defeat tomorrow would have been well-nigh certain. You know how much our people think of their guns; and if, when the fight began, the cannon had been silent, instead of pouring their contents into the ranks of the enemy, they would have lost heart at once, and would have been beaten almost before the fight began.

"We have no honours to bestow on you, Monsieur Stansfield, but in the name of La Vendee I thank you, with all my heart. I shall add, to my order respecting your fight of yesterday, a statement of what has taken place tonight; and I shall beg that all officers read it aloud to the parties that follow them."

"I agree most cordially with the general's words," Monsieur Bonchamp said. "Your defence yesterday would have been a credit to any military man, and this discovery has saved us from ruin tomorrow, or rather today. I will venture to say that not one man in five hundred would have taken the trouble to go out of his way to ascertain whether the words of a drunken man rested on any foundation."

There was, then, a short conversation as to the approaching fight. The number of men who had arrived was much smaller than had been anticipated, owing to the fact that the simultaneous invasion, at so many points, had the effect of retaining the peasants of the various localities for the defence of their own homes. Leigh learned that a mounted messenger had been despatched, shortly before he brought the prisoner down, to beg Monsieur d'Elbee to bring the force he commanded, at Chollet, with all speed to aid in the defence of Chemille; for if that town fell, he would be exposed to the attack of the united forces of Generals Berruyer and Leigonyer.

"Now, gentlemen, I think we had better get a few hours' sleep," Cathelineau said. "They will not be here very early, probably not until noon; for they may wait for a time before starting, in hopes of being joined either by Leigonyer or one of the other columns, and it is not likely that any news of the sharp reverse that Leigonyer has met with has reached them."

It was now two o'clock in the morning, and Leigh slept heavily, till roused at eight.

"You should have called me before, Andre," he said reproachfully, when he learnt how late it was.

"I thought it was better that you should have a good sleep, captain. Of course, if there had been any message to say that you were wanted, I should have woke you; but as no one came, and there is still no news of the enemy, I thought that it was better to let you sleep till now."

Pierre had started with his party, at five, to scout on the road by which the enemy was advancing. Leigh first hurried down to the river and had a bath, and then felt ready for any work that he might have to do. He then went to the house where Jean was lodged. The latter, who had not returned from his outpost work till day broke, was just getting up.

"Well, Leigh," he said, "I called in at Cathelineau's quarters to report. I found him already up. He told me the work that you had been doing, and praised you up to the skies. It seems to me that you are getting all the credit of the campaign. Really I feel quite proud of you, and we shall be having you starting as a rival leader to Cathelineau."

Leigh laughed.

"One does not often have two such opportunities in the course of a day, and I don't suppose I am likely to have such luck again, if the war goes on for a year. Where are you going to be today?"

"I am going to act as aide-de-camp to Bonchamp."

"And what shall we do, do you think?"

"Well, I should say you had best keep out of it altogether, Leigh. You and your band did much more than your share of fighting yesterday, and your pistols will be of no use in a fight such as this will be. Seriously, unless Cathelineau assigns you some post, I should keep out of it. Your little corps is specially formed to act as scouts and, as we are so extremely badly off in that respect, it will be far better for you to keep to your proper duties, than to risk your lives."

"How do you think the fight is likely to go, Jean?"

"It depends, in the first place, upon how the Blues fight; if they do well, they ought to beat us. In the next place, it depends on whether d'Elbee comes up in time. If he does, I think that we shall hold the place, but it will be stiff fighting."

It was not until noon that Berruyer's force was seen approaching. As soon as it was in sight the Vendeans poured out, and took up their station by the hill on which the guns were placed. In spite of what Jean had said, Leigh would have placed his band with the rest; had not Cathelineau sent for him, half an hour before, and given him orders which were almost identical with the advice of Jean.

"I wish you and your band to keep out of this battle, Monsieur Stansfield. Your force is so small that it can make no possible difference in the fortunes of the day and, whether we win or lose, your lads may be wanted as messengers, after it is over. They have done extremely well, at present, and need no further credit than they have gained. I beg, therefore, that you will take post with them somewhat in rear of the village, away on the right. I shall then know where to find you, if I have any messages to send; and moreover, I want you at once to send off one of your most active lads with this note to d'Elbee, urging him to come on at full speed, for the fight is likely to go hard with us, unless he comes in time to our assistance; and telling him I wish him to know that, even if I have to fall back, the church will be held till the last; and that as soon as he arrives I shall, if possible, again take the offensive, and beg that he will attack the enemy in flank or in rear, as he sees an opportunity. Upon the belfry of the church, half a mile on our right, you will be able to see how the battle goes; and can send off news to d'Elbee, from time to time."

"Very well, sir. I will despatch your letter at once, and then march out to the church, which I noticed yesterday."

"Here is a telescope," Cathelineau said. "We are well provided with them, as we took all that we could find, at Chollet and Vihiers. I think that, with its aid, you will be able to have a good view of what is going on."

In twenty minutes, Leigh had taken up his post in the belfry of the village church that Cathelineau had indicated. Andre and Pierre, whose party had returned an hour before, were with him. The rest of the band were in the story below them, from which a view was also obtainable. The three most severely wounded had started for their homes, early that morning. The others were fit for duty.

The fight began by a discharge of the guns of the assailants. Leigh could see that the defenders' guns had been somewhat withdrawn from their position on the top of the rising ground, where they would have been too much exposed to the enemy's fire; and their muzzles now only showed over the brow. During the course of the morning an earthwork had been thrown up, to afford protection to the men serving them. They did not return the fire until the enemy were within a distance of a quarter of a mile, then they commenced, with deadly effect.

The Blues halted, and Leigh could make out that a considerable number of men in the rear at once turned and ran. In order to encourage them they had been informed, just before they marched, of the plot that had been arranged to silence the guns; and this unexpected discharge caused the greatest consternation among the young levies. A body of cavalry were at once sent off in pursuit, and drove the fugitives back to their ranks, the troopers using the flats of their swords unstintingly.

Then the advance was resumed, covered by the fire of the guns and by volleys of musketry. These were answered but feebly by the firearms in the peasants' hands, and the Blues pressed on until, just before they reached the foot of the slope, the peasants charged them with fury.

The regular troops and a regiment of gendarmes had been placed in front. These stood firm, poured heavy volleys into the peasants as they approached, and then received them with levelled bayonets.

In vain the Vendeans strove to break through the hedge of steel. Cathelineau and his officers on one side, and the French generals on the other, encouraged their men, and for a quarter of an hour a desperate conflict reigned. Then the peasants fell back, and the Blues resumed their advance.

Three times Cathelineau induced his followers to renew the attack, but each time it was unsuccessful. The Blues mounted the hill, the cannon were captured, and the Vendeans fell back into the town. Here the ends of the streets had been barricaded and, in spite of the artillery and the captured guns now turned against their former owners, the assailants tried in vain to force their way into the town.

From every window that commanded the approaches, the men with muskets kept up an incessant fire. The mass of the peasants lay in shelter behind the barricades, or in the houses, until the enemy's infantry approached to within striking distance; and then, leaping up from these barricades, and fighting with an absolute disregard of their lives, they again and again repulsed the attacks of the enemy.

Berruyer, seeing that in spite of his heavy losses he made no way, called his troops from the assault and, forming them into two columns, moved to the right and left, and attacked the town on both sides. Here no barricades had been erected and, in spite of the efforts of the peasants, an entrance was forced into the town. Every street, lane, and house was defended with desperate energy; but discipline gradually triumphed, and the Blues won their way into the square in the centre of the town, where the principal church stood. As they entered the open space, they were assailed with a rain of bullets from the roof, tower, and windows.

As soon as the flanking movement began, Monsieur Bonchamp, seeing that the town was now certain to be taken, had hurried, with the greater portion of the men armed with muskets, to the church; which had already been prepared by him, on the previous day, for the defence. A great number of paving stones had been got up from the roadway and piled inside the church and, as soon as he arrived there with his men, the doors were closed, and blocked behind with a deep wall of stones.

Berruyer saw that the position was a formidable one and, ignorant of the number of the defenders, sent back for his guns, and contented himself for the time by clearing the rest of the town of its defenders. These, however, as they issued out, were rallied by Cathelineau and his officers. They assured the peasants that the day was not yet lost, that the church would hold out for hours, and that d'Elbee would soon arrive, with his force from Chollet, to their assistance.

Leigh, anxiously watching the progress of the fight, had sent messenger after messenger along the road by which d'Elbee would come. His heart sank, as he heard the guns open in the centre of the town, and knew that they were directed against the church. Still, there was no abatement of the fire of the defenders. An incessant fire of musketry was maintained, not only from the church itself, but from every window in the houses around it.

At last, he heard that d'Elbee's force was but a quarter of a mile away and, running down from his lookout, he started to meet it. It was coming at a run, the men panting and breathless, but holding on desperately, half maddened with the sound of battle.

"All is not lost yet, then?" d'Elbee said, as he came up.

"No, sir. The church holds out, and I could see that the peasants who have been driven out of the town have rallied, but a few hundred yards away, and are evidently only waiting for your arrival to renew the attack. I think, sir, that if you will run up to the belfry of the church with this glass, you will be able to understand the exact situation."

The officer ran up the tower, and returned in two or three minutes. Then he led his men down towards the southeastern corner of the town.

Leigh, on hearing that d'Elbee was close at hand, sent off two messengers to Cathelineau to inform him of the fact; and he now sent off another, stating the direction in which the reinforcement was marching.

"I am going to attack at that corner, instead of in the rear," Monsieur d'Elbee said to him; for now that the duty assigned to him had been performed, Leigh thought that he would be justified in joining in the attack, with what remained of his band. "If I were to get directly in their rear they would, on finding their retreat cut off, fight so fiercely that I might be overpowered. Even the most cowardly troops will fight, under those circumstances. Therefore, while threatening their line of retreat, I still leave it open to them. It is a maxim in war, you know, always to leave a bridge open for a flying foe."

In a few minutes they reached the town. None had observed their approach, the troops being assembled round the church. These were at once thrown into confusion, when they found themselves attacked with fury by a large force, of whose existence they had no previous thought.

The Vendeans fought with desperate valour. The new levies for the most part lost heart at once and, in spite of the efforts of Berruyer and his officers, began to make for the line of retreat. The movement was accelerated by an outburst of shouts from the other side of the town, where Cathelineau's force poured in, burning to avenge their former losses; and as they fell upon the enemy, Bonchamp led out the defenders of the church, by a side door, and joined in the fray.

Berruyer saw that all was lost. By great efforts he kept together the gendarmes and regular troops, to cover the retreat; and fell back, fighting fiercely. Bonchamp and his musketeers pressed hotly upon them. The peasants made charge after charge and, as soon as the force issued from the town, many of the peasantry set off at full speed in pursuit of the fugitives, great numbers of whom were overtaken and killed. Berruyer continued his retreat all night, and entered Saint Lambert before morning; having lost the whole of his cannon, and three thousand men, in this disastrous fight.

The joy of the Vendeans was unbounded. The stones were speedily removed from the shattered doors of the church, mass was celebrated, and the peasants returned thanks for their great victory.

The gains were, indeed, considerable. Three thousand muskets had fallen into their hands. They had recaptured the guns that they had lost, and taken twelve others. Their own losses had been heavy--eighteen hundred men had been killed, and a great number wounded. But of this, at the time, they thought but little; those who had died had died for their country and their God, as all of them were ready to do, and how could men do more?

On the Republican side, General Duhaus had been very dangerously wounded, and most of Berruyer's principal officers killed.

A council of war was held the next morning, at Chemille. For the moment, the victory had secured their safety; but while the peasants believed and hoped that the war was over, their leaders saw that the position was scarcely improved. They had, indeed, captured guns and muskets; but these were useless without ammunition, and their stock of powder and ball was quite exhausted. Already the peasantry were leaving in large numbers for their homes. Berruyer might return reinforced at any time, and effect a junction with Leigonyer; while the column that had captured Saint Florent would doubtless advance. It was therefore decided that Chemille must be abandoned, and that the officers should retire to Tiffauges until, at any rate, the peasants were ready to leave their homes again.

By evening that day the greater portion of the army had melted away and, on the following morning, the leaders also left the town they had so bravely defended. On the following day, indeed, Berruyer, having learned the position of Leigonyer, returned to Chemille and, two days later, was in communication with Leigonyer's force. The latter had occupied Chollet, which had been left devoid of defenders since the day they marched away.

On the other hand Quetineau had, on the thirteenth, been attacked at Aubiers, and had been forced to evacuate the place, leaving three guns behind him, retiring to Bressuire. The capture of Aubiers was the work of Henri de la Rochejaquelein. He had ridden to join Cathelineau, and met him and the other leaders retiring from Chemille. They were gloomy and depressed. They had won a battle, but they were without an army, without ammunition. Almost all the towns were in the possession of the Blues. It seemed to them that the struggle could not be much longer maintained.

The young count was too energetic and too enthusiastic to be seriously moved, and rode back to the residence of an aunt, at Saint Aubin. There he learned that Aubiers had been taken by the enemy. The peasantry around were in a state of extreme excitement. They had hoisted the white flag on their churches, and were ready to fight, but they had no leader.

Hearing that Rochejaquelein was at his aunt's house, they came to him, and begged him to take the command, promising him that in twenty-four hours ten thousand men should be ready to follow him. He agreed to the request. The church bells were set ringing and, before morning, almost that number were assembled. Of these, only two hundred had guns.

With this force he attacked Aubiers. The resistance of the enemy was feeble, and they were chased almost to Bressuire. Rochejaquelein was very anxious to capture this town, as his friends, the Lescures, had been brought from Clisson and imprisoned there; but he saw that it was of primary importance to carry assistance to Cathelineau, and he accordingly marched to Tiffauges. The church bells again rang out their summons; and Cathelineau, in twenty-four hours, found himself at the head of an army of twenty thousand men.

"I told you at Clisson that I should soon meet you again, Monsieur Martin," La Rochejaquelein said when, as he rode into Tiffauges at the head of his newly raised force, he met Jean in the street, "and here I am, you see. I am only sorry that I am too late to take part in the brave fight at Chemille."

"Right glad are we to see you, count," Jean replied. "This is my wife's brother, of whom I was speaking to you at Clisson. Cathelineau will tell you that he has been distinguishing himself rarely."

Henri held out his hand to Leigh, and said warmly, "I am glad to know you. It would be a shame, indeed, were any Vendeans to remain at home, when a young Englishman is fighting for their country. I hope that we shall be great friends."

"I shall be glad, indeed, to be so," Leigh replied with equal warmth, for he was greatly struck with the appearance of the young soldier.

Henri de la Rochejaquelein was but twenty-one years old, tall, and remarkably handsome. He had fair hair, and a noble bearing. His father had been a colonel in the army, and he himself was a cavalry officer in the king's guard. He was the beau ideal of a dashing hussar, and his appearance was far more English than French. He was immensely popular, his manner frank and pleasant, and he was greatly beloved by the peasantry on his family estates.

At this moment Cathelineau with his two generals came up, and Leigh retired from the circle. The arrival of the young count, with his strong reinforcement, at once altered the position. The leaders who had, since they fell back from Chemille, been depressed and almost hopeless, beamed with satisfaction as they talked with Henri, whose enthusiasm was infectious.

La Rochejaquelein accompanied them to his quarters. Hitherto he had only heard rumours of the fighting at Chemille, and Cathelineau now gave him a full account of the affair. Jean Martin had, at his invitation, accompanied him; and when Cathelineau had finished, Henri turned to him and said:

"Indeed you did not exaggerate, Monsieur Martin, when you said that your brother-in-law had already distinguished himself. In fact, there can be no doubt that the splendid defence he made at that little river, where he held Berruyer's whole force in check for upwards of three hours--and so forced him to halt for the night on the way, instead of pushing forward and attacking Chemille at once--saved the town, for it gave time to Monsieur d'Elbee to come up. Scarcely less important was his detection of the treachery of the man in charge of the artillery. I cannot but regret that so gallant a young fellow is not my countryman, for I should have felt proud of one so daring, and so thoughtful.

"When you do not want him for scouting work, Monsieur Cathelineau, I shall get you to lend him to me. I should be really glad to have him by my side. His face pleased me much. There was something so frank and honest about it and, after what he has done, I am sure that I shall always respect his opinion."

There was another consultation as to what should be their first operation, and it was resolved that Leigonyer should be attacked at once, before he could make a complete junction with Berruyer. The next morning, at daybreak, the whole force moved off. They were only just in time, for Berruyer had already ordered General Gauvillier, who commanded the force that had captured Saint Florent, to advance to Beaupreau. Berruyer was to march to Vezins, and he himself to Jallais, and to join Leigonyer at May.

On the previous evening Henri had, after the termination of the council, requested Jean Martin to take him to the house where Leigh and his little party were quartered.

"I have been hearing of your doings," he said, "and feel quite jealous that you, who are, I hear, four years younger than myself, should have done so much; while I, with all my family influence and connection, should as yet have done nothing but chase the enemy out of Aubiers. How is it that you, who have had no training as a soldier, should have conceived the idea of arresting the march of Berruyer's army, with a force of only two or three hundred peasants?"

"It was a mere matter of common sense," Leigh said, with a smile. "I knew that it was of the utmost importance that Chemille should not be attacked, until Cathelineau received reinforcements. At first, I had no thought of doing more than breaking down the bridge, and of perhaps checking the advanced cavalry; but when I found that the peasants who came along were quite willing to aid, it seemed to me that by cutting down the trees, so as to block the road and make a shelter for us, we might be able to cause the enemy considerable delay. I hardly hoped to succeed in holding out so long, or in inflicting such loss upon him as we were able to do. It did not require any military knowledge whatever, and I should not have attempted it had I not seen that, thanks to the forest, we should be able to retreat when we could no longer hold the barricade of felled trees."

"Well, you could not have done better if you had been a general. I have Cathelineau's permission to ask you to ride with me, when you are not engaged in scouting."

"I should be delighted to do so, but at present I have no horse. However, I can send one of my lads back to the chateau, to fetch the one that I generally ride."

"I have brought a spare animal with me," the young count said. "I brought it in case the other should be shot, and I shall be glad if you will ride it tomorrow, and until yours arrives; but I would not send for one until after tomorrow, for likely enough we may make some captures before nightfall.

"We are to march at three in the morning, and to attack Leigonyer. The great thing that we need is powder. Cathelineau says that there is scarcely a charge left among his men. Mine are not much better off. We should have had none with which to attack Aubiers; but I sent off during the night to a quarry, a few miles from my aunt's, and succeeded in getting forty pounds of blasting powder. It would not have been of much use for the muskets, but the fact of its being powder was sufficient to encourage the peasants; and the Blues made such a feeble resistance that its quality made no difference to us. It enabled those who had muskets to make a noise with them, and was just as effectual in raising their spirits in attacking the Blues as if it had been the finest quality. We got a few hundred cartridges when we took the place, but that will not go very far, and I hope that, tomorrow, we shall be able to obtain a supply from the enemy."

Before the hour for starting, the force had swelled considerably. The news that Monsieur de la Rochejaquelein had retaken Aubiers, and had come with twelve thousand men to assist Cathelineau, spread like wildfire. The peasants from all the country round flocked in and, when they started in the morning, the united force had swollen to over twenty thousand men.

As soon as the young count left him, Leigh sent all his band, under his lieutenants, with orders to proceed towards Vezins; to ascertain the progress Leigonyer had made, and the position of his forces, and to send back news to him. Just as the army was starting one of the boys returned, and said that a party of twelve cavalry, and a detachment of infantry, had just entered the chateau of Crilloire. Leigh at once informed Cathelineau, who sent off a hundred and fifty men to capture the place. They were ordered to travel at the top of their speed, and Jean Martin was in command of them.

The expedition was crowned with success. The infantry, who had been stationed outside the chateau, fled at once. Their commandant Villemet, Leigonyer's best officer, charged the Vendeans with his little body of cavalry. He was received with a volley. Two of his men were killed, and he himself and nine of his men were wounded. He managed, however, to burst through the Vendeans, and to overtake his flying infantry. These he rallied and led back to the chateau, which he found deserted; for Martin, as soon as he captured the place and cleared it of the enemy, had gone off with his men to join the main body.

Berruyer had also started early, and sent five hundred men to May, where he expected Leigonyer to arrive in a few hours; but before he reached the town the Vendeans attacked the advanced guard of the latter general, which consisted of two companies of grenadiers. These old soldiers fought well, and threw themselves into the chateau of Bois-Groleau.

Leaving fifteen hundred men to surround and attack the chateau, the main army pressed forward. Leigonyer, hearing of the disaster, sent forward two thousand men to succour the besieged force; but the Vendeans fell upon them and, after a short resistance, they broke and fled into Vezins.

The arrival of the fugitives caused a panic among the whole of Leigonyer's force assembled there, and they fled precipitately; two hundred and fifty men of the regiment of Finisterre, alone, remaining steady; and these, maintaining good order, covered the retreat of the guns, repulsing the attacks of the peasantry who pursued them. Fortunately for the Vendeans, a waggon laden with barrels of powder was left behind, in the confusion caused by their approach, and proved of inestimable value to them.

Had the Vendeans pursued the fugitives with vigour, the force would have been almost annihilated; but Cathelineau, learning from Leigh's scouts that Berruyer was already approaching Vezins, feared to be taken in the rear by him, and therefore fell back to May and Beaupreau.

The garrison that defended the chateau of Bois-Groleau repulsed the repeated attacks made upon them, but surrendered on the approach of the main army, their ammunition and the food they had brought with them in their haversacks being entirely exhausted.

Berruyer, on his arrival at Jallais, heard of the defeat of Leigonyer; and marched back in all haste to Chemille, where he had left his magazines. On hearing however that Leigonyer, on his arrival at Vihiers, had been deserted during the night by the whole of his troops and, finding himself in the morning with but a hundred and fifty men of the Finisterre regiment, had evacuated the town and retreated to Doug, Berruyer wrote to him to endeavour to gather his forces together again, and to return to Chemille.

But the news of another disaster convinced him that he could not maintain himself there. The Vendeans had marched, without delay, against Beaupreau, and attacked Gauvillier. That general had already heard of the defeat of Leigonyer, and the retreat of Berruyer. His force was greatly dispirited at the news, and offered but a feeble resistance to the fierce assault. The Blues were driven out of the town with the loss of their five cannon, and were hotly pursued to Saint Florent, losing a large proportion of their numbers on the way.

The news of this fresh disaster convinced Berruyer that he must fall back without delay, and he accordingly retreated with his whole force to Saint Lambert, whence he wrote to the Convention to declare the impossibility of doing anything without large reinforcements of regular troops, as no dependence whatever could be placed upon the National Guards and volunteers and, if the insurgents marched against him, he would be obliged to march to Ponts-de-Ce in order to cover Angers, where the alarm of the inhabitants was intense.

Thus the invasion that was to crush the Vendeans failed altogether, except that some advantages had been gained by the Blues along the line of coast, the troops being assisted by the fleet. At all other points, misfortune had attended them. Quetineau had been driven from Aubiers and, a great proportion of his force having deserted, he held Bressuire with so feeble a grasp that he could not maintain himself, if attacked. Leigonyer's army had practically ceased to exist, as had that which had advanced from Saint Florent. Berruyer had lost three thousand men, and was back again at the point from which he had started. Chollet and Vihiers had been recovered without a blow.

As the result of his failures, Berruyer was recalled to Paris, tried for his conduct, and narrowly escaped the guillotine.

As soon as Berruyer retired, Cathelineau advanced against Bressuire. News of his coming at once scared the Blues from the town, and they retreated to Thouars. They did not even wait to take their prisoners with them and, as soon as they had gone, the Marquis de la Lescure with his family rode off to their chateau, at Clisson. They had scarcely arrived there when la Rochejaquelein arrived, and acquainted them with the general facts of the insurrection.

"Cathelineau's army," he said, "consists of twenty thousand men and, on any emergency, it would swell to nearly twice that number. Twelve thousand Bretons had crossed the Loire, and were on their way to join him. In lower Poitou, Charette had an army of twenty thousand; and besides these, there were many scattered bands."

Lescure at once agreed to accompany la Rochejaquelein to Bressuire; and the Marquis of Donnissan, Madame Lescure's father, arranged to follow them, as soon as he had seen his wife and daughter safely placed in the chateau of de la Boulais.

Chapter 7
A Short Rest

Leigh Stansfield had ridden with Rochejaquelein during the march of the army to Vezins, and from there to Bressuire. He was charmed with his companion, who had been the first to dash, with a few other mounted gentlemen, into the streets of Vezins; and who had thrown himself, with reckless bravery, upon the retreating infantry and, as the peasants came up, had led them to the attack several times, until Cathelineau's orders, that the pursuit should be pushed no farther, reached him.

"That sort of order is very hard to obey," he said to Leigh. "However, I need not regret that these brave fellows should escape us. We have won the battle, if one can call it a battle; and I honour the men who, when all the others have fled like sheep, still cling together and defend their guns. At least a hundred of them have fallen, since they left the town; and we have lost double that number, and should lose at least as many more, before we finally overcame their opposition. If all the armies of the Republic were composed of such stuff as this regiment, I fear that our chance of defending La Vendee successfully would be small, indeed."

On rejoining Cathelineau, and hearing his reason for calling off the pursuit, Henri at once admitted its wisdom.

"After the defeat of Leigonyer, you will see that Berruyer will not long be able to maintain himself at Chemille," he said; "and when he hears the news, I fancy that he will retire at once; for he will know, well enough, that it will be useless for him to pursue us. Still, if he were to come down on our rear as we advanced, it would have a bad effect upon the peasants; and it is much better to avoid fighting, unless under circumstances that are almost sure to give us victory. We can almost always choose our own ground, which is an enormous advantage in a country like this. It is very fortunate that it is so, for we certainly could not raise a body of cavalry that could stand against those of the line; but in these lanes and thickets they have no superiority in that respect, for no general would be fool enough to send cavalry into places where they would be at the mercy of an unseen foe. At the same time, I must own that I regretted today that we had no mounted force.

With but a squadron or two of my old regiment, not a man of Leigonyer's force would have escaped; for the country here is open enough to use them, and I should certainly have had no compunction in cutting down the rascals who are always shouting for blood, and yet are such arrant cowards that they fly without firing a shot."

The day after the capture of Bressuire the Vendeans marched against Thouars, to which town Quetineau had retreated with his force. Thouars was the only town in La Vendee which was still walled. The fortifications were in a dilapidated condition, but nevertheless offered a considerable advantage to a force determined upon a desperate resistance. With the fugitives from Bressuire, and the garrison already in Thouars, Quetineau was at the head of three thousand five hundred troops; of these, however, comparatively few could be depended upon. The successive defeats that had been inflicted on the troops of the Republic, by the Vendeans, had entirely destroyed their morale. They no longer felt any confidence in their power to resist the onslaught of the peasants.

Quetineau himself had no hope of making a successful resistance. He had repeatedly written urgent letters to the authorities at Paris, saying that nothing could be done without large reinforcements of disciplined troops; and that the National Guard and volunteers were worse than useless, as they frequently ran at the first shot, and excited the hostility of the people, generally, by their habits of plundering. Nevertheless, the old soldier determined to resist to the last, however hopeless the conflict; and when the Vendeans approached, at six o'clock in the morning, they found that the bridge of Viennes was barricaded and guarded.

As soon as they attacked, the general reinforced the defenders of the bridge by his most trustworthy troops; a battalion, three hundred and twenty-five strong, of Marseillais, and a battalion of the National Guard of Nievre. So stoutly was the post held that the Vendean general saw that the bridge could not be taken, without terrible loss. He therefore contented himself with keeping up a heavy fire all day, while preparing an attack from other quarters.

The first step was to destroy the bridge behind the castle, and to make a breach in the wall near the Paris gate, thereby cutting off the garrison's means of retreat. At five o'clock a large body of peasantry was massed for an attack on the bridge at Viennes; and its defenders, seeing the storm that was preparing, retired into the town. The Vendeans crossed the bridge but, as they approached the walls, they were attacked by a battalion of the National Guard of Deux Sevres and a body of gendarmes and, taken by surprise, were driven back some distance. Their leaders, however, speedily rallied them; and in the meantime other bodies forced their way into the town, at several points.

To avoid a massacre of his troops, Quetineau hoisted the white flag. On this, as on all other occasions in the northern portion of La Vendee, the prisoners were well treated. They were offered their freedom, on condition of promising not to serve against La Vendee again; and to ensure that this oath should be kept for some time, at least, their heads were shaved before their release, a step that was afterwards taken throughout the war.

Quetineau was treated with all honour, and was given his freedom, without conditions. Although he knew well that neither his long services, nor the efforts that he had made, would save him from the fury of the Convention; he returned to Paris where, after the mockery of a trial, he was sent to the guillotine--a fate which awaited all those who failed, in the face of impossibilities, to carry out the plans of the mob leaders. Instead of blame, the general deserved a high amount of praise for the manner in which he had defended the town against a force six times as strong as his own.

Three thousand muskets, ten pieces of cannon, and a considerable amount of ammunition fell into the hands of the victors. This success left it open to the Vendeans either to march against Leigonyer--the remnant of whose army was in a state of insubordination at Doug, and could have offered no opposition, but must have retreated to Saumur--or to clear the country south and west.

The former would unquestionably have been the wiser course, for the capture of Saumur would have been a heavy blow, indeed, to the Republicans; but the peasants, whose villages and property were threatened by the presence of the Blues at Fontenay, Parthenay, and Chataigneraie, were so strongly in favour of the other alternative that it was adopted; and the force broke into two divisions, one moving towards Chataigneraie, and the other against Fontenay.

Parthenay was evacuated at once by the Republicans, as soon as news reached the authorities of the approach of the Vendeans. The latter, however, made no stay, but continued their march towards Chataigneraie. The town was held by General Chalbos, with three thousand men. After two hours' fighting Chalbos, seeing that his retreat was menaced, fell back.

He took up a position at Fontenay, where he was joined by General Sandoz, from Niort. The country around the town was unfavourable for the Vendeans, being a large plain, and the result was disastrous to them. The Republicans were strong in cavalry, and a portion of these fell on the flank of the Vendeans, while the remainder charged them in rear. They fell into disorder at once, and the cavalry captured a portion of their artillery.

The Republican infantry, seeing the success of their cavalry, advanced stoutly and in good order. In vain the leaders of the Vendeans strove to reanimate their men, and induce them to charge the enemy. The panic that had begun spread rapidly and, in a few minutes, they became a mob of fugitives scattering in all directions, and leaving behind them sixteen cannon, and all the munitions of war they had captured.

La Rochejaquelein who, after he had visited Lescure at Clisson, had rejoined the army with a party of gentlemen, covered the retreat with desperate valour; charging the enemy's cavalry again and again and, before falling back, allowing time for the fugitives to gain the shelter of the woods. The loss of men was therefore small, but the fact that the peasants, who had come to be regarded as almost irresistible by the troops, should have been so easily defeated, raised the Blues from the depth of depression into which they had fallen; while the blow inflicted upon the Vendeans was correspondingly great. It was some little time before the peasants could be aroused again.

Small bodies, indeed, kept the field and, under their leaders, showed so bold a face whenever reconnoitring parties of the Blues went out from Fontenay, that the troops were not long before they again began to lose heart; while the generals, who had thought that the victory at Fontenay would bring the war to a conclusion, again began to pour in letters to the authorities at Paris, calling for reinforcements.

On the side of the Vendeans, the priests everywhere exerted themselves to impress upon their flocks the necessity of again joining the army. Cathelineau himself made a tour through the Bocage, and the peasants, persuaded that the defeat was a punishment for having committed some excesses at the capture of Chataigneraie, responded to the call. In nine days after the reverse they were again in force near Fontenay, and in much greater numbers than before; for very many of them had returned to their homes, as soon as Thouars had been captured, and their strength in the first battle was but little greater than that of the Republicans.

Burning with ardour to avenge their defeat, and rendered furious by the pillage of all the houses of the patriots at Chataigneraie--to which town Chalbos with seven thousand troops had marched--it was against him that the Vendeans first moved. Chalbos, who had occupied his time in issuing vainglorious proclamations, and in writing assurances to the Convention that the Vendeans were so panic stricken that the war was virtually over, only saved his army by a long and painful night march back to Fontenay. Here the troops lay down to sleep, feeling certain that there could be no attack that day by the enemy.

At one o'clock, however, the Vendeans issued from the woods on to the plain, and the troops were hastily called to arms.

The Royal Catholic Army, as it now called itself, advanced in three columns. It was without cannon, but its enthusiasm more than counterbalanced this deficiency. The Vendeans received unshaken the discharge of the artillery of the Blues, pursuing their usual tactics of throwing themselves to the ground when they saw the flash of the cannon, and then leaping up again and rushing forward with loud shouts. The cavalry were ordered to charge, but only twenty men obeyed. The rest turned and fled. The infantry offered but a feeble resistance and, in ten minutes after the first gun was fired, the Republican army was a mob of fugitives. Fontenay was taken and, what pleased the peasants even more, their beloved cannon, Marie Jeanne, was recaptured, having been recovered by young Foret who, with a handful of peasants, charged the cavalry that were covering the retreat, and snatched it from their hands. After this victory the peasants, as usual, returned for the most part to their homes.

As there was no probability of further fighting at the moment, Jean Martin and Leigh started for the chateau. They had first asked Cathelineau if they could be spared.

"For the moment, yes. I hope that we shall be joined by the Count de Lescure, in a day or two. He will, of course, be one of our generals. He has great influence with the peasantry and, if he can but persuade them to remain under arms for a time, we will attack the enemy. Messieurs d'Elbee and Bonchamp, and I may say several of the gentlemen with me, are of opinion that if we are to be successful in the end, it can only be by taking the offensive, and marching against Paris. They urge that we should get Monsieur Charette to go with us with his army, cross the Loire, rouse all Brittany, and then march, a hundred thousand strong, against Paris.

"They say that although we have been most successful this time, and repulsed the invaders everywhere except on the coast, they will come again and again, with larger forces, till they overpower us. Possibly, if Monsieur de Lescure and Henri de la Rochejaquelein aid us with their influence and authority, we might persuade the peasants that it is better to make one great effort, and then to have done with it, than to be constantly called from their homes whenever the Blues are in sufficient strength to invade us. We shall tell them, too, that after the two repulses they have suffered, the Blues will grow more and more savage, and that already orders have been sent for all villages to be destroyed, and all hedges and woods to be cut down--a business that, by the way, would employ the whole French army for some years.

"However, as soon as our plans are decided upon, I will send a messenger to you. At present there is nothing requiring either you or your scouts, Monsieur Stansfield, and after the good service that they have rendered, it is but fair that they should have a short rest."

Patsey was delighted when her husband and Leigh arrived. She was under no uneasiness as to their safety as, after the repulse of Berruyer's army at Chemille, and the rout of Leigonyer, Leigh had sent one of the boys home, with the assurance that they were unhurt.

"I don't quite know how much to believe," she said, as they sat down to a meal, "of the reports that the boys have brought home. The first came and told me that on your arrival at Cathelineau's, he himself praised them all, and that Monsieur Bonchamp drilled them for an hour. Then came home two wounded lads, with a story about the great fight, in which they insisted that Leigh commanded, and that they kept the army of the Blues at bay for three hours, and killed hundreds of them. The next messenger told us a tale about Leigh's having discovered some treachery, upon the part of the man who was in charge of the artillery, and that he was in consequence shot. He insisted that Cathelineau had declared that Leigh had saved Chemille, because the enemy were so long delayed that Monsieur d'Elbee, with his band, had time to come up from Chollet and rout the Blues.

"Of course, I did not believe anything like all they said; but I suppose there must be something in it, for I questioned the boys myself; and though I had no doubt they would make as much as they could of their own doings, among their neighbours and friends, they would hardly venture to lie, though they might exaggerate greatly to me."

"Strange as it may appear, Patsey," Jean said, "they told you the simple truth and, as soon as we have finished supper, I will tell you the whole story of what has taken place since we left; and you will see that this brother of yours has cut a very conspicuous figure in our affairs."

"You are not joking, Jean?"

"Not in the smallest degree. I can assure you that if Leigh chose to set up as leader on his own account, a large proportion of the peasants would follow him."

"Ridiculous, Jean!" Leigh exclaimed hotly.

"It may seem ridiculous, but it is a real fact."

"The peasants, you must know, Patsey, choose their own leaders. There is no dividing or sorting them, no getting them to keep in regular companies; they simply follow the leader in whom they have the most confidence, or who appears to them the most fortunate. If he does anything that they don't like, or they do not approve of his plan, they tell him so. Leigh's defence of the stream against Berruyer's army created a feeling of enthusiasm among them, and I verily believe that his discovery of the plot to render the cannon useless was regarded, by them, as almost supernatural. Superstitious and ignorant as they are, they are, as you know, always ready to consider anything they can't understand, and which acts greatly in their favour, as a special interposition of Providence. I am bound to say that Leigh acted upon such very slender grounds that even Cathelineau, who is enormously in advance of the peasantry in general, was staggered by it; and told me he could not have believed it possible that anyone should, on such a slight clue, have followed the matter up, unless by a special inspiration."

"The thing was as simple as A B C," Leigh broke in.

"You will have to remain a silent listener, Leigh," his sister said, "when Jean is telling me the story. I cannot have him interrupted."

"Very well," Leigh said. "Then I will put on my hat, take a fresh horse from the stable, and ride off to see how the two wounded boys are going on."

"I can tell you that they are almost well; but still, if you don't want to hear Jean's story of all your adventures, by all means go round. I am sure that the tenants will be gratified at hearing that you rode over to see them, the very first evening you came home."

The Vendean leaders had for some time felt the necessity of having a generally recognized authority, and after the battle of Fontenay they decided to appoint a council, who were to reside permanently at some central place and administer the affairs of the whole district, provide supplies for the armies, and make all other civil arrangements; so that the generals would be able to attend only to the actual fighting. A body of eighteen men was chosen, to administer affairs under the title of the Superior Council; and a priest who had joined them at Thouars, and who called himself, though without a shadow of right, the Bishop of Agra, was appointed president. He was an eloquent man, of commanding presence, and the leaders had not thought it worth while to inquire too minutely into his claim to the title of bishop; for the peasants had been full of enthusiasm at having a prelate among them, and his influence and exhortations had been largely instrumental in gathering the army which had won the battle of Fontenay.

But although he was appointed president, the leading spirit of the council was the Abbe Bernier, a man of great energy and intellect, with a commanding person, ready pen, and a splendid voice; but who was altogether without principle, and threw himself into the cause for purely selfish and ambitious motives.

It was on the sixteenth of May that Fontenay was won, and on the third of June the church bells again called the peasantry to arms. The disaster at Fontenay had done more than all the representations of their generals to rouse the Convention. Seven battalions of regular troops arrived, and Biron, who had been appointed commander-in-chief, reached Niort and assumed the command.

He wrote at once, to the minister of war, to say that he found the confusion impossible to describe. There was an absence of any organization, whatever. The town was crowded with fugitives who, having distinguished themselves by the violence of their opinions and the severity of their measures, before the insurrection broke out, were forced to take refuge in the cities. The general reported that he had caused the assembly to be sounded again and again, without more than a tenth part of the troops paying the slightest heed to the summons.

The army was without cavalry, without waggons for carrying supplies, without an ambulance train--in fact, it was nothing but a half-armed mob. Biron himself was at heart a Royalist, and when he in turn had to meet his fate by the guillotine, openly declared himself to be one; and the repugnance which he felt on assuming the command against the Vendeans--which he had only accepted after a long delay, and after petitioning in vain to be allowed to remain at his former post--was heightened when he discovered the state of affairs, and the utter confusion that prevailed everywhere.

When sending the order for the bells to ring on the first of June, the superior council of the Vendeans issued a proclamation, which was to be read in all the churches, to the effect that provisional councils should be formed, in each parish, to provide for the subsistence of the women and children of men with the army. Receipts were to be given for all supplies of grain used for this purpose, which were to be paid for by the superior council. Those men who did not remain permanently with the army, as long as necessary, would be called upon to pay the taxes to which they were subject, prior to the rising.

The sales of the land belonging to the churches--which had been sequestrated on the refusal of the clergy to comply with the orders of the Convention--were declared null and void. As these had been bought by the upholders of the Revolution, for no devout Vendean would have taken part in the robbery of the church, the blow was a heavy one to those who had so long been dominant in La Vendee. These lands were, for the time, to be administered for the good of the cause by the parish council.

It was hoped that this proclamation would act beneficially in keeping the peasants in the field; as they would know that their families were cared for, and that if they only went out at times, they would subject themselves to taxation, and be regarded by the families of those who remained with the army as being wanting in zeal.

Upon rejoining the army, Leigh and his party of scouts learned, to their satisfaction, that it was intended to march against Saumur. They were now double their former strength, as the story of what they had done had roused the spirit of emulation among lads in the surrounding parishes; and Leigh could have had a hundred, had he chosen. He was this time mounted, in order that he might at times ride with Rochejaquelein, while at others he went out scouting with his party.

"I am heartily glad to see you back again, my friend," the young count said, shaking him warmly by the hand. "To be with you does me good, for the generals, and even Lescure, are so serious and solemn that I feel afraid to make a joke. You see, in the cavalry we have little responsibility except in an actual battle. In an open country we should scout ahead, and have affairs with the enemy's outposts; but in this land of woods, where one can seldom see more than twenty yards ahead, there is little use for us. Besides, with the exception of a score or two of gentlemen, I have no troops to command and, having health and good spirits, and enjoying life, I cannot go about as if the cares of life were on my shoulders. Your brother-in-law Martin is a capital fellow but, with a wife and child, he cannot feel so lighthearted as I do; though next to yourself he is the most ready to join me in a laugh. Sailors seem always to be lighthearted, and he certainly is no exception."

"He is a splendid fellow, count."

"Yes, he is a fine fellow; but you see, he is seven or eight years older than I am, while I feel with you that you are about my own age. By the way, it is high time that we dropped calling each other by our surnames, especially as mine is such a long one; so in future let us be' Henri' and 'Leigh 'to each other. Most of the peasants call me Henri."

"They generally speak of you as 'our Henri,'" Leigh said, "and would follow you through fire and water. I think the Vendeans are, as a whole, serious people; and they admire you all the more because you are so unlike themselves. If you do not mind my saying so, you remind me much more of the young English officers I used to meet, at Poole, than of Frenchmen."

"Yes, I have often been told that I am more English than French in appearance, and perhaps in manner; for in France most men have forgotten, for the past four years, what it is to smile; and I question whether a laugh would not be considered, in itself, sufficient to ensure a man's condemnation as an enemy of the Republic.

"Well, so we are going to Saumur! That is an enterprise worth undertaking. It may be considered as the headquarters of the Blues in these parts. There is a considerable body of troops there. If we capture it, we shall give a rare fright to Poitiers, Tours, and the other towns, and cause a scare even in Paris."

Leigh was requested to go forward at daybreak, with his band, to discover the situation of the enemy, who might come out from their situation to give battle before Doue. Leigonyer, who commanded here, had with him four good regiments; and occupied several strong positions on the right bank of the river Layon, and also a post called Rochette on the left bank.

The fact that the Vendeans were advancing against them was already known to Leigonyer for, confident as they now felt, the Vendeans made no secret of their destination, and the news was speedily carried by the adherents of the Convention, who everywhere acted as spies. Three such men were captured by Leigh's party, making their way to Leigonyer; and, being unable to give any account of themselves, were immediately shot.

Leigh had no difficulty in ascertaining the position of the enemy and, as the army was but two hours' march in the rear, he himself rode back to carry the news.

At ten o'clock the Vendeans arrived, and at once attacked the Blues; their main column throwing itself upon the centre of the position, which it speedily forced. Leigonyer's troops at Rochette and Verches were thereby threatened in flank; and Leigonyer, who was himself present, ordered the whole force to fall back to a position which he had before chosen as being favourable for giving battle behind Doue.

But the Vendeans pressed forward with such eagerness that the retreat speedily degenerated into a rout; and the troops, for the most part throwing away their arms, fled precipitately, carrying the reserve with them to Bourlan, a strong position in front of Saumur, where General Menou was stationed, and where he succeeded in rallying them.

Leigonyer, having from his previous experience great doubts as to whether he should be successful in his stand against the Vendeans, had taken the precaution to send back the waggons with the munitions and stores, together with the artillery. As his men had fled too rapidly to be overtaken, the numerical loss was not great. He himself, in his report of the fight, ascribed it to a cause that has been frequently used by the French to excuse their defeats; namely that it was due to treachery, for many of the men broke and fled, directly the action began; and these, he avowed, could have been none other than Vendeans who had disguised themselves, and enlisted for the purpose of causing discontent among the men, and confusion in their ranks, the first time they met the enemy.

Since the commencement of the campaign he had several times begged to be relieved of his command, and to return to the post that he occupied previously. He now repeated the demand, saying that he had lost the confidence of his men, and that a new commander would be far more likely to succeed with them. This time the request was granted, and General Menou was appointed to succeed him.

Fortunately for Leigonyer, the commissioners of the Convention reported most favourably of the activity and energy that he had personally shown and, although he was accused of treachery in the Assembly, this report saved him from the guillotine.

As soon as the fight was over, Cathelineau sent for Leigh.

"It is of the greatest importance that we should know what is passing at Saumur. We have learned, from one of the officers who is a prisoner in our hands, that Biron is at Tours, and is endeavouring to persuade the Paris battalions that have arrived there to march, at once, to Saumur. They have absolutely refused to do so, until the arrival of the cannon that were promised to them, before they left Paris. They may, by this time, be marching towards Saumur, with or without their cannon. General Salomon is at Thouars, with a considerable force, and it is possible that he also may march to aid in the defence of Saumur; and as he has, in addition to the new levies, a fine battalion of gendarmes, his arrival at Saumur would greatly increase the strength of the defence.

"I should say that half your scouts had better go to Thouars and, should there be any considerable movement of troops there, they should bring me word at the greatest possible speed. We shall tomorrow march forward and take post facing the enemy's positions, and on the ninth shall attack. I tell you this in order that your scouts may know where to find me.

"To you, with the other half of your party, I give the charge of watching Saumur. If one or two of them could cross the Loire and watch the road between Tours and Saumur, and bring me speedy word if they see a large body of troops coming along, we should know what force we have to encounter, and act accordingly."

"You shall have news, general," Leigh said and, saluting, at once joined his band.

Jean, who had been talking with him when the message from Cathelineau arrived, and had waited to hear what his orders were, said as he came up:

"You and your regiment are off on an adventure again, Leigh?"

"Yes, we are going to watch Thouars and Saumur, and to find out, if possible, if the battalions from Paris are on their way from Tours."

"The first will be easy enough but, unless you swim the Loire, I don't see how the second is to be managed."

"I should think that a boat might be obtained, at one of the villages on the river bank. Anyhow, I shall get across somehow."

Andre was ordered to take his party to Thouars.

"Remember," Leigh said, "there is to be no fighting; not a shot must be fired. I want you and another to enter the town, if possible, from the other side; to see whether there is any unusual excitement, and especially whether there is any stir among the troops that would seem to show that they are on the point of marching away. You are to remain there until you see some such movement. The lad that you are taking in with you must go out, every hour, to the spot where you have left the rest; and one of these must at once start with your report to the general, who will tomorrow be on his way to Saumur, and will halt not far from its works of defence. Having delivered his message, he is to return to you, for you must continue to send off messengers until you hear that there is fighting at Saumur. If the commander of the Blues at Thouars has not moved by that time, you need remain no longer, but return with your party and join the army."

After Andre had left, Leigh marched with Pierre and the others to a spot up the river, ten miles above Saumur.

"Can any of you swim?" he asked.

Three only of the party were able to reply in the affirmative.

"Do you think that you could swim across the Loire?"

All of them expressed great doubt of being able to do so.

"Well, at any rate, I must take you with me," he said. "To be able to swim a little is a good deal better than not to be able to swim at all, for by making a faggot you will gain such support as will enable you to get across.

"Now, Pierre, you must for the present remain here. Tomorrow morning you can go into the village, whose church tower you can see over there, and find out whether the people there are for us or for the Blues. If they are for us you can show them Cathelineau's order, of which you have a copy, and they will certainly provide you with a boat. In that case, cross the river with your party and take post on the opposite bank, keeping the boat with you, and a man who can row. Then, as soon as one of my messengers arrives there, you will send on my report to the general who, tomorrow evening, will be not far from Saumur. Do the same with each messenger that arrives.

"If, on reaching the bank opposite the village, they do not find you there, they will follow the opposite bank down until they are opposite to you. Then they will call, and you, unless anything has happened to drive you away, will reply. The messenger will then swim across with my report, as in the other case. You will send it forward at once, and he will return to the spot I shall appoint.

"I see there is another village, a mile below us. I shall go there with my three followers, tonight. We will manage to steal a boat and row across. I shall go to that village instead of the other, because the loss of a boat may cause anger and, even if well disposed to the cause, they might not receive you well. However, I shall tie the boat up on the opposite bank when I leave it, so that it will not drift away down the river; and when they see it in the morning, they will only have to send another boat across to fetch it over."

"I understand, captain, and will do my best to carry out your instructions. Even if I find that, at the village above, they are divided in opinion, I shall surely be able to discover, from their talk, some who are on our side, and who will arrange to bring a boat down to this spot; in which case your messenger, when he does not find us opposite the village, will follow the bank down till he does so."

"At any rate, Pierre, here are a couple of crowns, so that you can arrange with a man for the hire of the boat, and his services, for twenty-four hours, if necessary."

Chapter 8
The Capture Of Saumur

The arrangements being now completed, Leigh and his band lay down in a thicket near the bank of the river, and slept for some hours. At one o'clock in the morning Leigh rose and, with his three followers, started for the village. It was but twenty minutes' walk. Not a soul was stirring, not a light visible in any window.

They found that three or four boats were lying by the bank. Leigh chose the smallest of these and, loosening the head rope from the post to which it was fastened, took his place in her with the others. Accustomed as he was to rowing, from his childhood, he soon reached the opposite bank. Here he fastened the boat up, and struck across country until he reached the road. Then he sent one of his followers westward.

"You will follow the road," he said, "until within a mile of Tours; then you will conceal yourself, and watch who passes along. If you see a large body of troops coming, you will at once strike across country and make your way down to the village above that at which we crossed. You heard the instructions that I gave to Pierre. If you find him and the others there with the boat, you will report what you have seen. He will send another messenger on with the news to Cathelineau, and you will remain with him until I arrive.

"If he is not there, you will follow the bank of the river down to the other village. You will give a shout as you pass the spot where we halted. If no answer comes, you will probably find Pierre and the boat somewhere below. You will not miss him, for I have ordered him to post two of your comrades on the bank, so that you cannot pass them unseen. As in the first case, you will remain with him until I arrive, and your message will be carried to the general by another of his party.

"In case you do not find him at all, you will know that I have returned before you, and have taken him and the others on with me. In that case, you must make a faggot sufficiently large to support you in the water, and swim across. The river is low, and it will not be many yards out of your depth."

"I could swim that without the faggot, sir."

"Yes; but it is better to have it. I don't suppose that you have ever swum in your clothes, and you would find it heavy work; therefore you had better rely upon the faggot to keep you up and, with its aid, you will have no difficulty in crossing."

The morning now was breaking, for in June the nights are short and, after waiting for an hour, Leigh and his two companions--all of whom had divested themselves of their weapons and belts, which they had left in Pierre's charge--started for Saumur. In the presence of so large a number of troops, with scarcely any training and discipline, and with the excitement that would have been caused by the defeat of Leigonyer, and the prospect of an attack by the Vendeans, Leigh felt confident that three country lads ran no risk of being questioned. However, he took the precaution of learning the name of the village he passed through, six miles from the town; so that if any one should happen to ask where they came from, and what they were doing, he could give the name of a village, and say that they had merely come in from curiosity, hearing that there was likely to be a battle. Assuredly many country people would be coming for the same purpose.

They entered the town at six o'clock. It was already astir. The citizens, with anxious faces, were talking together in little groups. Soldiers were loitering about in the streets, totally regardless of the bugles and drums that were sounding in the marketplace, and at various points outside the town. The civil functionaries, in their scarves of office, hurried fussily about, but for once they were unheeded. But a week before, a denunciation by any of these men would have been sufficient to ensure the arrest and imprisonment, and probably the death, of anyone against whom they had a grudge. Now they were in greater danger than those who had dreaded and hated them.

At present there was no talk of politics among the groups of townspeople. Men who were the chief upholders of the regime of confiscation and murder, and others who in their heart loathed and hated it, were discussing the probabilities of an attack by the Vendeans, and what would happen were that attack to be successful. Would the town be given over to sack? Would there be a massacre and slaughter, such as Chalbos and other commanders of the Blues had inflicted in the Vendean villages through which they had passed? The Vendeans in arms were called, by the Blues, "the brigands." Would they behave like brigands, or would they conduct themselves as Royal and Catholic soldiers, as they called themselves?

As the hours passed, the streets became more crowded. Numbers of the country people came in to learn the news. Spies from Doue had already brought in word that orders had been issued, by Cathelineau, that the army should march at eight o'clock for Saumur; and all doubt that it was their intention either to attack the town, or to accept battle in the plain before it, was at an end. The assembly was sounded in all quarters of the town and, presently, parties of the mounted gendarmes rode through the streets, and drove the soldiers to their rendezvous.

Presently Leigh saw General Menou, and some other officers of rank, enter a large house.

"Who lives there?" he asked a woman who was standing near him.

"General Duhoux. He is in command, you know, but he has not recovered from a wound he got at Chemille, and is unable to ride."

Leigh had no doubt that a council of war was about to be held and, bidding his companions wait for him at the end of the street, he sauntered across the road, and sat down on the pavement by the side of the entrance. Leaning against the wall, he took from his pocket a hunk of the peasants' black bread and, cutting it up with his knife, proceeded to munch it unconcernedly. An officer and two or three troopers were standing by their horses' heads, in the road opposite the door, evidently awaiting orders.

In half an hour General Menou himself came out, and said to the officer:

"Sir, you will ride at once to Thouars, by way of Loudun, and deliver this despatch to General Salomon. It is most urgent. When you hand it to him, you can say that I begged you to impress upon him the necessity for losing not a moment of time. It is all important that he should arrive here tonight, for tomorrow morning we may be attacked. Take your troopers with you."

The officer and his men mounted at once, and rode off at full speed. Leigh remained quiet until Menou and the other officers rode out from the courtyard and proceeded down the street, followed by their escort. Then he got up, stretched himself, and walked slowly to the spot where his two comrades were awaiting him.

"I have learned what I wanted to know," he said. "Do you both make your way back to the spot where Pierre will be awaiting us, and tell him that I am going to swim the river, a mile above the town. He is to wait where he is until Lucien comes back from Tours--which will not be till twelve o'clock tonight, for his orders are to remain within sight of the town till six in the afternoon. If by that hour the troops there have not set out, they will not arrive until after we have captured Saumur.

"Saunter along quietly. There is no hurry."

After they had set out he, too, strolled out of the town, kept along the road for another half mile, and then struck off across the fields towards the river. Arrived there, he took off his heavy country shoes, tied them round his waist, and waded out into the river. He had but some thirty yards to swim. As soon as he reached the opposite bank, he poured the water out of his shoes, put them on again, and set out at a run. He had to make a detour, so as to get beyond the eminences on which the Republican troops were posted and, after running for a couple of miles, came down on the road.

A short distance farther he arrived at a village. A peasant, with a horse and cart, was standing in front of a cabaret.

"Do you want to earn two crowns?" he asked the man.

The latter nodded.

"Two crowns are not easily earned," he said. "I was just starting for Montreuil but, if it pays me better to go in another direction, I must put that journey off until tomorrow."

"I want you to carry me to Doue," he said, "at the best speed of which your horse is capable."

The countryman looked at him doubtfully. His clothes were not yet dry. Leigh saw that the man was not sure of his power to fulfil his promise. He therefore produced two crowns, and held them up.

"By Saint Matthew," he said, "it is the first silver I have seen for months. I will take you."

Leigh jumped up beside the peasant. The latter at once whipped up his horse, and started at a brisk trot.

"You know that the Catholic Army is there?" he asked.

"Yes, I know. I belong to it myself. I have been with it from the first."

"I would have taken you for nothing, if you had said so before," the man said. "We are all heart and soul with them, here; and if, as they say, they will come along here to attack Saumur, every man in the village will go with them. How is it that you are here?"

"I am an officer," Leigh said, "and have been, in disguise, into Saumur to see what is going on there; and am now taking the news back to Cathelineau."

Conversation was difficult, for the jolting of the cart was terrible, and Leigh found it next to impossible to talk. He was well content when the belfries of Doue came into sight. On arriving at the town, they drew up at the house where Cathelineau and the generals had their quarters. As he got down, he offered the peasant the two crowns.

"No, sir," the man said, "I will not take a sou for my service. We in this part have had no chance of doing anything, and I should be ashamed, indeed, to take money from those who have been fighting for the good cause.

"As you say they will advance tomorrow, I will wait here. It may be that my cart will be useful and, whether or no, I shall stay if it is only to get a sight of Cathelineau, whose name we all reverence."

"I will tell him of your goodwill. You had best remain here for a few minutes."

He was about to enter, when two armed peasants, who were guarding the door, stopped him.

"No one can enter. The general is in council."

"Do you not know me? I am Captain Stansfield."

The men drew back at once. It was not strange that they did not recognize him. He generally wore a sort of uniform, with a red sash round his waist, which was the distinguishing badge of the officers; but had always adopted a peasant dress, on setting out on an expedition. There was no one to announce him, and he entered a room where the leaders were sitting round a table.

They looked up in surprise. He was grimed with the dust, which had risen in clouds as he drove along, and his clothes bore signs of their immersion.

"Back again, monsieur?" Cathelineau exclaimed, "and with news, no doubt."

"Very important news, sir. I have been in Saumur, and have learned that an officer has started for Thouars, by way of Loudun, with orders to General Salomon to march instantly into Saumur, and that he is to arrive there tonight. I left the town five minutes after the messenger. Three-quarters of an hour later I struck the road, two miles this side of Saumur; and have been brought here in a cart, by a peasant. It is now four o'clock, and I do not think that the officer would arrive at Thouars before half past three."

"That is important news, indeed," Cathelineau said.

"Well, gentlemen, what do you think had best be done?"

"It seems to me that nothing could be better," Monsieur de Lescure said. "The enemy's column cannot start until five o'clock, at the earliest. It will be dark before they can arrive at Saumur. I know the road well. It runs in several places through woods and, where this is not the case, there are high hedges.

"Nothing could be more suitable for an ambuscade. I propose that half of our force should march, at once, and take post on the other side of Montreuil. It will be nearly sunset before Salomon can arrive at that town and, if we engage him at dusk, he will lose half the benefit of the discipline of the regiment of gendarmes who will, no doubt, accompany him."

"I quite approve of that plan, monsieur," Cathelineau said.

"Are you all of the same opinion, gentlemen?"

There was a general expression of assent.

"Will you, General Bonchamp, with Monsieur de Lescure, take command of that force? I myself will proceed, with the rest of our army, until past the point where the road from Montreuil falls into that from this town. In that way, if General Bonchamp fails to arrest Salomon's march, we can fall upon him; and on the other hand, if the firing should be heard at Saumur, and Menou leads out a force to assist Salomon, we can oppose him.

"General Dommaigne, your cavalry would be useless in the attack on Salomon, while it might be of great value if Menou comes out.

"You have rendered us another good service, Monsieur Stansfield. If Salomon had thrown another four thousand men into Saumur, including his regiment of gendarmes, it would have been a serious business to take the place; whereas with the troops Menou has, half of whom are Leigonyer's fugitives, I do not anticipate any great difficulty."

"I shall be glad, general, if you would speak a word to the good fellow who brought me here. I had bargained with him for two crowns but, when he found that I was one of your officers, he refused to receive anything; and moreover, he said that he would remain here with his cart, until tomorrow, as perhaps he might be useful in carrying stores. He expressed the greatest desire to see you."

"Certainly I will speak to him," Cathelineau said, as he sent out to give orders for the church bells to ring, and the horns to blow.

The man was standing by his cart, a short distance off, in the hope of catching sight of Cathelineau. The general at once walked up to him.

"This is General Cathelineau," Leigh said.

The countryman took off his hat, and dropped on his knees.

"Get up, my good fellow," Cathelineau said; "I am but a Vendean peasant, like yourself. I thank you for the good service that you have rendered, by bringing Monsieur Stansfield so quickly to us. The time it has saved may make all the difference to us and, in the future, you will have the satisfaction of knowing that you have played an important part in the capture of Saumur."

In five minutes the quiet street was crowded with men. The peasants had encamped in the fields round the town and, at the summons, caught up their arms and ran in hastily, feeling sure that the occasion was important, as they had been told that they were not to march until next morning.

The divisions commanded by Monsieur de Lescure and General Bonchamp speedily gathered round the distinguishing flags of those officers. Other leaders joined them with their followers, until some ten thousand men were gathered outside the town.

Leigh had changed his clothes and mounted his horse, Monsieur de Lescure having invited him to ride with him. As they were about to start, one of Andre's messengers arrived, with the news that an officer and three troopers had arrived at the town; and that, ten minutes later, the trumpets were sounding the assembly.

"It is well that we got your news first," Monsieur de Lescure said to Leigh, "for otherwise we could hardly have got our forces together, and been ready for a start, until it was too late to intercept Salomon."

The route of the column was by a byroad, between Doue and Montreuil. It was seven o'clock before they approached the town. Then, striking off the road, they marched through the fields until a mile and a half to the east of it, when they halted in a thick wood. They were now divided into three columns, of equal strength. That under Monsieur de Lescure occupied the wood on one side of the road, that under Monsieur Bonchamp the other side. The third column were posted in rear of the wood, and were to thickly line the hedges that bordered it.

It was just dusk when the force from Thouars came along. It consisted of three thousand six hundred men, with four pieces of cannon. It was allowed to pass nearly through the wood, when a heavy fire was opened upon it on both flanks.

The regiment of gendarmes which led the column showed great coolness and, animated by their example, the whole force remained steady. Darkness came on, but it was not until eleven o'clock that there was any change in the situation. Owing to the darkness in the forest, neither side was able to distinguish its foes. The men fired only at the flashes of the muskets.

Lescure then sent round four or five hundred men, who suddenly fell upon the baggage train of the enemy. The guard were completely taken by surprise. Many of the carters cut the ropes and traces, and galloped off, delighted to escape from a service into which they had, for the most part, been dragged against their will.

The alarm thus begun spread rapidly. The young troops who, encouraged by the example of the gendarmes, had so far stood their ground, at once lost heart. The darkness of the night, their ignorance as to the strength of the force that had attacked the rear, and the fear that all retreat would be cut off, would have shaken older soldiers than these and, in spite of the efforts of their officers, the wildest confusion soon reigned.

The Vendeans pressed their attack more hotly, and General Salomon, seeing that unless a retreat was made while there was yet time, a terrible disaster might take place, ordered the gendarmes to fall back in good order. The movement was effected without great loss. In the darkness it was impossible for Lescure and the other leaders to get their men together, and to press hard upon their retreating foes; and they were well satisfied at having carried out the object of their expedition, and prevented the force from Thouars from entering Saumur.

Word was sent to Cathelineau that Salomon had fallen back, and the peasants then lay down till morning.

Andre, with his little band, had joined the force when fighting began. They had, as soon as Salomon started from Thouars, followed his movements at a distance, from time to time sending off a messenger to Doue giving an account of the progress of the enemy. As soon as the firing broke out in the wood, Andre, with the twelve who still remained with him, joined the combatants and, finding that Leigh was with Monsieur de Lescure, was not long in discovering him.

"You have done very well, Andre," he said. "I don't think anything will come of this fighting. It is getting dark already, and I have no fear, now, that the Blues will break through. Neither party will be able to see the other, in this wood, and certainly you could do no good with your pistols. Practically, few are engaged on either side. The Blues have made one effort and, finding that we have a very strong force in their front, have given up the attempt to push forward. I don't believe that the new levies have courage enough to keep steady through a whole night's uncertainty.

"You had best draw off some distance and rest, till you hear, by the firing, that some change has taken place. If you hear that the Blues are retreating, follow them at a distance. It is important for the generals to know what course they are taking. They may halt in Montreuil, they may return to Thouars, they may retire to Niort or Parthenay.

"If they remain in Montreuil, let us know at once, because in that case we shall have to stay here, in case they should attempt to push on again. If they go farther, we need have no more concern about them. Still, it would be of great importance to our generals to know whether they return to Thouars, or retire farther south."

"Very well, captain; I will see that you are kept informed."

"You had better instruct your first messengers to come straight here. Cathelineau and the rest of the forces started, directly we did, and will halt at the junction of the roads, and are likely to remain there all day tomorrow. Therefore, if your messengers find the wood deserted, they have simply to follow the road, and they will either overtake us, or find us with Cathelineau."

"How long must we follow the Blues?"

"There is no occasion to go any great distance. I do not suppose that we shall pursue them. They could certainly defend themselves at Montreuil, and we should not risk suffering heavy loss, and having the men dispirited by failure, when all are needed for the work at Saumur. If you follow them far enough to determine whether they are retiring on Thouars, or are marching towards Niort, that is all that is necessary; and you will be able to rejoin us in plenty of time to see the fight at Saumur."

As Leigh thought would be probable, Monsieur de Lescure restrained the peasants from following in pursuit, when the Blues retreated. The latter had left two of their guns behind them, and a number of carts, laden with ammunition and provisions for the march, fell into the peasants' hands--the latter providing them with breakfast before they started, early next morning, rejoining Cathelineau's force two hours later. These had been apprised, some hours before, by one of the mounted gentlemen who had accompanied the column, of the success that had attended the operation; and they were received with great joy by their comrades, on their arrival.

Cathelineau, with General Bonchamp and a small escort of cavalry, had ridden towards Saumur to examine the positions occupied by the enemy, and to discuss the plan of attack. They now felt confident of success; unless, indeed, Biron should come up in the course of the day with the Paris brigade at Tours, together with its guns. The description that Leigh had given, of the confusion and want of discipline in the garrison, showed that it could not be relied upon for hard fighting; and as it was certain that the failure of Salomon to get through to its assistance would be known, in Saumur, early in the day, it could not but add to the dismay produced by the advance against the town.

This was indeed the case. As artillery had not been employed on either side, the sound of the conflict did not reach the town. However, as the officer who had taken the order to Thouars returned at seven o'clock; saying that Salomon was preparing to march, and would assuredly arrive some time in the evening, the anxiety increased hour by hour and, by midnight, the conviction that he must have been attacked by the enemy, and had failed to get through, became a certainty, and spread dismay through the town.

At five in the morning a mounted messenger brought a despatch from Salomon, saying that he had fought for four hours near Montreuil, against a large force of the enemy; and that, another column of these having fallen on his rear, he found it necessary to retire, as a panic was spreading among the National Guard, and a serious disaster would have happened, had he continued his attempts to push on. In the evening Generals Coustard and Berthier, who had been sent by Biron to act under Menou's orders, arrived in the town; and Santerre, the brewer of Paris, who had been the leader of the mob there and was now a general, arrived next morning.

Cathelineau's army was astir early. The leaders had been gladdened by the arrival, at five o'clock, of a messenger from Pierre, saying that one of his messengers had come in from Tours, and that, up to seven o'clock in the evening, no troops had left that city. It was, therefore, certain that the garrison of Saumur could receive no assistance from that quarter.

Breakfast was eaten, and the army then formed up in its divisions. Mass was celebrated, and it then set out for Saumur.

In that town all was confusion and dismay. The newly arrived generals were strangers alike to the town, its defences, and the troops they were to command. In front of the works defending Saumur ran the river Dives, which fell into the Loire, a mile or so below the town. It was crossed by a bridge; but so great was the confusion that, in spite of the representations of the civil authorities, no steps were taken either to cut or guard it.

It was not until three o'clock in the afternoon that the Vendeans approached the town, and General Menou sent two battalions of the line, one of volunteers, and eighty horse, under the orders of General Berthier, to take possession of a chateau in front of the position. Two hundred and fifty men were posted in a convent near it. Santerre commanded the force which was to defend the intrenchments at Nantilly, and Coustard the troops who occupied the heights of Bourlan.

At four o'clock the skirmishers on both sides were hotly engaged. The Vendeans advanced in three columns--the central one against the post occupied by Berthier, the left against Nantilly, and the right threatened to turn the position at Beaulieu.

Berthier allowed the force advancing against him to approach within a short distance of the chateau, and then poured a storm of grape into it, from a battery that he had established. Lescure, who was in command, was badly wounded. The head of the column fell into confusion, and Berthier at once attacked them, with his two regiments of the line, and for a time pressed the column back. His little body of cavalry, whom he had ordered to charge, fell back as soon as the Vendeans opened fire upon them; and the latter then attacked the line battalions, with such fury that Berthier was obliged to call up his regiment of volunteers. Cathelineau sent reinforcements to his troops, and these pressed on so hotly that Berthier, who had had a horse shot under him, was obliged to fall back; and the exulting Vendeans rushed forward and carried the faubourg of Fenet.

Dommaigne, with his cavalry, charged the cuirassiers and the German Legion. There was a sharp fight. Dommaigne was killed, and the colonel of the German Legion desperately wounded; but a body of the Vendean infantry, coming up, took the cuirassiers in flank with their fire, and they fell back into Saumur.

General Menou had been in the thick of the fight, and had three horses killed under him. He sent another battalion to reinforce Berthier but, as soon as they came within shot of the Vendeans, they broke and fled.

The two line battalions, reinforced by four companies of gendarmes, kept up a heavy fire. The artillery until now had zealously supported them, but their ammunition was failing. Menou and Berthier placed themselves at the head of the cavalry, and called upon them to charge; but instead of doing so, they raised their favourite cry of "Treason!" and galloped back to the town.

The line regiments and gendarmes, pressed more and more hotly, and finding themselves without support, withdrew in good order into Saumur. The Vendeans had now possession of all the works in the centre of the defenders' line. Coustard, seeing that the centre was lost, and that the Vendeans were moving towards a bridge across the Dives, by which alone they could enter the town, ordered two battalions with two pieces of cannon to hold it. He was not only disobeyed but, with shouts of "Treason!" they rushed upon him and, with difficulty, he escaped with his life.

The Vendeans seized the bridge, and established a battery for its defence. Coustard saw that it must be recaptured, as the town was now open to the enemy; and ordered a detachment of cuirassiers, commanded by Colonel Weissen, to carry the bridge. The two battalions of infantry now promised to follow.

Although he saw that to charge the battery with a handful of cavalry was to ride to almost certain death, Weissen gallantly led his men forward. The infantry followed for a short distance but, being taken in flank by a volley from a party of Vendeans, they broke and fled. The cavalry were almost annihilated, and Weissen was desperately wounded, two or three of his men alone riding back.

The main force of Coustard's division, in the redoubts at Bourlan, had not been attacked; and retired to Angers during the night. The rout of the rest of the defenders was now complete, and the town open.

La Rochejaquelein, by whose side Leigh and a small party of gentlemen rode, had made a succession of desperate charges into the midst of the fugitives; and he now said to Leigh and three other gentlemen:

"Come along, we will see what they are doing in the town."

Then, dashing forward at full speed, they passed through the gate, entered the main street, and found that it contained a battalion of infantry, retreating. So cowed were these that they opened their ranks and allowed the five horsemen to dash through them. Then they made a tour of the place, and returned to inform the Vendeans, who were just entering, that all resistance had ceased. As on two previous occasions, the flying Republicans owed their safety to the piety of the peasants who, instead of pursuing at once, rushed into the churches; where the cures, who had accompanied them, returned thanks for the victory that had been gained, and thus lost the half hour of daylight that would have been invaluable.

Cathelineau, after a consultation with Lescure and Bonchamp, decided that it would be useless to attempt a pursuit in the dark. Berthier's battalion was, too, unbroken. The generals, finding that there was no pursuit, might have rallied a considerable number of the others; when the peasants, coming up in the dark, could in turn have been repulsed with heavy loss. Saumur had been taken, with all its stores of cannon, ammunition, and provisions; and it was considered that, under the circumstances, it was best to be contented with the signal success they had gained.

Berthier and Menou indeed, although both severely wounded, had covered the retreat with the line regiments and gendarmes; and carried off with them seven cannon, which they came across as they passed through the town; and would have given the peasants a warm reception, had they followed them. The rest of the army were hopelessly scattered, and continued their flight all night; some towards Tours, others to Angers, their reports causing the wildest dismay in both towns.

Had Charette, who had always acted independently in lower Vendee, been persuaded at this moment to join hands with Cathelineau, there can be little question that they might have marched to Paris without encountering any serious resistance, and that their arrival there would have changed the whole course of events. Unfortunately, however, he was himself sorely pressed, by several columns of the enemy, and was with difficulty holding his own. The great opportunity was therefore lost, never to return.

The castle of Saumur was still in the hands of the Blues. Five hundred of the National Guards of the town, and about the same number of men of different regiments, threw themselves into it before the Vendeans entered, carrying with them what provisions they could lay hands upon. The wives of the National Guards soon surrounded the chateau, crying to their friends to surrender; and asserting that, if they did not do so, the Vendeans would give the town over to pillage and fire. For a time the commandant resisted their entreaties but, feeling that his position was desperate, and that there was no hope of relief, he surrendered.

In the morning the garrison marched out. The officers were allowed to retain their sidearms, and the men to return to their homes. Eighty cannon fell into the hands of the victors, many thousands of muskets, a large quantity of ammunition, and very many prisoners.

Here, as at other places, the peasants behaved with great moderation. The agents of the Convention, who had tyrannized the town so long, were thrown into prison, as were their chief supporters; but private property was untouched. On the following day there was a council, at which Lescure, seriously wounded as he was, was present. It was agreed that it was indispensable that one man should be appointed commander-in-chief. Many difficulties had arisen from independent action, by generals and leaders of bands more or less numerous, and it was necessary that all should act under the orders of a recognized head.

When this was agreed to, the question had to be decided as to who should be appointed to this responsible post. The claims of Lescure, la Rochejaquelein, d'Elbee, Bonchamp, Cathelineau, and Stofflet were almost even. Each had a large band of followers. All had been unwearied in their devotion to the cause.

It is probable that Lescure would have been chosen. He was the largest landed proprietor, and was of the highest rank--with the exception of

Rochejaquelein, who had, although the idol of the army, scarcely experience and ballast enough to take so responsible a position. Lescure himself, however, proposed that Cathelineau should be chosen. His influence was great, his talents unquestionable, and the simple honesty of his character, his modesty and untiring zeal in the cause, alike recommended him. Lescure felt that if he himself, Bonchamp, or d'Elbee were chosen, jealousies might arise and the cause suffer.

His choice was felt by all to be a good one, and Cathelineau was unanimously appointed to the post of commander-in-chief. No finer tribute was ever paid, to the virtues and talent of a simple peasant, than such a choice, made by men so greatly his superior in rank and station.

Chapter 9
Bad News

Neither Leigh nor Jean Martin was at Saumur, when this decision was arrived at. The very night that the town was taken, one of the former's band, who was wounded and, greatly against his inclination, had been left behind, arrived there on horseback. He was the bearer of terrible news.

Early on the previous day, a troop of the enemy's cavalry had arrived. They had apparently ridden all night, and without exciting any alarm on the way. They had made straight for the chateau, without going into the village. Beyond the fact that they belonged to the force operating from Nantes, none knew the route they had followed. They had doubtless expected to arrest Jean at the chateau but, on finding him absent, had seized his wife, had placed her in their midst, set fire to the chateau, and ridden off before any force could be gathered to oppose them. Jean and Leigh were horror stricken at the news.

"What is to be done?" the former exclaimed. "What can be done?"

"I should say," Leigh said, "that the first thing to do will be to tell the generals that we must, for the present, leave them. Then we must go to Nantes in disguise, find out where she is imprisoned, and see what can be done to rescue her."

"Certainly that is the best thing, Leigh. Let us start at once."

"It will be daylight in two hours, Jean, and that will make no difference. I will go and talk with my boys. They are asleep together on the steps of the church of Saint Marie. They may be useful to us, and I am sure would follow us anywhere."

Jean made no reply. He had buried his face in his hands, and deep sobs broke from him. Tears were streaming down Leigh's cheek as he spoke, but he put his hand upon Jean's shoulder and said, in a voice which he tried to keep steady:

"It is terrible, Jean, but we must not give up hope. We have beaten the Blues in the field, and it is hard if we cannot manage to beat them, somehow, in this business."

The other made no reply, and Leigh, feeling that it would be best to leave him to himself for the present, went downstairs.

The lad who had brought the message was seated against the wall, holding the horse's bridle in his hand. Being a stranger in the place, he did not know where to go.

"Come with me, Philippe. The others are all in the great square, a hundred yards away. They got their bread yesterday morning, and will have plenty of it left for you and the horse. It can take a drink at the fountain, in the centre.

"Ah," he exclaimed stopping suddenly, "you said nothing about the child, and we did not think to ask. Did my sister take it away with her, or was it left?"

"I did not hear, captain. My mother ran into the house crying, and said:

"'The Blues have come, and have set fire to the chateau and carried madame away prisoner. Take the horse and ride to the army, and tell Monsieur Martin what has happened.'

"I ran into the stable and saddled it, took two loaves of bread, one for him and one for myself, and started. I should have been here in the middle of the day, but I lost my way in the lanes last night, and had to stop till daylight and, even then, rode for a long time in the wrong direction."

Leaving the lad and horse in the middle of the square, Leigh went to the steps of the church. A great number of peasants were sleeping there. He was not long in finding his own band. He roused Andre and Pierre with some difficulty for, having both been up all the previous night, they slept heavily.

"Come with me," Leigh said, as soon as they were sufficiently roused to understand who was speaking to them. "I want to have a talk with you.

"I have some bad news," he went on, as they passed beyond the sleepers; "the Blues have been at the chateau. They have burned it down, and have carried off Madame Martin."

Exclamations of rage broke from both the lads. Patsey had, during the months she had spent on the estate, made herself extremely popular among the peasantry; whose cottages she constantly visited, and who always found her ready to listen to their tales of trouble, and to supply dainty food for the sick. The thought, too, that the chateau had been burned down was also a blow, for all the tenantry considered that they had a personal interest in the affairs of their seigneur.

"How was it that there was no defence?" Andre asked. "I know that most of the men were away, but surely enough might have been gathered to keep the Blues back, until madame escaped to the woods."

"It seems they rode by night, and arrived there soon after day broke. They had evidently come on purpose to seize your lord for, as soon as they found that he was not there, they went away at once, only stopping to set fire to the chateau. They were evidently in a hurry to be off.

"Here is Philippe Rehan, who has brought the news. He only knows what I have told you, as he mounted and rode off at once."

"I suppose they have taken our young lord, too?"

"Philippe does not know about that. He says they came from the direction of Nantes, and no doubt my sister has been taken there."

"What is to be done, captain?" Andre asked, as he and Pierre looked at each other helplessly, in face of this trouble.

"Monsieur Martin and I are going to leave, at once. We don't know what we are going to do yet, but we shall certainly try, by all means, to get her out of prison. How it is to be managed we have not even thought, but if it can be done, we shall do it. Now, I am sure that we can rely upon your assistance."

"We will do anything," Andre exclaimed; while Pierre said, "We will be cut to pieces for you, captain."

Leigh gave a hand to each.

"I am sure of it," he said. "And the band?"

"Every one of those we had at first we could answer for," Andre replied. "And I believe that the others can be trusted, too. They all esteem it a high honour to have been received into the band of Cathelineau's scouts. They knew that there would be danger, when they joined, and that they must be prepared to die for the cause. All would certainly be faithful; there would be no fear about that."

"I have not the least idea, at present, what I shall want you to do; but at any rate we shall go to Nantes, and it is there that you must meet us. We shall ride off in an hour's time. Let the others sleep till there is a general movement, then you can tell them what has happened, and that my orders are that you shall march home, at once. You can be there by tomorrow night, can you not?"

"It will be two long marches, but we will be there, captain."

"We shall not be much before you. By that time we shall have determined how we shall set about the matter, and shall be able to give you instructions; which will probably be that you are to meet us, at some point we will arrange, just outside the town. Of course, you will not go in a body, but singly or in pairs; crossing the river at various points, and travelling by different roads. Enter the town as if you belonged to villages round.

"I will ask Monsieur de la Rochejaquelein to let you have another pistol, each, before you leave. Of course, you will hide your arms under your clothes. I don't know that it will be necessary to use force; of course, at first we shall try bribery.

"At any rate, you will both be most useful in obtaining information. There are very many people who know Monsieur Martin by sight, and a few who know me. Possibly some of your band may have friends in Nantes; and these, if they are of our party, would be able to ask questions, and to find out the place in which my sister is imprisoned, much better than strangers could do.

"We have heard nothing of what is passing in Nantes for many weeks and, as they have sent troops to arrest Monsieur Martin, it is possible that his father may also be arrested. If he is at liberty, he would be sure to know where my sister is imprisoned."

The day was breaking now, and Leigh went next to the large house which had been set apart for the use of the generals. He knew Rochejaquelein's room, having been chatting with him till late, the evening before. The young count sat up in bed, as he opened the door.

"You have given me a start, Leigh," he said, with a smile. "I was dreaming that the Blues had retaken the town and, when the door opened, thought that it was a party come to make me prisoner.

"Is there any bad news? You look grave."

"Bad news as far as Jean Martin and I are concerned. A messenger arrived, two hours ago, with the news that a party of Blues from Nantes arrived at his chateau, without being observed, as they had travelled all night and reached it at daybreak. They had no doubt been specially sent to arrest Jean but, finding that he was away, they burnt the chateau, and carried off my sister a prisoner.

"We are going to start at once. I trust that you will explain, to the other generals, the cause of our absence."

"I am sorry, indeed, to hear your news," Rochejaquelein said warmly. "A curse upon the Blues! Why can't they content themselves with making war on men, without persecuting and massacring women?

"Certainly I will explain, to Cathelineau and the others, the cause of your absence. But what are you thinking of doing?"

"That we have not even considered. We mean to get her out of their hands, if possible; but until we see whether she has been really taken to Nantes--of which I have little doubt--which prison she is placed in, and how it is guarded, we can form no plan. If possible, we shall bribe the jailers. If not, we will try to rescue her by force.

"I am taking my band with me. I can depend upon them, and there is no one in Nantes on whom we can rely. They will, of course, enter the town singly; and will, I am sure, give us their loyal service, should we require it."

"If they serve you as well as they serve the cause, you could scarce have better assistants. I would that I could go with you. It would be an adventure after my own heart, but private friendship must give way to our country's needs. I hope, Leigh, that it will not be long before we meet again, and that I may hear that you have been successful."

Half an hour later, Leigh and Jean Martin started. The latter's first question, when Leigh returned, had been regarding the child. It was now nearly fifteen months old but, in the terrible shock caused by the news of his wife having been carried off, Jean had not thought of it till Leigh had left the room.

"The child is as nothing to me," he said, when Leigh had told him that the messenger had heard nothing of it. "It would have been, some day; but so far 'tis as nothing compared to Patsey. It slept with the nurse, and may possibly have escaped; unless, indeed, Patsey wished to take it with her."

"I do not think that she would do that," Leigh said. "No doubt it would have been a comfort, to have it with her; but she would have known that its chances of life would be slight, indeed, and for your sake she would have concealed it, if possible, before she was seized."

They reached the ruins of the chateau at noon next day, having stopped for the night at Chemille, in order to rest their horses and keep them in condition for another long ride, if necessary. The outhouse had been left standing. Francois came out, on hearing the sound of the horses' hoofs.

"Thank God you are back, master!" he said. "It has been a terrible time."

"Is the child safe, or was it taken with its mother?" Jean asked.

"He is safe, sir. Marthe saved it. When madame heard the Blues ride up, and looked out and saw their uniforms, she ran into Marthe's room and said:

"'Hide the child, Marthe! Run with it downstairs, without waking it, and put it in a cupboard in the kitchen. They will never think of searching for it there. Then return to your bed again. Tell your master, when he comes back again, I have left little Louis for him.'

"I was getting up when I heard the horsemen, and guessed that it was the Blues and, without waiting a moment, dropped from my window and ran past the stable, and hid myself in the shrubbery behind it. I had scarcely done so when I heard them come round the house.

"Then there was a great knocking at the door and, a minute later, a pistol shot was fired. I heard afterwards that madame told Henri to open the door. As he did so, the officer of the Blues shot him through the head.

"For ten minutes I heard nothing more. Then someone came to the stable, took out the two horses, and then set fire to it. Looking out through the bushes, I saw the smoke coming out from two or three windows of the chateau. Then I made off as quickly as I could, got into the church, and set the bells ringing; thinking that it might frighten off the Blues, though I knew that the men were all away, and there was no chance of help.

"Soon they came riding along at full speed, and I saw madame in the middle of them. As soon as they had gone, the women all ran out from their houses. We tried our best to put out the flames, but the fire had too much hold.

"As we were doing this, I saw Marthe with the child in her arms. It had been saved well-nigh by a miracle, she said, and she told me how her mistress had run in to her. She caught up the child, and then, thinking that if they saw its clothes they would search for it, she opened the drawers, seized them all, and ran down and put them and the child into the kitchen cupboard, as her mistress had told her, then ran back to her bedroom and began to dress.

"She heard her mistress call to Henri to go down and open the door. She heard the pistol shot, and the Blues pour into the house. She hurried on her clothes and went out. They were searching all over the chateau. The officer came up to her, with a pistol in his hand.

"'Where is your master?' he said.

"'I do not know,' she replied. 'He rode away from here ten days ago, and has not been back since.'

"'That is the tale your mistress tells,' he said.

"'It is true, sir. You go into the village and ask any of the women there, they will tell you the same thing. I will swear on the cross that it is so.'

"He seemed very angry, but turned away from her. Presently the mistress came down, under a guard of two soldiers and, as she passed, she said:

"'Goodbye, Marthe. Tell your master that I am thankful, indeed, that he was not here.'

"Then the officers told the men to set fire to the house, in a dozen places. They had all got bundles, having taken everything they thought of value. As soon as they had set fire to the curtains everywhere, and saw that the flames had got a good hold, they mounted and rode off.

"They had not searched the kitchen much, as they had only opened the closets large enough for a man to hide in and, not expecting to find anything worth taking, had not troubled themselves to look into the small ones; so Marthe had only to take the child out. Fortunately it had not awoke. When we found that it was hopeless to try and put the fire out, Marthe took the child over to the farm of Madame Rehan who, as soon as she got the news of the mistress being carried off, had sent her son away on horseback to tell you."

"Thank God, the child has been spared!" Jean Martin said, reverently. "We will go to the cure's.

"The boys will all be back tonight. Give the horses a good feed. We shall set out perhaps tonight, perhaps tomorrow morning."

"Ah, Monsieur Martin," the cure said, as they entered his house, "this is a sad homecoming for you. If we had known that the Blues were coming, but a quarter of an hour before they arrived, we could have got madame away to a place of safety. I knew nought about it until the church bells began to ring. Just as I was about to go out, five minutes later, to learn the cause, I saw them ride past with Madame Martin in their midst. We did not know that there were any of them within twenty miles of us, and thought that there was no chance, whatever, of their coming to a little village like ours."

"They came, no doubt, for me," Jean said gloomily. "If they had found Leigh and myself at home, they would not have taken the place so easily. He and I and the two men could have made a stout defence. I hear that there were not more than twenty of them, and I warrant that there would not have been many of them left, when the fight was over."

"I am sure," the cure said, "that if you had been there, and the place had been defended, all the women within sound of the church bell would have come in with arms, and would have fought like men in the defence of yourself and madame; but as it was, the whole thing was such a surprise, with everyone in bed and asleep, that the enemy were off before anyone could think of what had best be done. As it was, the women from all the farms round were here, armed with hatchets or pitchforks, half an hour after the bell began to ring. Of course, in the village here we knew that it was too late to do anything, but to flock to the church and pray for the safety of our good lady."

"Thank you, my friend. Leigh and I are going to Nantes, to see if anything can be done to get her out of prison. Leigh's band are coming also. Of course, they will travel singly. If of no other use, they will be better able to ask questions than we.

"I am going over now to Rehan's farm, to see my boy and to thank Marthe for saving him."

"It was well managed, indeed," the priest said. "I went over yesterday to see the child, and the nurse told me how its escape had been contrived.

It was a happy thought on the part of its mother, and the woman carried it out well.

"But before you go, you must take a meal. I am sure that you must want it."

"I will not say no to that," Jean replied, "for we have not broken our fast this morning."

In half an hour, the cure's table was most abundantly furnished for, as soon as the news spread through the village that the seigneur had arrived, and was at the house of the priest, the women brought in little presents--a dozen eggs, a fowl, or some trout that had been caught by the boys in the stream, that morning.

One or two of the women volunteered to assist the cure's servant. Three fowls were hastily plucked, cut asunder, and grilled over the fire. As soon as they were nearly ready, they were placed in front of the fire to be finished, while the trout took their place. The repast began with these, the fowls followed, and it was concluded with an omelette.

"I have not eaten such a meal, father," Martin said, "since I rode away. I think, after this, I shall be able to take a more hopeful view of matters. In that respect the meal will be thrown away upon Leigh, for he always takes the brightest view of everything, and has never ceased to assure me that we are sure to manage to get my wife out of the hands of these villains, somehow; and as he has so far always succeeded in what he has attempted, I feel a good deal of faith in him. I should be as hopeful as he, if I knew that the Henriette was in the river at Nantes, and that I had to my hand a dozen stout fellows I could thoroughly rely on."

After paying a visit to the farm, praising Marthe, and arranging that she should continue to live there, they returned to the village.

"We will go over to the chateau, Leigh, before we do anything else. I want to see how hot the ruins are."

"I should think that they must be pretty cool by this time, Jean. You see, it is nearly four days since it was burnt."

"I have no doubt that the walls will be cool enough; but there was a lot of woodwork about it. When the roof fell in it would smother the fire for a time, but it might go on smouldering, even now."

"But what does it matter, Jean?"

"It matters a good deal. I have with me only a hundred francs, in paper, which is not worth above a third of its face value. I have here four thousand in gold, which I brought with me from Nantes, as soon as the troubles began.

I buried it one day under the hearthstone of the kitchen, thinking it possible that the Blues might come here. The money is of the utmost importance now, for we may want it to bribe some of the jailers; and therefore I must get it, even if it delays us for a day."

They found indeed that, as they had feared, there was still fire among the mass of debris.

"We must quench it before we can do anything, Jean. I have no doubt that the women will help."

Francois was at once sent round and, in a short time, all the women in the place were assembled with pails. Martin and Francois worked the windlass of the well, the women carried pails of water, and Leigh threw the contents on to the smouldering mass above where he knew the kitchen fireplace must have stood. Clouds of steam rose and, from time to time, some of the women with rakes pulled off the upper layer of ashes. They worked till nightfall, by which time steam had ceased to rise.

"That will do for tonight," Jean said; "we will finish the job tomorrow morning. Your band will be here by that time, and will help us to get some of these heavy beams and timbers out of the way. We can then rake the smaller stuff out, and get at the fireplace."

At eight o'clock the band arrived. Leigh went down and spoke to them, and thanked them for the two long marches they had made. He had, during the afternoon, obtained a supply of bread and wine and, after they fell out, a meal was eaten before they started for their homes, promising to be back at six in the morning, to aid in the work of clearing away the debris.

Jean and Leigh spent a couple of hours in talk with the cure, and related to him the events that had passed since they had left. Then, thoroughly tired out, they retired to the room that had been prepared for them. The work that afternoon had been heavy; they had had a long ride previously, and neither had slept much the night before.

The next morning the work was recommenced. During the night the fire had crept in again, from the surrounding mass; but there were plenty of hands now, and in an hour it was again extinguished. The hearthstone was soon cleared and raised, and Martin brought out a crock, in which he had placed the gold.

"Now, Leigh," he said, "you had better have a talk with your boys, and arrange where they are to meet you. I should not press any of them who are unwilling to go. This is a private business, and I do not think that it would be right to urge them."

"Certainly not," Leigh agreed. "I am quite sure that all our boys will go with us, both for Patsey's sake, and because they are furious at the chateau being burnt down; as to the others, I shall put it to them that they are perfectly free to do as they wish. They can go with us, or they can rejoin the army, just as they like.

"If they go, I think that it would be as well that they did not enter the town; but should take up their quarters in a copse, or in a deserted house, a mile or two away, so that we could call them if we wanted them. Even in a town like Nantes, forty strange boys wandering about might be noticed."

Martin, after seeing that the workers all had refreshment, went to the cure's; as he never interfered in any way with the boys, thinking that it might lessen Leigh's authority, were he to do so.

"Now, I want to talk to you all," Leigh said, after they had drunk their wine and eaten their bread. "In the first place, do I understand that all who were first with me are ready to run a considerable risk to attempt, with us, to carry off Madame Martin from the hands of the Blues, and to save her from the fate that falls upon every one that they once lay a hand upon?"

"They are all willing, captain," Andre said. "We spoke to them again, just before we came in last night, and they all said that they were willing and anxious."

"Good. Remember, lads, that it is not too late to draw back now."

"We should not dare show our face in the village again," Pierre said, "if we were to hang back when there was a chance of our being of service to so good a lady."

"I thank you with all my heart," Leigh said. "I tell you fairly that I expected such an answer. Those who have shown such courage as you have done, and have been so loyal to the promises made me when I first enrolled you, would, I felt certain, not hang back now. Now, do you draw aside for a minute or two, while I speak to the others."

There was a movement, and the two groups stood apart.

"Your case is different from that of the others," he said. "In the first place, you have not been with me so long; and secondly--and this is more important--that Madame Martin is not the wife of your seigneur, and that you owe no duty to her. The enterprise on which we are going to start does not concern the cause for which we are fighting. It is a private business, and there is no occasion whatever for you to take part in it. You are free either to choose an officer among yourselves; or to rejoin the army, find Monsieur de la Rochejaquelein, and tell him that I sent you to him in order that he might find a suitable leader for you, among the gentlemen with him. I would rather that you talked the matter over among yourselves, and came and gave me an answer, in half an hour."

"Will you tell us what we shall have to do, captain?" one of them said.

"That I can hardly do, for I do not know myself. However, I think it probable that the greater portion of the band would remain outside the town. There are copses, down by the riverside, where you could wait in safety until you were wanted. Possibly you might not be wanted at all. Possibly you might be summoned to take part in so desperate an enterprise as storming one of the prisons. Of course it would be done at night, when we should have the advantage of a surprise. I can tell you no more than that.

"Now, my last word is, I shall not think any the worse of you, if you decide not to go with me."

It wanted five minutes of the time, when two of the boys returned to where he was talking with Pierre and Andre.

"We have decided, captain. You told us, when you marched away from Saumur, that Monsieur de la Rochejaquelein had approved of your taking us, and therefore we shall feel that we are still doing our duty to the cause. You have been kind, good, and thoughtful while we have been with you. All those of our own age in the army envied us who were of Cathelineau's scouts, and regarded our position as a great honour. Even if we were willing to go back, we could not do so, and tell the others that we had left you and our comrades when you were about to undertake some perilous service.

"But we do not wish it. We all desire to remain with you, and to follow wherever you may lead us, and to die in your service, if need be."

Leigh shook them warmly by the hand.

"Bravely said, and I thank you heartily. I am proud of my scouts, and am glad to see that my confidence in you is well founded. Call the others up."

After thanking these also, Leigh addressed the whole of them.

"Now, I will give you your orders. You must make your way by different routes to Nantes. There are many villages on the bank where you can find a boat that will take you across. Never travel more than two together. You must all take the green ribbons off your hats, leave your belts behind, and hide your pistols. If questions are asked you, reply that you are going to get work at Nantes, where you have friends, and that you are afraid to stay in your own villages.

"I will give each of you assignats for five francs. It would not do to give you silver. With this you can pay for your ferry across the water, and buy food on the way. It were best that, both on this side of the river and the other, you travel either by by-lanes or through the fields.

"When you get near Nantes, keep close to the river, and enter the last large copse before you get there. Andre or Pierre are likely to be there first, and will be on the lookout for you. They will join me in the town and bring you orders when necessary, and will send two or three of you in, daily, to buy food for the rest.

"I can give you no orders beyond that. Now, I hope I shall meet you all, in three days' time, at your rendezvous.

"Pierre and Andre, you will, on the evening after you arrive, enter Nantes, following the river bank. You will go along to a spot where a church faces the river. Sit down on its steps and wait for us, until the clock strikes ten. If we are not there, return and come back the next evening. If we are still not there, you will know that some bad luck has befallen us; and the band will then disperse, and you will all find your way up home.

"I should advise you all to travel by night, when you have once crossed the Loire. In that way you will avoid any risk of being questioned."

The boys then dispersed, and Leigh returned to the priest's. He and Martin had already talked over their disguises, and had agreed that those of fishermen would be the most appropriate; but until they could obtain the necessary clothes, they would go in the attire of fairly well-to-do people in a country town.

"We should only have to put on a tricolour scarf, Jean, and should look like municipal authorities."

"It would go against the grain to put that rag on," Martin said; "but your idea is a good one, and I would dress up as a general of the Blues, or as Robespierre himself, on such an errand as we are bound on.

"We cannot do better than go to Clisson. The place is in the hands of our people, and the village authorities will not dare to ask us any questions."

After dining with the cure, they mounted and rode to Clisson, arriving there at five o'clock in the afternoon. They went to the leader of the force there, as he was a friend of Jean's.

"I will send and get you the things," he said, when they told him the object of their visit. "It is just as well, if any of the people here are acting as spies for the Blues--which is likely enough--that they should not be able to give any description of you. We are all three about the same size, therefore I will go out and buy two suits.

"As to the scarves, I am more doubtful. I doubt if any shopkeeper here would admit that he had even a bit of tricolour ribbon in his possession."

"It will not matter about that," Martin said; "and, at any rate, when we get beyond the ground held by us, we shall find no difficulty whatever in getting a couple of cockades of those colours.

"Thank you very much indeed," he went on. "Here are five louis. I have no doubt that you will be able to lay them out well for us. But remember, please, that although we are all three the same height, I am some four or five inches bigger round the shoulders than Leigh; and want more room for my arms, also."

"I will remember," the other laughed. "Just let me pass this string round you, and then round Monsieur Stansfield, and tie two knots in it; and I will also measure you round the waist and leg."

In an hour he returned with one of his men, carrying two parcels.

"I had no difficulty in getting the clothes for your brother-in-law," he said, "but I had to go to two or three shops before I could get coat and breeches wide enough for you. What do you intend to do with your horses?"

"We shall ride into Nantes as we are, after nightfall, and shall put them up at a small inn. I know of one near the water. It is kept by a man who was at one time in my lugger, but he had his leg crushed in a storm, and had to have it taken off. He was a good sailor, so I set him up, and can rely upon him. He will get fishermen's clothes for us and, should we have to stay there any time, buy a boat and nets. We may want such a thing, badly."

The clothes were tried on, and found to fit fairly well. In our days the short-waisted coats with their long tails, and the waistcoats extending below the waist, would be deemed laughable; but as it was then the fashion among the middle classes, and especially the Republicans, Jean saw nothing ridiculous in it, while Leigh smiled at the figures they cut. Both had bright yellow breeches and stockings, and low shoes.

They waited till midnight at Clisson, and then mounted again, and by morning they were within a mile or two of a ferry, a short distance above Nantes. They stopped at a small village, and there purchased two tricolour cockades from the one shop it boasted, these forming conspicuous objects in the window, as a proof of the warm adherence of its owner to the Convention.

At the little cabaret they took breakfast, and saw that the horses were fed, then they rode on to the ferry. The boat was on the opposite side, and in half an hour it crossed. Then they took their places, and were ferried over. A party of soldiers were posted at the landing place.

"You are going to Nantes, I suppose, citizens?" the officer in command asked.

"We are. We come from Vallet, and are going to consult the commissary of the republic concerning some taxes that, as we consider, it is impossible for the town to pay, which the commissary there has imposed upon us."

"I should imagine that your errand is scarcely likely to meet with success," the officer said, with a light smile. "I hear the same complaints at Nantes, but have not heard that any remission has been made. Well, citizens, at any rate I can wish you luck on your errand."

It was still very early when they rode into Nantes, and but few people were about the streets. Trade was almost at a standstill. The town, which had been strongly Republican, was at once deeply discontented with the crushing taxation imposed upon it, and horrified at the constant executions that took place. Almost every house had soldiers billeted on it, as it was considered necessary to keep a large force there in order to overawe the south of Brittany and, if necessary, to send supports to the generals operating in the west of La Vendee.

There was scarcely any shipping in the river, and even the fishermen had almost given up plying their business; their best customers had fallen under the guillotine, and there was no demand for fish on fast days--for to practise any of the observances of religion was considered to be, in itself, a proof of hostility to the Convention. Therefore Jean and Leigh rode into the courtyard of the little inn without having attracted any attention, whatever.

Chapter 10
Preparations For A Rescue

"I have no accommodation for you here, citizens," a voice said, as Jean Martin and Leigh rode into the little courtyard, and a man with a wooden leg came out from the side door of the inn.

"I think you might be able to manage for us, Brenon," Jean said.

"Mon Dieu! it is--"

Jean held up his hand sharply.

"Yes, it is I, Citizen Gallon, from Vallet. It is not often that I stir so far from home, but I had business here."

"Well, well, I will see what I can do for you, comrade; but as you know, I don't profess to take in horses. My clients come from the waterside, and generally my stable is full of their baskets and ropes. However, I will see what I can do. I will tie them up in that shed, for the present, and then clear out a stall for them afterwards."

The horses were led to a shed, encumbered with fishing gear of all sorts.

"What madness has seized you, mon capitaine, to put your head into this lion's den?"

"I will tell you presently, Brenon, when we get inside. I am glad that you are able to take the horses in. We don't want to be stared at, or talked about. We have come along the river bank and, so far, we have been quite unnoticed."

"All the better, all the better; to be noticed here means to have one's head cut off. Now, I will take you to a little room upstairs, where there is no chance of anyone seeing you."

"Get us up, if you can, without our being noticed by your servants, Brenon. We shall be differently dressed when we come down again."

The man nodded.

"The boy is in the front room," he said. "There are three or four fishermen there, having their morning glass. I have no other servants. My wife does what is needful, for I was obliged to discharge the girl we had, everything has been so slack of late."

He led them up to a chamber looking on to the quay. Jean was puzzled at the man's manner, for he spoke in a confused and hesitating way. When he closed the door behind him, he stood rubbing his hands together nervously.

"Have you heard lately from Nantes, Monsieur Jean?"

"No, it is five weeks since I had any news; except, of course, what was known about the troops that were here. What is it, old friend? Is there bad news?"

"There is terrible news," Brenon said, "so bad that I don't know how to tell you."

"Speak out, old friend. I have had one blow so heavy that I can scarcely be hurt more than I am."

"Well, then, monsieur, your father has been arrested and is in the prison; and you know what that means!"

"Father arrested!" Jean exclaimed; "on what grounds? He never expressed an opinion as to public affairs. That at heart he hated what has been going on, I know; but he never spoke strongly, even to me, and when I have heard his opinion asked, he has always replied that he was a trader, and that a man could not give his attention to business if he worried himself over politics. He attended to his trade, and left it to those who liked, to manage the government of the country.

"What of my mother and sister?"

"They are safe, monsieur. He sent them off a fortnight before, in disguise, to La Rochelle; at least, so I have heard from the fishermen. And as the Henriette was lying there at the time, and sailed two days after, there is not much doubt but that they sailed in her for England.

"Your father was denounced before the committee of public safety as one who was hostile to the Convention. He was accused of having sent large sums of money to England, and was believed to have sent his wife and daughter there also, with the intention, of course, of following them; and the fact that you were known to be fighting in the ranks of the brigands, as they call the Vendeans, was also mentioned as an additional crime on his part."

"Then we have a double task to carry out, Leigh," Jean said grimly.

"Now I will tell you what we came here for, Brenon. Six days ago a small party of the Blue cavalry came, at night, to my chateau. I was away, but they carried off my wife as a prisoner, and burnt the house to the ground. So we have come here to see if we cannot get her out of prison."

"You have thought of such a thing as that?" the man exclaimed in surprise. "Ah, monsieur! It is well nigh an impossibility that you have undertaken. The villains know that there are hundreds of men, friends of the prisoners with whom they have crowded the jails, who would tear them down stone by stone, if they had the power; but in addition to the prison warders--not the men that used to be there, but men taken from the lowest class in the town--the prisons are watched by what they call the volunteers, fifteen hundred men belonging to the scum of the city--the men from the slaughterhouses, the skinners', and the tan yards Some of these are ever on guard round the prisons, night and day.

"There have been great changes here. A year ago, almost everyone thought that the Assembly was going to do wonderful things. No one knew exactly what. According to what they said, everyone was to be able to eat meat, seven days a week, to wear good clothes, and to do just as much work as pleased him and no more. Even the fishermen and sailors were fools enough to believe it.

"But there is a great change now. At first they approved of cutting off the heads of those who, they were told, were the cause of all misery and poverty; but when, every day, fresh prisoners were brought in, and it was not the nobles only but quiet citizens--tradesmen, manufacturers, doctors, and advocates--and every morning a score were carried out to be guillotined, men began to change their opinion; especially when they found that the more heads were cut off, the less work there was and the poorer they became. They began to talk among themselves and, when it came to executing women and children, as well as men, they turned round altogether.

"More than once the fishermen and sailors have tried to rescue prisoners on their way to execution. The commissioners of the republic have been hooted in the streets and, if they had had arms in their hands, our men would have turned the tables; but the town is full of troops now and, worse than all, they have enrolled this corps of volunteers, who are the terror of the place. They have spies everywhere, and no one dares whisper a word against the commissioners or the executions for, if but two or three men are standing by, the chances are that one of them is a spy."

"But surely my brother might have prevented my father's arrest, Brenon? He was one of the leading men at that Jacobin Club."

"He is still one of the leading men of the party," Brenon said gloomily. "He is established in your father's house, now, and is on the most intimate terms with the commissaries of the Convention."

"Is Monsieur Desailles still here? He was a young advocate, and a member of the Jacobin Club."

"Yes, he is a member still: but he is not in good odour with the extreme party. He is at the head of what they call the moderates. They say that sometimes these try to defend accused persons, and that is considered a terrible offence by the others. I should never be surprised to hear that he himself, and those with him, have been denounced as enemies of the state. This is an awful time, monsieur, and Heaven only knows what we shall come to.

"Now, is there anything that I can do for you, captain? You know well that you have but to say the word and that, whatever it is, I would do it, even if I were cut to pieces the minute afterwards."

"Thank you, old friend. It was because I knew that you were trusty and true that I came here. Now, the first thing that we want is fishermen's clothes. We only disguised ourselves in those things in order to pass safely through the Blues, and be able to cross the ferry. For the present they have done their work, and now we want a disguise that we can go about in, unnoticed. Of course, we don't want new things."

"I can get them easily enough, monsieur. My customers are all hard up. I know pretty well which are true men, and which are not."

"In the next place, I should like to buy or hire a boat to be at my disposal, as long as I stay here."

"There are boats and to spare, captain. Fishing goes on because men must live; though it can hardly be called living, for the prices of everything are fixed by law, now, and are fixed so low that the men can scarce earn enough to buy bread for themselves, and their families. Still, there are boats in plenty. Men have come down from towns and villages higher up, for they say that the troops are under no control and, when the boats come in after a night's fishing, they come down and help themselves and, if a man ventures to grumble, he gets a musket ball to pay him for his fish. The men here, at first, were against their fishing between this place and the sea; but the authorities stepped in, and said that the more food, the better for the people; and as the price was fixed, the men here saw that it made no difference to them. Still, like our own men, they are doing badly enough, and one could buy a boat for a mere song."

"It would be better to buy one from those men, Brenon, because the fact of our being strangers would not then be noticed. I want one rowing boat, as fast a craft as you can pick out.

"I also want to hire a boat with a cabin that will hold us both. Of course it will be a sailing boat, say of three or four tons burden. I intend that we shall live on board. It might be noticed if two strange sailors were often coming in and out of your place; whereas, if we were in a boat moored against the bank, no one would notice us. If you can get hold of such a boat, with a couple of men who seem to you to be honest fellows, strangers to the place, it will be a great thing; and we could occasionally go down the river, and do a little fishing."

"All that can be managed easily enough, captain. I know of one boat, just such a size; owned by two men, Rouget and Medart, who sailed in the Henriette for years, and only left her when you did, as they had wives and families here, and knew that she would not put in again for a long time. You could trust them as you do me."

"That would be the very thing. Make arrangements with them, on any terms they like. I will take her by the week. She carries a boat, I suppose?"

"Of course, monsieur, they could not do without one."

"If she is fast, well and good. If not, tell them to buy the fastest they can find. They can sell their own boat in part payment, or they can get her up on the quay and let her lie there, until we have gone, when they can either sell her or the new one.

"However, the clothes are the first thing. We cannot venture out in these, in the first place, because we might be questioned; and secondly, because we might be recognized; whereas in a fisherman's dress, with a wide oilskin hat and our faces dirtied somewhat, I don't think that anyone could know us."

They remained quiet until evening, and then sallied out in the disguises Brenon had obtained for them. Their first visit was to the house of Jean's friend, Desailles. It was arranged that Leigh should not go in, as Desailles would probably speak more freely to Jean, if alone. Jean had written his name on a piece of paper, folded it up, and carefully sealed it and, when he reached the house, he handed this to the woman who opened the door.

"This is for Citizen Desailles," he said. "I will wait. He may want to see me."

In a minute the servant returned, and requested him to come in. He was shown into a room where Desailles was sitting, with some papers before him. He did not speak until the servant closed the door. Then he leapt up, and held out both hands to his visitor.

"My dear Jean," he said, "what imprudence, what madness for you to venture here!"

"I don't think there is any fear of my being discovered. Even you, yourself, would scarcely know me."

"I know you, now you have taken that hat off; but I own that I did not recognize you before, and thought for the moment that you were but a messenger.

"Please do not talk loud. For aught I know, my servant has been bribed to act as a spy upon me, and may have her ear at the keyhole. To tell you the truth, Jean, things are coming to a crisis at the club. The violent party get more violent every day, and I am heartily sick of this butchers' work. I feel that, at any moment, I may be denounced."

"Then why on earth do you stay here, Jules? Why don't you come and throw in your lot with us?"

"I should have laughed at the idea, a year ago," he said; "for at that time, although I objected strongly to the doings in Paris, I yet believed that much good would come of the changes. Now I know that nothing has come of them but murder and misery, and the madness increases rather than diminishes. Hopeless as I own your struggle seems, to me, I would at least rather be killed in battle than executed here; but I would rather still get to England, if I could. As you know, I can play the violin well, and might be able to support myself, by its aid, if nothing else turned up."

"If you are thinking of going, Desailles, I will give you a letter to my father-in-law, at Poole. I hear that my mother and sister have escaped, and they have doubtless gone there, so you will not find yourself friendless.

"And now for the purpose that has brought me here. I had no idea, until I arrived, that these wretches had imprisoned my father; who is the last man to interfere in politics, and has, I am sure, never uttered a word of enmity against the Convention. I came to endeavour to rescue my wife who, as no doubt you have heard, has been seized and carried off in my absence, and my house laid in ashes. I suppose she has been brought here."

"Yes, I am aware of it," Jules said. "The party of horse who did it were specially sent from here. Of course you were the principal object of the expedition, but the officer was ordered to bring her, too--in the first place as your wife, in the second as an Englishwoman and therefore, of course, an enemy of France. You were denounced to the club; and as you were known to be one of the gentlemen who had joined the insurrection, and were fighting with Cathelineau and others, I knew that it would be useless to raise a voice on your behalf; having the satisfaction of feeling sure that you would be away from home when they got there, and hoping that your wife would receive notice of their coming, before they entered the house."

"Has she been brought here yet?"

"Yes, she arrived three days ago. She is in the old city prison, where your father is also confined."

"So far that is fortunate," Jean said.

"Now, how about my father? I should have thought that Jacques' influence would have been sufficient to protect him."

The young advocate smiled bitterly.

"Monsieur Jacques Martin poses as a Brutus, Jean. When your father was denounced in the club, he rose and said that he should take no part in the deliberations, that he was before all other things a patriot, and that he would not permit private affection to interfere with his duty as a citizen. In fact, my dear Jean, painful as it must be for you to hear, my opinion is that your brother has all along been playing a deep game, and that his object has been to grasp the whole of your father's business and property. It was a friend of his who denounced you at the club, when I before gave you warning; it was members of his clique who stirred the authorities up to send a small body of cavalry to capture you, and it was they also who denounced your father. Your brother is by far the most powerful of the committee of safety, as well as in the club. He assumes an air of perfect disinterestedness, and of a passionate love for the republic. His vote is always given for death. I think he takes Saint Just as his model, and repeats his assertion, that it is only by the destruction of the enemies of France that France can be freed.

"There is a cold bloodedness about him that sets my nerves tingling. I believe, myself, that the discovery that your father had largely reduced his stocks, and had sent the proceeds to England, decided him in either agreeing to, or bringing about, this denunciation; and that he deferred it only until he found that your mother and sister had escaped. That freed his hands, to some extent. Had they remained here, he would have been in a difficult position. Even in these days, when we are sated with horrors, he could hardly have permitted his mother and sister to be executed when, as everyone knew, he had power to save them. On the other hand, if they had remained they would have been obstacles to the success of his plan. As it is now, your father's house and all property belonging to him were declared confiscated; but the committee of safety passed a vote that, seeing the inestimable service rendered to the state by his eldest son, they would be bestowed upon him as a token of gratitude for his well doing."

"You scarcely surprise me," Jean said gloomily. "I never liked my brother--we had not a feeling in common, and for years he has never seemed to belong to the family; and certainly, since the troubles began, he has not set foot in my father's house. Still, I hardly believed that he would be such a scoundrel. I abhorred his opinions, but believed that he was at least sincere. I did not see what he could gain by a revolution. Now I understand his character better, and can see how cleverly he has played his cards. I cannot reckon myself with the scoundrel, deeply as he has wronged me and my father; but I should welcome the news that retribution had fallen upon him, by some other hand.

"And now, Jules, can you give me any advice whatever as to how to set about my scheme of getting them both out of prison?"

Jules shook his head.

"I fear, my poor friend, that that is impossible. The prison is, as you know, strong. There are, I should say, some forty warders, all ruffians and scoundrels. Any attempt to bribe even one of them would, almost to a certainty, be denounced; and it would probably be necessary to have at least half a dozen in the plot. As to force, it is out of the question. The building is very strong. There are always some twenty or thirty of the volunteers on guard outside, and an alarm would bring up five hundred in a quarter of an hour, to say nothing of the troops. What force could you bring that could have even a remote chance of success?"

"I have Leigh with me. You know him well, Jules. I rely much more upon him than I do on myself. He is full of plans and contrivances, and has rendered extraordinary services during the war. He has with him, or rather will have in the course of a day or so, a band of forty lads, of whom he is the captain, who have acted as scouts to Cathelineau. They will be in hiding, a mile or two out of the town."

Jules lifted his eyebrows.

"I am afraid that such a force as that would be of very little use to you, Jean--in fact, of no use whatever. If you had five hundred men, and could gather them for a sudden attack on the jail, and had a couple of cannon to blow in the gate, I should say it might be possible; and even then the chance of its being all done, and the fugitives got safely away, before the arrival of some three thousand troops would be very doubtful."

At this moment the servant brought in a note.

"Who brought this?" Monsieur Desailles asked.

"It was a woman, monsieur. She did not wait for an answer."

The advocate opened it. It was written in pencil.

"Dear Jules, Martin is on his feet denouncing you. Hostile vote certain. Escape at once."

After reading it, he handed it to Jean.

"That settles it," he said. "I am with you. Where are you staying?"

Martin told him, and said:

"It will never do for you to stay there. But I have arranged for a boat, with a cabin. We shall go on board at once. You can come with us. I had better go out first."

"It is better that we should not go together for, if the woman reports that I went off with a fisherman, a search might be made in all the boats. I will join you on the quay opposite the inn you speak of. I shall need a quarter of an hour to burn some papers. I have already a valise packed, with a couple of thousand francs, which is all the money I could obtain without creating suspicion. I have seen this coming for some time, and had no intention of making a martyr of myself, when my doing so would be of no advantage."

"Don't delay too long, Jules. I shall be in a fever until you join me."

"I know their way, Jean. There will be a half a dozen speeches, each vying with the other in abusing me. My friends will see the uselessness of trying to defend me, when the terrorists are three to one against them. If my friend slipped out, as is probable, directly your brother rose, I can calculate on a good hour. Actually, the club have no power whatever to order arrests, but they are so closely allied now with the committee of safety that they do not stand upon legalities, except in cases likely to attract a great deal of public attention."

Jules went to the door and let his visitor out. Jean joined Leigh.

"Desailles is going to join us. He has just been denounced, and will be with us in a quarter of an hour, on the wharf. It is very lucky that Brenon completed the arrangements today for the boat, and that Rouget and Medart will be expecting us this evening. I told them that I might not come until tomorrow morning, but this settles it. There will be a sharp search for Desailles, as soon as it is found that he is gone; and it is just as well that we should be off, too. I am very glad that I had the boat taken from her usual berth to a spot half a mile higher up, because there are sure to be inquiries whether any fishing boats put out during the night."

They walked fast back to the inn. Brenon, on being told what had happened, agreed that it would certainly be safest for them to go on board.

"I have two friends living here," he said, "both of whom are carriers, and keep eight or ten horses. Tomorrow morning, early, I will take one of your horses to one and the second to the other. No one will notice them there, whereas if a search is made--and I have no doubt a search will be made of the houses near the river--they will light upon them in my shed, and they would not believe my story that I had two citizens from Vallet living here--in the first place because it is an unlikely place to put them up, and in the second because no such citizens would be forthcoming. It is lucky that you told the men to get a cask of wine and a store of provisions on board, before starting.

"Well, you know, captain, that whenever you choose to land again, my house is at your disposal; and I will carry out what we arranged, that I should get together a score of men I can trust, and to each of whom I can promise a hundred francs, for a night's work in a good cause."

They packed up their former disguises, which might come in useful again. Their pistols they had already about them. They then went out on to the wharf again and, a few minutes later, were joined by Jules Desailles.

"I have been nervous ever since I left you," Jean Martin said, as his friend shook hands with Leigh. "I was afraid that a quarter of an hour's delay might be fatal."

"I lost no time. But I feel sure that it will be an hour before anyone is down after me; they are all too fond of listening to their own voices to close any discussion, in less than an hour after the proposer has sat down. I hope the boat is not far off, for this portmanteau of mine is heavy, I can assure you."

Martin took it up and swung it on to his shoulder.

"No, my dear Jean, I won't have it."

"Nonsense, Jules. The weight is nothing to me though, no doubt, to a man who never takes any exercise it would feel heavy."

"To say the truth, it is heavier than I expected. I went on packing up everything that I did not like to leave behind, until the thing was crammed full; and after I had locked it, and went to lift it, I was thunderstruck with the weight."

"Did your servant see you go out?"

"No; I rang for her, and told her that I was going out, and did not suppose that I should be back till late, and that she could go to bed when she liked--which I knew would be a few minutes after she got permission. She is a sort of human dormouse and, nineteen times out of twenty, I have had to wait for my breakfast. I was in a fright as I walked down here, lest some one who knew me might run against me, but happily I saw no one."

"They would not recognize you, if they had seen you," Jean laughed. "The idea of Monsieur Desailles, advocate, a gentleman somewhat particular as to his attire, dragging a portmanteau weighing a hundred pounds through the streets, would seem an impossibility."

"I have left that phase of my existence behind me," Jules laughed; "henceforth I am a man of war, a rebel, a brigand, as they call you, prepared for any desperate adventure, ready to rush up to a cannon's mouth."

"That is right, Desailles. I am glad to see that you take things so cheerfully."

"My dear Jean, I feel as if I walk on air since you have taken my portmanteau. I have been living in a state of suspense for months, hating these wretches and their ways; and knowing that I was gradually falling into bad odour with them, and that the blow would certainly fall, ere long. Over and over again I have thought of making my escape from it all; but you see, I am not a man of action, as you are. I did not see how the matter was to be effected--where to go or what to do. I was like a boy shivering at the edge of the bank, and afraid to plunge in; then another comes behind him and pushes him into the water, and he strikes out, and finds that it is not as cold as he expected, and forthwith enjoys it. I have cut loose from the past. I have become a rover and a waif, and I feel as lighthearted as a boy.

"Now, let me get hold of one end of that trunk, again."

"I have got it all right and, as you see, I have not yet changed shoulders. And if I want help, it is to Leigh I should turn, and not to you. After three months' campaigning, it may be that you will be able to hold up an end as well as he can, but you certainly cannot do so now. In another hundred yards we shall be at the boat, and they must be on the lookout for us."

In a short time they saw a fishing craft, with a boat astern of her. A man was standing on the deck.

"It is a dark night, my friends," he said.

"It will be lighter in the morning," Jean replied.

The man leapt ashore.

"Ah, captain, I am glad, indeed, to see you. Brenon did not tell us, until after he had made a bargain with us, who wanted our boat, or we should not have talked about payment. Not likely, after having sailed with you since you were a boy of fourteen."

"No, indeed," said another man, who had just raised his head out of the cabin hatch; "and we are not going to take it, either."

"We will talk about that afterwards," Jean said, as he stepped on board.

"I doubted whether it was you, captain, for Brenon had only spoken to us of two; and when I saw three of you, I thought that you must belong to one of the boats higher up. There are two or three of them, a bit farther on."

"I did not know, myself, until half an hour ago. This is my friend Monsieur Desailles, who is in the same danger from these butchers of the Convention as I am. First pass this box down, and then we will follow it."

They gathered in the little cabin. It was but some seven feet long.

"It will be close work, captain," Rouget said.

"It will do very well," Jean said cheerfully. "There is room for two of us to sleep on the lockers, and one on the floor. You have got the small boat behind you, I see."

"She is there," the man said, "and a good boat she is. We bought her from two fishermen, who had come down from Saint Florent. She is very well for up there, but she is scarce fit for fishing far below Nantes."

"I am glad that she did not belong to this place," Martin said. "The fishermen might have been surprised to see two strange men in a boat they knew; but so many have come down here, from the towns above, that we shall excite no attention. Now, the first thing to do is to get up sail, and drop down two miles past the town; then you can go about your fishing as usual. Only one of us will show upon deck at a time.

"Now, as to the matter on which we are here. Brenon told you that it was a dangerous business for which you would be required?"

"He told us that it was to hide two gentlemen whom the committee of public safety would be glad to get hold of; and I knew, of course, that to do such a thing was dangerous, but we did not like it any the worse for that. All honest men are horrified at the way these commissioners from Paris are carrying things on, and would be glad enough to aid in getting anyone out of their hands."

"But the danger is greater, in our case, than ordinary," Jean went on. "You heard that my father had been imprisoned?"

"We heard it, captain, and savage it made us, as you may guess. Everyone spoke well of him and, being your father, of course we felt it all the more."

"But that is not all, lads. A party of their cavalry went to my chateau in my absence, burnt it down, and brought my wife here a prisoner. Now, it is absolutely certain that they will both of them be condemned, for they have a personal enemy on the committee of public safety, and they will be murdered, unless we can get them out; and I and my brother Leigh, whom you all know, have come for that purpose."

"Well, captain, you can count upon both of us, heart and soul. But I don't see how it is going to be done. The prison is a strong place, and well guarded. I have no doubt that we could count on getting twenty stout men, along the wharf, but that would not be much use. They have more than that on guard and, before we could get into the prison, they would come swarming down, any number of them."

"We have forty young fellows from my neighbourhood, who will by tomorrow be hidden away in the wood, a mile and a half higher up the river."

"That will be a help, sir; but even with two hundred we should not be able to do much."

"We shall have plenty of time to talk it over, afterwards. Get the sail up and drop down the river. Keep close to the opposite bank. It is important that we should not be noticed, as we pass the town."

"Well, sir, there is hardly air enough to fill the sails. I should say that we had best tow her across to the other side, in the small boat; and then drift till we are fairly beyond the town. We are safe not to be seen then."

"Perhaps that will be the best plan, Rouget."

The men went out and, in two or three minutes, the sound of the oars could be heard.

"I can't say that the lookout is very hopeful, Leigh."

"I did not think that anyone would think it so, Jean; but it seems to me that it is just because everyone seems so confident that the prison is safe from attack, that we shall have a chance. The thing that is troubling me most is where we can get a barrel of gunpowder. We must have powder to blow open the gate. I expect that any of the doors we may find locked, inside, will give way if a pistol is fired through the keyhole; but to blow in the main gate of the prison we must get powder, and a good deal of it. That, however, is a matter in which we shall find that money will be of use.

"There are too many officials in the prison for us to hope to get any one out, without eight or ten being in the plot; and as these, we hear, are all fellows who are heart and soul with the Convention, it is not possible to attempt it in that way. But when, as you know, the Blues succeeded in bribing a Vendean to tamper with our guns, it ought not to be such a difficult thing to bribe one of these fellows, who is in charge of ammunition, to let us have a barrel or two of powder."

"That certainly seems to hold out a prospect of success, so far, Leigh. I have never been able to understand your confidence in success, but certainly the first indication of your plan seems to promise well. Now, let us hear some more of it."

"Well, this is my idea, Jean. I will choose a windy night, and send Andre and Pierre, with twenty of the boys, into the worst part of the town. Each shall carry a ball of yarn dipped in turpentine, mixed with sulphur and other inflammable things. They shall also carry another ball, having but a thin coating of the yarn, and powder inside so as to explode. When the clock strikes two, we will say, each of them will smash the window of some store, light both balls, and put them in. I want the explosion of one ball to scare anyone who may be sleeping there half out of their senses, and make them rush out of the house; which will leave plenty of time for the other ball to set on fire anything that it may light upon. Twenty fires, starting at once at different spots, will create a fearful scare. Many of the guards outside the prison--all of whom are drawn from the slums--will have come from that quarter and, as they have no idea of discipline, will, when they see the flames mounting up, leave their posts and rush off to see to the safety of their homes.

"Choosing a windy night, you may be sure that the fires would burn fast, and that the rest of the volunteers, and the National Guard, would soon be so busy that they would not trouble themselves about the prison, one way or the other. Thus I calculate that, of the fifty men on guard round the prison, there would not be twenty left at the outside; and they would be so busy staring at and talking of the fire that, with a sudden surprise, they could all be disposed of without difficulty. Then the gates of the prison would be blown in, and we should rush in, shoot down all the warders we meet--keeping one only as a guide--make straight for the rooms where your father and Patsey are confined, release them and as many others as the time will allow, telling them to rush down to the wharf and seize boats, or to escape in whichever way they like; while you, with your father and Patsey, would make straight down to our boat; while I, with the boys, would follow you and cover your retreat, if any of the Blues came up to pursue you."

"Leigh, you are a genius!" Martin exclaimed, bringing his hand down on the lad's shoulder with a force that almost knocked him from his seat.

"What do you think of that, Desailles, for a plan? I told you that I relied upon Leigh's head more than my own, and you see I had good reason for doing so. I doubt whether it could be done with his forty boys, but if we can get the powder, it seems to me that, with half as many sailors to help us, there is no reason why it should not succeed."

"But you might burn half the town down," Desailles said, gravely.

"If I was sure that it would burn the whole of it down, I should not mind," Leigh exclaimed. "But there is not much fear of that. If it cleared out the whole of the slums, where the supporters of the gang of murderers they call the committee of public safety live, I should rejoice most heartily. As there are several wide streets between them and the business quarters, and as they will have all the soldiers of the town to assist in fighting the flames, I do not think that there will be any fear of the fire spreading very far."

"Well, at any rate, Leigh, you have hit on a plan that offers a good chance of success. We shall find out, in a day or two, how many of the boatmen we can get to aid us, and how far they will be disposed to go. We must learn, in some way, how long it is likely to be before it is absolutely necessary to act. If we find that there is time, we can send some of the boys off to the army, to bring their fathers and brothers back with them. The sixty might not be enough, but with a hundred of our men, I think we should be pretty sure of success."

Chapter 11
The Attack On Nantes

When three or four miles down the river the boat was anchored, and the two men were called into the cabin, and Leigh's scheme explained to them.

"It is a big affair, sir," Medart said thoughtfully, when Jean had concluded. "Now, there is no love lost between us and the ruffians who carry out the committee's orders. They call us river rats, we call them sewer rats, and there has been many fights between the fishermen and these fellows, as far back as I can remember, and lately these have been much more frequent. If the plan was only to burn down their quarters, there are a good many who would lend a hand; because it could be done quietly, and they would have no particular reason for suspecting that it was the work of the fishermen. But as for going into the jail, that would be different. We should not have time, by what you say, to hunt up and kill all the warders; and it would therefore be known, at once, that we were concerned. Five or six of our fellows have already had their heads chopped off, on suspicion of having aided Royalists to escape. They don't mind whom they lay hands on, and they don't trouble themselves to search, but just seize the first they come to who, perhaps in a cabaret, has said a word against their doings.

"As to the trials, they are no trials at all. One of their fellows comes in and says, 'I heard this man abusing the authorities, and I accuse him also of being concerned in the escape of so and so.' It is no odds what the prisoner says. The fellow who acts as judge looks at the jury, who are all their creatures; they say 'Guilty 'and he says' Death!' and the accused are marched off again to the prison, to wait until their turn comes for the guillotine. Well you see, if this prison was broken into as you propose, and it was known that the sailors had a hand in it, the chances are that they would march a couple of hundred of us into the great square, which would be choke full of the National Guard and volunteers, and just shoot us down."

Jean was silent. The probability that things would go as the man said was so evident that he had no answer.

"I think the way to get over that difficulty," Leigh said, when he saw that Jean was puzzled, "would be for you all quietly to buy other clothes or, better still, for them to be bought for you by your wives. They should be such clothes as the peasants buy, when they come into the town. It would then be supposed that the attack was made by a party of Breton peasantry. As a good many other prisoners would escape, in addition to Monsieur Martin and your captain's wife, there would be no reason to suppose that the plot was specially arranged to aid their escape, or that any of the people of this town were concerned in the matter."

"That is so, Master Leigh," Rouget said. "It might be managed in that way. But I think that most of our chaps had better be told off for firing the town. I think that a good many might be willing to undertake that job, for I have heard it said, many and many a time, that they would like to burn the sewer rats out. There are other men who would, I am sure, rather join in the attack on the jail, if they could do so without putting the lives of all of us in danger.

"As to getting hold of an artilleryman, I don't know that that would be difficult. The men employed on that sort of work are all old soldiers, and many of these, though they dare not say so, hate what is going on just as much as we do. I have met one of them with Emile Moufflet, who served with you, captain, for two or three years. When we have been chatting together, he has said things about the committee that would have cost him his head, if he had been overheard. I know that his chum is in charge of some stores, but whether they are powder or not, I cannot say. But at any rate, Emile will be able to find out for me the name of several of them who have charge of powder; and he would be likely to know which of them had sentiments like his own, and how far they could be trusted.

"That would not take long, but to get hold of forty hands for the other work would take some time. One dare go only to men one is very intimate with, and get them to approach men whom they know well; for even among us, there are fellows who take the committee's money to spy over the others, and to find out whether any trouble is likely to come, or Royalists to be shipped off. One generally knows who they are, because they overdo their parts, and rail at the Convention more roundly and openly than an honest man would dare to do. Some of them one finds out that way; others, again, one spots by their always having money to spend. If they are too shrewd to betray themselves in that way, our wives find them out for us, by telling us that their women and children have new clothes, and we know well enough that there is no buying new clothes out of fish, at their present price. Besides, most of these fellows give up fishing altogether, and lounge about the wharves talking and smoking, and one knows that a man and his family cannot live on air. Still, there may be others who are too sly to let out their secret in either way, and therefore one must be very careful whom one speaks to. One would not think of telling anyone about what is intended until, just as it comes off, one could simply say that one has heard that there is something in the air, and that report says that every man who will lend a hand will earn--how much, captain?"

"Two hundred francs."

"When one sees how a man takes that, one can go a step or two further.

"Well, I should not think of letting out to a soul what the nature of the work would be, simply saying that every precaution will be taken to prevent its being known that any fishermen are engaged in it. All that will take time. I should say that it might be nigh a couple of weeks before one could get the whole thing arranged."

"What do you think, Desailles?" Jean said. "Shall we have a fortnight?"

Desailles shook his head.

"I could not say; you might have more than that, if the prisoners were taken in the regular order in which they were condemned. The jails are crowded and, as fresh captures are effected, room must be made for them. Of course the committee have a list, and they make a mark against the names of those who are to be executed, each day. It might be three weeks before your friends' turn comes, it might be only a few days."

"I tell you what, Rouget; you and your comrade had better land tomorrow morning, and set to work. You might say that three fishermen from Saint Florent, finding their boat too small, hired yours for a week to try their luck. If they succeed they will give you a fair price for her, if not they will simply pay the hire. You can say that the price is not much, but as it is as much as you can make at fishing, you thought that you might as well have an idle week on shore.

"Leigh and I can work her. As soon as day breaks you shall shoot your nets, so that we can see exactly how you work, and be able to catch an average amount of fish each day. I am sure that no one will know us in these disguises and, at any rate, we sha'n't be clumsy either with the sails or oars. You can say that, as we are strangers, you have agreed to sell our fish for us; which will be an excuse for your coming down to us, with the news of how you are getting on, each time that we come in."

"That will do very well, captain; but in that case, as a good deal of the fishing must be done at night, we had better get out the nets at once, and show you how they are managed."

For the next three days the work was carried on. Desailles had undertaken to obtain, from a friend of his on the committee of public safety, news of what was going on, and an early copy of the names of the prisoners told off for execution on the following day.

On the third day after their arrival, Martin and Leigh rowed up to the wood where they had directed the band to assemble and found that, with two or three exceptions, all had arrived. Four or five of them were at once told to return, to the estate and to the army, with a message from Jean begging all his tenants to leave, and join the party in hiding. Many of them would, no doubt, have returned to their homes within a day or two of the capture of Saumur. Letters had already been written to Bonchamp and Rochejaquelein to say that they were intending to attack the jail, and deliver a number of captives besides Jean's father and wife; and to beg that they would pick out some fifty or a hundred determined men, and send them on. On the morning of the sixth day, when the two sailors joined them, they were in a state of high excitement.

"There is great news, captain," Rouget said; "the whole city is in a state of tumult. It is reported that Cathelineau, with his army, is marching upon Nantes; and it is also reported--but this is not so certain--that Charette is marching to join them, with all his force."

"That is grand news, if true!" Jean exclaimed. "That would indeed favour our scheme! I doubt whether they will capture Nantes, for there is a big force here, and enough of them are seasoned troops to encourage the volunteers and National Guard to make a good fight of it. However we can, at any rate, take advantage of the attack to carry out our own plans. When the fighting is at the hottest, you may be sure that every armed man will be wanted at the work, and that there will not be many guards left behind at the prison. Our band here can dispose of them; and half a dozen men each, with fireballs, can add to the confusion by setting fire to warehouses and factories. The great thing now will be the powder."

"That we have managed already, captain," Medart replied. "As I told you, I spoke to Emile Moufflet the first morning I went ashore, and he said that it was at the magazines that his chum was employed. Yesterday evening he came to us, and said that if I gave him the two thousand francs that you had given me for the purpose, he would hand us over two barrels of powder, at eleven o'clock last night. We got them; and carried them, as you told us, to Brenon's; and helped him to bury them in his shed. We also got, as you ordered, a couple of yards of fuse."

"Bravo, Medart! everything seems going well for us."

The news of Cathelineau's advance was confirmed, on the following day, by the return of the lads who had been sent to fetch assistance. They brought with them eight or ten men from the estate; and reported that la

Rochejaquelein had remained at Saumur, with a portion of his army, to defend that town against a large force that Biron was assembling at Tours; while Cathelineau, having with him Bonchamp and Stofflet, was marching with the main force along the north bank of the river. They said, however, that his force was greatly diminished, for that large numbers of his men, objecting to fight outside their own country, had scattered to their villages. They, however, confirmed the news that Charette was reported to be marching north to join Cathelineau.

"That is the worst part of the whole business," Jean said, bitterly. "Our generals have no control over their men. They will fight when they want to fight, and return home when they choose. If Cathelineau had come along with a big force, he would have been joined by numbers of Bretons on the way and, if he had captured Nantes, by the greater part of Southern Brittany. Now that so many of his men have left him, it is quite possible that his attack may fail; and in that case the result will be disastrous. His army would disperse, the Blues would turn their whole force against la Rochejaquelein, and the cause that a fortnight since seemed half won would be lost.

"It shows, at any rate, that the idea of marching on Paris could not be carried out; for if men refuse to march, when they would be separated from their own country only by the river, to take Nantes, by which La Vendee is constantly threatened; certainly a greater portion still would have gone off to their homes, rather than join in what would seem to them so terrible an affair as a march on Paris. The peasants are good enough at fighting but, though they may win a victory by their bravery, they are certain to lose a campaign by their independent habits."

Feeling convinced that the approach of the Vendean army would enable their enterprise to be carried out by a much smaller body than had at first appeared necessary, Jean Martin told the two sailors that they had better abstain from broaching the matter to any more of their acquaintances. They had already obtained the adhesion of those of whose fidelity they felt absolutely assured and, should one of the others whom they intended to approach turn traitor, it would overthrow all chances of success, and might cause such alarm to the authorities that the executions would go on more rapidly than before, and the fate of their friends be precipitated.

Day by day the excitement in the city increased. Generals Beysser and Canclaux had, under their command, some ten thousand men. There was no chance of further reinforcements reaching them, but they felt confident that they could successfully defend the town with this force.

Had Charette marched to Ponts-de-Ce and, crossing there, joined Cathelineau, the danger would have been much more formidable; but instead of so doing he was advancing directly towards Nantes, on the south side of the river, the few places remaining in the hands of the Republicans being hastily evacuated on his approach. Here, however, he could give but slight aid to Cathelineau, for the bridge crossing the Loire could be defended by a comparatively small force, provided with cannon to sweep the approaches.

In order to reassure the townspeople and encourage the troops, the French generals, as the enemy approached, moved out with a large proportion of their force and threw up some intrenchments a mile and a half outside the town; feeling confident that they could withstand any attack in the open country.

As many of the peasants fled into Nantes, especially those who, in the villages, had rendered themselves obnoxious by their persecutions of those suspected of Royalist leanings, or who were personally obnoxious to them, Leigh was able to gather the whole of his party in the town. They were, like other peasants, to sleep in the open squares or down near the walls. They were always to go about in pairs, and to meet Pierre or Andre at places and hours arranged by them. They were supplied with money sufficient to buy bread, and were warned on no account to make themselves conspicuous in any way. With them were the men from Martin's estates who had answered to his summons.

Clothes had been bought for the twelve sailors engaged by Medart and Rouget. The fireballs had been prepared in the cabin of the fishing boat. Each of the fourteen fishermen was to carry two of these. Their leaders had carefully gone round the quarter, and had picked out the stores or warehouses into which the fireballs were to be flung. Among these were several wood yards No private houses were to be fired. That the flames would spread to these was likely enough, but at least there would be time for the women and children to escape.

Having decided upon the places to be fired, the sailors were one by one taken round, and the two buildings assigned to each pointed out, so that there would be no confusion or loss of time when the signal was given. Only two stores near the water had been marked down for destruction, namely, those belonging to the Martins. This was Leigh's work. As a firm the business was extinct. It was now the sole property of Jacques Martin, and there was no probability that Martin senior or Jean would ever recover a share in it. As in each of the stores a considerable quantity of spirits in addition to the wine was housed, not only would the loss be very heavy, but the interest excited in the vicinity would increase the confusion and alarm that would prevail.

Desailles was in daily communication with his friend. He learned that the list of prisoners was being taken, now, more in the order in which they stood. The farce of a trial had been gone through, in the case of Jean's wife, and she had of course been condemned. She stood a good deal lower on the list than his father. There was not much chance of the day of her execution being settled before the arrival of the Vendean forces. The number of names, however, above that of Monsieur Martin was rapidly decreasing, and there was imminent danger that he might be included in the fatal list before their arrival.

On the twenty-sixth of June the Vendeans arrived within a few miles of the town, and a formal summons was sent in to the generals. It was briefly refused. General Canclaux believed that he had so strengthened his advanced position, which was occupied by his best troops, that he would be able to repulse Cathelineau's force there. The Vendeans, however, being informed by the peasantry of the formidable nature of the intrenchments, decided that it would be dangerous to attack them; and consequently moved round so as to threaten the town from the north. Charette, on his side, moved his force up within cannon shot of the bridge.

At eight o'clock on the evening of the twenty-seventh, the sound of heavy firing was heard in Nantes. A column of the Vendeans had attacked Nort, a place lying to the north of the town. It was defended by six hundred troops of the line, and a body of the National Guard. They maintained themselves there during the night but, at daybreak, fell back upon the town, leaving their cannon behind them. A considerable body of troops moved out to cover their retreat.

Confident that the attack would begin that evening, every preparation for action was made by Jean and Leigh. The powder barrels were dug up, and holes bored for the fuses. The boys were all informed that the hour for action was at hand; and were ordered to lie down, at nightfall, in the open space facing the front of the prison, scattering themselves among others who would be sleeping there or, in expectation of the attack on the town beginning, would be standing in groups listening for it. Leigh would be among them.

As the hour neared twelve they were to gather in a body. The sailors were not to begin their work until the attack on the town commenced in earnest. Jean, with his twelve tenants, was to come up at twelve. The exact moment for the attack was to be decided upon by the progress made by the fires. When these had had their effect, Leigh was to fall upon the guard round the prison; and Jean, with his band, to run forward to the gate, plant the powder barrels against it, light the fuse and run back.

As soon as they had killed or driven away the guard, Leigh's party were to return to the front. There Andre, with half the band, were to station themselves, and to hold the gate against any armed body that might arrive; while Leigh, with the others, entered the prison and aided, if necessary, to overpower the warders and blow open the doors of the cells. The prisoners were all to be told that Charette's army was on the other side of the Loire, and that their best plan was to make their way down to the river, seize boats, and get across.

At five o'clock in the afternoon Charette's guns opened against the barricades that had been thrown up at the bridge. Canclaux, seeing that the attack upon the north had rendered it useless for him to retain the advanced post, ordered the troops there to fall back into the town, at ten o'clock in the evening; and at eleven the whole garrison were concentrated in Nantes.

Finding that, with the exception of the cannonade on both sides across the river, all remained quiet, Leigh passed the word round among his followers to remain as they were, until further orders. Jean and his men came up by twos and threes before twelve; and these, too, lay down as if to sleep, or seated themselves on the steps of the houses. Few of the inhabitants had retired to rest. They knew that at any moment the storm might break, and some awaited the attack with hope that the time of their release from the tyranny under which they had, for months, groaned, had come; while others trembled at the thought of the vengeance that, if the town were taken, would fall upon those who had been concerned in what had passed.

Martin and Desailles presently joined Leigh. As the time went on they began to fear that, for some reason or other, the Vendeans had determined to delay their attack until the next day. At half past two Charette's cannonade redoubled in vigour, and the rattle of musketry showed that his troops were advancing. The batteries of the defenders opened with equal violence, and their musketry answered that of the assailants on the opposite bank.

"I think that that must be the signal for Cathelineau to begin," Martin said.

And, ten minutes later, the attack commenced with fury upon the gates of Vannes, Rennes, and that by the river.

Every window was opened, and anxious faces looked out. The night was dark, and the few oil lamps alone threw a feeble light on the square. Suddenly a broad glare rose to the west, and the murmur, "There is a house on fire!" passed from mouth to mouth. In another few minutes flames were seen rising at a dozen points, and a cry of consternation arose.

"The brigands have entered the town! They are going to burn it to the ground."

Man after man of the little group of National Guards, who had been gathered talking in front of the door of the prison, was seen to detach himself from it and to move quietly away. Then those at the windows noticed four or five parties of men move forward, from among those who were standing talking; when within a short distance of the guard there was a sharp command, and these groups all rushed towards the gates together. There were shouts and cries, and then there was silence. Taken wholly by surprise, the guard had fallen under the knives of the Vendeans without having had time to fire a shot.

Then the majority of their assailants ran off, half one way, half the other, following the wall of the prison. Two pistol shots were fired, a moment later. The men who had remained at the gate drew back for some distance. There was a short pause, and then a tremendous explosion. All the people gathered in the place, save those who had carried out the affair, fled with cries of terror. Then Jean and his party dashed forward towards the shattered gates and entered the prison, and shot or cut down the frightened warders as these came running out, dazed and bewildered at the sound of the explosion. Jean seized one of them by the throat.

"Where are the keys kept? Answer, or I will blow out your brains!"

The frightened ruffian at once led the way to the chief warder's room. He had already fallen, being one of the first to run down. There were two bunches of keys.

"These are of the doors of the corridors," the man said, taking down one bunch. "The others are of the cells."

"Now, go before us and open them all--every one, mind."

They were soon joined by Leigh with his party, who had made short work of the few guards who remained at their post outside the prison.

"Set your men to blow in the doors," Jean said; "It would take half an hour to unlock them all, at this rate."

Pistols were at once applied to the keyholes, and the locks destroyed. There were a few separate cells, but the prisoners were for the most part crowded, twenty or thirty together, in the larger rooms. As he entered each room, Leigh shouted the directions agreed on to the prisoners. In a short time he came upon Jean who, as had been arranged, had first gone to the rooms where his father and Patsey were confined. Jean started with these at once, with six of his men, leaving Leigh and Desailles to see to the release of the rest of the prisoners.

As soon as all rooms had been burst open or unlocked, he and his party, with that at the gate, hurried away. The streets were light, as a sheet of flame rose from the stores of Jacques Martin. The musketry fire on the wharves showed that there were troops stationed there. As they hurried along, the shouts of alarm which rose in the town showed that the news of the attack upon the prison had spread rapidly. As soon as the released prisoners knew that they were well above the bridge, and the silence on the wharves showed that none of the troops were stationed there, shouts of delight arose. There were a good many boats moored to the bank, and the fugitives threw themselves into these.

"Get out your oars and row straight across," Leigh shouted. "If you drift down the stream, you will come under the fire of the troops there."

Then, having done their work, he and his band went up a hundred yards farther, where they knew that three large boats were lying. In these they took their places and started to row across the river and, in five minutes, reached the opposite bank. They sprang out, with a shout of joy at finding themselves again in their own country. Most of the fugitives also gained the opposite bank; but some boats, in which there were but few capable of handling the oars, drifted down the river, and lost most of their number from the fire of the troops on the bank, before they could land among the men of Charette's army.

Leigh with his boys soon joined the other party, who had landed a hundred yards higher up. It was a joyful meeting, indeed, between him and Patsey.

"Jean tells me it is all your doing that we have been got out," she said. "I felt sure you would manage it, somehow."

They had already arranged their plans. Jean, with his wife and father and his twelve men, was to start at once for Parthenay, where Lescure was in command. Leigh had determined to join Cathelineau, with as many of his band as chose to accompany him. Desailles would go with Jean.

The boys, on the choice being given them, almost all decided to accompany Leigh. They were excited at the success that had attended them, and the tremendous roll of fire round the town showed how fiercely their countrymen were fighting, and they longed to join in the conflict.

Saying goodbye to those who were going, Leigh and his party towed one of the boats a mile up the river, and then crossing, soon joined the party engaged. The Vendeans had already advanced some distance, but every house and garden was fiercely contested. Hour after hour passed, and the troops were beginning to be discouraged. It was broad daylight now, and the Vendeans pressed forward at all points, more hotly than ever.

The troops were falling into disorder, and would soon have become a disorganized mass; when a musket ball, fired from a window, struck Cathelineau in the breast as, with his officers, who had been considerably increased in number owing to the many gentlemen who had joined him at Saumur, he was leading on his troops.

A cry of dismay rose from those who saw him fall, and the news spread like wildfire among the peasants, who regarded him with an almost superstitious reverence, and had a firm belief that he was protected by Heaven from the balls of his enemies. His loss seemed to them an irretrievable misfortune. The fierceness of their attack diminished. Their ardour was gone, and the Blues, gaining courage as their assailants ceased to press them, took the offensive.

They met with but little opposition. The Vendean army, lately on the point of being victorious, was already breaking up and, ere long, was scattered over the country, its retreat being undisturbed by the enemy, who could scarcely believe their own good fortune at having succeeded, when all had seemed lost.

Cathelineau was carried off; but died, a fortnight later, from the effects of the wound. His death was a terrible blow to the cause. The failure to take Nantes had, in itself, been a great misfortune; but the Vendeans had suffered no more heavily than the enemy and, had Cathelineau been but spared, matters might still have gone well with them. The effect of his death, however, was for the time to dishearten the peasantry utterly; and had at this time terms of peace, which would have permitted them to enjoy the exercise of their religion, and to be free from conscription, been offered to them, they would gladly have been accepted.

Charette, after he saw that the attack upon Nantes from the north side of the river had failed, fell back with his force, as before, into Lower Poitou. The Vendeans, now under Bonchamp, who had also been wounded, retired along the north bank of the Loire, crossing the river at various points as they could find boats.

Before joining in the fight, Leigh had told his band that, in the event of failure, he should recross the river in the boat that had brought them over. They had all kept near him during the struggle. Eight of them had fallen, several others were wounded, and he himself had received a musket ball in the shoulder. As soon as he saw that the battle was lost, he withdrew from it and made his way with the boys to the river bank; recrossed the stream, and struck across the country. After proceeding some six miles they entered a wood, and lay down and slept for some hours, and then marched to Parthenay.

Here the band broke up and proceeded to their homes; while Leigh made his way to Lescure's headquarters, learned where his friends were lodged, and joined them.

Patsey gave a cry of alarm as he entered. Fugitives had arrived before him, and it was already known that the attack on Nantes had failed, and that Cathelineau was mortally wounded.

"What is it, Leigh?"

"I am wounded in the shoulder. It is nothing very serious, I think; though I suppose I sha'n't be able to hold a sword for some time."

A surgeon was soon fetched, the ball extracted, and the wound bandaged; and they then sat down to talk over the events that had occurred. Since they had been separated, Monsieur Martin had become a broken man. The fact that his son, who assuredly had it in his power to protect him, had given him over to the terrible tribunal, had been a harder blow to him than the prospect of death; and even the devotion that had been shown by Jean scarcely sufficed to comfort him.

Patsey was pale and thin. Her imprisonment had told upon her and, still more, the thought of what Jean must be suffering on her account, and her uncertainty as to the fate of her child. But even the twenty-four hours that had elapsed since she had left her prison had done much for her. The news that the child was safe and well had taken a load off her mind; and she felt proud, indeed, that her release, and that of so many others of her fellow prisoners, had been brought about by the devotion of her husband and her brother. Before the day was out, she was laughing and chatting as if nothing had happened.

On the following morning they started early, and reached home in the afternoon. They were received with delight by their people, although many of these had lost relations in the recent battles. A house in the village was placed at their disposal, Patsey riding straight on to see her child; with which, and its faithful nurse, she soon returned.

"And now, Jean," Patsey said when, with the cure and Jules Desailles, they sat down for a quiet talk that evening, "what is to be the next thing?"

"You should ask the Blues that," he replied. "So far as I can see, it will be a repetition of what has taken place. They will invade us again, and probably we shall beat them back. Each time they will come with larger forces and, at last, I suppose we shall have to endeavour to make our way to England. I am afraid there can be no question that that will be the end of it. Fight as we may, we cannot withstand the whole strength of France."

"Why can we not fly at once?" Monsieur Martin asked.

"The difficulty in reaching the coast, and of getting a passage, would be immense. Besides, so long as La Vendee resists, so long is it my duty to fight; and I am sure that Patsey would not wish me to do otherwise. I have been in it from the first, and must stay until the end, if I am not killed before that comes. If it were possible to send you and Patsey and Leigh away to England, I would gladly do so; but I am sure that she would not go, and I think I may say the same for Leigh."

"Certainly, Jean; as long as you stay, I stay. My life is far less important than yours, for I have no one dependent upon me. I quite agree with you that the war can end in only one way; but till that comes, all those who have been the leaders of these poor peasants ought to hold by them."

"I agree entirely with you both," Patsey added, and there was no more to be said.

Chapter 12
A Series Of Victories

More formidable foes than the peasants had yet met were approaching La Vendee. Mayence had surrendered to the allies, and the garrison there, which was a large one, composed of veteran troops, was allowed to march away, on each man taking an oath that he would not again serve on the frontier.

Outside France there was no idea of the desperate struggle that was going on in La Vendee. Had it been known, in England, that it needed but little aid for Brittany and La Vendee to successfully oppose the efforts of the Republic, men, money, arms, and ammunition would no doubt have been sent; but unfortunately the leaders of the insurrection, occupied as they were with the efforts they were making, had taken no steps to send a statement of the real facts of the case to the English government. The ports were all in the hands of the Republicans and, although in Paris public attention was concentrated on the struggle, the British government was very badly informed as to what was passing there. Had the allies been aware of it, the terms granted to the garrison at Mayence would have been very different; and they would either have been held as prisoners, or been compelled to take the oath that they would, in future, not serve the Republic in any way, in arms.

As it was, they were free to act in France, and were already on the march towards La Vendee. As before, arrangements were made for the district to be attacked simultaneously on all sides. La Rochejaquelein was so much weakened by the return of the peasants to their homes that he was obliged to evacuate Saumur, and this town was taken possession of by the division from Tours, consisting of twelve thousand five hundred infantry, sixteen hundred cavalry, and four hundred artillerymen, under General Menou.

The division of Niort comprised fifteen thousand six hundred infantry, and thirteen hundred and eighty cavalry. It was commanded by Chalbos, having Westermann with him. At Sables were four thousand three hundred infantry, two hundred and fifty cavalry, and three hundred artillery. They were commanded by General Boulard.

There was but small breathing time for the Vendeans. Westermann had moved towards Parthenay with a strong force and, but a few hours after the Martins had left it, Lescure was forced to fall back from the town. This was occupied by the Blues. They pillaged and burned a village near, although no opposition had been offered, and then sent off a force which burned Lescure's chateau at Clisson.

The Martins were engaged in conversation when a messenger ran in.

"I have an order from Monsieur Lescure," he said. "The church bells are to be rung throughout the district."

All started to their feet.

"Already?" Jean exclaimed. "Why, what has happened?"

"We have fallen back from Parthenay. The Blues under Westermann, eight thousand strong, have already occupied the town. The general's orders are that all are to join him at Moulin, in two days' time. Messengers have been despatched all over the country, and Monsieur de la Rochejaquelein has been sent for, to join General Lescure at Moulin."

"That gives us twenty-four hours, then," Jean said, with a sigh of content. "I will see that your message is carried on to all the villages near. There are plenty of boys of twelve or fourteen about the place."

But the bells rang that night to deaf ears. Many of the peasants were still absent, others had returned but a few hours before, worn out and dispirited. But when on the following day the news came that Westermann's troops were burning villages, and slaying all who fell into their hands, and that Monsieur de Lescure's chateau had been burnt, fury and indignation again fired them and, that night, the greater part of them set out for Moulin.

"I wonder what has become of our horses," Jean said, as he prepared to start. "We shall never hear any more of those we left at Nantes. We must go on foot this time, and trust to getting hold of a couple of horses, the first time we defeat the Blues."

He had that day been over with Patsey, her child, his father, the nurse, and Francois to the peasant's house, deep in the forest, to which he had before arranged that she should go, in case of need. All the party were dressed as peasants. The man and woman from whom the house was hired removed to another hut, a quarter of a mile away. Francois was to go down every day in the cart to the village, to get news and letters and buy provisions. The cure had arranged to send off one of the village boys, the moment that he heard that any party of the Blues were approaching; when the whole of the occupants of the village and the farms around it would be obliged to take to the woods, for it was evident that neither age nor sex was respected by Westermann's troops.

It was morning when Jean, Leigh, and Desailles arrived at Moulin. They were warmly received by Rochejaquelein and Bonchamp, to whom Jean introduced Desailles as a new comrade.

"I know nothing of fighting," the latter said; "but, gentlemen, I shall do my best."

"That is all that anyone can do," Rochejaquelein said heartily. "We may say that none of us, with the exception of Monsieur Bonchamp and a few others, had any experience in fighting when we began; but we have done pretty well, on the whole."

"Do you think that we have much chance of holding this place?" Jean asked. "They told us, as we came in, that at present there are not much more than eight thousand men here; and Westermann, they say, has about as many."

"That is so," Bonchamp said, "and I do not expect that we shall beat them; but we must fight, or they will march through the country, wasting and destroying as they go. It is only by showing them that we are still formidable, and that they must keep together and be prudent and cautious, that we can maintain ourselves. A succession of blows, even of light ones, will break a rock."

At two o'clock the enemy's forces approached, and the engagement soon became hot. Every hedge was lined by the peasants, every position strongly defended, and only evacuated when the horns gave the signal. At the end of two hours Westermann, after losing a considerable number of men, approached ground where his cavalry could come into play; and the leaders of all the bands had been warned that, when they fell back to this point, the horn was to be sounded three times, and that resistance was to cease at once and the bands disperse, to meet at a given point, two hours later. Seven of the ten cannon they had with them were safely carried off; and although compelled to retire from their position, the peasants were well satisfied with having withstood, so long, the attack of an equal number of troops, supported by an artillery much superior to their own.

Leigh had taken no part in the actual fighting. His right arm was tightly strapped, and bandaged across his chest; and he therefore acted only as the general's aide-de-camp.

"I'll tell you what it is, Jules," Jean said to Desailles, as they retired from the field; "if you are going to expose yourself in the way you have done today, your fighting will be over before long. When it comes to leading the peasants to an attack, one must necessarily set the men an example; but when on the defence, you see, the peasants all lie down behind the hedges and bushes, and show themselves as little as possible.

"And there were you, walking about as if you were in the principal street in Nantes! I do not say that we must not expose ourselves a good deal more than the peasants, in order to encourage them; but there is a limit to all things, and one must remember that we are very short of officers, and that the peasants, brave as they are, would be useless without someone to direct them."

"I have no doubt but you are right, Jean," Desailles said with a laugh; "but in fact, I don't remember giving a thought to the matter. I was almost bewildered by the roar of the battle and the whistling of the bullets. I felt like a man who had taken too much wine; which, in my student days, happened to me more than once. My blood seemed to rush through my veins, and I would have given anything for the order to come for us to throw ourselves upon the enemy."

"You will get over that," Jean laughed, "but the same feeling is strong among the men. One can see how eager they are for the order to charge. They use their muskets, but it is to use their bayonets that they are panting. They would make grand soldiers, if they were but well drilled and disciplined.

"Unless I am mistaken, you will see them at their favourite work, before many days are over. Westermann will get to Chatillon tonight. When he gets there, he will find no provisions for his troops, and will begin to wonder whether he is wise in thus penetrating so far into a nest of hornets.

"Bonchamp will give him two or three days to forget the mauling that we have given him. By that time our force will have increased, and it will be well for Westermann if he manages to carry half his force back with him."

The news of the burning of la Rochejaquelein's chateau, on the following day, excited the liveliest indignation. The young count himself received the news with greater indifference than did those around him.

"When a man carries his life in his hand, every day," he said, "he does not fret over the loss of a house. I do not suppose that I should ever have sat down quietly in possession of it, and the cousin who is my heir may have to wait a number of years before, if ever, he comes to take possession of the estate. Had circumstances been different, the loss of the old chateau, where my family have lived for so many years, would have been very grievous to me; but at present it affects me comparatively little.

"It is lucky that I sent off four men, directly the fight was over, with a letter to my steward, charging him to hand over to them the four horses that still remained in my stables. They arrived here an hour ago. I guessed that the Blues would be paying a visit there in my absence.

"One of them is for you, Monsieur Martin, and one for Leigh; the others I shall keep as spare chargers. I have had two shot under me already, and am likely to have more. In the meantime, if your friend Monsieur Desailles likes to ride one, it is at his service."

"I thank you very much, marquis," Jules said; "but I would prefer trusting to my own legs. My profession has been a peaceful one, and I have never yet mounted a horse, and certainly should feel utterly out of my element, in the saddle, with an animal under me excited almost to madness by the sounds of battle. Of the two, I think that I should prefer being on a ship, during a storm."

Rochejaquelein laughed.

"It is all a matter of training," he said. "As for me I feel twice the man, on horseback, that I do on foot. I have never tried fighting on foot, yet; and I should certainly feel altogether out of my element, the first time that I attempted it.

"However, I will not press the animal on you. I shall send it and the other to some cottage, in the heart of the woods, whence I can have them fetched when needed."

"I am sure that we are greatly obliged to you," Jean said. "As I told you, when relating our adventure in Nantes, we had to leave our horses behind us there though, had we captured the town, we should have recovered them. As it is, the Blues carried off the two I had left behind at the chateau, and I could only buy one other, as we came through. That I detailed for the use of my wife. I certainly had not expected to obtain another, until we captured some from the enemy. We are heartily obliged to you, not only for your generous gift, but for your thoughtful kindness in sending for them for us."

"Say not another word," Rochejaquelein said. "You are a sailor and I am a soldier, and between us there is no occasion for thanks or compliments. You would have done the same for me, and I am glad to be able to set you both on horseback again. And indeed, I am not sure that I was not a little selfish in the matter; for yesterday I missed the company of your brother-in-law greatly, and felt that I would give a good deal to hear his cheery laugh, and confident tone."

As usual, the army dispersed after its victory; but there were but a few days' quiet, for on the fourteenth it gathered to oppose the advance of a strong French column, from Brissac; and on the morning of the fifteenth, early, just as the troops were getting into movement, the Vendeans burst down upon them.

Their numbers were not large, for the notice had been short, and only the peasants of the surrounding district had had time to gather. Nevertheless they attacked with such energy, led by Rochejaquelein and d'Elbee, that they fought their way into the middle of the camp, captured the headquarters with its correspondence and treasury, and scattered several battalions in utter confusion.

On the return of the advanced guard, under Santerre, the situation changed; the fugitives were rallied and, after long and fierce fighting, the Vendeans drew off.

"We must admit another failure," said Rochejaquelein; who had, with his little troop of mounted men, been in the thick of the fight; charging again and again into the midst of the enemy, and covering the retreat, when it began, by opposing a determined front to the enemy's cavalry; "a failure, but a glorious one. They were superior to us in numbers; and yet, if it hadn't been that their advanced guard returned while our men were scattered, intent upon the plunder of their headquarters, we should have won the day. However, we shall have reinforcements up, in a couple of days."

On the seventeenth, the French column resumed its march. Santerre's command led the way to Vihiers, which they reached without opposition. The rest of the division arrived in the afternoon. They had left, at their previous halting place, the heavy baggage; with a portion of their artillery ammunition. Scarcely had they arrived at Vihiers when a tremendous explosion told them that the guard left behind had been overpowered, and their store of ammunition destroyed.

A feeling of uneasiness and alarm spread through the army. Santerre's battalion were at once attacked by Rochejaquelein, who had but a small body of men with him, but who thought to take advantage of the alarm which the explosion would naturally cause among the enemy. Santerre's battalion, however, stood firm, and the Vendeans were drawn off. In the night, however, the main body of the peasants arrived and, at one o'clock next day, made their attack.

Menou himself, with the rest of his command, had now come up. Some of the battalions, as before, stood steadily; but the rest of the army, dispirited by the perseverance with which the Vendeans, in spite of failure and losses, were ever ready to renew their attack, speedily lost heart.

In two hours the right fell back in disorder, the panic spread and, in a short time, the rout became general. In vain the officers endeavoured to check the fugitives. So great was their terror that, in three hours, the panic stricken mob traversed the distance between Vihiers and Saumur.

Thus the second great invasion of La Vendee had met with no greater success than the first. The two strong columns that had advanced, in full confidence of success, had returned utterly discomfited. Westermann's division had been all but annihilated. The army from Saumur had lost great numbers of men, and had for the time ceased to be a military body. The Bocage, with its sombre woods, its thick hedges, and its brave population, seemed destined to become the grave of the Republican army; and the order to advance into it was, in itself, sufficient to shake the courage of those who boasted so loudly, when at a distance.

It was the grave, too, of the reputation of the French generals. One after another they had tried, failed, and been disgraced. The first general, Marce, was superseded by Berruyer; Berruyer by Biron, who was recalled and guillotined. Westermann was also tried, but having powerful friends, was acquitted. Generals of divisions had come and gone in numbers. Some had been dismissed. Some, at their own urgent request, allowed to return to the districts they commanded before the outbreak of the insurrection. But one and all had failed. One and all, too, had never ceased, from the time they joined the army of invasion, to send report after report to the Convention, complaining of the untrustworthiness of the troops, the bad conduct and uselessness of the officers, and the want of a sufficient staff to maintain discipline and restore order.

Indeed, the bulk of the revolutionary troops possessed little more discipline than the Vendeans themselves and, being uninspired, as were the latter, by a feeling either of religion or of patriotic enthusiasm, they were no match for men who were willing to give their lives for the cause.

The Vendeans were far better armed than when they commenced the struggle. Then the proportion of men who were possessed of muskets or firearms of any kind was extremely small; but now, thanks to the immense quantity which had been captured in the hands of prisoners, thrown away by fugitives, or found in the storehouses of the towns, there were sufficient to supply almost every man of the population with firearms; and in addition, they possessed a good many pieces of artillery.

Unfortunately they had learned little during the four months' fighting. Their methods were unchanged. Love of home overpowered all other considerations; and after a victory, as after a defeat, they hurried away, leaving with their generals only the officers and a small body of men, who were either emigres who had returned from England to take part in the struggle, or Royalists who had made their way from distant parts of France, for the same purpose.

After the capture of Saumur, too, a good many Swiss and Germans, belonging to a cavalry regiment formed of foreigners, had deserted and joined the Vendeans. Thus a small nucleus of an army held together, swelling only when the church bells summoned the peasants to take up arms for a few days.

But while the Royalists of La Vendee remained quiescent, after they had expelled the invaders; the Republicans, more alarmed than ever, were making the most tremendous efforts to stamp out the insurrection.

Beysser, who had commanded at Nantes, was appointed to succeed Menou. Orders were given that the forests and hedges of La Vendee were all to be levelled, the crops destroyed, the cattle seized, and the goods of the insurgents confiscated. An enormous number of carts were collected to carry faggots, tar, and other combustibles into La Vendee, for setting fire to the woods. It was actually proposed to destroy the whole male population, to deport the women and children, and to repeople La Vendee from other parts of France, from which immigrants would be attracted by offers of free land and houses. Santerre suggested that poisonous gases should be inclosed in suitable vessels, and fired into the district to poison the atmosphere.

Carrier, the infamous scoundrel who had been appointed commissioner at Nantes, proposed an equally villainous scheme; namely, that great quantities of bread, mixed with arsenic, should be baked and scattered broadcast, so that the starving people might eat it and be destroyed, wholesale. This would have been carried out, had it not been vigorously opposed by General Kleber, who had now taken the command of one of the armies of the invasion.

The rest of July and the first half of August passed comparatively quietly. General Toncq advanced with a column into La Vendee, and fought two or three battles, in which he generally gained successes over the peasants; but with this exception, no forward movement was made, and the majority of the peasants remained undisturbed in their homes.

Soon, however, from all sides, the flood of invaders poured in. No fewer than two hundred thousand men were now under the orders of the French generals, and advanced from different directions, in all cases carrying out the orders of the Convention, to devastate the country, burn down the woods, destroy the crops, and slay the inhabitants. Five armies moved forward simultaneously, that commanded by Kleber consisting of the veteran battalions of Mayence.

But everywhere they were met. Charette had marched to the aid of the Vendeans of the north, and the country was divided into four districts, commanded by Charette, Bonchamp, Lescure, and la Rochejaquelein. Each of these strove to defend his own district.

The war now assumed a terrible aspect. Maddened by the atrocities perpetrated upon them, the peasants no longer gave quarter to those who fell into their hands and, in their despair, performed prodigies of valour. They had not now, as at the commencement of the war the superiority in numbers. Instead of fighting generally four to one against the Blues, the latter now exceeded them in the same proportion.

But the peasants had changed their tactics. Instead of rushing impetuously upon the enemy's lines, and hurling themselves upon his artillery, they utilized the natural features of their country. As the Republican columns marched along, believing that there was no enemy near, they would hear the sound of a horn, and from behind every hedge, every thicket, every tree, a stream of musketry would break out. Very soon the column would fall into confusion. The lanes would be blocked with dead horses and immovable waggons. In vain would the soldiers try to force their way through the hedges, and to return the fire of their invisible foes. Then, as suddenly as the attack commenced, the peasants would leap from their shelter and, with knife and bayonet, carry havoc among their enemies.

These tactics prevailed over numbers, even when, as in the case of Kleber's division, the numbers possessed military discipline, training, and high reputation. For a month, fighting was almost continuous and, at the end of that time, to the stupefaction of the Convention, their two hundred thousand troops were driven out of La Vendee, at every point, by a fourth of that number of undisciplined peasants. Never, perhaps, in the history of military warfare did enthusiasm and valour accomplish such a marvel.

The second half of September was spent by the peasants at their homes, rejoicing and returning thanks for their success; but already a heavy blow was being struck at their cause. Charette, hotheaded, impetuous, and self confident, had always preferred carrying out his own plans, without regard to those of the leaders in Upper Vendee; and he now quarrelled with them as to the course that had best be pursued, and left, with the forces that he had brought with him, to renew the war in the south.

But although the peasants rejoiced, their leaders knew that the struggle could not long continue. The number of fighting men--that is to say, of the whole male population of La Vendee capable of bearing arms--had diminished terribly; indeed, the number that originally responded to the summons of the church bells was decreased by fully a half. Food was scarce.

Owing to the continued absence of the peasants the harvest had, in many places, not been garnered; and wherever the Republican troops had passed, the destruction had been complete. A large portion of the population were homeless. The very movements of the Vendeans were hampered by the crowds of women and children who, with the few belongings that they had saved, packed in their little carts, wandered almost aimlessly through the country. Many of the towns were in ruins, and deserted; in all save a few secluded spots, as yet unvisited by the Republicans, want and misery were universal.

There was no thought of surrender, but among chiefs and peasants alike the idea that, as a last resource, it would be necessary to abandon La Vendee altogether, and to take refuge in Brittany, where the vast majority of the population were favourable to them, gradually gained ground.

Generals Beysser, Canclaux, and Dubayet were recalled by the Convention for their failure to obtain success, and l'Echelle was appointed to the command, having Kleber and Westermann as leaders of his principal divisions.

Jean Martin and Leigh had joined their friends, in their retreat in the forest, after the repulse of all the Republican columns. They had heard, while engaged in the thick of the fighting, of the death of Monsieur Martin. He had never recovered from the effects of his imprisonment at Nantes, and instead of gaining strength he had become weaker and weaker. The terrible uncertainty of the position, the news that constantly arrived of desperate battles, and the conviction that in the end the Vendeans would be crushed, told heavily upon him. He took to his bed, and sank gradually.

"I am not sorry, my child," he said to Patsey, the day before he died, "that I am going to leave you. I was wrong in not taking Jean's advice, and sailing for England with my wife and daughter. However, it is useless to think of that, now.

"I can see terrible times in store for all here. It is evident that no mercy is to be shown to the Vendeans. It has been decreed by the Convention that they are to be hunted down like wild beasts.

"Had I lived, I should have been a terrible burden to you. I should have hampered your movements and destroyed any chance, whatever, that you might have of escaping from these fiends. It would have been impossible for me to have supported the fatigues and hardships of a flight, and I should have been the means of bringing destruction on you all. It is therefore better, in every respect, that I should go.

"I pray that Heaven will protect you and Jean and your brave brother, and enable you to reach England in safety. You will bear my last message to my wife and Louise. You will tell them that my last thought was of them, my last feeling one of gratitude to God that they are in safety, and that I have been permitted to die in peace and quiet."

"It is a sad homecoming this time, Jean," Patsey said, as her husband and Leigh rode up to the door.

"It is indeed, Patsey; and yet, even when the news came to me, I could scarcely grieve that it was so. I had seen how he was fading when I went away, and was not surprised when I heard that he had gone. For me it is one care, one anxiety, the less, in future.

"Patsey, we will be together. I cannot leave you here, when Leigh and I are away. The child shall go with us and, when all is lost, we will escape or die together."

"I am glad to hear you say so, Jean. It has been terrible waiting here, and knowing that you were in the midst of dangers, and that even while I thought of you, you might be lying dead. I shall be glad, indeed, to share your fate, whatever it is."

For three weeks the little party lived quietly in the cottage. There were many discussions as to the future. It was agreed that, in case of a final reverse, it would be better that they should travel alone.

"The more of us there are, the more certain to attract observation," Jean said. "We must go without Francois and Marthe. Their chance of safety will be greater if they either return to their villages, or take up their abode with the family of some woodman--or rather, Marthe's safety would be greater. As to Francois, he has long been eager to join in the fighting, and it is only his fidelity that has constrained him to remain in what he considers is a disgraceful position, when every other man who can bear arms is fighting. We will therefore take him with us and, when the day of battle comes, he will join the fighting men and, if we are defeated, must care for his own safety.

"When we fight, I shall always leave you at a village, a mile or two away. You will have the horse ready to mount, and we shall join you at once, if we are defeated."

"We ought to be disguised, Jean," Leigh said.

"It would be well," Jean said, "but I hardly see what disguise would be of use to us. Certainly not that of peasants, for in that dress we should be shot down, without question, by the first party of Blues we came across.

Even if we succeed in reaching the river and crossing it, we may be sure that the authorities will be everywhere on the lookout for fugitive peasants. It would be better to be shot, at once, than to await in prison death by the guillotine."

"I should say that it does not matter a bit how we are dressed, till we reach the river. We know now pretty nearly every lane in the country," Leigh said, "and I should think that we ought to be able to reach the Loire."

"That is where the difficulty will begin. In the first place there will be the trouble of crossing, and then that of making our way through the country. Certainly we could not do so as Vendean peasants."

"I should say, Jean, that the best disguises would be those of fairly well-to-do townspeople; something like those we wore into Nantes, but rather less formal--the sort of thing that ordinary tradesmen, without any strong political feeling either way, would wear. I don't say that we shall not be suspected, however we are dressed, because no one in his senses would be travelling about just at present; but when once we get beyond Tours, if we go that way, we might pass without much notice.

"Which way do you think that we ought to go, Jean?"

Jean shrugged his shoulders.

"I don't see that there is any choice. There would be very little chance of escaping from any of the ports of Brittany, and La Rochelle would be still more hopeless. As far south as Bordeaux we should be in a comparatively peaceful country, and I should hope to find friends there. The eastern frontier is of course the safest to cross, but the distance is very great and, in the towns near the border, a very sharp lookout is kept to prevent emigres escaping.

"There is a rumour that Lyons has declared against the Convention, but if we got there it is certain that it would be but La Vendee over again. Lyons cannot resist all France and, as soon as they have done with us here, they will be able to send any number of troops to stamp out these risings.

"Undoubtedly, if we could get there, Toulon would be the best place. I have heard for certain that they have driven out the extreme party, and have admitted the English fleet. Once there, we should be able to take berths in a ship bound somewhere abroad--it matters little where--and thence get a passage to England. Most probably we shall be able to arrange to go direct from Toulon, for there are sure to be vessels coming and going with stores for the British fleet."

"But that would be a terrible journey, Jean," his wife said.

"Yes, I think that would be quite out of the question. It seems to me that our best chance would be either to cross the Loire and then make for Le Mans, and so up through Alencon to Honfleur--that way we should be east of the disturbed district--or, if we found that a vast number of fugitives had made their way into Brittany, as is almost certain to be the case, we might bear more to the east, and go up through Vendome and Chartres and Evreux, and then branch off and strike the Seine near Honfleur. In that case we should be outside the district where they would be searching for fugitives from here.

"Once on the seashore, or on the Seine, it would be hard if we could not steal a fishing boat, and cross the Channel. However, one must of course be guided by circumstances. Still, I do think that it would be as well to buy the disguises Leigh suggests, without loss of time. I will ride over to Chatillon, tomorrow, and get them."

Chapter 13
Across The Loire

Marthe was filled with grief, when she heard that it had been decided that it was better that she should return to her native village; but her mistress pointed out to her that, if all went well, she could rejoin them. If things went badly, and they escaped, they would send for her wherever they might be; but in case disaster compelled them to fly, three persons were as many as could hope to travel together, without exciting suspicion. The nurse however begged that, at any rate, she might go with them to the headquarters of the army.

"Everyone is going," she said; "and they say that, if we are beaten in the next battle, they will cross the Loire and take refuge in Brittany, for the Blues will not leave a soul alive in La Vendee. I should have nowhere to go to here, and will keep with the others, whatever happens. If you are with them, madame, I can rejoin you; if not, I hope to be with you, afterward."

It was indeed an exodus, rather than the gathering of an army, that was taking place. The atrocities committed by the invaders, the destruction of every village, the clouds of smoke which ascended from the burning woods, created so terrible a scare among the peasants that the greater portion of the villages and farms were entirely deserted, and every road leading to Chollet, which was the rendezvous where the fighting men were ordered to gather, was crowded with fugitives. Francois walked by the horse's head. Patsey, the nurse, and the child, with a trunk containing articles of absolute necessity, occupied the cart. Jean and Leigh rode ahead.

The company of Cathelineau's scouts no longer existed. More than half of them had fallen in the late battles. Their services were no longer required as scouts, and the survivors had joined their fathers and brothers, and formed part of the command of Bonchamp.

On the fourteenth of October the enemy's columns were closing in upon Chollet. Those round Mortagne were marching forward, when the advanced guard, under General Beaupuy, were suddenly attacked by the Vendeans, while entangled in the lanes. The head of the column fought well; but those in the rear, finding themselves also attacked, and fearing that the retreat would be cut off, retired hastily to Mortagne. The column would have been destroyed, had not Beaupuy promptly sent up large reinforcements. After a long and obstinate fight the Vendeans were driven from the woods and, the Republican artillery opening upon them, they were compelled to retire to Chollet.

Here no halt was made. Kleber had also been fiercely attacked, but had also, though with much difficulty, repulsed his assailants. The next morning the Republicans entered Chollet, which they found deserted by the enemy.

On the seventeenth, their whole force being now concentrated there, they were about to move forward towards Beaupreau; when the advanced guard was hotly attacked and, in a short time, the combat became general. For a time the Vendeans bore down all opposition, but as the whole of the Republican force came into action, their advance was arrested.

The battle began soon after one o'clock. It raged without intermission till nightfall. No decisive advantage had been gained on either side, and the result was still doubtful, when a panic took place among the multitude of noncombatants in the rear of the Vendeans. The cry was raised, "To the Loire!"

The panic spread. In vain the leaders and their officers galloped backwards and forwards, endeavouring to restore confidence, and shouted to the men that victory was still in their grasp. In the darkness and din they could only be heard by those immediately round them, and even these they failed to reanimate; and the men who had for seven hours fought, as Kleber himself reported, like tigers, lost heart.

Lescure had fallen in the fighting on the fourteenth. Bonchamp and d'Elbee were both desperately wounded at the battle at Chollet, and were carried off by their men. La Rochejaquelein, with whom Jean Martin and Leigh were riding, had made almost superhuman efforts to check the panic; and they fell back, almost broken hearted, with a band of peasants, who held together to the last. On the previous day Leigh had escorted Patsey to Beaupreau, and it was to this town that the fugitives made their way, arriving there at midnight.

"Thank God that you are both alive!" Patsey said, bursting into tears as her husband entered the room in which she was established.

"We can hardly believe it ourselves," Jean said. "It has been a terrible day, indeed. Our men fought nobly, and I firmly believe that we should have won the day, had not an unaccountable panic set in. What caused it I know not. We were doing well everywhere, and had begun to drive them back and, could we have fought on for another half hour it was likely that, as usual, a panic would have seized them.

"However, Patsey, they would have gathered again stronger than ever, and it must have come to the same thing, in the long run. Now put on your disguise, at once. We will lie down for two hours, and see you off before daybreak. I do not know whether la Rochejaquelein, who must now be considered in command, since d'Elbee and Bonchamp are both desperately wounded, will gather a force to act as a rearguard. If so we must stay with him; but I do not think that even his influence would suffice to hold any considerable body of peasants together. All have convinced themselves that there is safety in Brittany.

"At any rate, the enemy will need a day's rest before they pursue. They must have suffered quite as heavily as we have."

The night, however, was not to pass quietly. At two o'clock two officers, who had remained as piquets, rode into the town with news that Westermann's division, which had marched through Moulet and had taken no part in the action, was approaching. The horn sounded the alarm, and the fugitives started up and renewed their flight. Marthe could not be left behind now, nor did the others desire it; and until they had crossed the Loire there could be no separation, for the whole country would swarm, in forty-eight hours, with parties of the enemy, hunting down and slaying those who had taken refuge in the woods.

Jean and Leigh had lain down in the cart, to prevent any of the fugitives seizing it. The two women and the child were hurried down, and took their places in it. Francois, who had escaped, had fortunately found them; and took the reins, and the journey was continued.

There was no pursuit. It was only a portion of Westermann's force that had arrived, and these were so exhausted and worn out, by the length of their march and by the fact that they had been unable to obtain food by the way, that they threw themselves down when they reached the town, incapable of marching a mile farther.

At Beaupreau there had been no fewer than five thousand Republican prisoners, kept under guard. On the arrival of the routed Vendeans, the peasants, as a last act of retaliation, would have slain them; but Bonchamp, who was at the point of death, ordered them to be set free.

"It is the last order that I shall ever give," he said to the peasants assembled round his litter. "Surely you will not disobey me, my children."

The order was obeyed, and the prisoners were at once sent off; and as the Republican column marched out from Chollet, the next day, they encountered on the road their liberated comrades. The sentiments with which the commissioners of the Convention were animated is evidenced by the fact that one of them declared, in a letter to the commander-in-chief of the army, that the release of these prisoners by the Vendeans was a regrettable affair; and recommended that no mention, whatever, should be made of it in the despatches to Paris, lest this act of mercy by the insurgents should arouse public opinion to insist upon a cessation of the measures that had been taken for the annihilation of the Vendeans.

The fugitives, a vast crowd of over one hundred thousand men, women, and children, reached Saint Florent without coming in contact with the enemy. The Republican generals, indeed, had no idea that the peasants had any intention of quitting their beloved country; and imagined that they would disperse to their homes again, and that there remained only the task of hunting them down. A company had been left on a hill which commanded Saint Florent, but they had no idea of being attacked, and had not even taken the precaution of removing the boats across the river.

As soon as they arrived, the Vendeans attacked the post with fury, and captured it. Twenty boats were found, and the crossing was effected with no little difficulty. There were still two or three thousand, principally women and children, to be taken over, when a party of Republican dragoons arrived. Numbers of the women and children were massacred; but the great bulk, flying precipitately, regained the country beyond the heights of Saint Florent, and took refuge in the woods.

The multitude were, for the present, safe. There was no strong force of the enemy between Nantes and Saumur, and they halted for the night, dispirited, worn out, and filled with grief. They had left their homes and all they cared for behind. They were in a strange country, without aim or purpose, their only hope being that the Bretons would rise and join them--a poor hope, since the terrible vengeance that had been taken on La Vendee could not but strike terror throughout Brittany, also.

Jean Martin and Leigh had seen Patsey and the nurse placed in one of the first boats that crossed.

"Do not go far from the spot where you land," they said. "We shall stay here, until all is over. If the Blues come up before all have crossed, we shall swim across with our horses; be under no uneasiness about us."

Taking the horse out of the shafts of the cart, and putting a saddle that they had brought with them on its back, they left the three animals in charge of Francois; and then aided other officers to keep order among the crowd, and to prevent them from pressing into the boats, as they returned from the other bank, in such numbers as to sink them. All day the work went on quietly and regularly, until so comparatively few remained that hope became strong that all would cross, before any of the enemy arrived.

That hope was destroyed when, suddenly, the enemy's cavalry appeared at the edge of the slope, and came galloping down. The officers in vain tried to get the few men that remained to make a stand. They were too dispirited to attempt to do so, and the little throng broke up and fled, some one way, some another.

Fortunately an empty boat had just returned, and into this the other officers leapt; while Jean, with his two companions, led the horses into the water. They had already linked the reins. Francois was unable to swim but, at Jean's order, he took hold of the tail of the horse in the middle; while Jean and Leigh swam by the heads of the two outside horses, and without difficulty the other side was gained. Patsey, who had had her eye fixed upon them all day, was standing at the spot where they landed.

They were near the town of Ancenis, and a portion of the Vendeans entered the place, which was wholly undefended. The inhabitants were in abject terror, thinking that the town would be sacked; and were surprised to find that the peasants did no one any harm, and were ready to pay for anything that they required. So long, indeed, as any money whatever remained, the Vendeans paid scrupulously. When it was all expended, the chiefs did the only thing in their power, issuing notes promising to pay; and although these had no value, save in the good faith of the Vendeans, they were received by the Bretons as readily as the assignats of the Republic--which, indeed, like the notes of the Vendeans, were never destined to be paid.

Had the army plunged into Brittany after the capture of Saumur, there can be no doubt that the peasantry would everywhere have risen; but coming as fugitives and exiles, they were a warning rather than a source of enthusiasm; and although small numbers of peasants joined them, the accession of force was very trifling.

Jean Martin, his wife, and Leigh held an anxious consultation that evening. They had found a poor lodging, after attending a meeting of the leaders, at which la Rochejaquelein had been unanimously elected commander-in-chief; Bonchamp having died, while d'Elbee, wounded to death, had been left at the cottage of a Breton peasant, who promised to conceal him. The young soldier had accepted the fearful responsibility with the greatest reluctance. He, and those around him, saw plainly enough that the only hope of escape from annihilation was the landing of a British force to their assistance. Unhappily, however, England had not as yet awoke to the tremendous nature of the struggle that was going on. Her army was a small one; and her fleet, as yet, had not attained the dimensions that were, before many years, to render her the unquestioned mistress of the seas.

The feeling that the Revolution was the fruit of centuries of oppression; and that, terrible as were the excesses committed in the name of liberty, the cause of the Revolution was still the cause of the peoples of Europe, had created a party sufficiently powerful to hamper the ministry. Moreover, the government was badly informed in every respect by its agents in France, and had no idea of the extent of the rising in La Vendee, or how nobly the people there had been defending themselves against the whole force of France. It is not too much to say that had England, at this time, landed twenty thousand troops in Brittany or La Vendee, the whole course of events in Europe would have been changed. The French Revolution would have been crushed before it became formidable to Europe, and countless millions of money and millions of lives would have been saved.

Throughout France there was a considerable portion of the population who would have rejoiced in the overthrow of the Republic, for even in the large towns its crimes had provoked reaction. Toulon had opened its gates to the English. Lyons was in arms against the Republic. Normandy's discontent was general, and its peasantry would have joined those of Brittany and La Vendee, had there been but a fair prospect of success.

England, however, did nothing, but stood passive until the peasantry of La Vendee were all but exterminated; and indeed, added to their misfortunes by promising aid that never was sent, and thus encouraging them to maintain a resistance that added to the exasperation of their enemies, and to their own misfortunes and sufferings.

"What are we going to do?" Patsey asked, as her husband and Leigh returned from the meeting.

"That is more than anyone can say," Jean replied. "We shall, for the present, move north. We are like a flight of locusts. We must move since we must eat, and no district could furnish subsistence for eighty thousand people, for more than a day or two.

"There can be no doubt that the impulse to cross the Loire was a mad one. On the other side we at least knew the country, and it would have been far better to have died fighting, there, than to throw ourselves across the river. It was well nigh a miracle that we got across, and it will need nothing short of a miracle to get us back again.

"Of one thing we may be sure: the whole host of our enemies will, by this time, be in movement. We should never have got across, had they dreamed that such was our intention. Now that we have done it, you may be sure that they will strain every effort to prevent us from returning. Probably, by this time, half their forces are marching to cross at Nantes. The other half are pressing on to Saumur. In three or four days they will be united again, and will be between us and the river.

"Were we a smaller body, were we only men, I should say that we ought to march another twenty miles north, then sweep round either east or west and, while the enemy followed the north bank of the river to effect a junction, we should march all night without a halt, pass them, and hurl ourselves either upon Saumur or Nantes, and so return to La Vendee. But with such a host as this, there would be little hope of success. I fancy that we shall march to Laval, and there halt for a day or two. By that time the whole force of the enemy will have come up, and there will be another battle."

"And we, Jean?"

"I see nothing but for us to march with them. We know nothing of the movements of the enemy and, were we to try to make our way across the country, we might run into their arms. Besides, Leigh and I have both agreed that, at present at least, we cannot leave Rochejaquelein."

"We could not, indeed, Patsey," Leigh broke in. "If you had seen him this evening when, with tears in his eyes, he accepted our choice, you would feel as we do. It was all very well for us, before, to talk of making off; but now that the worst has happened, if it were only for his sake, I should stay by him; though I think that Jean, with the responsibility of you and your child, would be justified in going."

"No," Patsey said firmly, "whatever comes, we will stay together. As Jean said, you cannot desert the cause now. As long as there are battles to fight we must stay with them, and it is not until further fighting has become impossible that we, like others, must endeavour to shift for ourselves."

"Well spoken, Patsey!" her husband said. "That must be our course. So long as the Vendeans hang together, with Rochejaquelein at their head, we must remain true to the cause that we have taken up. When once again the army becomes a mass of fugitives we can, without loss of honour, and a clear consciousness that we have done our duty to the end, think of our safety. I grant that, if one could find a safe asylum for you and our Louis in the cottage of some Breton peasant--"

"No, no!" she interrupted, "that I would never consent to. We will remain together, Jean, come what may. If all is lost, I will ask you to put a pistol to my head. I would a thousand times rather die so than fall into the hands of the Blues, and either be slaughtered mercilessly, or thrown into one of their prisons to linger, until the guillotine released me."

"I agree with you in that, Patsey. Well, we will regard the matter as settled. As long as the army hangs together, so long will we remain with it; after that we will carry out the plans we talked over, and make for the coast by the way which seems most open to us."

The next day was spent, by Rochejaquelein and his officers, in going about among the peasants. They did not disguise from these the extreme peril of the position, but they pointed out that it was only by holding together, and by defeating the Blues whenever they attacked them, that they could hope for safety.

"It was difficult to cross the Loire before," they said; "it will be tenfold more difficult now. Every boat will have been taken over to the other side, and you may be sure that strong bodies of the enemy will have been posted, all along the banks, to prevent our returning. You have fought well before. You must fight even better in future, for there is no retreat, no home to retire to. Your lives, and those of the women and children with you, depend upon your being victorious. You have beaten the Blues almost every time that you have met them. You would have beaten them last time, had not a sort of madness seized you. It was not we who led you across the Loire; you have chosen to come, and we have followed you.

"At any rate, it is better to die fighting, for God and country, than to be slaughtered unresistingly by these murderers. You saw how they fell upon the helpless ones who were unable to cross with us; how they murdered women and children, although there was no resistance, nothing to excite their anger. If you die, you die as martyrs to your faith and loyalty, and no man could wish for a better death.

"All is not lost, yet. Defeat the Blues, and Brittany may yet rise; besides, we are promised aid from England. At any rate, La Vendee has been true to herself through over six months of terrible struggle. La Vendee may perish. Let the world see that she has been true to herself, to the end."

The fugitive priests with the army seconded the efforts of the officers and, by nightfall, a feeling of resolution and hope succeeded the depression caused by the terrible events of the preceding thirty-six hours; and it was with an air of calmness and courage that the march was recommenced, on the following morning.

The instant that it became known that the Vendeans had crossed the Loire, a panic seized the Republicans at Nantes; and messengers were sent to implore the commander-in-chief to march with all haste to aid them should, as they believed, the Vendeans be marching to assail the town. Kleber with his division started at once, followed more slowly by the main body of the army.

Another column advanced to Saint Florent and, obtaining boats, crossed the river and entered Angers; to the immense relief of the Republicans there, who had been in a state of abject terror at the presence, so near them, of the Vendeans. Kleber marched with great rapidity, passed through Nantes without stopping, and established himself at the camp of Saint Georges.

The news of what was termed the glorious victory at Chollet--although in point of fact the Republicans fell back, after the battle, to that town--caused the greatest enthusiasm in Paris, and the Convention and the Republican authorities issued proclamations, which were unanimous in exhorting the army to pursue and exterminate the Vendeans.

By the twenty-third, the whole of the French army was in readiness to march in pursuit. Kleber was still in the camp of Saint Georges, Chalbos was at Nantes with a corps d'armee, Beaupuy was at Angers.

The Vendeans had marched through Cande and Chateau-Gontier, and had without difficulty driven out the Republican force stationed at Laval. L'Echelle, the commander-in-chief, was profoundly ignorant, supine, and cowardly; and owed his position solely to the fact that he belonged to the lower class, and was not, like Biron and the other commanders-in-chief, of good family. Remaining always at a distance from the scene of operations, he confused the generals of divisions by contradictory orders, which vied with each other in their folly.

On the twenty-fourth, Kleber marched to Ancenis, and on the following day he, Beaupuy, and Westermann arrived at Chateau-Gontier. Canuel's division from Saint Florent had not yet come up. The troops were already tired, but Westermann who, as Kleber in his report said, was always anxious to gain glory and bring himself into prominence, insisted on pushing forward at once; and prevailed over the more prudent counsel of the others, as he was the senior officer.

When they approached Laval, Westermann sent a troop of cavalry forward to reconnoitre. He was not long before he came upon some Vendean outposts. These he charged, and drove in towards the town.

No sooner did they arrive there than the bells of the churches pealed out. It was now midnight but, before the army could form into order, the Vendeans poured out upon them, guided by the shouts of the Republican officers, who were endeavouring to get their troops into order. The combat was desperate and sanguinary. The peasants, fighting with the fury of despair, threw themselves recklessly upon the Republican troops; whose cannon were not yet in a position to come into action, and whose infantry, in the darkness, fired at random. Fighting in the dark, discipline availed but little. Kleber's veterans, however, preserved their coolness, and for a time the issue was doubtful.

Had Westermann's cavalry done their duty, victory might still have inclined towards them; but instead of charging when ordered, they turned tail and, riding through a portion of their infantry, spread disorder among them. Westermann, seeing that it was hopeless to endeavour to retrieve the confusion, ordered a retreat; and the army fell back to Chateau-Gontier, where they arrived in the course of the day. Here they found the commander-in-chief who, disregarding the exhausting march the troops had already accomplished, and their loss of spirit after their defeat, ordered them to return to Vihiers, halfway to Laval.

It was nightfall when they reached this place, but Westermann pushed the advanced guard some two leagues farther. Kleber, seeing the extreme danger of the position, refused to advance beyond Vihiers; and sent orders to Danican, who commanded the advanced guard, to fall back to a strong position in advance of Vihiers.

Danican had taken command only on the previous day, and the soldiers, believing that this order was but an act of arbitrary authority on his part, refused to move; and the bridge over the river Ouette, in front of Vihiers, remained unguarded save by a squadron of cavalry. Kleber had just returned from visiting the post, when he received a despatch from l'Echelle, bidding him give the order they had decided upon between them to the other two divisions. As no such arrangement had been made, Kleber was in ignorance of what was meant; but he sent a messenger to Beaupuy, who was at Chateau-Gontier, and to Bloss, who commanded a column of grenadiers, to join him as soon as possible.

Bloss arrived early the next morning at the camp. Beaupuy moved forward but, as his whole force had not yet come up, he did not arrive at the camp at the same time.

At eleven that night l'Echelle and the four generals now in the camp held a council. Westermann was extremely discontented, at finding that the heights were not occupied; but as Kleber remarked, the troops were utterly dissatisfied at the way in which they had been handled, and at the unnecessary and enormous fatigues that had been imposed upon them, and it was impossible to demand further exertions. Savary, one of the generals at the council, was well acquainted with Laval, and gave the advice that a portion of the army should follow the river for some distance, and then take possession of the hills commanding the town.

When Beaupuy arrived, his division moved forward at once, as an advanced guard; but as the army was moving a messenger arrived from l'Echelle, issuing orders in absolute contradiction of the plan that he had agreed to, when the council of war broke up. The orders were obeyed, but the generals again met, and sent off a messenger to l'Echelle to remonstrate against the attack in one mass, and a march by a single road, on a position that could be attacked by several routes; and to recommend that at least a diversion should be made, by a false attack. Westermann himself carried this remonstrance, but the commander-in-chief paid no attention to him.

Advancing, it was found that the Vendeans had taken up a position on the neglected heights. The cannon opened on both sides, and Beaupuy was soon hotly engaged. Kleber advanced his division to sustain him. L'Echelle, coming up, arrested the further advance of the division of Chalbos. Savary rode back in haste, to implore l'Echelle to order Chalbos to move to the right and attack the left flank of the enemy; but by this time the unfortunate wretch had completely lost his head and, instead of giving Chalbos orders to advance, ordered him to retreat, and himself fled in all haste.

Two columns, that were posted a few miles in the rear, received no orders whatever, and remained all day waiting for them. Kleber, seeing the division of Chalbos retiring in great disorder, felt that success was now impossible; and placed two battalions not yet engaged at the bridge, to cover the retreat. But the panic was spreading, his orders were disobeyed, and the veterans of Mayence, as well as the divisions of Beaupuy, broke their ranks and fled.

In vain the officers endeavoured to stay the flight. The panic was complete. Their guns were left behind, and the Vendeans, pressing hotly on their rear, overtook and killed great numbers. Bloss with his grenadiers, advancing from Chateau-Gontier, tried in vain to arrest the flight of the fugitives; and he himself and his command were swept away by the mob, and carried beyond the town.

A few hundreds of the soldiers alone were rallied, and prepared to defend the bridge of Chateau-Gontier; but la Rochejaquelein had sent a portion of his force to make a circuit and seize the town, so that the defenders of the bridge were exposed to a heavy fire from houses in their rear.

Kleber, with a handful of men, held the bridge; and was joined by Bloss, who had been already wounded while passing through the town. He advanced to cross; Kleber and Savary in vain tried to stop him.

"No," he said, "I will not survive the shame of such a day," and, rushing forward with a small party, fell under the fire of the advancing Vendeans.

The pursuit was hotly maintained. Keeping on heights which commanded the road, the Vendeans maintained an incessant fire of cannon and musketry. It was already night, and this alone saved the Republican army from total destruction. Beaupuy received a terrible wound in the battle, and a great number of officers were killed, in endeavouring to stop the panic.

At last the pursuit ceased and, for a few hours, the weary fugitives slept. Then they continued their retreat, and took up a strong position near the town of Angers, which was crowded with fugitives.

L'Echelle came out to review the troops who, by the orders of their generals, had already formed in order of battle; but was received with such yells of hatred and contempt that he was forced to retire. The representatives of the convention offered Kleber the command of the army, but he refused, saying that Chalbos was of superior rank, and that it was he who should take the command. They agreed to this, and sent to l'Echelle, telling him to demand leave of absence, on account of his health.

A council of war was then held. The representatives of the Convention were favourable to a fresh advance of the army, but Kleber protested that, at present, there was no army. He said that the soldiers were utterly discouraged, that some battalions had but twenty or thirty men with the colours, that all were wet to the skin, utterly exhausted, many without shoes, and all dispirited. Therefore he insisted that it was absolutely necessary that the army should be completely reorganized, before undertaking a fresh forward movement.

Their loss had indeed been extremely heavy, Kleber's division alone having lost over a thousand men. Beaupuy had suffered even more heavily; while the divisions of Chalbos, and the grenadiers of Bloss had also lost large numbers. The total loss, including deserters, amounted to over four thousand.

The whole of the cannon of the two first divisions had fallen into the hands of the enemy, the artillerymen having cut the traces. A large number of ammunition waggons, and a quantity of carts laden with provisions, had also been captured.

Chapter 14
Le Mans

The victory won by the Vendeans was one of the most important of the war. Never had they fought with greater bravery. Never did they carry out more accurately and promptly the orders of their generals. Napoleon afterwards pronounced that the tactics pursued by la Rochejaquelein showed that he possessed the highest military genius.

It was night, alone, that saved the routed army of the Republic from absolute destruction. It is probable that, at the time, the Vendean general had no idea of the completeness of the victory that he had won, or of the disorganization of the enemy. Had he known it, he would doubtless have attacked them again on the following day; when he would have experienced no resistance, could have captured Angers without firing a shot, and could, had he chosen, have recrossed the Loire. The Vendeans, however, well content with their success, returned to Laval, and there enjoyed a week's quiet and repose.

The crushing defeat that the Republicans had experienced caused an immense sensation at Paris, and in the towns through which the Vendeans would pass on their way to the capital, which was at the time actually open to them.

Patsey was delighted, when Jean and Leigh returned unwounded.

"You both seem to bear a charmed life," she said. "Leigh has indeed once been hit, but it was not serious; you have escaped altogether. What is going to be done next?"

"We are going to rest here for ten days or so. There is plenty of food to be had, and the rest will do wonders for the men. Of course, we rode back with la Rochejaquelein. His opinion was, as it always has been, that a march on Paris will alone bring this terrible business to a close; but he knows that even his authority will not suffice to carry out such a plan. As long as they are in Brittany they are among friends, and are still near their homes; but to turn their backs on these, and march on Paris, would appear so terrible an undertaking that, reckless as they are of their lives in battle, nothing would induce them to attempt it."

After ten days' delay, the Vendeans commenced their march towards the coast. The battle at Vihiers was fought on the twenty-seventh. By the sixth of November they had captured the towns of Ernee and de Fougeres, defeating at the latter place three battalions. Dol was next captured. Mayenne opened its gates without resistance.

The greatest efforts were made, by the Republicans, to place the seaports in a state of defence. Cherbourg would have been the best point for the fugitives to attack, as here they would have found an abundance of powder, of which they were in great need, and cannon; and here they might have defended themselves until the promised help arrived from England. Granville, however, had been fixed upon by the British government; and the march thither was shorter, therefore it was against Granville that the attack was directed.

A considerable portion of the force, with the artillery, were left at Avranches. Although assured that the march to the sea was made in order to obtain succour there from England, there was much fear among the peasants that the intention of the chiefs was to embark, and to leave the army to its fate. Consequently they advanced against Granville with less energy and enthusiasm than usual.

However, half a league out of the town they came upon a portion of the garrison, and repulsed them so successfully that they entered one of the suburbs with them. The garrison had, for the most part, shut themselves up in a fort which commanded the town; having erected a strong palisade across the streets leading to it. Four hundred men occupied this post.

The Vendeans had no axes to cut down the palisades, nor powder to blow then in. They were therefore obliged to content themselves with a musketry fire against it. As the garrison were well supplied with ammunition, and kept up a constant fire, they suffered heavily.

When night came, the Vendeans scattered among the houses to find food, fire, and shelter; and all night the batteries on the heights played upon them.

In the morning the Republicans redoubled their fire. It became evident that the town itself could not be taken, and the mass of the Vendeans, without orders from their chiefs, began to retire, and in a short time the whole were in rapid retreat to Avranches.

There the cry was raised, "Back to La Vendee!"

La Rochejaquelein, after halting his force on the main road a few hours, called upon the men to follow him to Caen; but only one thousand did so. On arriving at a village he learned that the bulk of the army, instead of being behind him, had marched towards Pontorson. He was therefore forced to retrace his steps and to follow them and, on overtaking them, found that they had already carried the bridge, driven away the enemy, and occupied the town.

The enemy were closing round them, but the capture of Pontorson deranged the plans of the Republicans. The place had been held by four thousand men and ten pieces of cannon and, as it could be approached only by a narrow defile, it was believed that it would be impossible for the Vendeans to force their way into it. However, after three hours' fighting, their desperate valour won the day, and the Republicans were routed, with the loss of most of their cannon.

The affair, indeed, appeared to the peasants to be a miracle granted in their favour; and with renewed heart they marched the next night to Dol. Kleber was with a large force in this neighbourhood, but the impetuosity of Westermann again upset his plans. As soon as the latter heard that Pontorson had been carried by the Vendeans, and that they had marched to Dol, he pursued them with three thousand infantry, two hundred cavalry, and four cannon. He arrived within a short distance of Dol at six in the evening and, without waiting for the infantry to come up, charged into the town, and for a moment spread confusion among the Vendeans.

They, however, soon recovered from their surprise, and drove the enemy out with loss. Westermann's infantry took no part in the action. Kleber was occupied in closing every route by which the Vendeans could leave Dol; but Westermann, who had held no communication with him, and knew nothing of his plans, marched with Marigny's division, with six thousand men, to attack the town.

This he did at two o'clock in the morning. The Vendeans at once rushed to meet them, and first tried to turn the right; but they failed here, and also in an attack on the left. They fought, however, so fiercely that Westermann withdrew his troops to the position that they had occupied before attacking. The Vendeans, however, gave them no time to form in order of battle but, heralding their charge with a heavy musketry fire, rushed down upon them. The enemy at once broke and, leaving their cannon behind them, continued their flight till they reached Pontorson.

In the meantime Marceau was advancing with his division by another road; and the Vendeans, hearing this, ceased their pursuit of Westermann's routed division and moved against him and, at four o'clock in the morning, attacked him when within a league of Dol. A combat ensued that lasted for three hours. The Vendeans then drew off, on learning that the division of Muller was on the point of joining that of Marceau.

Together these divisions could have forced their way into Dol, but Muller was hopelessly drunk and, being the senior officer, the greatest confusion arose and, had the Vendeans known what was taking place, they could have gained a decisive victory.

Marceau, seeing that he could do nothing to restore order, rode at full speed to Kleber's headquarters; and at daybreak the two generals arrived at the spot, and found the two divisions mingled in supreme disorder, the brigades and battalions being mixed up together. Finding that nothing could be done with them, there, Kleber drew them off; their confusion being almost converted into a rout, by the fire of about a hundred Vendeans. A council of war was held, and eighteen hundred men, with two guns, were sent to Pontorson to join Westermann's defeated division.

That general was ordered to advance again, at once, upon Dol. Kleber opposed this, and the rest of the council coming at last to his opinion, orders were sent to Westermann to remain on the defensive, and await fresh orders. Westermann, however, as usual, disregarded these and, marching through the night, approached the town and arrived, early in the morning, at a village close to it.

The sounding of the church bells told that the Vendeans had discovered the enemy, and in a few minutes these were seen rushing, as usual, to the attack. In spite of the reinforcements that had reached them, Westermann's troops fought worse than they had done two nights before. The reinforcements were the first to give way. The advanced guard speedily turned and fled. Westermann and Marigny, with a small party of cavalry, fought desperately to cover the retreat. Marigny however fell, and the whole force became a mass of fugitives.

Kleber, on his way the next day to reconnoitre the town, met the Vendeans advancing. Scattering rapidly, these occupied the ridges, and attacked the brigade that formed his advanced guard so fiercely that it broke and fled. Kleber sent to fetch some battalions of the troops of Mayence and, as soon as they arrived, with some battalions of grenadiers, formed them in order of battle. Other troops came up, and they prepared for a serious engagement.

At this moment the Vendean column that had defeated Westermann showed itself, on the right flank of the Republicans, and threatened their rear. Kleber ordered some of the battalions to take post further back, to cover the line of retreat. Other battalions, seeing the movement, and believing this to be a signal for retreat, followed.

The grenadiers alone stood firm, and defended themselves for three hours. In the meantime the greater portion of the Republican army was already in full flight, and a retreat was ordered. The troops remaining on the field retired at first in good order but, as the victorious Vendeans pressed on, this speedily became a rout.

Marceau, gathering together such soldiers as still retained their presence of mind, endeavoured to defend the bridge of Antrain; but the Vendeans, pressing forward, swept them away; and the fugitives fled, in a confused mob, as far as Rennes.

The Vendeans, on entering Antrain, at once scattered in search of food; disregarding the orders and entreaties of la Rochejaquelein and Stofflet, who urged them to press hotly upon the routed enemy, and so to complete the victory they had won. At Antrain they learned that the wounded, who had been left in hospital at Fougeres, had been murdered in their beds by the Blues; and they accordingly shot all the prisoners they had taken in the battle.

The victory seemed to open the way to the Loire, and the Vendeans steadily marched south through Mayenne and Laval, and arrived in front of Angers. But the city was no longer in the defenceless state in which it was when they first crossed the Loire. As soon as it was perceived to be the point for which the Vendeans were marching, four thousand troops were thrown into it, and all preparations made for a stout defence.

"If they defend themselves as they ought to do," la Rochejaquelein said to two or three of his officers, among whom was Jean Martin, "there is no hope of taking the town. We have neither cannon to blow down the walls, nor means of scaling them. Thirty-six hours is the utmost we can hope for our operations. Kleber and the rest of them will be up by that time. However--it is our sole hope--possibly a panic may seize them when we attack; but even cowards will fight behind walls and, after our failure at Granville, I have little hope of our taking Angers, especially as they must know how soon their army will be up."

The affair was a repetition of that at Granville. The Vendeans at once obtained possession of one of the suburbs. Twenty pieces of cannon opened fire upon it from the walls, while from the houses the Vendeans replied with a musketry fire. During the night a number of men laboured to undermine the wall by one of the gates, and partially succeeded. But day broke before the work was completed, and the defenders planted several cannon to bear upon them.

The Vendeans were too much discouraged to make any further effort; and when, a few hours later, news came that the Republican army was fast approaching, and would reach the ground in an hour's time, they again got into motion, and pursued their hopeless journey in search of some point where they could cross the river, if only to die in their beloved land.

On the following day Kleber was reinforced by a column, eight thousand strong, from Cherbourg; and a reconnaissance was made along the road by which the Vendeans had retreated. They found everywhere the bodies of men, women, and children who had succumbed to cold, fatigue, and misery. Westermann's cavalry set out in pursuit, Muller following with his division to support him.

Marceau was now appointed commander-in-chief, pending the arrival of Turreau and Rossignol. The latter had, almost from the commencement of the war, intrigued against every general concerned in the operations, especially against Kleber. He was himself utterly without military talent, and owed his position simply to his devotion to the Convention, and his readiness to denounce the men who failed to satisfy its anticipations of an easy victory, or who showed the slightest repugnance to execute its barbarous decrees.

With the exception of some three thousand men, who marched at the head of the Vendean column, the fugitives were now utterly disheartened. Many hid their muskets and, cutting sticks, thought that, being no longer armed, they would not be molested by the enemy. Each night numbers stole away, in groups of twos and threes, in the hope of finding a boat on the bank of the river. Others scattered among the villages, their appearance exciting compassion; but fear of the troops was more powerful, and the men for the most part were seized and held prisoners.

Of the hundred thousand men, women, and children who had crossed the Loire, more than half were dead. Of those who remained, fully fifteen thousand were women and children.

On the march, Leigh always rode by the side of his sister, generally carrying the child before him. Jean, as one of the leading officers, now rode with Rochejaquelein at the head of the column. Patsey suffered less, on her own account, than on that of the poor people who had to journey on foot. The cold was intense and, except when they entered a town, it was impossible to obtain provisions. The horses were worn out and half famished, a great proportion of the fugitives were without shoes, and the clothing of all was in rags.

In order to spare her the sight of the misery prevailing among those who marched in the rear of the column, Leigh always rode with his sister in the rear of the leading division. He himself, for the most part, walked on foot; lending his horse to some wounded man, or exhausted woman.

When the column left Angers it had been intended to march to Saumur and cross there, but the news arrived that a strong Republican force had gathered there; and it was determined to change the course, and to march through La Fleche to Le Mans. By this sudden and unexpected movement, Rochejaquelein hoped to gain time to give his followers two days' rest.

The immediate result, however, was to excite a feeling of despair among a great portion of them. Their backs were now turned to La Vendee, and it seemed to them that their last hope of reaching their homes had vanished. Rochejaquelein's idea, however, was that in their present state of exhaustion it was impossible to hope to cross the Loire--guarded as it was at every point, and with over one hundred thousand men between him and La Vendee--and he intended, after giving them the much needed rest, to march round through Chateaudun, to come down on the Loire above Orleans, and so to make his way back into Poitou.

Had he had with him only men, the project, difficult as it seemed, might possibly have been accomplished. Unembarrassed by baggage trains or cannon, the peasants could have out marched their pursuers; but hampered by the crowd of wounded, sick, women, and children, the movement must be regarded as the inspiration of despair.

Indeed, even the fighting men were no longer in a state to bear the fatigue. Bad and insufficient food had played havoc with them. Dysentery was raging in their ranks, and many could scarce drag themselves along.

"We cannot conceal from ourselves that it is nearly over," Jean said, when he told his wife and Leigh that the route was changed. "We shall get to Le Mans, but the Republicans will be on our heels, and one cannot doubt what the issue will be. Doubtless a small body will hang together, and still try to regain La Vendee; but we shall have done our duty. After our next defeat I will leave the army.

"I shall not go without telling la Rochejaquelein of my intentions. He has more than once spoken to me of you both, and it was but two days ago that he said to me:

"'Martin, you are not like the rest of us. You have an English wife, and your brave young brother-in-law is English, also. You have to think of them, as well as of La Vendee. You can make your home in England, and live there until better times come.

"'It is no longer a question of defending our country. It is lost. Charette is there now, and still fighting; but as soon as we are disposed of, all these troops that have been hunting us down will be free to act against him, and he too must be crushed. The peasants have nowhere else to go; and it is not with a desire to defend their homes--which no longer exist--but to die in their native land that they seek to return. You have from the first done your utmost for La Vendee, but there can be no occasion that you should throw away your life, and those of your wife and brother, now that the cause is utterly lost, and all hope is at an end.

"'Think this over. I do not say that it is possible for you to escape; but the longer you stay with us, the more difficult will it become.'

"So you see, I am sure that when I tell him that, feeling that we can no longer be of use, I am determined to make at least an endeavour to reach England with you, he will approve."

"I think he is right, Jean. No one can say that you have not done your duty to your country to the utmost, or can blame you for now doing what you can for your family."

Just as they neared La Fleche, a squadron of the enemy's cavalry fell upon the rear of the column. They killed many of the fugitives, but were too small in number to threaten the safety of the column, which kept on until it reached the bridge across the Loir. This had been broken down, but fire was opened against the cannon planted on the other side. The gunboats that were guarding the river were driven away; and a party, moving up the bank, found two little boats, and began to cross.

A detachment of Republicans hurried to attack them; but the Loir, an affluent of the Loire, was narrow, and the musketry fire of the main body drove them away, until two or three hundred men had crossed. La Rochejaquelein went over and took the command, and on their advance the Republicans took to their heels. Rochejaquelein then recrossed, and drove off the cavalry that were harrassing the rear.

Working desperately, a strong party threw beams across the broken bridge, and the Vendeans occupied the town at daybreak. The weary fugitives slept till midday, when the enemy's cavalry reappeared; but Rochejaquelein with some mounted gentlemen attacked and defeated them, and pursued them for some distance.

In the evening a force under Chalbos approached the town, but the Vendeans sallied out and speedily scattered them. They then broke down the bridge that they had repaired, and started for Le Mans; which they captured after three-quarters of an hour's fighting.

Two days later, Kleber was in front of the town. Westermann and Muller's divisions first approached. The two days' rest had reanimated the Vendeans, and Muller's infantry were driven back three miles; but large reinforcements came up, and the peasants were forced to fall back again. Then Westermann's cavalry charged into the town, carrying dismay among its defenders; but la Rochejaquelein and his officers soon reanimated them, and the cavalry were driven out of the town, itself. They and the infantry that had come up were able, however, to maintain themselves in the suburbs.

By this time la Rochejaquelein was aware that the armies of Brest, Cherbourg, and the west were all upon him. All through the night the battle went on, without interruption. The Republican columns could gain no ground, and were frequently obliged to give way; but behind the Vendean line of defence, panic was gaining ground among the fugitives. Three or four thousand escaped by the road to Laval, but the retreat of the rest was cut off by the cavalry.

In the morning, Kleber's division came up. They at once relieved Marceau's division, which had been fighting all night, and renewed the attack. The resistance was feeble. A few hundred men disputed every foot of the way, and died with a consciousness that they had at least covered the retreat of the rest.

A hot pursuit was at once organised and, while all taken in the town were massacred at once, Westermann's cavalry pursued the fugitives in all directions, covering the plain with corpses, and pressing hard on the rear of the force that still held together.

Jean Martin had, the day before the Republican attack, gone with Leigh to la Rochejaquelein's quarters; and told him that he intended, if the town was captured by the enemy, to endeavour to save the life of his wife by flight.

"You are quite right," Rochejaquelein said warmly. "I entirely approve of your determination. As long as ten of my men hold together, it is my duty to remain with them; for I have accepted the position of their commander, and I must share their fate to the end. But it is different with you. As the cause of La Vendee, for which you have fought, is lost, your first duty now is to your wife. I trust that you will all three succeed in making your way to England, and enjoy there the peace and rest that none can have in unhappy France. I thank you for your gallant services.

"And I thank you in the name of La Vendee, Leigh, for the manner in which you have fought for her; and also for the companionship that has so often cheered me, during our last days.

"As for myself, I have no wish to live. I should feel dishonoured were the army I led to be exterminated, and I, who accepted the responsibility of leading it, to survive. We have the consolation, at least, that never in history has a people fought more bravely against overpowering odds than La Vendee has done; and though at present we are called brigands, I am sure that the world will acknowledge that we have fought like heroes, for our country and our faith. Unfortunate as we may be, I am proud to be one of those who have led them so often to victory.

"When will you go, my friend?"

"I intend to be with you to the last," Jean said. "When the fight begins, Leigh and my wife will be ready, at a point agreed on in the rear of the town. When all is lost, I shall join them there. We shall ride until beyond pursuit, and then put on our disguises."

"Then I will not say goodbye to you now," Rochejaquelein said.

"Goodbye, Leigh. May Heaven keep you, and take you safely home again."

Leigh was too much affected to speak and, after a silent grasp of the hand of the gallant young soldier, he returned with Jean to the quarters they occupied.

"Now for our plans," Jean said. "They are as vague as ever, but we must settle now. It is quite evident that the alarm is so widely spread, here in the west, that it will be well-nigh impossible to pass through even a village without being questioned. Alencon on the north has a strong garrison, at Mayenne on the west is a division, and the whole country beyond will be alive with troops on the search for fugitives. It is only to the east that the road is open to us.

"I should say that the safest way will be to travel so as to cross the Loir between Chateaudun and Nogent, and then come down on the road running south from Fontainebleau through Montargis. Travelling south through Nevers, we should excite no suspicion. If questioned, we can say that we are going to visit some friends at Macon. The unfortunate thing is that we have no papers; and I think that our story had best be that we belong to Le Mans, and fled in such haste, when the town was captured by the Vendeans, that we escaped just as we stood, and omitted to bring our papers with us.

"Fortunately we all speak French without accent, and there is nothing about us to give rise to suspicion that we belong to La Vendee. If we can think of a more likely story, as we go along, all the better. When we get as far as Macon, if we ever get there, we can decide whether to endeavour to cross the frontier into Switzerland, or to go down to Toulon.

"Now remember, Patsey, my last injunctions are that, when you perceive from the rush of fugitives that all is over, and that any firing that may still be going on is but an attempt to cover the retreat, you must not wait for me but, as soon as the sound of combat approaches, you will ride off with Leigh. You need not suppose, because I do not join you, that I am killed. The enemy may have pushed so far through the town that I may find it impossible to join you. But from whatever cause I tarry, you are not to wait for me.

"If I am shot, it will be a consolation to me to know that you will be away under your brother's protection. If I escape, I shall, if I make my way to England, have the hope of meeting you there; and shall not be haunted with the fear that you have delayed too long, and have sacrificed your lives uselessly. I want you and him to give me your solemn promise that you will act thus, and will, as soon as he considers that further delay will be dangerous, ride off. Remember that this is my last wish, this is my last order."

"I will do as you wish, Jean," his wife said firmly. "God has preserved us three thus far, and I trust that He will continue to do so. I shall have the less hesitation because I think that, alone, you will have perhaps a better chance of escaping than with us. At any rate, we will carry out your instructions. But should we miss each other, is there no place where we can arrange to meet?"

"I do not see that it is possible to make any arrangements, Patsey. You may be turned out of your course, by circumstances which it is impossible to foresee; and the same may be the case with myself. Suppose we named a seaport, there would in the first place be difficulty in finding each other. You might see some opportunity of getting across the water and, if you lost that, the chance might not occur again; and the delay might cost you your lives. I trust that we shall not be separated, dear, but I see clearly that if such a misfortune should happen, it were best that we should each make our own way, in the hope of meeting at Poole.

"You may be sure that I shall join you, if possible; for I see that, if separated, your difficulties will be far greater than mine. You, too, would have the burden of the child. But let us suppose that I was wounded, but got away and managed to obtain shelter in some Breton cottage. You might be waiting for me, for weeks, at an agreed point. Now, while travelling, you might escape many questions; but were you to stop even for a few days at any town or village, you may be sure that you would be questioned so closely, by the authorities, that there would be little chance of your getting on. I should know that, and should be fretting my heart out."

"Yes, I see 'tis best that we should do as you say, Jean. God forbid that we should be separated, but if you do not come to the rendezvous, I promise you that we will, as you wish, go on by ourselves."

"And now, dear, we will divide our money. We have still three hundred louis left. I will take one hundred, and you shall take the rest. You are much more likely to want money, if we are separated, than I.

"You had best sew the greater part up in your saddle, Leigh."

"I think we had better divide it as much as possible, Jean. We can put seventy-five louis in each of our saddles, and the weight would not be so great that anyone who happens to handle one of them would notice it. I can put another five-and-forty in the belt round my waist, and keep the odd five in my pocket for expenses. Of course, if we decide to abandon our horses, I will make some other arrangement."

"The best plan, Leigh, will be for us to change the louis for assignats at the first opportunity. Gold is so scarce that each time you offered to pay with it, it would excite suspicion. I have no doubt that I can buy assignats here. We have taken a quantity from the enemy, and la Rochejaquelein will, I am sure, be glad to obtain some gold for them. It will be a double advantage:

we shall have less weight to carry, and shall be able to pay our way without the gold exciting suspicion. The assignats now are only a quarter of their face value, so that for two hundred louis I should get eight hundred louis in assignats, of which I would take two hundred, and you could take the rest."

"That would certainly be an excellent plan, Jean, for two hundred louis in gold would be a serious weight to carry and, if found on us, would in itself be sufficient to condemn us as intending emigres."

Jean at once took two hundred louis, which had hitherto been carried in their wallets, and went out. He returned in an hour.

"That is satisfactorily settled," he said. "Blacquard, who is in charge of the treasury, was delighted to obtain some gold, and has given us five times the amount in assignats. Of this I will take two hundred and fifty louis' worth. You will have seven hundred and fifty louis in assignats, and we will divide the hundred louis in gold. Of the latter, you had best sew up twenty in each of your saddles, and you can carry ten about you. People are so anxious for gold that, in case of need, you can get services rendered for it that you would fail to obtain for any amount of paper."

The greater portion of the assignats and the gold, as agreed, was sewn up in the saddles; some provisions packed in the valises; and Jean and Leigh went out together, and fixed upon a spot where they were to wait. The preparations were all finished, when firing broke out. Jean kissed his wife.

"May God's blessing keep you," he said. "I trust that we shall meet again, when the fighting is over."

Then he kissed his child, wrung Leigh by the hand, and rode off to join the general. The women, children, and the men who had thrown away their arms, the sick and wounded, were already leaving the town.

"Marthe, you must go now," Patsey said to the faithful nurse.

They had bought a horse for her from a peasant who had captured it, a riderless animal that belonged to one of Westermann troopers.

"Here are fifty louis in assignats. I wish that you could have gone with us, but that is not possible. Francois is waiting outside, and will take care of you, as we have agreed. The best possible plan will be to separate yourselves from the others as soon as possible. The Blues are sure to be keeping close to them. Ride straight for the river by by-lanes and, if you cannot obtain a boat, swim your horse across, and then make for home. If we get safely to England, we will write to you, as soon as these troubles are over, and you can join us there."

"God bless you, madame. It breaks my heart to part with you and the child, but I see that it is for the best."

Leigh fetched the horse round, and assisted her to mount behind Francois. The two women, both weeping, were still exchanging adieus when Leigh said to Francois:

"Ride on; the sooner this is over, the better for both."

The man nodded.

"God bless you, young master! I will look after Marthe. As soon as we get away from the rest, I shall get off and run by her side. The horse would never carry two of us far."

So saying, he touched the horse with his heel, and they rode off.

Chapter 15
In Disguise

Leigh returned into the house with his sister.

"Cheer up, Patsey," he said; "it is very hard parting, but I have every hope that they will succeed in getting safely home. Francois is a sharp fellow. They have a good stock of food, and they won't have to go into any village and, being only two, they will have a far better chance of crossing the river than if they kept with the others."

"How they are fighting!" Patsey said, a few minutes later.

Indeed the roar of musketry was unceasing, and was mingled with the louder cracks of the field guns.

"Our men are holding their own," Leigh replied. "The firing is no nearer than it was half an hour ago.

"Now, you had better lie down, Patsey. I will keep a sharp lookout and, the moment I see any signs of our men retiring, we will mount. I know there is no chance of your sleeping, but it will rest you to lie down, and we shall have a long ride before us, tomorrow."

Patsey nodded, but after he had gone out she did not lie down, but threw herself on her knees by the couch, and prayed for the safety of her husband. Hour after hour passed. From time to time Leigh returned and, towards morning, told Patsey that it was time that they should mount.

"Our men have not begun to give way yet," he said, "but they say that Kleber's division has just arrived. There is a lull in the fighting at present, but no doubt they will relieve the division that has been fighting all night, and our men cannot hope to hold out for long. I have just brought the horses round to the door. Now, I will strap the valises on while you wrap Louis up warmly."

In five minutes they started for the point agreed on. Before they reached it, the firing broke out again with increased violence. In an hour numbers of men began to make their way past them. One of them halted. He was one of Jean's tenants.

"Ah! madame," he said, as he recognized her--for it was now broad daylight--"I fear that all is lost. You had best ride at once. The Blues will not come just yet, for la Rochejaquelein, with four or five hundred of his best followers, will hold the place till the last, so as to give us time to get away."

"Did you see my husband, Leroux?"

"He was with the general, madame. They and the horsemen charged again and again, whenever the Blues pushed forward."

"Thank God he is safe so far!" Patsey said. "Goodbye, Leroux; we may not meet again."

"We shall meet in heaven, madame," the man said reverently. "They may take away our country, they may kill our cures, they may destroy our churches, but they cannot take away our God. May He protect you, madame!" and, pressing the hand she held out to him, he hurried on.

Faster and faster the fugitives passed them, but for an hour the combat continued unabated; then the exulting shouts of the Blues showed that they were making way. The gallant band of Vendeans were not, indeed, retiring; but they were being annihilated. Patsey had said but little during the anxious time of waiting. From time to time she murmured:

"Will he never come? Oh, God, send him to us!"

Presently a mounted officer rode past.

"Ride on! ride on!" he shouted. "The Blues will be here in a minute!"

"We must go, Patsey," Leigh said as, without drawing rein, the officer rode on.

"No, no; wait a few minutes, Leigh. He will surely come soon."

Presently, however, a number of peasants, their faces blackened with powder, ran past.

"The Blues are on our heels!" they shouted. "They will be here in a minute; they are but a hundred yards away."

"Come, Patsey," Leigh said. "Remember your promise. We must go; it is madness waiting any longer."

And as he spoke one of the peasants, running past, fell dead, shot by a musket ball from the rear. Leigh seized Patsey's bridle and, setting his own horse in motion, they rode on. They were but just in time for, before they had ridden two hundred yards Leigh, looking round, saw the Republicans issuing from the town.

"Pull yourself together, Patsey!" Leigh exclaimed. "We may have their cavalry after us, in a minute or two. Remember, Jean trusts you to carry out his instructions."

Patsey drew herself up, struck the horse with her whip, and galloped on at full speed. They soon left the road followed by the rest of the fugitives, and turned down one leading east. The din of battle had ceased now, but a scattered fire of musketry showed that the enemy were engaged in their usual work of shooting all who fell into their hands.

After riding for an hour at full speed they drew rein at a wood and, entering it, dismounted and put on their disguises. They had no fear now of pursuit. The enemy's cavalry must have made a very long march to reach the town, and their horses must be worn out by their previous exertions; while their own had had forty-eight hours' rest, during which time they had been well fed and cared for. Moreover, any pursuit that was made would be in the direction taken by the bulk of the fugitives.

Mounting again, they rode on. It was but a narrow country road that they were traversing and, during the day, they only passed through two or three small hamlets.

"Are the brigands coming this way?" they were asked.

"No," Leigh replied. "They are fighting at Le Mans. If they are beaten they won't come this way, but will make south. We thought it best to leave the town. When fighting is going on in the streets it is time for quiet people to be off."

They rode forty miles before night, and then entered a wood; having agreed that, until they got farther away from the scene of action, and struck the road running south, it would be better not to enter any place where they would be questioned. Choosing an open space among the trees, Leigh took off the bridles to let the horses pluck what grass they could, after giving to each a hunch of bread from their store. Then he returned, with the blankets that had been rolled up and fastened behind the saddles.

"Now, Patsey, you must eat something and drink some wine. You must keep up your strength, for the sake of Louis and Jean."

Patsey had spoken very few words during the day. She shook her head.

"I will try for Louis's sake," she said; "as to Jean--" and she stopped.

"As to Jean," he said, "we have every reason to hope for the best. Many things may have happened to prevent his joining us. The Blues may have pushed in between his party and us, and he may have found that he could not rejoin us. His horse may have been shot and he obliged to fly on foot.

He has gone through all these battles from the first, and has never been wounded. Why should we suppose that he has not done the same now? I feel sure that if he had lost his horse he would not have tried to join us, for he would have thought that he would have hampered our escape.

"Jean is full of resources, and has everything in his favour. He is not like the others, who have but one aim, to get back to La Vendee and die there, and whose way is barred by the Loire. He has all France open to him and, if he gains a port, has but to get some sailor clothes to pass unnoticed. He is well provided with money, and has everything in his favour. When he once gets away from Le Mans, the road would be open, for we may be sure that the enemy will all gather in the rear of the remains of our army."

"I see all that," Patsey said; "and if I were but sure that he got safely away, I should feel comparatively easy. However, Leigh, I will try and look at the best side of things. If Jean is killed he has died gloriously, doing his duty till the last. If he is not, he will some day be restored to me."

"That is right, dear," he said. "You have always been so hopeful and cheery, through all this business, that I am sure you will keep up your courage now. We have every reason to hope and, for my part, I confidently expect to see Jean, safe and sound, when we arrive home. Now let us set to; we both want something badly."

Patsey did her best and, being indeed faint from hunger, having eaten nothing since the evening before, she felt all the better and stronger when she had finished her meal; and was able to chatter cheerfully to little Louis, who had ridden before Leigh all day, and who was now just beginning to talk. Then they spread a blanket on the ground and, lying down together for warmth, covered themselves with the rest of their wraps; and Leigh was glad to find, by her steady breathing, that the fatigue of the last twenty-four hours had sufficed to send his sister to sleep, in spite of her grief at her separation from her husband.

The next day they crossed the road leading to Tours, between Chateaudun and Chartres. Once over this there was no longer any occasion for haste. There was no fear of their connection with the struggle in the west being suspected, and they had now only to face the troubles consequent on travelling unprovided with proper papers.

Late that evening they entered the town of Artenay, on the main road from Paris to Orleans, coming down upon it from the north side. Here they entered a quiet inn. The landlord was a jovial, pleasant-faced man of some sixty years of age; and his wife a kind, motherly-looking woman. As usual, the travellers signed the names they had agreed upon in the book kept for the purpose, Patsey retaining her own name, and he signing as Lucien Porson.

The landlady, seeing that Patsey was completely worn out, at once took her off to her room.

"Ah! I thought that monsieur was too young to be madame's husband," the landlord said.

Leigh laughed.

"I am her brother," he said. "Her husband is a sailor, and she is to join him at Toulon."

"I see the resemblance," the landlord said. "It is a long journey indeed for her, and with a child under two years old, and in such weather."

"But you forget that such a place as Toulon no longer exists. It has been decreed that the town that received the English and resisted the Republic is to be altogether destroyed, except of course the arsenal, and is henceforth to be known as 'the town without a name.'"

The tone, rather than the words, convinced Leigh that his host was not an admirer of the present state of things. Leigh shrugged his shoulders slightly, and said, with a smile:

"Perhaps France will change her own name. Surely a Republic cannot put up with the name that has been associated, for centuries, with kings."

The landlord brought his hand down, with a heavy smack, on Leigh's shoulder.

"Ah," he said, "I see that you are too young, as I am too old, to care for the present changes. With anyone in the town I should not venture to say anything; but I am sure, by your face, that you can be trusted."

"And I can say the same to you, landlord."

"Are your papers, by the by, in good order?"

"Frankly, we have no papers."

The landlord gave a low whistle, expressive of surprise and consternation.

"And how do you expect to travel, monsieur? How you have got so far as this, I cannot make out; for at any tavern where you put up you might, of course, have been asked for them."

"We have not put up at any towns, as yet; but have slept at little places, where no questions were asked."

"But you can't get on like that, monsieur. Even in the small villages, they are on the watch for suspected persons. You must have papers of some sort."

"That is all very well," Leigh said; "the question is, where to get them?"

"What story do you mean to tell?"

"If we had been stopped anywhere on our way here, we should have said that we belonged to Le Mans; that, like most of the other inhabitants, we fled before the Vendeans entered, and in such haste that I forgot all about papers; and indeed could not have got them, had I thought of it, as all the authorities had fled before we did."

"That story, added to your appearance and that of madame as respectable citizens, might succeed sometimes, with those who are not anxious to show their zeal; but as most of these functionaries are so, you would probably, if it was a village, be sent on under a guard to the next town, and if it were a town would be thrown into prison. And you know, to get in a prison in our days is--"

"Equivalent to a sentence of death," Leigh put in as he hesitated.

"You must get papers somehow--something that would pass at any rate in the villages, where as often as not there is not a man who can read. I will see what I can do. A cousin of mine is clerk to the mayor. He is a good fellow, though he has to pretend to be a violent supporter of the Convention.

"I don't know how you are situated, monsieur, but times are hard, and all salaries terribly in arrears; and when they are paid it is in assignats, and I need hardly say that when you pay in assignats you don't buy cheap."

"We have money," Leigh said, "and I would pay any reasonable sum, in gold, for proper papers."

"Sapristi! You might almost tempt the maire himself, by offering him gold. Only he would suspect that you must have more hidden away, and that by arresting you, he could make himself master of the whole, instead of only a part; but since you offer gold, I have no doubt that my cousin would not mind running some little risk. How much shall I say, monsieur?"

"I would, if necessary, give forty louis."

"That is more than his yearly salary," the innkeeper said; "half of that would be ample. I will go to him at once. It is important that you should get papers of some kind, for at any moment anyone might come in and demand to see them."

"Here are ten louis. I have more sewn up in my saddle, and can give him the other ten later on, when I get an opportunity to go to the stable unnoticed."

"That will do very well, monsieur. I will be off at once."

It was an hour before he returned, and Leigh and Patsey had just finished supper. As there were two or three other persons in the room he said nothing, but signified by a little nod that he had succeeded. A quarter of an hour later the other customers, having finished their meal, went out.

"Here are your papers," he said, as he handed a document to Leigh.

It was a printed form, blanks being left for the names, description, and the object of journey.

"Arthenay Mairie,

"To all concerned--

"It is hereby testified that citizen Lucien Porson, and his sister citoyenne Martin, both of good repute and well disposed to the Republic, natives of this town of Arthenay, are travelling, accompanied by a child of the latter, to Marseilles, whither they go on family affairs, and to join citoyenne Martin's husband, a master mariner of that town."

The destination had been altered when they heard of the state of things at Toulon. The document was purposed to be signed by the maire, under his official seal.

"There is only one difficulty," the landlord said, as Leigh and Patsey warmly thanked him; "and that is that, although it will pass you when you have once left this town, it would be dangerous to use it here; and you may at any moment be asked for it. But my cousin, who is a charming fellow, pointed out the difficulty to me, and said:

"'The best thing will be for me to take a couple of men, and pay the official visit to him, myself.'

"I expect that he will be here in a few minutes."

"Then, as the stableman has gone out at last--at least I see no lights there--I will go and get the rest of the money."

"Yes, I met him a hundred yards off, on my way back. There is no one about. I will take a lantern and go out with you."

In ten minutes they returned, Leigh having the ten louis required in his pocket. A quarter of an hour later the door opened, and a man wearing the scarf which showed him to be an officer of the municipality entered, followed by two men with the cockade of the Republic in their hats.

"This is citizen Porson and citoyenne Martin, his sister," the landlord, who accompanied the party, said.

The functionary walked up to the table and said gruffly, "Your papers, citizen."

Leigh handed him the document. He glanced through it.

"That is right," he said. "Citizen Porson and citoyenne Martin, of the arrondissement of Paris, travelling to Marseilles, duly signed by the maire of the arrondissement and duly sealed. That is all in order. We are obliged to be particular, citizen; there are many ill disposed to the Republic travelling through the country."

"Will you sit down, citizen, and take a glass of wine with me? Landlord, draw two stoups of wine for these two good citizens."

The two men followed the landlord out to the public room.

"I should think, Jeannette," Leigh said to his sister, "you had better to retire to bed. You have had a long day's ride, and must, I am sure, be tired out."

As soon as she had left the room, Leigh dropped the ten louis into the adjoint's hand.

"I thank you with all my heart," he said. "You have done a good action, and I can assure you that it can do no harm to the Republic, against whom I have no intention of conspiring. There is no fear, I suppose, that the maire's signature may be questioned?"

"There is no fear whatever of that, because the signature is precisely similar to that which occurs on all official documents. The maire is without doubt an excellent Republican, and a devoted servant of the Convention, but he is altogether ignorant of letters, and the consequence is that I sign all official documents for him. So you see there was no trouble whatever in filling in, signing, and sealing this letter. The only matter that concerned me was that, if by any chance you should be arrested as a suspect, possibly a demand might be made as to how you obtained this pass. However, even that did not trouble me greatly; for as I myself open and read the maire's letters, I should have no difficulty in keeping him altogether in the dark as to the purport of any letter that might come, and should myself pen an answer, with explanations which would no doubt be found satisfactory."

"And now can you tell me, sir, which in your opinion would be the best port for me to make to, to leave the country? It matters little whether we go by land or sea."

"It would be more easy for you to make your way to a port than across the frontier," the adjoint said, "but when you reach a port, your difficulties would but begin. In the first place, our trade with foreign countries is almost at a standstill, and every vessel that goes out is rigidly searched for concealed emigres.

"On the other hand, once across the frontier your troubles would be at an end; but every road is closely watched, every village is on the lookout, for the orders are precise that all persons leaving France shall be arrested and detained until in a position to prove their identity, and to place the truth of the reason given for journeying beyond all doubt. I do not say that it might not be possible to bribe peasants to take you by unfrequented paths over the Jura; but the journey would be arduous in the extreme, and probably impossible to be performed on horseback.

"But for my part, if I were in your position and desired to leave the country, I should go north instead of south. I should go in the first place to Paris, stay there in quiet lodgings for a little time until you became known, and you might then get your papers visaed to enable you to continue your journey to Calais or Dunkirk. Money will go just as far among the incorruptibles of Paris as it will here. You might obtain a passage down the Seine, to Rouen or Havre."

"That would certainly suit us best. I regret, now, that I had the paper made out for Marseilles."

"That can easily be remedied, monsieur. If you will walk back with me to the mairie, I will write a fresh paper out, and destroy the one I have given you. But what shall I say is your object in journeying to Paris? You are too young to be going to purchase goods and, indeed, would hardly be taking a woman and child with you for such a purpose.

"Now, monsieur, frankly tell me who you are. I have some relations in Paris, quiet bourgeois, who keep a small shop near the markets. If I were to give you a letter to them, saying that you have business in Paris, and have asked me to recommend someone who would provide you with quiet lodgings, no doubt they would willingly take you in. But I would not involve them in danger. You might be recognised as being members of some family who are proscribed, and in that case not only would my friends get into trouble but, as they would, of course, say that you were recommended to them by me, I might find myself in a very unpleasant position."

"There is no fear of anything of that sort. I and my sister are both English. She married the son of a merchant at Nantes, and I came over with her to learn the business. There have, as you know, been troubles in that part of France. We endeavoured to escape, but she was separated from her husband--who has, I greatly fear, been killed--and we, of course, are both anxious to rejoin our family in England."

"How long have you been in France, monsieur? You speak the language well."

"We have been over here nearly three years."

"Well, I do not think that there is any risk; unless, of course, you are caught in the act of trying to make your escape. But I think that it would be as well that my friends should be prepared for your coming. I know a man who is leaving for Paris tomorrow. I will give him my letter, and ask him to deliver it personally, as soon as he gets there; then you can follow, twenty-four hours later. Now that it is known that I have examined your papers, and found them correct, there will be no further inquiry about you and, at any rate, you could stay here for a day or two without any questions being asked."

"That would be an admirable plan, monsieur; and I cannot tell you how much I am obliged to you."

"Say no more about that, monsieur; you have paid me well for it and, moreover, I am not a bad fellow, though at present I am obliged to appear to be a strong supporter of the people in Paris. Now, if you will put on your hat and come along with me, I will leave you a short distance from the hotel de ville, to which I have access at all hours. I shall of course simply put, in the passport, that you are travelling to Paris on private matters, and that you will stay with your friend, citizen Tourrier, in the rue des Halles."

A quarter of an hour later Leigh returned to the auberge, furnished with the required paper. The adjoint had said, on handing it to him:

"I shall not come round tomorrow. We met as strangers yesterday, and it is as well I should not appear to be intimate with you. But should you find yourself in any difficulty, send for me at once, and I will soon set matters right."

"Is it all satisfactorily arranged, monsieur?" the hotel keeper asked, when Leigh returned.

"Perfectly. Your friend has done even more than he promised."

And he told him of the change that had been made in the plans.

"That is certainly better. I have been wondering, myself, how you would ever be able to get away from Marseilles. Now it seems comparatively easy. I have no doubt that my cousin's friends in Paris will be able to get you another pass, or to put you in the way of travelling to one of the ports;

though no doubt it will be almost as difficult to get away, from there, as from Marseilles."

"I think that could be managed, landlord. I am a pretty good sailor, and there ought to be no great difficulty in getting hold of a boat and making out to sea and, when once away, I could steer for England, or get on board some vessel bound there."

He tapped at his sister's door. She was still up.

"You are very late, Leigh."

"Yes, but you will be able to sleep as long as you like tomorrow, as we are not going to start till next day, and are then going north instead of south. Our paper has been changed for Paris, instead of Marseilles; and we are going to the house of a cousin of the man who gave me the pass, so we shall be safe so far; and ought to have no difficulty, whatever, in journeying from there either to Havre or one of the northern ports. I will tell you all about it, tomorrow."

They passed the next day quietly, and both felt better for the short rest. In addition to the pass, the adjoint had given Leigh a note to his cousin. It was unsealed, and read:

"My dear Cousin,

"The bearer of this is Monsieur Porson, and his sister, Madame Martin, of whom I wrote to you. You will find them amiable people, who will give you but little trouble. I have assured them that they will find themselves very comfortable with you, and that you will do all in your power for them, for the sake of your affectionate cousin.

"Simon Valles,

"Adjoint to the maire of Arthenay."

They journeyed by easy stages, stopping at Etampes, Arpajon, and Longjumeau, and rode on the fourth day into Paris. They had no difficulty in finding the shop of Monsieur Tourrier. It was a grocer's and, as soon as they alighted from their horses, its owner came out and greeted them heartily.

"Madame and monsieur are both most welcome," he said. "I have received a letter from my cousin Simon. I am glad, indeed, to receive his friends. Fortunately our rooms upstairs are unlet. Strangers are rare in Paris, at present."

He called a boy from the shop, and told him to show Leigh the way to some stables near. He then entered the house, accompanied by Patsey with her child. Here she was received by Madame Tourrier, a plump-faced businesslike woman, and was not long in finding out that she was the real head of the establishment.

"I have got the rooms ready for you," she said. "We were surprised, indeed, to get a letter from Simon Valles; for he is a poor correspondent, though he generally comes to stay with us for three days, once a year. He is a good fellow, but it is a pity that he did not go into trade. He would have done better for himself than by becoming adjoint to the maire of Arthenay. It has a high sound, but in these days, when men are paid their salaries in assignats, it is but a poor living. However, I suppose that it is an easy life, for I don't think hard work would suit Simon. The last time he was up we tried to persuade him that he would do better here, but he laughed and said that people's heads were safer in Arthenay than they were in Paris. But that is folly; the Convention does not trouble itself with small shopkeepers. It knows well enough that we have work enough to do to earn our living, without troubling ourselves about politics; yet if the truth were known, a good many of us are better to do than some of those they call aristocrats. This is a busy quarter, you see, and we are close to the markets, and the country people who come in know that we sell good groceries, and on cheaper terms than they can get them in their villages. We should do better, still, if my husband would but bestir himself; but men are poor creatures, and I don't know what would become of them, if they had not us women to look after their affairs."

They now reached the rooms, which were small but comfortable, and the price which Madame Tourrier named seemed to Patsey to be very moderate.

"You see, your room is furnished as a sitting room also, madame, and you and your brother can talk over your affairs here. As to your meals, I could provide your cafe au lait in the morning, but I can't undertake to cook for you. But there are many good places, where you can obtain your meals at a cheap rate, in the neighbourhood. How long do you expect to remain in Paris?"

"That I cannot say, at present. My husband is a sailor, but I have not heard from him for a long time. At Arthenay there is but small opportunity of learning what happens outside, and it may be that I shall have to travel to Havre to obtain news of him; although I am troubled greatly by the fear that his ship has been lost, or captured by the English. We have never been in Paris before, and my brother naturally wishes to stay a short time, to see the sights."

Madame Tourrier shook her head.

"There are but few sights to see," she said. "The churches are all closed, or at least are turned into meeting places and clubs. It is not as it was before the troubles began; there are few amusements, and no reviews or pageants. I do not say that it is not better so. I have no opinion on such subjects. I have never once been to the hall of representatives. I have no time for such follies and, except on Sunday afternoons, I never stir out of doors. Still, no doubt, it will all be new to him, and as you have horses you can ride over to Versailles, and other places round. There is not much of that now; people think of nothing but the Convention, talk of nothing but of the speeches there, and of Robespierre and Saint Just and Danton. It seems to me that they are always quarrelling, and that nothing much comes of it.

"Now if you will excuse me, madame, I will go down to the shop again. My husband cannot be trusted there a minute and, if my back is turned, he will be selling the best sugar for the price of the worst, then we shall lose money; or the worst sugar for the price of the best, and then we shall lose customers."

So saying, she hurried away. In a few minutes Leigh came up.

"I was told where to find you," he said. "Madame is in the thick of business, and there were half a dozen customers waiting to be served. Monsieur was standing a few yards away from the front of the shop. It was he who gave me instructions for finding your room.

"'It is best,' he said, 'that madame should be asked no questions while she is busy. I always go out myself, when customers come in. She is one of the best of wives, and manages affairs excellently, but her temper is short. She likes to do things her own way and, as it pleases her, I never interfere with her.'"

"I think he is wise not to do so," Patsey laughed. "I can see already that she is mistress of the establishment. But from what I have seen at Nantes, I think that it is generally the women who look after the shops and mind the businesses. However, though she speaks sharply, I should say that she is a kind-hearted woman. However, we may be very thankful that we have obtained a shelter where we can live, safely and quietly, until we have fixed on our plans for the future."

But although Monsieur Tourrier was, in all matters connected with the business, but as a child in the hands of his wife, he was far better acquainted with what was passing around them; and when Leigh mentioned to him that he intended to ride out to Versailles, he at once warned him against doing so.

"My dear monsieur," he said, "I know nothing of the state of things at Arthenay, and for aught I know people may go out riding for pleasure there; but it would be little short of madness to attempt such a thing here. At present things have got to such a state that for any man to seem richer than another is, in itself, a crime. Here all must be on an equality. Were you to ride out, every man you pass would look askance at you. At the first village through which you rode you would be arrested, and to be arrested at present is to be condemned. There are no questions asked, the prisoners are brought in in bunches, and are condemned wholesale. I say nothing against the condemnation of the aristocrats; but when perhaps two or three aristocrats are brought up with half a dozen journalists, and a dozen others who may have been arrested merely out of spite, and are all condemned in five minutes, it is clear that the only way to live is to avoid being arrested, and the only way to avoid being arrested is to avoid attracting attention.

"If you were really going on a matter of business, it would be different, but to ride to Versailles merely to see the place would be regarded as ample proof that you were an aristocrat; and no one would regard your papers as anything but a proof that these had been obtained by fraud, and that you were either an aristocrat, or a spy of Pitt's, or a Girondist, and certainly an enemy of the Convention. Therefore, monsieur, if you wish to go anywhere, walk, or go out in a market cart, for to ride might be fatal."

"I will take your advice," Leigh said. "I did not think that things were so bad as that."

"They could not be worse, monsieur; it would be impossible. But we who are quiet men think that it cannot go on much longer; even the sans-culottes are getting tired of bloodshed. There is no longer a great crowd to see the executions, and the tumbrils pass along without insults and imprecations being hurled against the prisoners.

"The men of the Convention, having killed all the Girondists, are now quarrelling among themselves. Robespierre is still all powerful, but the party opposed to him are gaining in strength, and there is a feeling that, ere long, there will be a terrible struggle between them and, if Robespierre is beaten, there are many of us who think that the reign of terror will come to an end. We who are too insignificant to be watched talk these things over together, when we gather at our cafe, and there is no one but ourselves present; and even then we talk only in whispers, but we all live in hopes of a change, and any change must surely be for the better."

Chapter 16
A Friend At Last:

Day after day, Leigh went out into the town. More than once he saw the fatal tumbrils going along in the distance, but he always turned and walked in the opposite direction. Once or twice, having changed his clothes for those of a workman, he fought his way into the public galleries of the Convention and listened to the speeches; in which it seemed to him that the principal object of each speaker was to exceed those who had gone before him in violence, and that the most violent was the most loudly applauded, both by the galleries and the Assembly.

Patsey was most anxious to be off, but he urged that it would not do to show haste. She did not leave the house at all, while he was out almost all day. At the end of the fortnight, he told Monsieur Tourrier that he had now finished his business, and asked him if he could obtain from the maire of the arrondissement a pass down to Havre.

"It is a pity that you did not get your pass direct from Arthenay," he said. "You say that your sister wants to make inquiries about a husband there, and that you are taking her down, and you also say that you are a sailor."

"Yes."

"Then, I should think that the best thing for you would be to dress yourself as a sailor again. It will seem more natural than for you to be in that civilian dress. I can go with you, and say that you were strongly recommended to me by the maire's adjoint at Arthenay, and that your papers are all en regle. If he asks why you did not have your papers made out in the first place to Havre, say that you had hoped to have been joined by your brother-in-law here; but as he has not arrived your sister is anxious about him, and wishes therefore to go on to Havre, which indeed he has requested her to do, as it was uncertain whether he would be able to leave his ship.

"I know, of course, that it is all right, or my cousin would not have recommended you so strongly to me; but in these days everyone is suspicious, and one cannot be too cautious. I will get one of the market authorities to go up with me. I am well known to them all, and 'tis likely that none of the people at the mairie will know me, seeing that I am a quiet man, and keep myself to myself."

Leigh had no trouble in buying a sailor's dress, at a shop down by the wharves and, having put this on, went up with Monsieur Tourrier and one of the market officers to the mairie. As the former had anticipated, there was no difficulty. Leigh's pass was examined. The market official testified to the grocer as being a well-known citizen, doing business with the market people, and taking no part in public affairs; while Monsieur Tourrier showed the letter that he had received from his cousin, the adjoint at Arthenay.

"What is the name of the ship which your sister's husband commands?" the maire asked.

"The Henriette, a lugger. Formerly she traded with England but, since the war broke out, she trades between the ports on our western coast."

"And you have been a sailor on board her?"

"Yes, citizen."

The maire nodded, and made out the pass for Jeannette Martin, travelling to join her husband, the captain of the lugger Henriette; for her brother, Lucien Porson; and for Louis Martin, aged two years, son of the above-named citoyenne Martin.

As they agreed that it would now be best to travel by water, Leigh next went to the stables and, as the horses were both good ones, obtained a fair price for them. The next morning they went on board a sailing craft going down the river and, after a cordial adieu from their host and hostess, and a promise to take up their abode there, on their return through Paris, they went on board. Leigh had sold the saddles with the horses; having, on the journey to Paris, removed the bundles of assignats concealed in them.

The accommodation on board was very fair. Patsey occupied a roomy cabin aft, the rest slept in a large cabin forward; for before the troubles began, the majority of people travelling from Paris down to Rouen or Havre went by water, and although the boats were mainly constructed for the carriage of merchandise, the conveyance of passengers formed an important part of the profits. At present, however, there was but little travelling, and Patsey had the women's cabin to herself; while one other male messenger, with the master and two hands, had the forward compartments to themselves.

The master explained that, at ordinary times, his two men occupied a tiny place boarded off from the hold, or in summer slept on deck; but that, as there were so few passengers, they lived with the rest "for," as he growled under his breath, "the present."

The voyage was slow but not unpleasant. There was scarce wind enough to fill the two sails carried by the boat, but the captain and his two hands frequently got out sweeps, to keep the boat in the middle of the current. They stopped for a day at Rouen, while the cargo destined for that town was landed. Patsey and Leigh were glad to spend the day in the town, visiting the cathedral, taking their meals at a restaurant, for the cuisine on board the boat was not of the highest character.

"We used to keep a regular cook," the captain lamented. "In those days we often carried several passengers; but at present, when we seldom have more than one or two, we cannot afford it. The Revolution is no doubt a grand thing, and has greatly benefited the nation, but it has weighed hardly on us. There are but half the boats on the river there used to be, and they are hardly paying expenses, now that no one travels. Those that go to sea are worse off still for, what with the falling off in trade, and with the English cruisers all along the coast, there is little employment for seamen, save in the privateers. However, they don't starve; for the greater portion of the men on the coast have to go in the ships of the Republic."

On the sixth day after leaving Paris, they arrived at Havre. Here they had no difficulty in obtaining lodgings, in a small auberge near the port. Their pass was, on their arrival, sent to the authorities of the town and duly stamped. Leigh's first inquiries were for the Henriette. He found that she was well known in the port, and had sailed for La Rochelle, six weeks before.

"She does not very often come up here," one of the sailors said. "Sometimes she is months between her visits. As likely as not, she may have been captured on her way down. Her port is Bordeaux and, if you wanted to find her, you had much better have gone straight there than come to this place."

"I do want to find her," Leigh said. "Is there any chance of finding a ship going down south?"

"Well, you might find one," the man said; "but you would have to take your chance of getting there. Many of the ships are laid up, for the risk of capture is great. It is small craft that, for the most part, make the venture. They creep along inshore, and either run into a port or anchor under the guns of a battery if they see a British cruiser outside. Drawing so little water, they can keep in nearer than a cruiser would dare to; and as they all can take the mud, they do not mind if they stick on the sands for a tide."

Leigh returned with the news to his sister.

"What do you think, Patsey?" he said. "I do not say that we cannot cross from here in a boat, though I have learned that the entrance to the Channel is guarded by gunboats. If we passed safely through these, we should have serious risk and many hardships to undergo. I hear that there are numerous French privateers, and we might be picked up by one of them, instead of by an English cruiser. I am afraid that our passes, in that case, would not avail us in the slightest.

"Now, if we go down to Bordeaux, we have only to wait till the Henriette comes in. Possibly she may be there when we arrive. In that case, I am sure that Lefaux will be willing to take us out, and either put us on board a British cruiser, or land us in England."

"Certainly we will go to Bordeaux," Patsey said. "We may find Jean there. If he escaped that night he would make for the Loire and, as he is a good swimmer, he would get over without difficulty, and he would then try to make his way towards Bordeaux."

"That may be so, Patsey; but I would not be too sanguine about our finding him there. It was so much nearer for him to have made for one of the northern ports that he might very well have done so and, as soon as he managed to obtain a sea outfit, he would no longer be suspected of having anything to do with the Vendeans."

They had learnt before this that, after the fight at Le Mans, the Vendeans had made for the river, had desperately fought their way through the forces that barred their march, had come down on the banks, but had failed to find any means to cross it. Then they had turned into Brittany again for a short distance, had fought two or three more desperate battles, and had again reached the Loire. There was but one leaky boat to be found. In this la Rochejaquelein, with a few of his officers, had crossed the river to bring back some boats that were moored on the opposite bank. Directly they got across they were attacked, but la Rochejaquelein, with two or three others, effected their escape.

After this the Vendeans no longer kept together. The women and children, wounded and invalids, hid themselves in the woods; where they were hunted down like wild beasts, and either slaughtered at once or sent to Nantes, where thousands were either executed or drowned by the infamous Carrier, one of the most sanguinary villains produced by the Revolution. Many of the men managed to cross the river either by swimming on rough rafts or in boats. In La Vendee the war was still going on, for Charette had marched up again from Lower Poitou, and was keeping a large force of the Republican troops engaged.

"I will try not to hope too much," Patsey said. "But at any rate, I am for going down to Bordeaux for, apart from the chance of finding Jean there, it seems much safer than putting out to sea in a little boat."

"I certainly think so," Leigh replied. "Now I will go out and make inquiries as to what craft there may be, bound south."

He returned in a couple of hours.

"I have arranged for our passage, Patsey. She is a fast-looking little craft, with very decent accommodation. She is in the wine trade, and brought a cargo safely up last week, and will start again the day after tomorrow. She carries a crew of eight hands; and I have made inquiries about the captain, and hear a very good report of him, and he seemed to me a first-rate fellow. When I mentioned the name of the Henriette he said that he knew her well, and was acquainted both with the present captain and with your Jean. He had heard, from Lefaux, that her former owner had been denounced, and had been obliged to fly from Nantes to a chateau that he had in La Vendee. The Henriette has never been into Nantes since, but went down to Bordeaux, and was there registered in another owner's name, and Lefaux had worked for him ever since.

"'I fancy,' he said, 'she sometimes makes a run with brandy to England. She was in that business before, and had, Lefaux said, been chased many a time by English cutters, but had always managed to give them the slip.'

"I was half inclined to tell him that I was Jean's brother-in-law, but I thought it better not to until we had been to sea for a day or two, and had learned a little more about him."

The next day Leigh went to the mairie and explained that, not having found the ship commanded by citoyenne Martin's husband, and thinking it likely that they would hear of him at Bordeaux, they had taken passage by the Trois Freres, which sailed the next day. The addition was made to his papers without a question, and the next morning they went on board. They were heartily received by the captain.

"You ought to bring us luck, madame," he said; "I mean citoyenne, but the old word slips out of one's mouth, sometimes. It is not often that I have a lady passenger. There are few who travel now and, before the war broke out, people preferred taking passage in larger ships than mine. Still, I will do my best to make you comfortable, and I can assure you that Leon, my cook, is by no means a bad hand at turning out dainty dishes. He was cook in an hotel, at one time; but he let his tongue wag too freely and, having to leave suddenly, was glad enough to ship with me. Fortunately he likes the life, and I do not think anything would tempt him to go back to an hotel kitchen again."

"I am not particular, I can assure you," Patsey said. "In these times we all have to rough it. Still, I own that I like a good dinner better than a bad one."

"We shall put in to a good many little ports," the skipper said. "Sailing as close as we do inshore, I always make a port if I can, as evening comes on; and we are therefore never without fresh meat, fish, and vegetables."

"How long shall we be going down?"

"That I cannot tell you. It all depends upon the wind. We may, too, be kept in port for two or three days if there is an enemy's cruiser anywhere about. We may get there in ten days, we may take three weeks."

Before the boat set sail, a commissary with two men came on board and examined the passes of the passengers, and searched below the hatches to make sure that no one was hidden there. As soon as they had completed their inspection the sails were hoisted, and the Trois Freres started on her way down the Channel. The wind was light and blowing from the southwest, and they were just able to lay their course, and anchored for the night off the mouth of the Vire river.

"I suppose tomorrow you will get round the Cape de la Hague, captain?" Leigh said.

"No, we shall not attempt that. The coast is a very difficult one, with furious currents. We shall bring up off Cherbourg and start at daylight; and shall, I hope, be well down towards the bay of Avranches by nightfall. There is no fear of a British cruiser till we get out towards Ushant. They do not care about coming inside the islands; what with the fogs, the rocks, and the currents, it is safer outside than in. Besides, there is little to be picked up except coasters like ourselves, and fishing boats. There is hardly any foreign trade between Havre and Brest. It is from there down to the mouth of the Gironde that their cruisers are so thick. From Ushant to Boulogne there are plenty of them, but these are chiefly occupied in guarding their ships going up and down the Channel from our privateers, which run out from every port: Dieppe and Havre, Granville, Avranches, and Saint Malo."

The skipper had by no means over praised his cook, who turned them out a better dinner than any that they had eaten since the troubles began, with the exception only of those they had had at Arthenay.

"He takes a pride in it," the captain said, "and you will never get good work done in any line, unless by a man who does so. A sailor who is careless about the appearance of his ship is sure to be careless about the keeping of the watch, and is not to be trusted in matters of navigation. When you see a craft with every rope in its place, everything spotlessly clean, the brass work polished up, and the paint carefully attended to, you may be sure that the skipper is as particular in more important matters. It is just so with our man. It is a little bit of a galley, but his saucepans shine like gold, everything is clean and in its place. He grumbles if we run short of anything, and is a good deal more particular about my dinner being just what it should be than I am myself.

"Sometimes when we have rough weather I say to him, 'Make me a soup today, Leon. I shall be well content with that, and it is not weather for turning out a regular dinner.'

"He always replies gravely, 'Monsieur, anyone can cook when the sea is calm. It is on an occasion like this that one who knows his business is required. Monsieur will dine as usual.'

"And up comes dinner, with three or four courses, cooked to perfection. For myself, I would rather snatch a few mouthfuls and go up on deck again; but this would hurt Leon's feelings if he saw it, and he might even consider that he must seek another employer, for that his talents were wasted upon me; so I go through it all with exemplary patience. I would not lose him for anything, not only because I own I like good food, but the Trois Freres has such a reputation for good living that, if I am in port, passengers will wait for days to sail with me, instead of going by other craft.

"And then, too, I have no trouble with my crew, and it is rarely, indeed, that I change one of my hands; for although their meals are of course much simpler than mine, they are all perfect in their way.

"It takes a great deal of trouble off my hands, too. Instead of my having a dozen little accounts to go into, at every port we enter, I allow him a certain sum and he manages on that--so much a day for my own table, so much for each passenger, and so much for the crew. How he does it, I don't know. I find that it is cheaper than it used to be, before his time; and yet I have all sorts of dainties I never dreamt of, then.

"I say to him sometimes, 'Leon, you must be ruining yourself;' but he smiles and says, 'I am well content, captain; if you are satisfied, I am so.'

"He buys the fish off the boats as they come in, and I can understand that he gets them far more cheaply than if he waited till they were hawked in the streets. He is great at omelets and, when he has a chance, he is ashore before the countrywomen come into the market; and will buy the whole stock of eggs, a pound or two of butter, and three or four couples of fowls from one woman, who is glad to sell cheaply and so be free to return home at once. At Bordeaux he lays in a stock of snipe and other birds from the sand hills and marshes, oysters, and other such matters. He is a great favourite with the crew and, in cold weather or stormy nights, there is always hot soup ready for them.

"He has only one fault. As a rule, the cooks are expected to help get up the anchor and sails, but he will not put a hand to sailors' work. He says that a cook must not have a rough hand, but that it should be as soft as a woman's. Personally, I believe that is all nonsense. However, as we have a fairly strong crew, I do not press him on the subject; though sometimes, when I tail on to a rope myself, and see him leaning quietly against his galley smoking his pipe, I am inclined to use strong language."

"I don't think that is much to put up with, captain," Patsey said with a smile, "if he always cooks for you such breakfasts and dinners as we have had today; and I do think that there is, perhaps, something in what he says about rough hands."

"Well, I feel that myself," he said. "Still, it is a little aggravating, when everyone else is working hard, to see a man calmly smoking, and never raising a finger to help."

The next day they kept very close inshore. More than once a white sail was seen in the distance, which the captain pronounced, from its cut, to belong to a British cruiser.

"The weather is fine, you see, and the wind is steady, so they are coming rather farther into the bay than usual. We shall see more of them, as soon as we are round that cape ahead, for they keep a very sharp lookout off Cherbourg."

It was not, however, until they had rounded Ushant that any British vessel came near enough to cause them uneasiness. There were two large frigates cruising backwards and forwards off Brest, and a brig-of-war came within shot, as they were doubling Penmarch Point.

"There is plenty of water for her, here," the skipper said. "However, she will hardly catch us, before we are under shelter of the batteries of Quimper."

"I should have thought that she would hardly think you worth the trouble of chasing."

"It may be that they think we are carrying fresh meat from Saint Malo to Nantes. There is a good deal of trade that way, this time of year, when meat will keep good for a week. Or it may be that they want to get news of what ships there are in Brest. However, it is certain that he is in earnest; he is politely requesting us to lower our sails."

He laughed as a puff of white smoke broke out from the brig and, a second or two later, a ball dashed up the water fifty yards ahead of them. The emotions with which Patsey and Leigh watched the brig differed much from those of the captain. They would gladly have seen the lugger overhauled and captured, but they soon saw that there was little chance of this. The lugger was a fast boat, the wind just suited her, and the brig fell farther and farther astern until, as the former entered the bay of Quimper and laid her course north, the brig hauled her wind and turned to rejoin the vessels off Brest.

Keeping close to the land, they passed L'Orient and Quiberon and Vannes without stopping, and did not drop anchor again until they entered the bay on the eastern side of the island of Noirmoutier. The next day they passed out through the narrow channel of Froment, and had gone between the island and the mainland, for a distance of two miles, when they saw a large brig making in towards the shore.

"Another of those cruisers," the captain exclaimed. "This is more serious, for there is no bay we can run into, and the fellow is bringing the wind down with him. Our only chance is to anchor under the guns of Saint Jean des Montes; we shall be lucky if we get there in time."

The brig came up fast, and was within a mile when the lugger caught the wind; then running along rapidly she held her own until off Saint Jean, when she ran in as close as her draught would permit, and anchored. Two French privateers were already lying in there, one having dropped anchor only a few minutes before the Trois Freres arrived.

"I expect it was that fellow that the brig was in chase of, and I am not by any means sure that we have done with her, yet. They are as likely as not to try to cut out one, if not both, of these privateers. Of course it would look like madness, with the guns of that battery on the height protecting them, but they have done such things so often that one can never say that one is altogether safe from them."

The brig stood in until two or three guns in the battery opened fire, when she turned and made out to sea again.

"That means nothing," the captain said. "Of course she would not attack in daylight. I dare say she will sail pretty nearly out of sight, so as to make the privateers believe that she had no intention of meddling with them. If I was sure that was her game, I would get up sail again, as soon as it is dark, and make for Oleron; but it is likely enough that she may think that that is just what the privateers will do, and will sail in that direction herself, so as to cut them off before they get there, and force them to fight without the protection of a shore battery.

"There is the bell for breakfast! Leon would not be two minutes late, if there was an action going on close to us."

Half an hour later they went on deck again.

"At any rate, the sea has saved us the trouble of discussing the matter," the captain said. "We are aground. The tide turned just before we got here. It is now half past twelve, and we shall not be afloat again for nearly twelve hours.

"Well, there is one thing: if they are thinking of trying to cut out the privateers, they are not likely to do it before two or three o'clock in the morning. As soon as we float I shall haul out, a cable's length or two, so as to ensure our being able to get off; and if they do attack, I shall get up my sails at once, and run south. They will be too much occupied to give us a thought. Whereas if I stay here, and they capture the privateers, they might take it into their heads to come on board and set fire to the lugger; which, as I am part owner, would be a very serious matter to me."

It was apparent that the privateers had no thought of the brig returning, at any rate at present, as boats went backwards and forwards between them and the shore.

"What do you think, Leigh?" his sister asked quietly, as they were sitting alone together.

"I do not know in the least," he said. "Our best chance is that the two Frenchmen seem to be so confident that they are safe under the guns of the fort, that they will take no very great precautions. One of them mounts eight guns, the other ten, and they ought to be a match for the brig, even without the forts; for we could see, by her ports, that she only carries sixteen guns. However, I think myself that she will very likely have a try at them. It will be a very dark night, for the sky is overcast and there is no moon."

It was between ten and eleven when, just as they were about to turn in, the captain ran in.

"Quick, madame, you must hurry on your clothes! I heard a sound just now that could only be made by a boat. As we are still aground, I shall bring a boat alongside and land. There is nothing like being on the safe side!"

The two privateers were lying a quarter of a mile farther out, and there were still lights burning on board them.

"The fools!" the captain growled, as Leigh and his sister came on deck; Leigh carrying little Louis, who had been put to bed fully dressed. Indeed, no time had been lost, for his mother and Leigh had agreed that it would be better to lie down in their clothes, in case of an alarm being given.

"The fools!" the captain repeated. "If they had extinguished every light, as they ought to have done, the boats would have had difficulty in finding them. Now, they could not miss them if they tried.

"Now, madame, will you please take your place in the boat with me? I am sure that there are boats coming along. Of course the oars are muffled, and there is enough sea on to prevent us hearing the splash. I think the noise I heard was caused by one of the stretchers giving way."

Reluctantly Patsey and Leigh took their places in the boat. Just as they reached the shore, a shout was heard on board one of the privateers and, a moment later, came the sound of a British cheer. It was followed by a hubbub of shouts, then muskets flashed out from the decks, and almost immediately came the sounds of conflict. A blue light was struck on the deck of one of the privateers and, by its light, those on shore could obtain a view of the conflict. The boats had boarded from the shore side. Two of them lay alongside each of the privateers, and the crews could be seen climbing up by the chains and leaping down upon the decks.

"They deserve to be taken," the captain said. "They have not even triced up their boarding nets."

A confused medley of sounds came to the shore; with the shouts of the French sailors were mingled the clash of cutlasses and the crack of pistols. The British sailors fought, for the most part, silently. On the heights above, blue lights were burning in the battery, and men could be seen standing on its crest watching the combat below, but powerless to assist their friends.

It was but five minutes after the outbreak of the combat when a loud British cheer, followed by a dead silence, showed that one, at least, of the privateers had been captured. The fighting still continued on the deck of the other craft but, from the vessel that had been captured, a number of sailors leapt down into one of their boats, and rowed to the assistance of their comrades. The reinforcements apparently decided the issue of the fight, for in a couple of minutes the British cheer was again heard, and the blue light was promptly extinguished, as were all the other lights on both vessels. Scarcely was this done when the guns from the battery boomed out.

"It is of no use their firing," the captain said. "I don't think they can depress the guns enough to bear upon them.

"There, they are making sail!" he went on, as the creaking of blocks was heard. "Of course they have cut the cables. They would not waste time in getting up anchors, with the forts playing upon them. However, it is mere waste of powder and shot on such a night as this. I don't suppose the gunners can make them out, now; for a certainty they won't be able to do so, as soon as they have moved off another quarter of a mile. Of course a stray shot may hit them, but practically it is all over.

"I think that we can go on board again. I did not think of it before, but they would hardly set fire to us, for the light would enable the gunners to see them till they were a long way out.

"There is no doubt those Englishmen can fight. Our men are all right when they are under sail, and it is a question of exchanging broadsides, but the success of so many of their cutting out expeditions shows that, somehow or other, we lose heart when we are boarded. We must have had nearly twice as many men as there were in those four boats, and yet it seemed to be a certainty, as soon as the English got among them.

"Our craft had much better have sailed out together when the brig came in this morning, and fought her fairly. They ought to have been more than a match for her. No doubt they would have done so if they had thought that they would be attacked tonight; but they relied upon the battery, and allowed themselves to be taken completely by surprise.

"I could see, even from this distance, that most of them were fighting in their shirts; and I expect that they were sound asleep when the attack began, and men roused in that sudden way can never be relied upon to do their duty as they would do, if prepared to meet it."

The party were soon on board the lugger again. Just as daylight was breaking there was a trampling of feet on the deck, and Leigh, going up, found that sail was being hoisted. Keeping close to the shore they ran down, without putting in anywhere, to La Rochelle. Here they waited for a day and then, keeping inside the Isle of Oleron, entered the Gironde and, the next day, anchored in the Garonne, off the quays of Bordeaux.

After thanking the captain very heartily for his kindness during the passage, they landed, showed their papers to an official on the quay, and then, being unhampered by luggage, walked quietly away. As there was nothing particularly noticeable in their appearance, they attracted no attention whatever. It was five o'clock when they landed, and already becoming dusk. They waited until it was quite dark and then, having inquired for the house of Monsieur Flambard, the merchant to whom Jean had assigned the Henriette, they knocked at his door.

It was a handsome house, not far from the quays. The lower portion was evidently occupied by the offices. As a servant opened the door, Leigh, seeing that his sister hesitated to speak, inquired if Monsieur Flambard was at home.

"He is," the man said shortly, "but he does not see people on business after the office is closed."

Leigh saw that his dress, as a sailor, did not impress the man.

"I think he will see us," he said, "if you take the name up to him. Will you tell him that Citoyenne Martin wishes to speak to him."

A minute later the merchant himself, a handsome man of about the same age as Jean Martin, came down.

"Ah! madame, I am glad indeed to see you," he said; for he had more than once been up to Nantes, during the time she was living there, and had been frequently at the house. "I have been in great anxiety about you."

"Has Jean been here?" she asked, in a tone of intense anxiety.

"No, madame, I have heard nothing of him for many months; not, indeed, since his lugger first came down here, with his letter and the deed of her sale to myself. Did you expect to find him here?"

"I hoped so, although there was no arrangement between us to meet here. Still, I thought that he would have made his way down here, if possible, as he would then be able to escape in the lugger."

"He may have found it more difficult than he thought," Monsieur Flambard said, soothingly. "But do not let us be standing here. Pray, come up. My wife will be glad to welcome you, for she has often heard me speak of Martin's English wife."

Leigh had been standing behind Patsey while they spoke but, as the merchant closed the door, his eye fell upon him.

"Ah, monsieur, now I recognize you. You are Monsieur Leigh Stansfield, the brother of madame. I welcome you also, cordially."

So saying, he led the way upstairs.

Chapter 17
A Grave Risk

Nothing could be kinder than the reception of the fugitives by Madame Flambard. She had heard so much of Patsey, she said, from her husband, to whom she had been married six months before, that she had quite shared his anxiety about the fate of Jean Martin, who had more than once been mentioned as being one of the leaders of the Vendeans. She soon went off with Patsey to put the child to bed and, while they were away, Monsieur Flambard took Leigh into his smoking room.

"Before," he said, "I ask you anything about your adventures, I must explain to you the state of things here. Until November last Bordeaux, and indeed the whole of the Gironde, was moderate. All our deputies--who have now, as perhaps you know, either fallen on the scaffold or been hunted down like wild beasts--belonged to that party. They were earnest reformers, and were prominent among the leaders of the Revolution. They went with the stream, up to a certain point. They voted for most of the sanguinary decrees, although in time they strove to mitigate the horrors inflicted by the extreme party; but after a long conflict the latter, supported by the mob of Paris, obtained the ascendency, and the Girondists underwent the same fate that had befallen so many others. For myself, I cannot pity them. They were all men of standing and of intelligence but, without perceiving the terrible results that must follow, they unchained the mob and became its victims.

"Up to that time there had been but few executions here, and the power remained in the hands of the moderate party. Two months since, however, there was a local insurrection. The party of the terror suddenly rose, seized the members of the council, and threw them into prison. Other prominent citizens were seized, and the guillotine began its bloody work in earnest. Since that time every citizen of position or standing lives in momentary danger of arrest. Not a day passes, but a dozen or so are seized and dragged off. I grant that, at present, there is nothing like the wholesale butchery that goes on at Nantes under that fiend Carrier; it is only those who have wealth and property that are seized. Not only in this town, but in the whole department, the agents of those who assumed power are busy. It is the Gironde, and therefore hateful to the party of Robespierre; and the proprietors of the land, who have hitherto been left unmolested, are being brought in daily.

"The trial is of course a mere farce. The prisoners are murdered, not because they are moderates, but because they are rich; and their wealth is divided among the members of the council, and the mob who support them. So far I have been unmolested. I have never taken any part in politics, business being sufficient to occupy all my time. Another thing is that I employ a considerable number of men, in addition to the crews of some ten vessels which belong to me. I believe that I am popular generally on the wharves, and it is the knowledge that my arrest might promote a tumult, and might reverse the present order of things, that has led to my being left alone so far.

"Fortunately my servant, who let you in, has been in the family for the past five-and-thirty years, and is devoted to me. Had it been otherwise the position would have been a dangerous one. A report to the council that a young man in the attire of a sailor, accompanied by a lady and child, had arrived, and been at once received, would suffice to set them in motion. I should be accused of having a suspect, probably one of the emigres hidden here, and it would be difficult for me to explain your reception. You must, in the first place, attire yourself in clothes such as are worn by the mate of a privateer. I suppose you have papers, or you would not have been permitted to land."

Leigh took out the passes and handed them to him. Monsieur Flambard glanced through them.

"You must have managed well to have got hold of these passes, and they certainly put the matter on safer ground. However, I should find some difficulty in explaining how I came to show hospitality to two persons who, by a strangely roundabout course, had made their way from Arthenay. It is a little unfortunate that your sister kept her own name. Had it been otherwise, I might have said that her husband was captain of one of my ships. But he is unfortunately not unknown here. After Martin's flight from Nantes, a claim was made by the committee of public safety at Nantes for the Henriette. Fortunately your brother-in-law had dated his bill of sale to me a fortnight before he left. The trial took place here and, as in those days law and justice still prevailed in the civic courts, the decision was given in my favour.

"It was urged on the other side that the transaction was invalid, as Martin must have parted with his vessel knowing well that he was a traitor to the Republic, and that his property would be confiscated. However, we got the best of them. There was no proof whatever that Martin was conscious that he was suspected of being disaffected, and we claimed that he had only sold it as, having married, he had decided to give up the sea and to settle upon his estates in La Vendee. Of course, at that time La Vendee had not risen, and it was not a crime worthy of death to own an estate there. Still, the case attracted attention, and the fact that my guest was a Madame Martin might recall the circumstances, and at once awake a suspicion that she was the wife of one of those who had led the insurgents of La Vendee; in which case her life and yours would be certainly forfeited, and my receiving you would be regarded as amply sufficient evidence of my connection with the insurgents.

"Now, for our sakes, as well as yours, I think that it would be strongly advisable that you should take up your abode elsewhere. Believe me that it is no want of hospitality, but a measure of precaution, both for your sake and ours. Tomorrow morning I should have to send in a statement that two guests have arrived here, and it is therefore most desirable that you should move without delay. Fortunately the wives of two or three of my captains live here; one of these especially, an excellent woman, has a house much larger than she needs, and takes in lodgers, generally captains whose families do not reside here, when their ships are in port. Therefore the fact that a sailor, with a sister and her child, have taken rooms there will excite no suspicion, whatever. She will, as a matter of course, send in your name to the police of the town, together with your passes. They will be marked and returned without, probably, being glanced at."

"I think that that will be an excellent arrangement, sir," Leigh said, "and I quite see that our stay here might be awkward for you, as well as us."

"I will at once go with you; that is, as soon as you have told your sister the reason why it will be better for you to establish yourselves elsewhere than here. I may tell you that I, myself, have been quietly making preparations for flight; but it is not all my captains whom I can trust. The Henriette, which I expect here shortly, has been delayed; but on her arrival I propose that we shall all cross the Channel together. I hear the ladies' voices in the next room. It were best that we got this painful business over, at once."

Madame Flambard was greatly distressed, when Leigh gave his sister an account of the conversation they had had, and the resolution at which they had arrived; but Patsey at once saw that it was most desirable that the change should be made, and assured her hostess that she fully recognized that their safety would be imperilled by staying at their house.

"It would be a cruel kindness, on your part, to insist upon our stopping here, Madame Flambard. We know that it is from no lack of hospitality that we are leaving, but that you are making a real sacrifice, in order to procure our safety.

"Shall I put on my things at once, monsieur?"

"By no means. I will go with your brother, first, to see if Madame Chopin has other lodgers. If so, I will go to the wife of one of my clerks, who also lets a portion of a house; or, if you would not mind poor accommodation, to another of the captains' wives as, in your brother's character of a sailor, it would be more natural for you to go to such a lodging, which may very well have been recommended to you by the skipper of the lugger in which you came here. When we have arranged things, we will return. It is but a quarter of an hour's walk, for the house stands near the river, above the bridge."

He at once set out with Leigh. On arriving at the house, they found that there were at present no lodgers there.

"This young sailor has brought a letter of recommendation to me, Madame Chopin. He has a married sister and her child with him, and I am sure that you will make them very comfortable, and can supply them with what they may require. They have just arrived by sea, from Havre; the length of their stay is uncertain. This young man is looking for a berth as mate, and shall have the first vacancy on one of my vessels. His sister may stop with you for some time, as she is hoping that her husband will return here, though he is so long overdue that I fear his ship has been either lost or captured by the English."

"I will do my best to make them both comfortable, Monsieur Flambard, and thank you for recommending them to me."

Leigh saw the rooms, which consisted of two bedrooms, and a third room which was similarly furnished; but Madame Chopin said that she would take down the bed and put some other furniture into it, so that they could use it as a sitting room.

"We should prefer that, madame; for my sister at times is greatly depressed, and we should prefer being alone."

"I can quite understand that," the woman said. "Well, you will not be troubled with society here, as I have only these three rooms to let so that, unless my husband comes home before you go, we shall be quite alone."

"I shall return with my sister in an hour's time," Leigh said; "that will not be too late for you?"

"No, monsieur, it is little past eight o'clock yet, and it will take me fully two hours to get everything straight and tidy."

"Very well, then, we will say ten o'clock," Monsieur Flambard said. "I will keep Monsieur Porson, as he has news to give me concerning the friend who recommended him to me."

On their return to the merchant's, they sat chatting for an hour over the adventures through which Leigh and his sister had passed, and the manner in which they were separated from Jean Martin.

"I think you have every reason to hope, madame," Monsieur Flambard said cheerfully. "Jean is not the sort of fellow to let himself be caught in a hole; and I expect that, when he found that he could not rejoin you, he at once struck north, either for Dunkirk or Calais, and has probably managed to be taken over in a fishing boat or a smuggler and, if he failed in doing so, he would probably make off in a boat single handed. I think that you have every reason to hope that you will find him at Poole, when you arrive there; but even should he not be there, there will be no reason for despair. He may have had difficulty in getting away. He may have been impressed for the naval service. At any rate, I have great faith that he will turn up, sooner or later. Certainly, when he has once managed to get a seafaring outfit, he will be safe from any fear of detection as one of the terrible Vendean insurgents."

At a quarter to ten little Louis was taken out of bed, wrapped up in a cloak, and carried by Leigh. Monsieur Flambard insisted on again accompanying them. The streets were now almost deserted, and they soon arrived at Madame Chopin's.

"I quite forgot to ask if you would want anything, before going to bed; but I can make you a cup of good coffee, if you would like it."

"Thank you, but we have eaten but an hour ago."

Saying goodnight to Monsieur Flambard, they went up to their rooms, their hostess leading with a candle. She had made the most of her time, since Leigh left the house. White curtains had been put up at the windows, and everything looked beautifully clean; and Patsey uttered an exclamation of pleasure when she entered the room.

"This does indeed look fresh and homelike," she said. "Thank you for taking so much trouble, madame."

The next morning Leigh procured a jacket and waistcoat, with brass buttons; and a cap with a gold band. He then sauntered along the wharves and went aboard the Trois Freres, and told the skipper that no news had been received of his sister's husband. It had been agreed that it was best that they should not go to Monsieur Flambard's house, but that the merchant should call at the lodging, after dark. When Leigh returned to the midday meal, he found that the papers had come back from the mairie, duly stamped and countersigned, and that as no one had been to the house to make inquiries, it was evident that no suspicion had been excited.

During the next four or five days Leigh went but little into the town, contenting himself with keeping near the wharves, watching the vessels loading or discharging cargo, and spending much of his time on board the Trois Freres. On the afternoon of the fifth day he saw a lugger approaching and as it came near, he made out, to his great delight, that it was the Henriette. As soon as she dropped anchor in the stream, her boat rowed to the wharves. Lefaux was sitting in the stern and, as soon as he landed, went off in the direction of Monsieur Flambard's office.

Leigh did not go near him. He thought that it would be better that the honest sailor should learn that he and his sister were there from the merchant, before he spoke to him; as any imprudent remark on the sailor's part might be caught up by one of the spies of the committee, and lead to trouble. As he expected, Monsieur Flambard came round with Lefaux, that evening.

"I am heartily glad to see you again, madame," he said, as Patsey shook him by the hand; "and you too, Monsieur Stansfield. I began to think that I never should do so, and I only wish that Monsieur Jean was here, too. Still, I feel confident that he has got safely away; trust a sailor for getting out of a scrape. You must have gone through a lot, madame, but you don't look any the worse for it."

"Except anxiety for my husband, I have gone through nothing to speak of. I had a horse to ride, and generally a shelter to sleep under, and for myself I had little to complain of; but it was terrible to see the sufferings of the peasant women and children, and of the many men broken down by sickness. And there was, too, the anxiety as to the safety of my husband and brother, in each battle that took place. But of hardship to myself there was very little."

"Well, madame, I hope that I shall soon have the pleasure of sailing into Poole again, with you and Monsieur Leigh on board; and also with my good master, Monsieur Flambard, and his wife."

"When will you be off again?" Patsey asked eagerly.

"That is what I have come to talk with you about, Madame Martin," Monsieur Flambard said. "I have pretty good information as to what passes, at the meetings of the wretches who call themselves the committee of public safety, and I hear that there will very shortly be a seizure of a number of prominent citizens, and my name has been mentioned. They are only hanging back until they can decide upon what shall be the pretext, since none of those named have taken any part in politics here. All those who have done so have been already seized. However, the blow may come at any moment.

"The Henriette has already begun to discharge her cargo. Fortunately, there is not much of it. The moment that she has finished she will drop down below the rest of the shipping, and be ready to start at any moment. If we find that the matter is not absolutely pressing, we will go quietly on board as soon as she is ready, and sail at once; as there will then be no fear of her being stopped.

"If, however, I find that the order for our arrest is on the point of being issued, I will send her down and let her lie beyond Fort Medoc and Blaye. If it were discovered that I was missing, a few hours after she had started, it would be suspected at once that I had gone in the Henriette. Mounted messengers would carry the news down to both forts, and the boat would be forced to heave to, as she passed between them.

"Therefore I shall have a light carriage, with two fast horses, kept in readiness a quarter of a mile outside the town; and a relay of horses fifteen miles on, which is about halfway, and join the ship below the forts. If, as may possibly happen, I am suddenly arrested in the streets, I shall have my servant near me. He will have his orders, which will be to hurry back home to tell his mistress to put on the disguise of a peasant woman, that has already been prepared for her, and to go with her at once to the carriage; and another man, whom I can also thoroughly trust, is to come here and say to you, 'It is a bad day.'

"Then you and your sister and the child will at once start to join my wife. She has most reluctantly consented to carry out this plan for, as I tell her, it will add to my sufferings a hundredfold, were she also to be arrested."

By dint of great exertions the Henriette was unloaded by the following evening and, half an hour after her last bale was ashore, she dropped down the river with the tide. She was to anchor off a small village, two miles beyond Fort Medoc; and if inquiry was made as to why she stopped there, Lefaux was to say that he was to take in some wine that Monsieur Flambard had bought from a large grower in that district, and that the lugger was then going to Charente to fill up with brandy for Havre.

Leigh had, the day before, gone with the merchant into the extensive cellars which adjoined the house.

"There is not a man here," Monsieur Flambard said, "who would not do all in his power for me. Some of them have been with the firm nearly all their lives. I treat them well, and I am happy to say that not one of them has taken any part in our last troubles. Indeed, I am told that is one of the matters that, if I am arrested, will be brought against me. It will be said that it was a proof of my enmity to the Convention that none of my people took the side of the patriots.

"However, it tells both ways. I have over forty men here. They have, of course, friends among the porters and others working on the wharves; and a disturbance might take place, were I arrested. However, the scoundrels have now got such absolute power that, no doubt, they feel that they could disregard any local rising and, indeed, with the plunder of my store before them, they could reckon on the devotion of the greater part of the mob of the town."

On the morning after the Henriette had sailed, the merchant took Leigh down to a little wayside inn, half a mile below the town, where he had placed his carriage and horses; and gave instructions to his coachman that he was to place himself under Leigh's orders.

"At whatever hour of the day or night he comes, you will start at once with him, and the lady and child who accompany him. You will know in that case that I am not coming, but have been arrested."

"But, master--"

"It must be as I say, Pierre. Once I am arrested--and it is almost certain my wife would be arrested with me--nothing can be done to help, and it would be a great satisfaction to me to know that my friends have escaped. There will be in that case no need of extreme haste, for no one knows that they are in any way connected with me, and there will be no inquiries for them."

Leigh told Patsey that afternoon that, in the event of the Flambards being arrested, he might possibly, instead of coming himself, send a messenger to her; and that she must then start at once, and await his coming in front of the church, at the end of the street in which the merchant's house stood.

"You had better have a letter written to our landlady, inclosing the sum due to her and a week's rent in advance; and say that we are hastily called away to Blaye, but may return in a few days, and begging her to keep the rooms vacant for a week, for which you leave the money. You had better write the letter at once, so that if you get my message you can leave instantly. There is nothing like being prepared for everything. Of course the arrest of the Flambards would not really affect us in any way, or add to our danger; but if the coachman were to hear of it before we got there, he might disregard his master's orders, and return at once with the carriage."

Leigh had in his mind the very short notice that Desailles had had of his danger, and how narrowly he escaped being arrested, although he had a friend who kept him acquainted with what was going on. He thought that it was still more likely that the arrest of the Flambards would take place suddenly. It would probably be decided upon by two or three of the men, who were the leaders of the party of terror; and no word would get about as to their intentions until the arrest had been absolutely made, in which case the captives would be lodged in prison before the matter would be known, and all fear of an emeute be thereby prevented. He had therefore decided upon what was the best course to pursue, and posted himself in the street, where he could observe anyone who entered or left Flambard's house.

It was already getting dusk when he saw two commissaries of the committee, with six armed men, stop before the door and knock. It was opened. Two of the men remained outside, and the rest entered. He ran to the stores. The head cellarman had gone round the place with him and his master, and Leigh at once went to him.

"Lefranc," he said, "your master and mistress have just been arrested. Two commissaries and six armed men have gone into the house. There is time to save them yet. They have a carriage in waiting, a short distance away; and if we can overpower these men and tie them up, so that they cannot give the alarm until morning, Monsieur Flambard and his wife will get safely away. They have a vessel waiting for them in readiness, down the river."

"I am your man, sir, and every one here."

"Half a dozen will be enough. Pick out that number of strong fellows, whom you can rely upon. Let them all take off their aprons, and tear up this black silk handkerchief and, as we leave the cellar, let each man put a piece over his face, to act as a mask. There is a private door leading to the house, is there not?"

"Yes, monsieur."

"Well, draw the men off quietly, so that the others shall not notice them; and tell them to go to that door, and to put on their masks there. Let each man take some weapon, but not a mallet, or anything used in the trade. Let them bring some stout rope with them."

The man nodded and hurried away, and Leigh went to the end of the stores abutting on the house, and stopped at the door he found there. In a minute the men began to arrive. They had, as he directed, thrown aside their leather aprons and put on blouses; so that they differed in no way, in appearance, from ordinary working men. One or two were armed with hammers, others with long knives. Each carried a piece of black handkerchief in his hand, long enough to go from the forehead down to the mouth. Leigh tied these on with strings, cutting holes with his knife through which they could see.

When the six men and the foreman had assembled, they entered the house. The old servant was standing in the hall, wringing his hands in distress.

"Where are they?" Leigh asked.

"In the master's study, sir. They are searching the drawers."

"Come on quietly," Leigh said to the men. "We must take them by surprise."

The door of the study was standing open, and lights burned within. Leigh had already instructed his followers to go at once for the armed men, and to knock them down before they had time to use their muskets. Going noiselessly up, they entered the door with a sudden rush.

The two commissaries were engaged in emptying the contents of the table drawers into a basket. The armed ruffians had leant their muskets against the wall, and had seated themselves in comfortable chairs. Flambard stood with his arm round his wife, looking disdainfully at the proceedings of the commissaries.

In a moment the scene changed. Before the men could even rise from their seats they were knocked down, bits of sacking thrust into their mouths, and their arms tied. Leigh had levelled one of the commissaries by a blow in the face, and the foreman had struck down the other with a hammer. These were also securely tied.

The Flambards stood, a picture of astonishment. The whole thing had passed so instantaneously that they could scarcely realize what had happened. When they did so, Madame Flambard, who had hitherto preserved her calmness, burst into tears; while her husband embraced Leigh with passionate gratitude.

"Now, monsieur," the latter said, "you had better collect at once any money and jewels you wish to take with you, while we are making sure of these ruffians.

"Now, my men," he went on, "take these fellows into different rooms; but first let me see that the ropes are securely tied; although, as sailors, you are not likely to make any mistake that way. Still, it is as well to be on the safe side."

He himself then examined the fastenings, and added a few more cords.

"Now, when you have got them into separate rooms, tie their feet to a heavy piece of furniture. Make a slipknot at the end of another rope, put the noose round the neck, and fasten the other end to another piece of furniture, that there may be no chance of their getting loose, till their friends come to their assistance."

He saw all this securely done. Then he said:

"There is one more thing to see to. In time those fellows at the door will be getting impatient, and will begin to suspect that all is not right. We must get them inside, and then tie them up with the others. Stand back behind the door as they enter and, as I close it, throw yourselves upon them. One of you grip each of them by the throat, and another seize his musket and wrench it from him. The rest will be easy."

The men placed themselves as directed, and Leigh then opened the door and said:

"You are to come in. They will take some little time over the papers, and there is plenty of good wine for you to amuse yourselves with."

With an exclamation of satisfaction, the two men entered.

"It is very dark in here," one said, as Leigh closed the door. "Why didn't you get a light?"

The words were scarcely spoken when there was a rush, a sudden exclamation, the sound of a short struggle, and then silence.

"Keep hold of them tightly, while I fetch a candle," Leigh said and, running upstairs, soon came down with the light.

The two guards were standing helpless in the hands of their captors, and gripped so tightly that they were unable to utter the least sound.

"Now, put the gags into their mouths and truss them up, as you did the others."

Leaving the men to carry out his orders, he ran upstairs again.

"Everything is arranged now," he said. "The whole of the fellows are bound, and the road is free for you. I should go out by the back way, for there is sure to be a little crowd in front of the house, attracted by the sight of the guard standing outside. I do not think that there is any extraordinary hurry, but in an hour or so, if either of the men who have ordered your arrest is waiting at the prison, he may get impatient, and send down to see what detains the party here.

"I am going, in the first place, to have the servants bound, so that they may not be suspected of having aided in this business. As soon as that is done, I shall hasten to my lodging and bring my sister and the child to the inn where you have your carriage. Of course, you will have the horses put in as soon as you get there. I shall not be very long behind you, as I shall take the first fiacre and drive down to that end of the town, and then discharge him. As I am not in any way associated with you, even if inquiries are made, our movements will throw no light upon yours."

The conversation took place in the bedroom where Madame Flambard was, with her husband, packing up a few necessaries.

"As we go downstairs," he went on, "I shall make some remark about our going straight on board. That will put them on the wrong scent, and they will waste a lot of time searching all the craft in the river. I do it principally because I want them to believe that you have been rescued by a party of sailors. You heard me say that, as sailors, they would be accustomed to tie the knots tightly; and of course my uniform will help to lead them astray. The men with me were really some of your cellarmen, under Lefranc."

"We shall be ready in three minutes. Fortunately we have not much beyond my wife's jewels that we want to save. Like your wife's brother, I have already made provision in England for this."

"I will be off as soon as I see the servants tied up."

He ran downstairs again. The two men and the maids willingly suffered themselves to be tied up, when Leigh explained to them the reasons for which it was done.

"Mind," he said, "if questioned, you say you believe that the men who rushed in and fastened you up were sailors."

Before the work was done Monsieur Flambard came down and, standing at the door which communicated with the cellars, shook hands with his rescuers as they went out; and thanked them most heartily, in the name of himself as well as his wife, for the service that they had rendered. The men, before they passed through the door, took off their masks. It had already been arranged that they should at once scatter, and return quietly to the places where they had been at work, and in so large a place it was not likely that their absence had been noticed, as it would be supposed that they had gone to another part of the cellar, and it was not above twenty minutes since they had left it.

As soon as they had gone out, the door was locked on the inside. Leigh and the Flambards went out at the back entrance into another street, and there separated, Leigh hurrying back to his lodgings. Madame Chopin opened the door.

"Madame," he said, "I have good news for my sister. I hope that we shall be able to obtain news of her husband at Blaye; for he may, if my information is correct, have sailed up the Dordogne, and we may catch him as he comes down again. If my information is not correct, we shall return here. I will therefore, if you will allow me, pay you our reckoning at once, and also the rent of the rooms for another week; so that if we return, we may find them unoccupied."

"But you are not going to start this evening, surely, monsieur?"

"Yes; I have arranged for a passage on a boat that is on the point of starting, and have not a moment to lose."

He ran upstairs to Patsey.

"They have gone on to the carriage," he said. "Put on Louis's things and your own. I will tell you all about it, as we go."

He then went down again and settled up with his landlady, who was profuse in her exclamations of regret at their departure. In a couple of minutes Patsey came down. She had the letter that she had written in her hand. Leigh took it from her.

"I have already settled up with our kind hostess," he said. "Say goodbye, dear, at once, or the boat may be starting without us."

A minute later they were out of the house. Leigh carried Louis, and led the way to a spot near, where two or three fiacres were always standing. He took the first, and told the driver to put them down in a street at the lower end of the town, the name of which he had noticed when he went with Monsieur Flambard to the inn where the carriage was standing.

When he got to the end of the street he told the driver to stop, saying that he was not sure of the number. Paying the man his fare, they walked slowly down the street until the fiacre had driven off; and then, returning, took the road leading into the country.

Ten minutes' walking brought them close to the little inn. They met the carriage coming along slowly, three hundred yards before they arrived there. It stopped at once.

"You are here sooner than I expected, madame," Monsieur Flambard said, as he alighted and helped Patsey.

As she took her place by the side of Madame Flambard, the latter threw her arms round her neck.

"Thank God this awful time is over!" she said. "It is to your brother we owe it that we are not, both, now in that terrible prison."

"Leigh is good at breaking prison," Patsey said. "He rescued me from the gaol at Nantes."

By this time her husband and Leigh had taken their places. Louis, still soundly asleep, was transferred to his mother's lap; and the carriage, turning, went back at the full speed of the horses.

Chapter 18
Home

"Why did you come down the road?" Leigh asked Monsieur Flambard, as the carriage flew past the little inn. "We had not arranged for that, and in the dark we might have passed it without knowing that it was yours."

"We were on the lookout for you, and had no fear of missing you. I decided to drive back to the town as we went out. I believe the innkeeper to be an honest fellow, and he has been one of our customers for a number of years; but I thought it just as well to throw dust in his eyes. Therefore, as I got into the carriage, I said in his hearing:

"'Don't go through the main streets of the town, but drive round and strike the road beyond it. Keep on to Langon. We shall stop there tonight.'

"We drove off fast, and only broke into a walk just before you met us. The innkeeper would have gone into the house again, before we met; and as I noticed that the shutters were up, he certainly would not have supposed that the vehicle which passed was our carriage, coming back again.

"Well, thank God we are all safe and together! In three hours we shall be at the village. Lefaux was to keep a boat ashore, and to be himself at the inn. There is only one in the village."

The road was a good one, and the horses fast, and in less than an hour and a half they reached the spot where the relay of horses had been stationed. Five minutes sufficed to make the change and, in a little under three hours after starting, they arrived at the village two miles below Fort Medoc. They stopped at the first house.

"Now, Gregoire," Monsieur Flambard said, as they alighted, "here are five louis for yourself. You had better drive back to the place where we changed horses, and put up there for the night. Tomorrow you can go quietly back to Bordeaux. Don't get there until late in the afternoon. Return the carriage and the other two horses to the stables where you hired them, and take my two horses back to our stables.

"You are sure to be questioned, and can tell them the truth. Say that you acted by my orders, and had no idea of the reason for which I had hired the carriage and the extra horses; that you knew that I often made flying visits to the vineyards, and you thought I wanted to see some proprietor of Medoc, on business, and to return as quickly as possible; and were much surprised when you saw that madame went with me. Do not say anything about our picking up my friends on the road."

"I understand, monsieur, and I will stick to that story. God bless you, sir, and you, madame; and I trust that, before long, you will be back again with us."

"I hope so, Gregoire, but I fear it will not be for some time to come."

They now walked forward, Leigh hurrying on in front until he came to the little village inn. It was already closed but, on his knocking violently at the door, a window above was opened.

"What are you making such a noise for, at this time of night?"

"I have come to call Captain Lefaux," he said. "A messenger has just brought an order, from Bordeaux, that he is to get up anchor at daylight."

"I will call him," the landlord said, and in three minutes Lefaux came out.

"We are all here, Lefaux," Leigh said, "and we want to go on board and get up anchor at once, and to be as far down the river as we can, before daylight."

"The saints be praised that you have all escaped, Monsieur Stansfield! We will lose no time. I have two men sleeping in a cottage, close to where the boat is made fast. They sleep on the ground floor, and I can tap at the window and get them out. I told them to turn in as they stood, as they might be wanted at any moment."

The others had now come up, and together they went down to the boat. The tide had turned about an hour before, and the boat was afloat.

"Now, I will fetch the men out," the skipper said, and in five minutes he came down with them.

They untied the head rope of the boat, from the stump to which it was fastened, and hauled it in.

"That is the lugger, I suppose?" Leigh said, pointing to a dark object, a hundred yards from the shore.

"That is her, sir, and it won't take us long to get under weigh. Everything is ready for hoisting sail."

They rowed off to the Henriette, and Leigh could hardly restrain a shout of joy at finding himself once again on board her. The crew had been unchanged since they left Nantes and, tumbling up on deck as they heard the boat coming off, greeted Leigh most heartily; and respectfully saluted Patsey and their owner. They would have broken into cheers, had not their skipper sharply silenced them.

"It will be time enough to cheer when we reach the open sea, lads," he said; "and we will do so more heartily still, when we land Madame Martin, Monsieur Leigh, and the owner and his wife either on English ground, or the deck of an English ship."

"You mistake, captain," Monsieur Flambard said. "As you know, the lugger was only passed over to me by Monsieur Martin to escape confiscation. There is no longer any need that I should appear as owner; and in fact Madame Martin, as representative of her husband, is the owner of the Henriette, and I and my wife are passengers on board her."

"I hope that you will find it all right below, madame," Captain Lefaux said. "Captain Martin's cabin--we have always called it so--is ready for you and Madame Flambard. Monsieur will take the spare cabin, and Monsieur Leigh mine."

"I will sleep on one of the sofas in the saloon, captain. I should not feel comfortable if I turned you out; and besides, I like being able to pop quietly on deck, whenever I feel inclined: so that is settled."

"Now we will have a tumbler of hot brandy and water," the captain said. "You have had a cold drive."

"What will you take, ladies?"

Both declared that they wanted nothing but to get to bed, and they at once retired to the after cabin with little Louis, who had slept without waking, ever since he had been lifted from his bed at Bordeaux. The captain had given orders, as soon as he came on board, to have the sails hoisted and, as Monsieur Flambard and Leigh sipped their grog, they had the satisfaction of hearing the water rippling past; and of feeling, by the heel of the boat, that there was sufficient wind to send them along at a good rate.

"What is she making, captain?" Leigh asked, as he went up to take a last look round.

"About five knots, but the wind is getting up. There was scarcely a breath when I turned in, at ten o'clock."

"How far do you call it to the mouth of the river?"

"It is about forty miles to the tower of Cordouan. Once past that, we reckon we are at sea."

"Eight hours going, at five knots. It is nearly twelve now. It will be daylight when we get there."

"I hope that we shall be there before that, sir. You have not allowed for the tide, nor for the wind increasing. I reckon we shall be there by six, and day does not begin to break till an hour later."

"I want to get past without being seen. There are always a couple of gunboats lying there. I fancy that they know us pretty well by this time, but sometimes as we go out they make us lie to, and come on board to see that we are not taking off suspected persons, and that any passengers we have tally with those on the manifest. If they should take it into their heads to do that in the morning, it would be awkward; and I am anxious to get past without being seen. Once out of gunshot I do not mind. I fancy that we can show our heels to either of the gunboats."

Leigh and Monsieur Flambard turned in. The latter slept soundly, but Leigh went frequently on deck.

"She is doing well," the captain said gleefully, "she is going fully seven knots an hour. You see, Master Leigh, I still keep to Captain Martin's terms, and count by knots instead of by leagues. The tide is giving us another two knots. I reckon that, at the rate we are going, we shall keep it pretty nearly down to the mouth of the river. Seven and two are nine, and as I have just been looking up the chart, and as I find that it is but thirty-seven from the village where we started, we shall do it in five hours at the outside.

"The river is wide at the mouth, and by heading south directly we get there, and running so for a couple of miles before we put straight out to sea, there will be no chance whatever of our being seen. Once away, we shall of course lay a course inside the islands till we are off Finisterre; then we can either strike out into the Channel, or coast along as far as Cape la Hague, and thence sail straight for Poole. But there is no occasion to discuss that, at present."

Satisfied with the assurance of the captain, Leigh turned in again at two o'clock, and this time slept soundly. When he awoke the motion of the vessel told him he was at sea, and he saw that it was broad daylight. Leaping off the sofa, he saw by his watch that it was eight o'clock, and he was speedily on deck. The mate was in charge.

"The captain turned in half an hour ago, sir. Do you wish him to be called?"

"Certainly not. Where are we now?"

"We are just passing between the island of Oleron and the mainland."

"Oh, yes, I see. When I came down, of course we saw it from the other way; and I did not recognize it, at first. So we managed to get past Cordouan without being seen?"

"Yes, we rounded the south point of the river before six o'clock, laid her head southwest for an hour and, just as it became light, changed our course north and passed three miles to seaward of the tower. They doubtless supposed that we were coming up from Bayonne. At any rate, they paid no attention to us."

"The wind is blowing pretty strongly."

"Yes, sir, we should have had a rough tumble of sea if it had been from the west, and should have had to lie up under shelter of the island; but as it is blowing right off shore, it is just about the right strength for us, and we shall make a quick run of it if it holds.

"I hear there is no news of Captain Martin, monsieur?"

"No, I am sorry to say there is not; but I have every hope that we shall find he has got to Poole before us."

"We are all hoping that nothing has happened to him. Of course, we heard that he was fighting in La Vendee and, as every one of us comes from one port or another there, we only wished that we had been with him."

"You were well out of it, Edouard. It was a terrible business. No one could have fought better than your people did, but they had all France against them; and few, indeed, of those who were engaged from the first can ever have returned to their homes. And even when they get there there can be no safety for them, for Carrier and his commissioners seem to be determined to annihilate the Vendeans altogether."

The mate indulged in many strong expressions as to the future fate of Carrier and his underlings.

"We heard of that attack on the jail, Master Leigh. I guessed that you were in that, for among the prisoners who were delivered the names of Monsieur Martin and Madame Jean Martin were mentioned."

"Yes, Captain Martin and I were in the thick of it. There was very little fighting to do, for we chose a time when the troops were all busy with Cathelineau's and Stofflet's attack; and we had really only to open the door of the prison, to get them out."

"The captain has been telling us that Monsieur Flambard was also in danger of arrest. It is atrocious. Everyone knows that he is a good master, and I never heard a word said against him."

"That has very little to do with it," Leigh said. "His crime was that he was rich, and the scoundrels wanted his money. They did arrest him, but he was rescued before they got him out of his house, and fortunately everything had been prepared for his flight. At the present moment they are searching high and low for him, and I expect that no craft there will be permitted to leave till she has been thoroughly ransacked, to make sure that he and madame are not hiding there."

"Ah, they are bad times, monsieur. It may be that things were not quite as they might have been, though for my part I never saw anything to grumble at; nor did any other Vendean, as far as I ever heard; but if things had been ten times as bad as they were, they would have been better than what is going on now.

"Why, monsieur, all Europe must think that we Frenchmen are devils. They say that more than a hundred thousand people have been put to death, not counting the loss in La Vendee."

"Which must be quite as much more, Edouard; and it is no consolation to know that the loss of the Blues must have been fully equal to ours."

"How is it to end, monsieur?"

"I think that the first part will end soon. As far as I could find out as we travelled through the country, and in Paris, even the mob are getting sick of this terrible bloodshed. That feeling will get stronger, until finally I believe that Robespierre and his gang will be overturned. What will come after that, I don't know. One may hope that some strong man will rise, drive out the Convention, and establish a fixed government. After that, I should say that no one can guess what will follow."

"There is one consolation, monsieur. No change can be for the worse."

"That is absolutely certain."

He went to the galley.

"Well, cook, when are you going to let us have some breakfast? I am famishing, for I have eaten nothing since twelve o'clock yesterday."

"It will be ready in twenty minutes, monsieur. I was just going to ask you if you would call the ladies, or whether you will take the cafe au lait and eggs to their door."

"I will go and ask them."

He went and knocked at the cabin door.

"Patsey, cafe au lait will be ready in twenty minutes. Will you and Madame Flambard take it in your cabin, or come into the saloon?"

"I am just dressed, and shall be up on deck with Louis in two or three minutes. Madame Flambard will not get up. It is her first voyage, and she will not take anything to eat."

He was just going to knock at the merchant's door, when there was a shout from within:

"I have heard what you are saying, and shall be dressed in ten minutes."

Patsey was soon on deck.

"This is splendid, Leigh! And now that we have got away so wonderfully, I feel more hopeful than I have done before that Jean, also, will have made his escape.

"Well, Louis, what do you think of this? You had better keep hold of your uncle's hand, as well as mine, or you may get a nasty tumble."

"Nasty, bad ship, mama?"

"It is because the wind is blowing hard, and the sea is rough. We had smooth water on our last voyage, you know."

"Louis not like him," he said positively; "very bad ship."

"You will be all right, if you keep hold of your uncle's hand. He will walk up and down with you."

"This is good, indeed," Monsieur Flambard said. "If we go on as well as we have begun, we shall have nothing to grumble at."

The voyage to Ushant was accomplished without any adventure. The lugger was so evidently French that two or three privateers, who passed close by, paid no attention to them; and although they saw the sails of more than one British cruiser, they either escaped observation or were considered too insignificant to be chased.

On the voyage they had agreed that, when they came to Ushant, they would be guided by the wind. If it continued to blow as it had done, from the east, it would be a great loss of time to beat in to Saint Malo, and they would be within sight of England long before they could make in there.

As the wind was unchanged, they therefore laid their course from Ushant for the Isle of Wight. Before they had been many hours out they saw an English brig of war, making toward them. They did not attempt to escape, but slightly changed their course so as to head for her.

As the brig approached, they lowered their mainsail. The brig was thrown up into the wind, a couple of lengths away.

"Send your boat on board!" the captain of the brig shouted.

They had indeed already got the boat over the side.

"You may as well come with me," Leigh said, as he stepped into her. "Monsieur Flambard will take care of Louis while you are away."

Seeing that there was a woman in the boat, the brig lowered its accommodation ladder, and the captain was standing at the gangway.

"We are English, sir," Leigh said. "The lugger is owned by my sister's husband, if he is alive. If not, I suppose it belongs to her. We are escaping from France, with two French friends. My brother-in-law was a Vendean, and has fought through the war. We were with him until, at the attack on Le Mans, we were separated. We hope to meet him at Poole. The vessel traded between that port and Nantes until the war broke out. Some members of the family are already established there, and our father is a magistrate, living within a couple of miles of the town."

"I am sorry, madam, that I cannot offer you a passage; but I must not leave my cruising ground."

"Thank you, sir. We are doing very well in the lugger. We intend to register her as a British vessel; and the crew, who are all Vendeans, will probably remain in our service until things settle down in France."

"And were you through the war too, madam?" the captain asked Patsey.

"Not through the whole of it," she replied. "Our chateau was burned down by the Republicans, and I was carried to the prison at Nantes; and should have been guillotined had not my husband and brother rescued me, when the Vendeans were attacking the town. I remained at the farmhouse, until the Vendeans could no longer maintain themselves in La Vendee and crossed the Loire; then I accompanied my husband."

"Well, madam, I congratulate you heartily on your escape. We heard terrible tales, in England, of what is going on in France."

"However terrible they are, they can hardly give you an idea of the truth. At Nantes, for instance, the guillotine is too slow; and hundreds of men, women, and children are put into boats, which are sunk in the middle of the river. It is too horrible to think of."

"Is there anything that I can do for you, madam? Anything in the way of provisions with which we can supply you?"

"No, thank you, we have everything that we can want."

"Then I will detain you no further," he said, "and can only wish you a pleasant voyage. I see, by the course you are steering, that you are making for the Isle of Wight. You ought to be there tomorrow afternoon."

The boat returned to the lugger, the sails were filled again and, at four next afternoon, the Henriette passed Handfast Point, and headed for the entrance to Poole harbour. As the distance from home lessened, Patsey's excitement increased hourly. She could not sit down for a minute, quietly, but walked restlessly up and down the deck. She had scarcely spoken when Leigh said, after a long look through the telescope:

"I can make out the house on the hill, quite plainly, Patsey."

At any other time Patsey, who dearly loved their old home, would have shown the liveliest interest; but just then her thoughts were all of Jean, and she could spare none for anything else.

"They must have made us out, by this time," she said, as they passed Durleston.

"I should think so, but I don't suppose they watch as we used to do in the old days. The revenue men up there--" and he nodded up the cliff "--must of course see that we are French; and if there are any of them who were here, three or four years ago, no doubt they know us again, and must be wondering what brings us here."

They had scarcely passed Durleston when Patsey sprang on to the rail, holding fast by the shrouds, and gazed intently at the narrow entrance of the channel, between the island and the mainland.

"There is a boat coming out," she exclaimed.

"The coast guard are sure to have launched their boat, as soon as they made us out. They would naturally come out to inquire what a French lugger is doing here."

He went forward with his telescope, and took a long look at the boat.

"Yes, it is the coast guard, rowing six oars."

In a minute or two he went back to his sister.

"Do get down, Patsey," he urged. "Of course they may have news of Jean, but you must not be disappointed, too much, if they have not. You know that we have agreed, all along, that very likely we shall be the first back; and no news cannot be considered as bad news. It will only mean that we must wait."

She shook her head, but did not reply.

"There are three men in the stern," she said at last.

Leigh sprang up onto the rail behind her.

"Yes, there are three sitters."

Suddenly one of the men stood up. The boat was still too far away for the figure to be distinguished. Leigh would have called to the captain, to use his glass; but he feared to hold out even a hope, to Patsey, that Jean might be in the boat.

A minute later the standing figure began to wave his arms wildly.

"It is Jean, it is Jean!" Patsey cried. "He has made me out."

It was well that Leigh had taken his place beside her, for suddenly her figure swayed; his arm closed round her and, calling to the captain to help him, he lowered her and laid her on the deck.

"My sister has fainted. Bring a bucket of water."

Madame Flambard took Patsey from him.

"She thinks she sees her husband in that boat," Leigh said. "Pray try and get her round, before it comes up. I think it must be he; but if it should not be, we will take her below, directly we are sure. It will be a terrible blow to her to be disappointed, now; but possibly they may have news of him, and that would be almost as good as his being here."

"She could not have recognized him, at this distance," Monsieur Flambard said.

"No, she did not; but he would have recognized her. At least, he must have seen that there was a woman standing upon the rail, watching them; and it was hardly likely that, coming in his own boat, it should be anyone but her. I don't see why anyone else should have waved his arms, suddenly, in the way that he did."

He took the bucket of water from Lefaux's hands.

"We think it is Captain Martin," he said. "Run up the shrouds and take a look through the glass."

Then, taking a double handful of water, he dashed it into his sister's face.

"But, monsieur--" Madame Flambard began to remonstrate.

"Oh, it does not matter about her being wet a bit," Leigh said. "The great thing is to bring her round.

"There, she is opening her eyes. I never saw her faint before. She is not that sort."

At this moment, there was a joyous shout from the skipper:

"It is Captain Martin, himself! Hurrah, boys! It is the captain."

The crew broke into joyous shouts.

"It is Jean, Patsey," Leigh said, sharply. "Thank God, it is he.

"Steady, steady!" he added, as his sister suddenly sat up, and held out her arms to be lifted to her feet. "Are you all right, dear? He will not be alongside for some little time. Don't try to get up for a minute or two."

As Madame Flambard supported her, he ran down into the cabin, poured out a little brandy and water, and ran upstairs again with the glass.

"There, dear, drink this. You must be strong enough to greet him, as he comes alongside."

She drank it up, and then he helped her to her feet. She stood leaning on the rail, but unable to see the boat through her tears. Leigh ran up a few of the ratlines and waved his cap and, two or three minutes later, the whole crew, clustered along the side, raised a loud cheer as the boat came near.

Patsey held out her arms to Jean, who had, after his first eager signal, dropped back into his seat; and sat there, with his face covered in his hands, until within two or three hundred yards of the lugger. Then he had stood up again. He waved his cap in reply to the cheers of the crew, but his eyes were fixed upon Patsey.

As the boat came alongside he sprang on to the channel, swung himself over the rail, Patsey falling into his arms as his feet touched the deck. The others all drew back and, for two or three minutes, husband and wife stood together. Then Jean, placing Patsey in a chair, turned and embraced Leigh warmly.

"I felt sure that you would bring her back safely," he said. "I never allowed myself to doubt it, for a minute; and as soon as I made the lugger out, from the height there, I was sure that she was on board; and ran down to the coast guard station, and Captain Whittier and the crew were in her, in a couple of minutes.

"Where is Louis?"

"Here he is!" Monsieur Flambard said, coming forward with the child in his arms.

Louis knew his father at once, and greeted him with a little shout of pleasure.

"And you, too, Flambard?" Jean said, after he had kissed and embraced his boy. "I am glad indeed that you, too, have escaped from that inferno they call France."

"Yes, and my wife too, Martin; and, like your wife, we owe our safety to Leigh."

Although they had not met before, Jean and Madame Flambard shook hands as warmly as if they had been old friends, filled as they were by a common happiness.

Captain Whittier now came on board. He had hitherto remained in the boat, in order that the family meetings should be got over before he showed himself.

"I am glad to see you, Master Leigh," he said, shaking hands as he spoke; "though I certainly should not have known you again. You ought no longer to be called Master Leigh, for you are a grown man. We have talked of you, often and often; and it was not until Captain Martin arrived, a week ago, that we had any idea of what had become of you.

"Everyone will be glad to know that you are safely back; and you too, Mrs. Martin. Everyone has missed Miss Patsey, as they still call you when they speak of you."

Jean had been shaking hands with Lefaux and the crew, and now returned.

"I don't know how we stand with this craft, captain. She has come into port of her own free will, and not as a prize. I claim that she is the property of a French Royalist, now an emigre; and as England, so far from being at war with French Royalists, is their ally, I intend to transfer her to my wife, and to have her registered as an English ship."

"Well, I suppose that you will have to settle that with the authorities, Captain Martin; but I should think that you are right, for other French craft have come across with emigres, and have always been allowed to return. Is there any cargo on board?"

"None," Leigh said. "She left Bordeaux the moment she discharged the cargo she brought there."

As they dropped anchor off the island another boat came alongside, with Mr. Stansfield and his two sons, and there was again a scene of tender greeting between them, her, and Leigh.

"Where is Polly?" Patsey asked.

"She was married, two years ago," her father said, "to Harry King, the son of the banker, you know. Of course, she lives in Poole now.

"And so this is your little boy?"

"Yes, but he cannot understand you, at present. We have always talked French with him since the troubles began as, had he spoken a word or two of English, it might have been fatal to him, and to us; but he will soon pick it up, now he is among you all."

It was a happy party, indeed, that evening at Netherstock, where Mr. Stansfield had insisted that Monsieur and Madame Flambard should stay, till they could find a lodging to suit them in Poole. Madame Martin and her daughter, Louise, arrived a few minutes after the others had reached the house; as Jean had sent off a boy to tell them, as soon as he made out the lugger; and a little later Patsey's sister, Polly, came over from Poole.

At first, innumerable questions were asked on each side; and then Leigh related all that had happened, since they left Le Mans. Monsieur Flambard interrupted, when it came to the point where Leigh had rescued him and his wife, and gave full particulars of it to Jean, who translated it to the others. Then it came to Jean's turn.

"I was with Rochejaquelein," he said. "We had made our last charge down on the head of the enemy's column. It was hot work. Desailles was shot through the head, close by my side and, as we rode off, I felt my horse stumble, and knew that it was hit. Almost at the same moment my sword fell from my hand, my right arm being broken by a musket ball.

"La Rochejaquelein had given orders that this charge was to be the last. He knew that, by this time, the main part of the army would have left the town. My horse lagged behind the others, and I was just turning it to ride to our meeting place, when it fell under me.

"I decided at once not to attempt to come to the rendezvous. In the first place, I felt sure that you had already followed out my instructions; and in the next place, had I joined you, I should have ruined your chance of escape. Being dismounted, I should have hampered your flight and, even had we escaped pursuit, your having a man with a broken arm with you would, everywhere, have roused suspicion. I therefore determined to go as far as I could, and then hide in a wood and shift for myself.

"I got a peasant, who was running past me, to stop for a moment and bind my arm tightly with my sash. It was broken high up. I walked, for two or three hours, in the direction opposite to that in which the army had retreated. The peasant who had bound my arm up accompanied me. I found that he came from a farm near us. He had recognized me at once, but I had not noticed who it was. I told him to try and save himself, but he would not hear of it.

"'Monsieur will require my aid,' he said, 'and it is my duty to render it. Besides, I am as likely to escape one way as the other. Monsieur knows more about the roads than I do, and will be able to direct me.'

"Of course, I assented, for I was glad indeed to have him with me. As soon as we hid up in a wood, he cut two strips of bark off the trunk of a young tree, cut off the sleeve of my coat and shirt, put the arm straight and, with a strip torn off my sash first bandaged it, and then applied the two pieces of bark as splints, and finally bound another bandage round them.

"He had carried with him the blanket and valises he had taken off the saddle. The latter contained a bottle of wine, and some food, and on this we lived for three days. Then I determined upon starting. He went out in the evening and managed to buy, at a cottage, two loaves of bread and a couple of bottles of wine. We divided these. Then I put on my disguise, and we started in different directions, he making south for the river, which I trust the good fellow managed to reach and cross safely, while I struck north.

"My wine and bread lasted me for four days, by which time I had arrived at Louviers, on the Seine. I was now a hundred miles from Le Mans, and altogether beyond the line of action. I felt comparatively safe. My arm was so painful, however, that I felt that, at whatever risk, I must see a surgeon.

"I went first to an inn, where my appearance as a stranger, and without means of conveyance, excited the surprise of the landlord.

"'You are hurt, monsieur,' he said.

"'Yes; my horse fell under me and threw me heavily, and broke my arm. Before I could recover myself, it had run away. Fortunately a peasant who was going by bandaged my arm up, and I was able to walk on here. Who is the best surgeon in the place?'

"He mentioned the name of the doctor, and said that he had the reputation of being very skilful and kind. He offered to send for him but, being close by, I said that I would rather go to him.

"The man's face gave me confidence, as soon as I entered. I knew that it would be of no use to tell him the story of a fall, and I said at once:

"'Monsieur, I believe doctors are like confessors, and that they keep the secrets of their patients.'

"He smiled.

"'Monsieur has a secret, then?'

"'I have,' I said. 'I have had my arm broken by a musket ball--it does not matter how or when, does it?'

"'In no way,' he said; 'my business is simply to do what I can for you.'

"'It is seven days old,' I said, 'and is horribly painful and inflamed.'

"He examined the wound.

"'The bone is badly broken,' he said. 'It is well for you that it has been bound up with some skill, and that these rough splints have kept it in its place. Of course, what you require is rest and quiet. Without cutting down to the bone I cannot tell how badly it is splintered and, in the state of inflammation that it is now in, I could not venture upon that. I can only rebandage it again, and give you a lotion to pour over it, from time to time.

"Tell me frankly what you are. You can trust me.'

"'I am a sailor,' I said, 'captain of my own craft. I am also a Vendean and, as the cause is now lost, I am making my way down to the sea. I hope, in some way or other, to make my escape to England, where I have friends, my wife being an Englishwoman. What I require more than anything is a suit of sailor's clothes.'

"'I will do what I can to help you, my friend. I am not one of those who think that France can be regenerated by the slaughter of the whole of the best of her people, and by all power being given to the worst.

"'Let me see; I cannot go and buy sailor's clothes myself, but my old servant can be trusted absolutely. There is a shop down by the river where such things are sold. I will get her to go down there, and say that she has a nephew just arrived from sea, and that she wants to give him a new rig out; but as he has hurt himself, and cannot come, she must choose it. What is your height?'

"'About five foot ten,' I said.

"'And how broad round the shoulders?'

"'Forty-three inches. I have plenty of money to pay for all that is necessary, and more,' and I took out my roll of assignats.

"'Since you are well provided,' he said, 'I will take some. The people are very poor, and we all suffer together. They pay me when they can and, so that I can make ends meet, I am well content.'

"In an hour the woman returned, with a suit of rough sailor's clothes, and you may imagine how glad I was to put them on, the doctor helping me on with the jacket.

"'Now,' he said, when I had dressed and eaten some food the old servant had set before me, 'it happens that at daybreak tomorrow one of my patients, the master of a river boat, is starting on the turn of tide for Honfleur. I will first go round to the auberge, and tell the landlord that your arm is badly broken, and that I shall keep you here for the night, as you will require attention; then I will go to the captain, and arrange for your passage. When I tell him that you are a patient of mine, and that I should be obliged if he would find you some quiet lodging at Honfleur, where you can remain till your arm is better and you are fit to be about again, I have no doubt he will manage it. He is a good fellow, and I shall let him understand that you don't want inquiries made about you.

"'Now, you had better lie down on a bed upstairs, and try to sleep. I will call you in time to go down to the boat.'

"'There is no fear of my getting you into trouble?' I asked. 'I would rather go on to Honfleur by road at once, than do so.'

"'There is no fear of that; the maire is a friend and patient of mine. And if, as may be the case, the landlord mentions the arrival of a stranger, and his coming to me; I shall simply tell the maire that, your arm being badly broken, I kept you for the night, and then sent you on by boat; and that as for papers, not being a gendarme, I never thought of asking you for them.'

"The next morning he dressed my arm again, and then himself took me down to the boat, and handed me over to its skipper. He absolutely refused any payment for his services; but I insisted on his receiving a couple of hundred francs, in assignats, for the use of his poorer patients.

"The skipper carried out his instructions to the letter. We got to Honfleur after dark, on the day after starting, and he went with me to the cottage of a widow of his acquaintance.

"He said to her, 'Mother, I want you to take care of this young sailor. He has broken his arm, and wants nursing. He does not want his being here to be known, because he is afraid he might be packed off in one of the ships of war, as soon as he recovers. I suppose you can manage that?'

"'Oh, yes,' she said; 'I have very few visitors, and no one would guess that I have anyone upstairs.'

"'He has plenty of money to pay your charges. Now I will leave him with you, and will look in tomorrow, to see how he is getting on.'

"I stayed there a fortnight, by which time the inflammation had pretty well subsided. No one could be kinder than the old woman was. She used to bathe my arm by the hour, and she fed me up with broth.

"At the end of that time I felt ready for work, though my arm was of course useless. So, having paid my account, I went down boldly to the river and crossed to Harfleur, and then went on to Havre. I stayed there for a couple of days, at a sailors' cabaret; where they supposed that I belonged to a vessel in port, and no questions were asked.

"Finding that it would be difficult to pass the gunboat lying there, I walked up to Fecamp, picked out a likely looking boat afloat by the quay; and at night got on board, rowed quietly out, and then managed to get the sail hoisted. The wind was offshore, and by the morning I was out of sight of the French coast. I laid my course for Portsmouth, and landed there that evening. Being fortunately able to speak English, I had only to leave the boat tied up to the quay, and go up to a small inn close by. I slept there, crossed to Gosport, and walked to Southampton the next morning; and got into Poole on the following day, and soon found where my mother and sister were staying.

"So you see I had, altogether, very little adventure on my way from Le Mans. Since then, I have spent most of my time up here sweeping the water with your father's glass. I had been watching the Henriette, for hours, before she came near enough for me to be sure that it was she; though of course, I could see that she was a French-rigged boat.

"As soon as I made her out I sent off word to my mother, and ran down to the coast guard station. I felt sure that you were on board, for otherwise the lugger would not have come over here. Still, of course, I could not be absolutely certain until I saw that the figure I could make out, standing on the rail, was that of a woman."

It was some little time before their plans were finally decided upon. It was evident that, at present, no trade could be done in French wines. However, as Jean, his mother, and his friend Flambard had sufficient capital to enable them to live without trade, for some time, they agreed that they should establish themselves at once, in London, as wine merchants. Flambard had correspondents in Spain and Portugal, from whom he could obtain wine of these countries; and they agreed that Poole did not offer opportunities for carrying on any considerable trade. Both insisted that Leigh should become a member of the firm and, a month after their arrival at Poole, the party moved up to London.

Madame Martin, her daughter, Jean and his wife took a house, between them, at Hackney; and Monsieur Flambard and his wife established themselves in another, a few hundred yards away.

From time to time came scraps of news from across the Channel. La Rochejaquelein and Stofflet, after being separated from their followers when crossing the Loire, had gathered a small band together, and gained some successes over parties of the enemy. Two grenadiers, after one of these skirmishes, were on the point of being shot by the peasants when Henri came up to save their lives. One of the prisoners, however, recognizing the gallant leader of the Vendeans, raised his musket and shot him dead.

It was not for two years after this that the struggle was finally brought to a conclusion, for the heroic people of La Vendee continued to resist all the efforts of their enemies; until Stofflet and Charette were captured and executed, the one in February, 1796, the other in the following month. The moderation and judgment of General Hoche finally brought about the end of a war which stands unexampled, in history, for the noble resistance offered by a small body of peasants to the power of a great country.

As soon as Monsieur Flambard heard, from his correspondents abroad, that a consignment of wine was on its way they took an office; for it had already been agreed that, having no connection for sales to private customers, they would work only as wholesale merchants, dealing with the trade and with large hotels and other establishments, contenting themselves with the smallest possible rate of profit until they made a connection; and at the end of two or three years, they were doing a considerable business.

The Henriette sailed for France, shortly after their arrival in Poole, as the crew preferred returning home. Lefaux was to trade as before and, being so well known at all the western ports, was certain of obtaining freights. He was to pay wages and all other expenses, and to transmit the balance as opportunity occurred.

Three years later, when the internal affairs of the country had calmed down, Jean managed to get a letter sent to the priest of their village, asking him to inquire about Marthe; and after a considerable time an answer was received, saying that she and Francois had reached home in safety, had been married shortly after their return, and were doing well; having, with their joint savings, purchased at a very low price one of Jean's confiscated farms.

Ten years later the firm of Flambard, Martin, & Stansfield were doing a large business, and when the war came to a termination, and trade with Bordeaux, Charente, and Nantes was renewed, Monsieur Flambard returned to Bordeaux and, having a large connection there, the firm soon became known as the largest importers of foreign wines in London.

Madame Martin had, long before that, died. Patsey was the mother of three boys and two girls, and Leigh had a separate establishment of his own, and had been for fifteen years a married man. Mr. Stansfield was still alive, and things went on at Netherstock in very much the same fashion as before Patsey left home.

Jacques Martin had been one of the many who were guillotined when the terror came to an end, after the death of Robespierre.